**Andrea Laurence** is an
romances filled with sec
of reading and writing st
West Coast girl transplan
to share her special blend of sensuality and dry, sarcastic humour with readers.

*USA TODAY* bestselling author **Janice Maynard** loved books and writing even as a child. But it took multiple rejections before she sold her first manuscript. Since 2002, she has written over forty-five books and novellas. Janice lives in east Tennessee with her husband, Charles. They love hiking, travelling and spending time with family.

You can connect with Janice at:
www.janicemaynard.com,
Twitter.com/janicemaynard,
Facebook.com/janicemaynardreaderpage,
Facebook.com/ janicesmaynard
Instagram.com/janicemaynard

**Maureen Child** writes for the Mills & Boon Desire line and can't imagine a better job. A seven-time finalist for a prestigious Romance Writers of America RITA® Award, Maureen is an author of more than one hundred romance novels. Her books regularly appear on bestseller lists and have won several awards, including a Prism Award, a National Readers' Choice Award, a Colorado Romance Writers Award of Excellence and a Golden Quill Award. She is a native Californian but has recently moved to the mountains of Utah.

# Saving His Blackmailed Lover

ANDREA LAURENCE
JANICE MAYNARD
MAUREEN CHILD

MILLS & BOON

All rights reserved including the right of reproduction in whole or in part in any form. This edition is published by arrangement with Harlequin Books S.A.

This is a work of fiction. Names, characters, places, locations and incidents are purely fictional and bear no relationship to any real life individuals, living or dead, or to any actual places, business establishments, locations, events or incidents. Any resemblance is entirely coincidental.

This book is sold subject to the condition that it shall not, by way of trade or otherwise, be lent, resold, hired out or otherwise circulated without the prior consent of the publisher in any form of binding or cover other than that in which it is published and without a similar condition including this condition being imposed on the subsequent purchaser.

® and ™ are trademarks owned and used by the trademark owner and/or its licensee. Trademarks marked with ® are registered with the United Kingdom Patent Office and/or the Office for Harmonisation in the Internal Market and in other countries.

First Published in Great Britain 2019
by Mills & Boon, an imprint of HarperCollins*Publishers*
1 London Bridge Street, London, SE1 9GF

SAVING HIS BLACKMAILED LOVER © 2019 Harlequin Books S. A.

*Expecting The Billionaire's Baby* © 2017 Harlequin Books S.A.
*Triplets For The Texan* © 2017 Harlequin Books S.A.
*A Texas-Sized Secret* © 2017 Harlequin Books S.A.

Special thanks and acknowledgement are given to Andrea Laurence, Janice Maynard and Maureen Child for their contributions to the *Texas Cattleman's Club: Blackmail* series.

ISBN: 978-0-263-27660-2

0719

**MIX**
Paper from
responsible sources
**FSC® C007454**

This book is produced from independently certified FSC™ paper to ensure responsible forest management.

For more information visit: www.harpercollins.co.uk/green

Printed and bound in Spain
by CPI, Barcelona

# EXPECTING THE BILLIONAIRE'S BABY

## ANDREA LAURENCE

To My Fellow TCC Authors—

I loved sharing a little blackmail between friends.
Looking forward to working with you all again!

And To Our Super Editor Charles—

If you can keep up with all twelve stories, you're
officially a superhero. I'm going to buy you a cape.
Maybe some tights.

# One

"You can do this, Cecelia."

Cecelia Morgan attempted to encourage herself as she looked over her portfolio for the hundredth time. Tomorrow, she was presenting her design plans to the board of directors of the new Bellamy Hotel. This was a big step for her and her company, To the Moon. The company she started after college specialized in children's furniture, bedding and toys. From the beginning she had targeted a high-end market, catering to wealthy parents who were looking for luxury products for their children.

The company had been a success from the very start. What had begun as a small online boutique had exploded into a series of stores across the United States after a celebrity posted on social media about how much they loved one of TTM's nursery designs. Cecelia had been forced to open her own production facility and warehouse outside her hometown of Royal, Texas, to keep up with the demand.

The portfolio on the desk in front of her, however, could take To the Moon to the next level. Designing furniture, toys and accessories for pampered little ones had been her first love, but now Cecelia was ready for her business to mature along with her tastes. The Bellamy Hotel was her chance to make this a reality.

The Bellamy was a brand-new five-star resort opening right outside Royal. Owner Shane Delgado had contacted Cecelia about decorating and furnishing the hotel about a month ago, after a previous designer had been fired well into the process. This would be a big step for Cecelia. If she could secure the contract with The Bellamy, it would give her the footing she needed to branch out into the luxury adult furniture market.

As her daddy always said, if you're not moving forward, you might as well be moving backward. She was successful, but that wasn't enough for the Morgans. Her subsidiary of To the Moon—Luna Fine Furnishings—could change everything for her.

She was shocked that Shane had reached out to her, given he was pretty clear he'd dismissed her as part of the mean girls clique, along with her best friends Simone and Naomi. Admittedly, she wasn't very nice to his girlfriend Brandee and recent gossip had been less than flattering about Cecelia and her friends.

Some even suspected them of being behind the recent blackmailings. Shane was taking a huge leap of faith inviting her to submit her ideas for this incredible opportunity; she wasn't about to screw this up.

Cecelia gathered up everything into her portfolio binder and slipped it into her leather briefcase. She'd probably gone over it a hundred times already. She needed to stop fiddling with it and just let it lie. It was perfect. Some of her best work yet. As usual, she was putting too much pressure on herself. Her parents certainly didn't help matters. They always held Cecelia, their only child, to very high standards and never accepted anything less than perfection.

She supposed that was why she was so successful. Brent and Tilly Morgan were practically Texas royalty and had raised their daughter to follow in their footsteps. She went to the best private schools, rode horses and competed in dressage in high school, and went on to graduate summa cum laude with a business degree from a prestigious Ivy League university. Anything less for the younger Morgan would've been unacceptable.

While her parents had been supportive both emotionally and financially when it came to her company, Cecelia always worried that their support came at a price. If Luna Fine Furnishings wasn't the success that she hoped for, she might never hear the end of it. The last thing she needed was for her father to pat her on the back and tell her that maybe she needed to just stick with the baby things. You know…woman stuff. Or worse yet, to hand the business over to someone else and focus on settling down with Chip Ashford to make actual babies instead of baby furniture.

She wasn't opposed to settling down with Chip—he was her fiancé after all—but she certainly didn't want to throw away everything that she'd worked for in the process. Chip was a Texas senator, and he had been very supportive of her business so far. But Cecelia got the feeling that once they got married, Chip might feel the same way as her parents did.

It wasn't that she didn't want kids. Cecelia wanted her own children more than anything. But she was confident that she could be both a mother and the CEO of her own company. She didn't intend to set one ambition aside for the other.

A chime sounded on Cecelia's phone. She reached for it and tapped the screen to open up the Snapchat notification she'd just received for a private message. It took her a moment to realize what she was actually looking at. The picture was of a document with small text, but the header at the top brought a sinking feeling to her stomach. It read "Certificate of Birth" with the seal of the state of Texas on the bottom corner. The message across the screen was far more worrisome.

Somebody has got a secret.

Cecelia looked once more at the photo before it disappeared. It was then that she realized that this wasn't just any birth certificate, it was *her* original birth certificate. The one issued before she was adopted by the Morgans.

For a moment, Cecelia almost couldn't breathe. Her adoption had always been kept a secret. Everyone, including members of her extended family, believed that Cecelia was Brent and Tilly's biological daughter. Even Cecelia had believed it until her thirteenth birthday. That night, they'd told her that she was adopted but that they had kept it a secret for her own protection. The unfortunate truth was that her birth mother had been a junkie, and child services had taken Cecelia away from her when she was only a few weeks old. Her mother had overdosed not long after that, and she was put up for adoption. The Morgans thought that it was best if Cecelia's birth mother and that dark past were kept secret.

But someone had found out.

Cecelia didn't know how—she hadn't even seen her original birth certificate before. A new one had been issued when her adoption was finalized, so someone had done some serious sleuthing to find it.

Another image popped up on her screen. This one was a message written in letters cut from magazines like some sort of ransom note. She supposed that in some way, it *was* a ransom note. It demanded that twenty-five thousand dollars be wired to an account within twenty-four hours or her secret would be exposed to the entire town. It was signed, Maverick.

Considering everything that had been happening in Royal, Texas, lately, she should've known she would be targeted eventually. Maverick had been wreaking havoc on the lives of Royal residents for the past few months. This anonymous blackmailer had been the talk of the town, and everyone at the Texas Cattleman's Club had suspicions about who it could be. The most recent suspects had been Cecelia herself, along with Naomi and Simone.

Cecelia was a busy woman. She ran her own business, served as arm candy for her fiancé's various political events, was busy keeping up appearances for her parents and for Chip... She hardly had time in her schedule to get a manicure, much less to research and dig up dirt on her fellow residents. Her busy schedule and high standards made her come off as a bit snobbish, and Cecelia supposed she was, but she was no blackmailer. Unfortunately, the only way to prove it was to let everyone know that she was Maverick's latest victim.

That certainly wasn't an option. She couldn't have the whole town knowing that her entire life was a lie.

Unfortunately, this wasn't just her secret. Her parents had built their lives around their perfect "biological" daughter. They'd lied to countless family members and friends to keep up the charade, but they'd only done it to protect her. Paying Maverick was probably the only way to shield Brent and Tilly from the fallout.

But hers wasn't the only family she had to worry about. The Ashfords would have a fit. Chip came from a certain kind of family, and he believed that Cecelia was cut from the same cloth. Would Chip call off the engagement if he found out the truth? Their relationship was more about appearances and family alliances than love, but she hoped that Chip cared enough about her not to throw everything away if her secret got out. As far as she was concerned, she was a Morgan, through and through.

And as a Morgan, it was her responsibility to safeguard her and her family's reputation, or tomorrow's presentation would go down in flames. Her reputation where Shane was concerned was hanging on by a thread as it was. Surely, he wouldn't want a scandal to interfere with his hotel's grand opening.

But when did it stop? Would Maverick be content with the first payment, or would he drag this out until Cecelia was broke and her business was bankrupted?

Cecelia clutched her head in her hands and fought off a pending migraine. She'd suddenly found herself stuck between a rock and a hard place, and there was no easy way out of this. She either paid Maverick, or the truth of her adoption would be spread all over town. The clock was ticking.

She wasn't sure what her path forward would be, but Cecelia knew what she was doing next. In her life whenever a crisis arose, Cecelia always called her daddy. This conversation, however, was one that needed to be had in person. She didn't know how Maverick had found out about her adoption, but if her phone lines were tapped or her computer was being monitored, she couldn't risk anything but face-to-face communication.

It took Cecelia over an hour for her to reach her parents' mansion outside Houston. It was nearly ten o'clock by the time she arrived, but her parents would still be awake. As expected, she found her father sitting in his library. He was reading a book and smoking one of his favorite cigars.

Brent Morgan looked up in surprise when he noticed his daughter standing in the doorway of his library. "What are you doing here, sweetheart? Your mother didn't tell me were stopping by tonight."

Cecelia took a few steps into her father's favorite room and took a seat in the leather chair across from him. "She doesn't know I'm here. I'm in trouble, Daddy."

Furrowing his brow, he set aside his book and stubbed out his cigar. "What is it? Are you and Chip having problems?"

"No, this isn't about Chip." With a sigh, Cecelia told her father about the message she had received. His expression had morphed from concerned, to angry, to anxious as she spoke. "I've got twenty-four hours to wire them twenty-five thousand dollars, or everyone is going to know the truth."

"Our family can't afford a scandal like this. And imagine the pain this would bring to the Ashfords. Surely this isn't what you want. You're just going to have to pay him," he said, matter-of-factly.

Cecelia hated being put in a position where she had no options, and being under Maverick's thumb was the last place she wanted to be. The only real way to combat blackmail was by exposing the truth before the attacker could. If they beat Maverick to the punch they could put their own spin on her adoption and why they'd lied about it.

"Are you sure, Daddy? I mean, I know you and Mother were trying to protect me, but I'm a grown woman now. I'd rather the story not get out. However, would it be the end of the world if people discovered I was adopted? Does it change anything, really?"

"It absolutely does!" her father said with his face flushing red, making his salt-and-pepper hair appear more starkly white against his skin. "We've lied to everyone we know for thirty years. This would ruin our reputation. And what would the Ashfords think? They wouldn't understand. Neither would my customers or my friends. I could lose business. Hell, you could get thrown out of the Texas Cattleman's Club. It's social suicide, and your mother's heart couldn't take the scandal. No," he insisted. "This stays a secret. Period. I will loan you the money if you need it to pay the blackmailer, but you *will* pay him."

Cecelia noted the finality in her father's tone. It had been the same when she was an unruly child, the same when she was a teenager testing her boundaries. She was an adult now, but Brent Morgan was still in charge. She didn't have the nerve to go against him then, and she certainly didn't have the nerve to do it now. She'd come here for his advice, and she'd be a fool not to take it.

"No, I have the money. I'll make the transfer in the morning. I just hope it is enough to put an end to all of this."

"It has to be," her father said. "I refuse to have our family turned into laughingstocks."

Cecelia sighed in resignation and got up from her seat. "I'll take care of it, Daddy."

Deacon Chase turned his restored 1965 Corvette Stingray down the main street of Royal, Texas. It'd been thirteen years since he'd looked at this town in his rearview mirror and swore he'd never set foot in this narrow-minded, Texas dust trap again. The whole flight over from France, he questioned why he was coming back. Yes, it was good business, and working with his old friend from high school, Shane Delgado, had always been a pleasant experience. But when Shane mentioned that he wanted to build a resort in their hometown of Royal, he should have passed.

Then again, when else would he get the chance to show the town and the people who rejected him that he was better than them? Sure, back then he'd just been a poor kid with few prospects. He was the son of a grocery store clerk and the local car mechanic. He'd gotten to go to private school with all the rich kids only because his parents had been adamant that Deacon make something of himself, and they'd put every dime they had toward his schooling. Even then he had worked in the cafeteria to bridge the gap in tuition. Nobody else had expected much out of him, and those were the people who even acknowledged he existed. As far as most the residents of Royal were concerned, Deacon had never fit in, never would fit in and needed to accept his station in life.

No one had expected him to take his hobby of restoring cars and parlay the skills and money into restoring houses. They certainly hadn't expected him to take the profit from those houses and put it into renovating hotels. Now the kid who worked in the cafeteria was a billionaire and the owner of the most glamorous resort in Cannes, France, the Hotel de Rêve, among others.

The only person in Royal who had ever believed in him was Cecelia. Back in high school, she'd pushed him to be the best person he could be. Considering that she'd held herself to such high standards, he'd been flattered that she saw so much potential in him when most of the people in high school either ignored him or taunted him. Cecelia had said he was a diamond in the rough. *Her* diamond in the rough.

It'd certainly blown the minds of all the boys at school that Cecelia had chosen Deacon instead of one of them. What could he offer her after all? A free carton of milk with her lunch? It turned out that he'd had plenty to offer her. He could still remember how many hours they'd spent lying in the back of his pickup truck talking. Kissing. Dreaming aloud about their future together. Deacon and Cecelia had had big plans for their lives after graduation.

Step one had been to get the hell out of Royal, Texas. Step two had been to live happily-ever-after.

As Deacon came to a stop at the traffic light at the intersection of Main Street and First Avenue, he shook his head in disgust. He had been a fool to think any of that would ever happen. He might have fancy hotels and expensive suits, sports cars and a forty-foot yacht docked in the French Riviera, but Deacon knew, and everybody else knew, that Cecelia was too good for him.

It hadn't taken long for Cecelia to figure that out, too.

The light turned green, and Deacon continued down the road to where his father's old garage used to be. When he'd made his first million, Deacon had moved his parents out of Royal and into a nice subdivision in central Florida. There, they could enjoy their early retirement without the meddling of the snooty residents of Royal. His father had sold the shop, and now a new shopping center was sitting where it used to be. A lot had changed in the last thirteen years.

Deacon couldn't help but wonder how much Cecelia had changed. He tried not to cyberstalk her, but from time to time he couldn't help looking over the Houston society pages to see what she was up to. The grainy black-and-white pictures hardly did her beauty justice, he was certain. The last time he'd seen her, she'd been a young woman, barely eighteen. Even then, Deacon had been certain that she was the most beautiful woman he would ever see in person. He would bet that time had been kind to his Cecelia.

Not that it mattered. The most recent article he'd stumbled across in the paper had included the announcement of her engagement to Chip Ashford. He remembered Chip from high school. He was a rich, entitled, first-class douche bag. Deacon was fairly certain that that hadn't changed, but if Cecelia was willing to marry him, she certainly wasn't the girl that he remembered. Back then, she'd hardly given Chip the time of day.

Mr. and Mrs. Morgan must be so proud of her now. She'd finally made a respectable choice in a man.

Turning off the main drag, Deacon headed down the narrow country road out of Royal that led to his latest real estate acquisition. The rustic yet luxurious lodge that was to serve as his home base in the area stood on three acres of wooded land several miles outside town. He'd bought the property sight unseen when he decided to take on The Bellamy project with Shane. He couldn't be happier with the place. It was very much his style, although it was a far cry from the elegant European architecture and design that he'd become accustomed to.

He hadn't really needed to buy the home. Deacon had no real intention of staying in Royal any longer than he had to. But the businessman in him had a hard time passing up a good deal, and it seemed a shame to throw money away on renting a place while they built the hotel. He had no regrets. It was his happy retreat, away from the society jungles of Royal.

When he pulled up in front of the lodge, he was surprised to find Shane Delgado's truck parked out front. Deacon parked the Corvette in his garage, then stepped out front to meet his friend and business partner.

Deacon hadn't had many friends back in school. Basically none. But his side business of buying and restoring cars had drawn Shane's attention. Shane had actually bought Deacon's very first restoration, a

1975 cherry-red Ford pickup truck with white leather seats. Deacon had been damn proud of that truck, especially when Shane had handed over the cash for it without questioning his asking price. They'd bonded then over a mutual love of cars and had continued to keep in touch over the years. When they both ended up in the real estate development business, it was natural for them to consider working together on a few projects.

"What's wrong now?" Deacon asked as he joined Shane at the bottom of his front steps.

While the construction of The Bellamy had gone relatively smoothly, Deacon was the silent partner. Shane bothered him with details only when something had gone awry. He joked with Shane once that he was getting to the point that he dreaded the sight of his friend's face.

"For once," Shane said with a smile, "I'm just here to hang out and have a drink with my friend. Everything at the hotel is going splendidly. Tomorrow, Cecelia Morgan will be presenting her designs to the board, based on your recommendation. Assuming we like what Cecelia did, and I hope I'm not going too far out on a limb here, we'll be moving forward and getting that much closer to opening the hotel."

Deacon slapped his friend on the back of the shoulder. "I wouldn't have brought her on board if I didn't think she was the best designer for the job. Come on in," he said as they started up the massive stone stairs to the front door. "Have you eaten?" he asked as they made their way into his office for a drink.

Shane nodded. "I have. Brandee is constantly feeding me. By the end of the year, I'm going to weigh three hundred pounds."

"You're a lucky man," Deacon said as he poured them both a couple of fingers of whiskey over ice. Shane had recently gotten involved with Brandee Lawless, the owner of the nearby Hope Springs Ranch. She was a tiny blonde spitfire, and one hell of a cook. "I'd be happy to have Brandee feeding me every night."

"I bet you would," Shane said. "But you need to just stick with your cultured European women."

Deacon chuckled at his friend's remark. He had certainly taken advantage of the local delicacies while he was in Europe. Even though it'd been years since he and Cecelia had broken up, it had soothed his injured pride to have a line of beautiful and exotic women waiting for their chance to be with him. He would never admit to anyone, especially Shane, that not a one of them held a candle to Cecelia in his mind.

Deacon and Shane sat there together, sipping their drinks and enjoying each other's company. They didn't get a lot of opportunities to just hang out anymore. Deacon's office, however, just begged for gentlemen to spend time in comfortable chairs and shoot the shit. The walls were lined with shelves containing leather-bound books that, frankly, came with the house and Deacon would never read. They did create a nice atmosphere, though, along with the oil paintings of landscapes and cattle that hung there. It was all very masculine Texas style.

"Can I ask you something?" Shane asked.

"Sure. What?"

"You do know that Cecelia's business specializes in children's furniture, right?"

Deacon tensed in his chair. Perhaps his office made Shane too comfortable, since he felt like prying into Deacon's motivations for wanting Cecelia for the job. "Yeah, I know. I also know that she's managed to turn her small company into a furniture and accessories juggernaut since she started it. She's always had a good eye for design."

"She does, I won't argue that. But hiring her to decorate The Bellamy is a huge risk. She and Brandee aren't exactly fans of each other. And what if she and her friends are actually behind the cyberattacks? That's not the kind of publicity we'd want for our hotel. I don't have to remind you how much we stand to lose if our gamble doesn't pay off."

"That's why we just asked her to submit a proposal along with the two other design firms. We haven't hired anybody yet. If she's out of her depth in this, or acts suspicious in any way, we thank her for her time and send her on her way. It's not ideal, but not the end of the world, either."

Shane narrowed his gaze at him. He obviously suspected that Deacon had ulterior motives in wanting Cecelia involved in the project. Deacon understood. He wasn't entirely sure that he didn't.

"I'm not sold on either of the other firm's designs. She's last to present, so if she flops tomorrow, it's going to set the project back weeks while we find yet another designer and they start from scratch. We have hotel bookings starting day one. Every delay costs us money."

Deacon just nodded. He was well aware that he was taking a risk. But for some reason, he had to do it. Perhaps he was a glutton for punishment. Perhaps he was looking for any excuse to see her again. He wasn't sure. The only thing he was sure of was that everything would turn out fine. "Relax, Shane. The project will finish on time and on budget with the amazing decor you're hoping for."

"And how do you know that?" Shane asked, sounding unconvinced.

"Because," Deacon said confidently, "Cecelia hasn't failed at anything in her entire life. She's not going to start now."

# Two

"Welcome, Miss Morgan. Please have a seat."

Cecelia took two steps into the boardroom and stopped short as she recognized the man's voice. She looked up and found herself staring into the green-and-gold eyes of her past. She couldn't take a single step farther. Her heart stuttered as her mind raced to make sense of what she was seeing. It wasn't possible that Deacon Chase, her first love, was sitting at the head of the boardroom table beside Shane Delgado.

Deacon had disappeared from Royal almost immediately after they graduated from high school. No one in town had seen or heard a word from him since then. She remembered being told that his parents had moved to Florida, and she had occasionally wondered what he had made of himself, but she hadn't had the heart to look him up and find out. She knew that it was best to keep Deacon a part of her past, and yet here he was, a critical element to the success of her future.

Cecelia realized she was standing awkwardly at the entrance to the conference room with the entire board of directors staring at her. She snapped out of it, pasting a wide smile on her face and walking to the front of the room where an empty seat was waiting for her. Beside him.

"Thank you, everyone, for having me here today. I'm very pleased to have the opportunity to present my designs for The Bellamy Hotel to the board. I'm really in love with what I have put together for you all today, and I hope it meets your expectations."

Deacon's cold gaze followed her around the room to where she had taken her seat, but she tried not to let it get to her. The man had every reason to hate her, so she shouldn't expect anything less.

She knew that Shane had a silent partner in The Bellamy project, but she'd never dreamed that it would be Deacon. She had a hard time believing it was even Deacon sitting there, considering how much he'd changed since she saw him last.

His lanky teenaged body had grown into itself, with broad shoulders and muscular arms that strained against the fabric of his expensively tailored navy suit. His jaw was more square and hardened now, as though he was trying to hold in the venomous words he had for her. The lines etched around his eyes and into his furrowed brow made it look like he didn't smile much anymore.

That made Cecelia sad. The Deacon she remembered had been full of life, despite the miserable hand that he had been dealt as a child. Back in high school, he'd had so much potential in him, Cecelia just couldn't wait to see what he was going to do with his future.

Now she knew. It appeared as though Deacon had done extremely well for himself. He had gone from the kid working in the cafeteria to the man who held her future in his hands.

Opening her portfolio, she sorted through her papers and prepared to give the presentation she had practiced repeatedly since Shane had called and offered her a chance to bid on the job. She pulled out several watercolor renderings of the designs, placing them on the easel behind her. Then, taking a deep breath and looking at everyone but Deacon, Cecelia began her presentation.

It was easy for her to get lost in the details of her plan for the hotel. Discussing fabric choices, wooden furnishing pieces, style and design was what she knew best. She had a very distinct point of view that she wanted to express for The Bellamy to separate it from all the other high-class resorts in the Houston area.

Judging by the smiles and nods of the people sitting around the conference room table, she had hit it out of the park. The only person who looked less than impressed, of course, was Deacon. His eyes still focused on her like lasers, but his expression was unreadable.

"Does anyone have any questions?" She looked around the room, ready to field any of the board's concerns. No one spoke up.

Shane finally stood up and walked around the table to shake Cecelia's hand. "Thank you so much, Cecelia," he said with an oddly relieved smile on his face. "I admit I was reluctant to believe you were the right designer for the job, but I must say I'm very impressed. You've done a great job. You're the last to present your designs, so we will have to discuss your proposal, and then we will get back to you about contracts. If we decide to go with Luna Fine Furnishings, how long do you think it will be before you can start work on the hotel?"

Her heart was pounding, but whether it was from Shane's question or Deacon being mere inches away, she couldn't say. "I have already started putting the major furniture pieces into production at my manufacturing facility," Cecelia said. Several of the designs were tweaks of her existing furniture, and it was easy to get them started. "I also put in an order for the fabric, and it should arrive tomorrow. I took the risk, hoping that you would accept my proposal. If you don't like what I've done, I'm going to have to find a new home for about two hundred and fifty dressers."

The people around the table chuckled. Shane just smiled. "A risk-taker. I like it. Well, hopefully we will find a good home for all those dressers. We hope to open the resort by the end of the month. Do you think you can make that happen?"

By the end of the month? Cecelia's stomach started to ache with dread. Even with construction complete, that was an extremely tight schedule. Two hundred and fifty suites in a month! Although she was expecting the fabric for the curtains and upholstered chairs, it would still take time to make the pieces. She wasn't about to say no, however. She could sleep when April was over. "Absolutely. We may have to have our craftsmen working around the clock to get all the pieces together and the wallpaper on the walls, but I think we can make it happen."

Cecelia tried to keep her focus on Shane, but Deacon's appraising gaze kept drawing her attention away. He still wasn't smiling like everyone else. But he wasn't glaring at her angrily anymore, either. Now he was just watching. Thinking, processing. She had no idea what was going on inside Deacon's brain because he hadn't spoken since he welcomed her into the room. Part of her wished she knew. Part of her didn't.

"That all sounds great. If you will give us just a few minutes, we're going to meet and will be right with you. Would you mind waiting in the lobby?"

"Not at all." Cecelia gathered her things up into her portfolio and, with a smile, stepped out of the room. The moment she shut the door behind her she felt like a weight had been lifted from her shoulders. Somehow, having that wall between her and Deacon seemed to make a difference. Thankfully, his laser-like vision couldn't reach her through the drywall and the expensive wallpaper of Shane's offices.

No question, he had rattled her. He'd probably intended to. After everything she'd done to Deacon, she deserved it. For the first time, she started to doubt that she would land this job. Yes, Shane had personally approached her about it, but perhaps Deacon had agreed to it just so he could have the opportunity to reject her the way she'd rejected him all those years ago.

She poured herself a glass of water at the nearby beverage station and took a seat, waiting anxiously for their decision. She was surprised they were moving so quickly, but if they needed the hotel done by the end of the month, there really wasn't a choice. She was the last designer to present her ideas, so the time to decide was here.

About ten minutes later, the door opened and a flow of board members exited the room. Cecelia waited patiently until her name was called and then stepped back into the conference room. The only person left in there was Deacon. She struggled to maintain her professional composure as she waited for him to finally speak to her. Now that they were alone, she was expecting him to lay into her about why she didn't deserve the job.

Instead, he smiled politely and stuffed his hands into his pants pockets. "I won't prolong the torture, Ms. Morgan. The bottom line is that everyone is very pleased with your designs and the direction that you'd like to take for The Bellamy. Shane has gone upstairs to have our contracts department write up something, and we will have it couriered over to your offices as soon as it's ready. Presuming, of course, that you will accept the job."

She'd be crazy not to. The budget that Shane had discussed with her was more than enough to cover materials and labor expenses and provide a tidy profit for her to add to her company's bottom line. She and her team would be working hard to earn it, but the very future of Luna Fine Furnishings was riding on the success of this project. *No* simply wasn't an option. She didn't want to seem too eager, however, especially where Deacon was concerned. "I'm happy to hear that you're pleased. I look forward to reviewing the contracts and touching base with you and Shane."

He nodded. "I understand the schedule is a bit hectic. The ground floor of the hotel has a business suite with several offices available for future hotel management. We're happy to offer you an on-site office location to help you better manage your team and their progress."

That would help. Especially if there was a cot in it where she could sleep. Perhaps she could finish a room so she could stay in it. "That would be lovely, thank you." She hesitated a moment before she spoke again. "May I ask you something?"

Deacon raised his brow in curiosity. "Of course."

She knew she should take the offer and run, but she wanted to know why they'd chosen her. Why *he'd* chosen her. "I am very grateful for this opportunity, but I'm curious as to why you chose to go with me instead of an established design firm. I'm sure you're aware that I've specialized in nursery and children's furnishings for the last few years. This is my first foray in adult luxury design."

Deacon nodded and thought over his response. "Shane and I requested your proposal because we knew the quality would be high. To the Moon is known for producing the best you can buy for a child's room. There's no reason for us to believe it would be any different with your adult designs. You're the best at whatever you choose to do, Cecelia. You always were."

There was a flicker of pain in his eyes as he spoke, but it was quickly masked by the return of his cold indifference to her. "If you'll excuse me," he said, before turning and marching quickly from the conference room.

Cecelia was left standing there, a little shell-shocked from their encounter. He said she was the best at what she did, but she could read between the lines—*except when it came to us*. She excelled in business but was a miserable failure when it came to love.

Deacon might be willing to hire her to do a job she was well capable of, but it was clear that he wasn't about to forgive her for what she'd done to him.

Deacon had made a mistake.

The minute Cecelia had strolled into that conference room, it had felt as though someone had punched him in the stomach. He'd tried to maintain the appearance of the confident, arrogant businessman, but on the inside he felt anything but. His chest was constricted, and he couldn't breathe. His heart was racing like he was in the middle of a marathon. He had thought he would be immune to her after all this time, but he was wrong.

Cecelia had been wearing a smart, tailored ivory-and-gold suit that accented every curve of her womanly figure. That certainly wasn't the body he remembered. She was still petite, but she had grown up quite a bit since he saw her last. He was still attempting to recover from the tantalizing glimpse of her cleavage at the V of her blouse when she smiled at him and flipped her long blond curls casually over her shoulder.

Instantly, he knew he was lost.

What the hell was he thinking coming back here? And an even better question, why had he insisted that Shane give Cecelia the opportunity to compete for the design job? He had all but guaranteed that he would come face-to-face with her like this. It was a terrible idea.

Cecelia had begun her presentation talking about fabrics and furniture details he really didn't give a damn about. He'd hardly heard a word she said. His mind was clouded with the scent of her perfume, reminding him of hot nights in the back of his pickup truck. It was the same scent she'd worn in high school. He'd had to save up for two months to be able to afford a bottle of it for her birthday.

Now all he could think about was her naked, willing body sprawled out beneath his own, his nose buried in her throat, drawing her scent deep into his lungs. They had dated for only six months during their senior year, but they had been some of the best months of his life. Deacon hadn't been sure what he was going to do with his life or if he was ever going to make something of himself, but he instantly knew that he wanted Cecelia to be a part of his future. He couldn't remember how many times they'd made love, but he knew it hadn't been enough.

Looking at her during the presentation, as she'd gestured toward a watercolor rendering of a guest suite, all he could see was the younger Cecelia sitting on his tailgate smiling at him.

Suddenly, every muscle in his body had tensed, every nerve firing sparks of need through him. Occasionally, Cecelia's gaze would flick over him and his throat threatened to close. He'd gripped the arm of his executive chair, trying to ground himself and calm down. It had been no way to act during a professional board meeting. If she had finished her briefing early, he wouldn't have been able to stand up to thank her without embarrassing himself.

Deacon thought that returning to Royal as a successful real estate developer would change things. But every ounce of cockiness and confidence seemed to fly out the window the moment he'd laid eyes on Cecelia. Suddenly, he was an awkward teenager again. His old insecurities washed over him. He hadn't been good enough for her then, and for some reason he didn't feel good enough for her even now.

Of course, it hadn't helped that their last conversation on graduation night had been her breaking up with him. He didn't know exactly what had made her change her mind. Up until that point, she'd been very enthusiastic about their plans and their future together. Then, suddenly, she'd turned a one-eighty on him and walked away.

Deacon had always known he wasn't the kind of boy the Morgans wanted for their daughter. He didn't come from a good family, he was poor and he worked with his hands. He was certain that Brent and Tilly were thrilled that Cecelia had chosen someone like Chip Ashford, former captain of the football team, Texas senator, son of one of the most respected and wealthy families in Houston. He had a bright future ahead of him, no doubt.

Damn him for putting himself in this position, knowing he would be drawn to Cecelia as he always had been, but once again unable to have what he wanted.

He had to remind himself that he hadn't returned to Royal to seduce Cecelia. That wasn't why he'd asked her to do this presentation, either. He had come back to prove to her, and everyone else in the small-minded little town, that he was better than them. To show them that he could take his humble beginnings and still manage to create an empire faster than any of them could manage to inherit. He'd come back to make Cecelia regret her decision. To make the Morgans regret their decision. Nothing more.

When he completed his mission and opened his new hotel, Deacon would return to Europe, indulge his vices and forget all about the cliquish and unimportant people of Royal, Texas.

Well, he doubted he'd forget about Cecelia.

He'd only *thought* it was hard being around Cecelia while she did her presentation. Being alone with her had been agonizing. What was he going to do now that she would be working at his hotel nonstop until it opened? He wouldn't be able to get away from her even if he wanted to. And he didn't.

He felt like an idiot as he strolled down the hallway to the office Shane had provided for him while he was in town. He felt like he'd run away from Cecelia. He should've been more confident, indifferent, as though she'd had no impact on him at all.

Just as he sat down at his desk, Shane appeared in his doorway. "A successful day, I'd say! We not only have a hotel, but the guests won't be sleeping on the floor. What do you say we go down to the Texas Cattleman's Club and celebrate with a drink?"

Deacon arched a brow at his friend. He'd never set foot in that building before. He hadn't even been good enough to clean their pool back in high school. "I'm not a member," he pointed out. "And I'm sure there are plenty of people in the club who would see to it that I never get to be one of them."

Shane dismissed him. "You are certainly welcome as my guest. And if you really wanted to be in the club I could sponsor you. I'm sure few people would have the nerve to speak up against me. Lately, the uproar has been more about the Maverick scandals, and I'm pretty sure that doesn't involve you. Aside from that, there are still a few folks sore that women can become members of the club. You should've heard some of the bitching when the billiards room was converted to a day care. I'm sure they'd be happy to admit you and counteract the appearance that it's turning into a henhouse instead of a clubhouse."

Deacon had never entertained the idea of joining the club. And all things considered, he really didn't want anything to do with an organization that had just decided in the past few years that women were worthy of participating. But he wouldn't be rude about it because he knew Shane was a member and enjoyed it. "No thanks. I think I'm going to finish up a few things here and call it a night. There is a T-bone steak in the fridge that's begging to be grilled tonight, and I can't disappoint it."

Shane smiled. "Okay, if you insist. But I'm going to drag you down there one day, though."

"Why? What's so great about a bunch of people sitting around in cowboy hats—which I don't own—talking about cattle and horses—which I'm not interested in?"

"Well, for one thing, the restaurant makes the finest steaks you'll ever eat. The bartenders pour a perfectly balanced dry martini. It's a nice place to hang out, have a drink and chat with friends."

Deacon supposed that to anyone else, it would sound very inviting. "Well, you're my only friend in town, so again, I'll pass. You go on and eat a finely prepared steak on my behalf."

Shane finally gave up, nodding and throwing up a hand in goodbye.

Deacon watched him go, relieved that he managed to get out of dinner. He had many reasons for avoiding the clubhouse, but the biggest one was Cecelia and Chip. He knew that both of them were members, and he had no interest in running into either of them tonight. Not after she'd spent the afternoon twisting his insides into knots.

No, he needed a little time before he saw Cecelia again. He needed to remind himself how badly she'd hurt him and how much he wanted her to regret what she'd done. To keep his head on straight, he had to stay away from her.

A steak, a stiff drink and a Netflix binge would do it.

He hoped.

# Three

When Cecelia got back to her office later that afternoon, she found a giddy Simone waiting for her in the lobby. Cecelia loved Simone, she was one of her best friends in the whole world, but after the day she'd had—hell, after the week she'd had—she wasn't really in the mood. She had to jump on this Bellamy job right away if they were going to make the grand opening deadline.

Simone obviously didn't care, ignoring the stressed-out vibes Cecelia knew she was sending out. She followed Cecelia down the halls of To the Moon to her private office. "Have you heard the latest news?" Simone asked after she slipped into the room behind her.

Cecelia dropped her things down on her desk and

plopped, exhausted, into her chair. "Nope. There's news?"

Simone rubbed her hands together in excitement and rushed over to sit on the edge of her desk. "So," she began, "word is that Maverick is at it again. A message went out on social media to everybody in the Texas Cattleman's Club today."

Cecelia held her breath as she waited to hear the latest news. She'd been too busy with The Bellamy project to check her phone. Had Maverick taken her money and spread her secret anyway? "So, what did the message say?"

Simone pulled her cell out of her purse and flipped through it to find the message. Locating it, she handed the phone over to Cecelia. The message was short and blessedly vague. It read: Someone in the Texas Cattleman's Club is not who they say they are.

Cecelia shrugged it off and handed the mobile back to Simone, feigning disinterest. "That's hardly big news. I'd say half the people there aren't who they pretend to be."

Simone returned her phone to her bag. "And to think that folks still believe we're the ones behind the attacks!"

"I have to say I'm thankful this last message went out when I couldn't possibly have sent it. I've got a room full of witnesses."

Simone just shrugged. "That doesn't mean they don't still think Naomi and I are the culprits, that we're all in on it together. If I had the time, I just might be the kind to do it. You've got to give the guy credit. Royal has been pretty dull lately. Maverick has brought more excitement to town in the last few months than we've had since the tornados hit."

Excitement? Cecelia certainly wouldn't consider extortion or extreme weather exciting. They were both terrifying in their own right. "You know, you might not want to act so excited when that stuff comes out. It makes us look guilty."

"Hey, I thought you would enjoy this more. What's wrong with you today? You don't seem like your usual self."

Cecelia wanted to shout, *"Because the real Maverick is blackmailing me! That message was about me!"* But she wouldn't. Instead she said, "I'm just stressed out and tired. I had that big presentation today at The Bellamy."

Simone perked up again. "So, how did it go? Did you dazzle Shane with your designs? Is he going to dump Brandee and run away with you? Please tell me that at the very least he wasn't rude."

"He was fine. And Brandee didn't even come up. You could say that I dazzled him, since they offered me the contract. It seems I also dazzled his silent partner, Deacon Chase."

Simone's nose wrinkled in thought as she tried to place the name. "Deacon Chase. Why do I know that name?"

"Because," Cecelia explained, "that was my first boyfriend in high school."

Simone's eyes grew as wide as saucers. "Are you

kidding me? Is *that* Deacon Chase Shane's silent partner? Didn't you lose your virginity to him?"

Cecelia looked around nervously to make sure that none of her employees overheard their discussion. Getting up from her chair, she ran to her office door and shut it. "Say it a little louder, Simone. Yes, Deacon was my first." Those weren't exactly helpful memories considering he was in town at the moment, but they were true. Deacon had been the first boy she ever loved. The last boy she'd ever loved.

"Does Chip know he's in town?"

"Does that matter?" Cecelia asked. "Chip and I didn't date in high school. We didn't even date in college. He's got no reason to worry about Deacon."

Simone wasn't convinced. "Yeah, but he knows you two dated and were pretty serious. You don't think it's going to bother him that Deacon is back in Royal?"

If there was only one thing that Cecelia knew about Chip, it was that his ego was bigger than the state of Texas. In his opinion, Deacon was from a lower class of people. He wasn't competition in Chip's eyes, and never would be. "I don't think it would bother Chip. I mean, I agreed to marry Chip. I broke it off with Deacon after graduation, so I don't know why he would feel threatened by him."

Simone shook her head. "Chip may not have been threatened by the Deacon we knew back in high school, but if he is Shane's partner in the hotel, he's done well for himself. That may change things."

Cecelia wasn't sure about that, but she didn't really have time to worry. "Well, I'm sure that Deacon won't stay. He will be long gone once the hotel is finished. Speaking of Chip, I've got to get out of here. He and I are meeting for dinner tonight at the club. We're celebrating my new contract with the hotel."

"Excellent. I've really got to get out of here, too. I just stopped by on my way out of town to share the latest gossip. I'm meeting Naomi at the airport. We're flying out tonight to that fashion show in LA. We'll be there for a couple of days. You be sure to keep us posted if anything new happens with Maverick."

"I will, although I'm not sure you'd be so excited about his next attack if he were blackmailing *you*." Cecelia certainly didn't feel that way now that she was his latest victim.

"Oh, I'm sure he'll get to me eventually. He'll get to all of us eventually."

Simone practically skipped out of Cecelia's office as if Maverick's threats didn't bother her. Cecelia hadn't been bothered, either, until a few days ago. Now the worry was front and center.

He had to be alluding to her in his latest message. She had wired the money the way her dad had instructed her to, and yet he hadn't backed off. It was exactly what she was afraid of. Once you stepped into the cycle of blackmail, there was no good way to get out of it. She wouldn't be surprised to see another message tonight asking for more money. Despite what her father had told her, Cecelia knew she had to use a different tact with Maverick.

Her parents didn't want her to tell Chip the truth, but that might be her only option if Maverick didn't back down. Chip's family was not only wealthy, but they had connections. If she confided her secret in him perhaps he could help to protect her. The Ashfords could crush Maverick like a bug...*if* they wanted to. She hoped they would, because she didn't know who else to turn to. She would have to tell him tonight at dinner before things got worse.

She was counting on him to be her savior.

Cecelia was a ball of nerves as she pulled her BMW into the parking lot of the Texas Cattleman's Club.

The club wasn't where she would've chosen to have this important discussion with Chip, but he had made the arrangements without asking her. Inside, she found Chip seated in the far corner booth of the dining room. She let the host escort her back to the table. Chip got up as she approached and gave her a short embrace and a chaste kiss on the cheek. "There you are, kitten. You're late. I was starting to worry."

Cecelia looked at her watch as she sat down and it was exactly five thirty. She wasn't about to argue with him, though. To Chip, if you didn't arrive five minutes early, you were late. "I'm sorry. I got hung up with Simone. She wanted to talk to me before she left for California with Naomi."

Chip settled into the booth across from her and smiled. "And what did the lovely Simone have to tell you today?"

Cecelia considered her words. "Well, I wanted to wait to talk to you about this until after we ordered."

"I already ordered for us both," Chip interjected. "I got you the grilled mahimahi since you're watching your weight for the wedding."

Cecelia tried to swallow her irritation. She hated when Chip made decisions for her. Especially when those decisions were based on imaginary weight she had no intention of losing, *thankyouverymuch*. It was a portent of her future with him that she tried hard to ignore. She feared she would be going from spending all her time trying to please her parents, to trying to please her husband.

"Then I suppose I don't have to wait," she said, ignoring his comments. "Simone told me that Maverick is blackmailing somebody new."

Chip nodded thoughtfully and accepted the gin and tonic the waiter brought him before placing a glass of white wine in front of Cecelia. "I saw something come up this afternoon, but I was too busy to pay much attention to it. What does that have to do with Simone? Is she his latest victim? I wouldn't be surprised if she got into some trouble."

Cecelia steeled her nerves, thankful for the glass of wine even though she would've preferred a red. She took a healthy sip before she started the discussion. "No, he's actually blackmailing me."

"What?" Chip shushed her, leaning into her across the table. "Not so loud, people will hear you." He scanned the dining area for anyone who might hear. Fortunately, it was still early for the dinner crowd at the club. The closest table was involved in a lively discussion about steer and not paying any attention to them. "What is going on?" he asked when he seemed certain it was safe to continue their discussion.

Cecelia followed suit, leaning in and speaking in low, hushed tones. "I got a message from him. It seems he found something out about me from a long time ago, and he's trying to blackmail me with it. Well, I supposed he's been successful since I've already made one payment to him, but it doesn't seem like it was enough, given the post this afternoon."

Chip's expression was stiff and stoic, without any of the sympathy or concern for her that she was hoping for. "What is he blackmailing you about? You told me you had a squeaky-clean past. It's absolutely critical, if you're going to be the wife of a senator, that you don't have anything in your life that can be detrimental to my career."

Cecelia sighed. How did this become about him and his career? "I know. It's not really something I think about very often. It was completely out of my control. My parents chose to keep it secret to protect me, but in the end, I don't think it's that bad. It's hardly a skeleton in my closet, Chip."

Chip eyed her expectantly, but she hesitated. She hadn't said the words out loud in thirteen years. Only ever said them once, the night she confided in Deacon. Somehow she wasn't sure this would go as well. "I'm adopted," she whispered.

Chip flinched as though she had slapped him across the face. "Adopted? Why didn't you tell me?"

Cecelia gritted her teeth at his reaction. She could already tell this was a mistake. "No one was ever to find out. I was adopted by the Morgans when I was only a few weeks old. They decided to raise me as their own child and have never told anybody about my history…because of who my mother was."

"What's wrong with your mother?"

"She had a drug problem. I was taken away from her when I was only two weeks old. My parents told me that she was so distraught, she overdosed not long after that."

A furious expression came over Chip's face. "Are you telling me that your mother was a junkie?"

There was no way to make that part go down easier. "I guess so. She was never a part of my life, but yes, my mother had a serious and deadly drug problem."

Chip didn't appear to even hear her words. "I cannot believe you would lie to me about something like this." He flushed an ugly red with anger. She'd never seen her polished and professional fiancé like this. "I thought you were like me. I thought you were from a good family and would make a perfect wife. But you're nothing but an impostor playing a role. How could you agree to marry me when you were keeping something like that a secret?"

Cecelia's jaw dropped open in shock. She thought he might be surprised by the news, maybe even concerned about the potential backlash, but she certainly didn't think that he would accuse her of deceiving him. "I am not an impostor, Chip Ashford. You have known me my whole life. I was raised by the Morgans in the same Houston suburb you were. I went to all the best schools like you did. I am nothing like my birth mother, and I never will be. I couldn't control who my mother was any more than you could."

Chip just shook his head. "You can dress it up, but a liar is always a liar."

Cecelia's blood ran cold in her veins. "Chip, please, don't be like this. I didn't intentionally deceive you. My parents just thought it was best that no one know."

"Thank goodness for Maverick," Chip said. "Without him I never would've found out the truth about you. You and your parents would've let me marry you knowing that everything I believed about you was a lie."

Her eyes welled up with tears she couldn't fight. Was Chip about to break up with her over this? She couldn't believe it, but that's what it sounded like. "Chip..."

"Don't," he snapped. "Don't look at me like that with tears in your eyes and try to convince me that you are a victim in this. I'm sorry, Cecelia, but the engagement is off. I can't marry somebody I can't trust. You're a liability to every future campaign I run, and I'm not about to destroy my career for a woman who is living a lie."

Cecelia looked down at the gigantic diamond-and-platinum ring that she'd worn for the past six months of their engagement. She hadn't particularly liked the ring, but couldn't say so. It was gaudy, but it was as expected for someone of his station. She didn't want to keep it, not when his words were like a knife to the heart. She grasped it between her fingers and tugged it off her hand, handing it across the table.

Chip took it and stuffed it into his pocket. "Thank you for being reasonable about that."

At least one of them could be reasonable, she thought as the pain of his rejection slowly morphed into anger. She never would've confided in Chip if she'd known he would react like this. Now, all she could hope for was damage control. "I hope that I can still count on you to keep this secret," Cecelia said. "Odds are it will get out eventually, but I would prefer it to be on my terms if you don't mind. For my parents' sake."

Chip got up from the table and shrugged it off. "What good would it do me to tell anybody? I've wasted enough time here. Have the waiter put dinner on my tab." He turned on his heel and marched out of the restaurant, leaving Cecelia to sit alone with their cocktails, a basket of bread sticks and an order for food they wouldn't even eat.

A hollow feeling echoed through her as she looked at his empty seat. Cecelia thought she would be more upset about her broken engagement, but she was just numb. The truth was that she didn't love Chip. Their relationship was more about strategic family connections than romance, but it still smarted to have him dump her like this when she was at her lowest point. They had planned a future together. They discussed how after The Bellamy deal they were going to sit down and make some solid wedding plans. Instead of finally getting one step closer to the family that she longed for, she was starting over.

Even if Chip kept his word and didn't spread her secret all over town, it would be embarrassing enough for everyone to find out about her broken engagement. Everyone would speculate about why they broke up if neither of them was talking. She wondered what Chip would tell them.

In the end, she was certain that her secret would come out anyway. One way or another everyone was going to find out that Cecelia was the adopted daughter of a junkie. Royal was a place where everybody was always in everyone else's business. They had all the drama and glamour that the Houston society provided, with all of the small-town nosiness that Cecelia could do without.

When the truth came to light, she wondered who would still be standing beside her. The members of the Texas Cattleman's Club were supposed to be like a family, but they were a fickle one.

Then there was the matter of her real family. How would her parents ever recover from the fallout? They'd built their lives on maintaining a perfect facade. Would their family, circle of friends and business contacts ever forgive the decades-long deception?

Reeling from the events of the evening, Cecelia picked up her purse and got up from the table, leaving a stack of bills to cover the tab. She could've let Chip pay for it all, but she didn't want to face the waiter and explain why she was suddenly alone with a tableful of food coming out of the kitchen.

As she got into her car, she leaned back against the soft leather seat and took a deep breath. At this moment, she needed her friends more than ever. But as Simone had said earlier, she and Naomi were already on a plane to California. They wouldn't be back for several days.

She couldn't talk to her parents about this. They would be more distraught about her breakup with Chip than how painful this was for her. She loved her parents, but they were far more concerned with appearances than anything else. She was certain that when word of her broken engagement got around to them, she would get an earful. She could just imagine her mother scrambling to get back in the Ashfords' good graces.

At the moment, Cecelia didn't really give a damn about the Ashfords. If they couldn't accept her the way she was, she didn't want to marry into their family anyway. So what if she wasn't of the good breeding that Chip thought she was? She was still the same person he had always known. The woman he had proposed to.

As she pulled her car out of the parking lot of the club, she found herself turning left instead of right toward the Pine Valley subdivision where she lived in a French château-inspired home. There wasn't much to the left, but Cecelia was in desperate need of a stretch of road to drive and clear her mind.

After a few miles, she realized that maybe all this was for the best. Perhaps Maverick was doing her a favor in the end. It was better that she and Chip break up now, while they were still engaged, than to have a messy divorce on her hands. And God forbid they'd started a family. Would Chip reject his own children if he found out that they were tainted by their mother's inferior bloodline?

Cecelia shuddered at the thought. The one thing she wanted, the one thing she'd always wanted, was a family of her own. She longed for blood relatives whom she was bound to by more than just a slip of paper. People who would love her without stipulations and requirements. Her parents did love her, of that she had no doubt. But the Morgans' high standards were hard to live up to. She had always strived to meet them, but lately she wondered how they would feel about her if she fell short. Would they still love and protect their perfect Cecelia if she wasn't so perfect?

As she made her way to the edge of town, she noticed lights on in the distance at the old Wilson House and slowed her car to investigate. She didn't realize anybody had bought that property. No one had lived in the large, luxurious cabin for several years, but someone was definitely there now.

She wasn't sure why she did it, but she turned her car down the winding gravel road that led to the old house. Maybe it was Maverick's secret hideout. There, out front, she spied a fully restored 1965 Corvette Stingray convertible roadster. She knew nothing of cars, but she remembered a poster of one almost exactly like this on Deacon's bedroom wall in high school. That one had been cherry red—his dream car.

This one was a dark burgundy, but she knew the

moment she saw it that the car belonged to Deacon. Instantly, she realized there was no place else she wanted to be in the whole world.

Deacon had known the truth about her. Years ago when they were in high school and completely infatuated with one another, they had confessed all their secrets. Cecelia had told him about her adoption and about her mother. She had even shown him the only picture she had of her mother. The old, worn photograph, given to her by her parents on her thirteenth birthday, had been found in her mother's hand when she died. It was a picture of her holding her brand-new baby girl, just a week before she was taken away.

Cecelia had spent a lot of time staring at that photo, looking for the similarities between her and her mother. Looking for the differences that made her better. She'd always been mystified by her mother's happy smile as she held her baby. How could she throw that all away? Every now and then she pulled the photo out to look at it when she was alone. Deacon hadn't judged her. Deacon had accepted her for who she was—the rich, spoiled daughter of the Morgan family and the poor, adopted daughter taken away from her drug-addled mother. Deacon had loved her just the same.

In this moment, she wanted nothing more than to feel that acceptance again. Without thinking, she drove up to the front of the house and got out of her car. She flew up the steps and knocked on the front door, not knowing what his reaction would be when he saw her. Judging by their interaction earlier that day, she didn't expect a warm welcome.

But she didn't care.

A moment later, the large door opened wide, revealing Deacon standing there in nothing but a pair of worn blue jeans. She had admired his new build during her briefing that day, but she could only guess what he was hiding beneath his designer suit. Now his hard, chiseled physique was on display, from his firm pecs to his defined six-pack. His chest and stomach were sprinkled with golden-brown chest hair she didn't remember from their times together in the past. Her palms itched to run her hands across him and see how different he felt.

Then her eyes met his, and the light of attraction and appreciation flickered there. Cecelia felt a surge of desire and bravery run through her, urging her on, so she didn't hesitate.

Before Deacon could even say hello, Cecelia launched herself into his arms.

# Four

The last thing Deacon expected when he opened his front door was to find Cecelia standing there. If he had suspected that, perhaps he would've put a shirt on. Or perhaps not.

Instead, he'd been standing there half-naked when he opened the door and looked into the seductive gray eyes of his past. She'd seemed broken somehow, not as confident as she'd been during her earlier presentation. She'd appeared to almost tremble as her eyes glistened with unshed tears. Before he could ask what was wrong, or why she was here, she'd launched herself at him, and was kissing him.

At that point all Deacon could do was react. And in that moment, with the woman he had once loved in his arms again after all this time, he couldn't push her away. Their encounter that afternoon had only lit the fires of his need for her once again. The years of anger and resentment took a back seat to desire, at least for the moment. He had no idea what had brought her to his doorstep tonight, but he was thankful for it.

Now her mouth was hot and demanding as she continued to kiss him. These were nothing like the sweet, hesitant kisses of their teenage years. Cecelia was a grown woman who knew exactly what she wanted and how to get it. And from the looks of it, she wanted Deacon.

She buried her fingers in the hair at the nape of his neck, pulling him closer as she pressed her body against his bare chest. He could feel the globes of her full breasts molding against the hard wall of his chest through the thin silk of the blouse he had admired earlier that day. As her tongue slipped into his mouth, he felt a growl form in the back of his throat. She certainly knew how to coax the beast out of him. He tried not to think about how Chip Ashford could've been the one to teach her these new tricks.

That was the thought that yanked Deacon away from Cecelia's kiss. He took a step back, bracing her shoulders and holding her away from him. "What are you doing here, Cecelia?" he asked. "Shouldn't you be making out with your rich fiancé right now, instead of me?"

Cecelia silently held up her hand, wiggling the bare finger that had previously held the gigantic diamond he'd noticed that afternoon at the presentation. So, that meant the engagement was off, and just since he'd seen her last. That was an interesting development, although one he was certain had little to do with his arrival in town. Only in his fantasies would Cecelia cast aside Chip for him.

"May I come in?" she asked, looking up at him through thick, golden lashes.

His tongue snaked out over his lips as he nodded. "Sure." He took a step back, wondering what could've broken the engagement and driven Cecelia back into his arms, but before he could ask, she was on him again.

This time he had no reason to stop her. They stumbled back through the doorway, and he kicked it shut behind them. Without hesitation, he lifted Cecelia and started carrying her toward the bedroom. She clung to him, unwilling to separate her lips from his as he navigated through the house.

When they reached his bedroom, he sat her gently down at the edge of his king-size bed. Cecelia immediately started undoing his belt, sliding it from his jeans and tossing it to the floor. There was no question that this was what she wanted. And frankly, if he were being honest with himself, it was what he wanted, too.

He certainly didn't expect it to be dropped into his lap like this, but only a fool would ask questions instead of accepting the gift he'd been given. As she started to unbutton his pants, he reached for her hand and pulled it away.

"I've got this," he said.

Cecelia just smiled and began to undo her own blouse, button by button, exposing more of the creamy, porcelain skin he'd always admired. She was one of the few women he'd ever met who truly had a flawless complexion. There were no freckles, no moles—not even a scar. The Morgans would never allow their precious daughter to be injured. Her skin was like that of a china doll—smooth...even...perfect.

He remembered running his hands over it years ago and it feeling like silk against the rough, calloused palms he'd earned from working on cars. As she slipped her blouse off her shoulders and exposed the ivory satin of her bra, he ached to touch it and the flesh beneath it.

Her breasts nearly overflowed the cups as she breathed hard with wanting him. He took a step back as she stood to unzip her pencil skirt. The fabric slid over her ample hips and pooled at her feet. The sight of her nearly nude stole his breath away. She was just as beautiful and perfect as he remembered. Only now, she was a fully grown woman with all the curves that a man at his age could finally appreciate. As a teenager, Cecelia had been his first, and he'd hardly known what he was doing. He wouldn't have been able to handle a woman like Cecelia back then.

Cecelia's steely-gray eyes were fixed on him as she reached behind herself and unlatched her bra. Her breasts spilled free, revealing tight, strawberry-pink tips that were just as he remembered them. Thirteen years was too long to wait, and he couldn't resist reaching out to cup them in his hands. The hard peaks of her nipples pressed into his palms as he squeezed and massaged her sensitive flesh.

Cecelia sighed with contentment, leaned into his touch, tipped her head back and shook her blond waves over her shoulders. "Yes," she whispered. "I need your touch, Deacon. I need it now more than ever."

Deacon didn't respond. Instead, he dipped his head and took one of her tight buds into his mouth. He teased at it with his tongue until Cecelia was gasping and writhing against him. He wrapped his arm around her waist, holding her body tight against his, and then slipped one hand beneath her silky ivory panties.

He was surprised to find her skin completely bare and smooth there, providing no barrier for his fingers to slip between her sensitive folds and stroke her center. Cecelia gasped and her hips bucked against his hand, but he didn't stop. Instead he drew harder on her nipple, stroking her again and again until she came apart in his arms.

Cecelia cried out and clawed at his shoulders, more wild and passionate beneath him than she'd ever let herself be. She had gotten in touch with her sexuality, and he was pleased to be benefiting from it.

When her body stilled and her cries subsided, he lowered her gently onto the bed, laying her back against the brocade comforter. She watched beneath hooded eyes as he unbuttoned his jeans and slipped them off, along with the rest of his clothing. She watched him with appreciation as he sought out a condom from the nightstand and returned to where her body was sprawled across his mattress. He set the condom beside her on the bed, using both hands to grasp her panties and slide the fabric over her hips and down her legs.

With her completely exposed in front of him, Deacon could only shake his head in wonder. How had he gotten to this place tonight? He had anticipated grilling a steak on the back porch, drinking a few beers and watching the news. Instead, he would gladly go without his dinner and feast on Cecelia instead.

He opened the condom and rolled it down his length and then crawled onto the bed, positioning himself between her still-quivering thighs.

This was the moment he'd waited for, fantasized about, since the day he and Cecelia had parted ways. The last time they'd made love had been the night before their high school graduation. He'd had no idea that the next day Cecelia would be breaking up with him. He'd had no idea that he was holding her for the last time, kissing her for the last time, until it was too late. Then, all he could do was long for what he lost and search for it in the arms of other women.

"Please," Cecelia begged. "Don't make me wait any longer."

Deacon was more than happy to fulfill her wish. He slowly surged forward, pressing into her warmth until he was fully buried inside her. He gritted his teeth, fighting to keep control, as her tight muscles wrapped around him. She felt as good as he remembered. Maybe better.

Cecelia drew her knees up, wrapping her legs

around his hips and holding him close. She reached up for him, cupping his face in her hands and drawing his mouth down to her own. He began to move, slowly at first, and then picking up speed. Her soft cries and groans of pleasure were muffled by his mouth against hers.

It didn't take long for the tension to build up inside him. Cecelia was eager and hungry for him, and he was near his breaking point. He moved harder and faster as she clawed at his back. The sharp sting was a painful reminder that although he was enjoying this, he needed to remember who he was with. The Cecelia of his past, of his fantasies, was long gone. The woman beneath him was harder, shrewder and lacking the sweet innocence he'd always associated with her.

No matter what he tried to tell himself, Deacon knew that she was just using him. Whatever had happened between her and Chip tonight had driven her into his arms. She probably wanted to forget about everything that was going wrong in her life and was using Deacon as a reminder of when things were better. It had worked. Whatever tensions and worries she'd arrived with on his doorstep were gone.

Admittedly, his mood had improved, too. As Deacon focused on the soft warmth of her body, the stress of the day melted away and a new kind of tension took its place. Cecelia's cries grew louder beneath him, signaling that she was close to another release. He wasn't far behind her. Reaching between them, he stroked her center, pushing her over the edge once again.

"Deacon!" she cried out, writhing under him.

The tightening of her muscles around him drew him closer to his release. He thrust into her three more times, hard and fast, and it was done. His jaw dropped open with a silent scream as he poured himself into her willing body.

When it was over, Deacon pulled away from her and flopped back onto the bed. Staring up at his ceiling, he had a hard time believing everything that had just happened. He'd come back to Royal in the hopes that Cecelia might regret dumping him all those years ago.

This was way better.

Cecelia awoke with a start. She sat up in bed, her heart racing in her chest, as she looked around the unfamiliar room. For a moment, she couldn't figure out where she was, but the morning light streaming across the furniture and the shape of the man in bed beside her pieced it together.

Suddenly everything came back to her at once. She'd slept with Deacon. No, she'd thrown herself at Deacon and he'd had the courtesy not to turn her down and make her look like a fool. What was she thinking, running to him like that? Of all the people in Royal?

Then again, who else did she have to turn to? She couldn't blame last night on alcohol, but apparently the emotional trauma of her breakup with Chip was enough to dull her inhibitions. With the arrival of dawn, her good sense returned to her, and she realized that last night, however amazing, had been a terrible mistake.

She pulled back the blankets and slipped silently from the bed. She crept through the room, collecting her clothing, and carried it with her to the hallway, where she pulled the bedroom door closed behind her and got dressed.

She looked back at the door and pictured the man asleep beyond it only once before she disappeared down the hallway and out the front door. She practically held her breath until she had started her car and made it down the driveway without Deacon showing up at his front door to see her leave. It was better this way. Neither of them had to face the reality of last night and what it meant, which was a big nothing.

They were both under stress, and the sex had done its job and gotten it out of their systems. Hopefully, she would be able to finish her work at The Bellamy without this becoming a problem for her. She had enough to deal with, with the fallout of her broken engagement and the threat of Maverick looming overhead. She didn't need any weird sexual tension buzzing between them while she was trying to pull off the design coup of the century.

Two hundred and fifty guest suites in less than a month was no laughing matter. It would take all of Cecelia's focus and drive to make it happen. She didn't have time for any distractions in her life, but she most certainly didn't need Deacon, who would be at the hotel every day, reminding her of what they'd just done while she tried to work.

And yet, by the time she reached Pine Valley Estates, she was feeling guilty about running out. That was no way to treat Deacon, especially after how welcoming he'd been last night. He'd had every right to slam the door in her face when she showed up at his doorstep without warning. She was the one who had broken up with him because he wasn't good enough for her. How dare she just show up and throw herself into his arms and expect him to welcome her? And yet he had.

Now she felt worse than ever.

She pulled her car into the garage at her château just around the time her alarm normally would wake her. There was no time for her to dwell on her mistakes. She needed to shower, change, grab a double-shot latte and get to work on her first day of The Bellamy project.

Cecelia made a stop at her office to collect the things she would need while she was working at the resort. With her laptop bag slung over her shoulder and a small file box of necessary paperwork and designs in hand, she headed back out to the receptionist's desk.

Her secretary, Nancy, was sitting there when she arrived. "Good morning, Miss Morgan," she said.

"Good morning, Nancy. Mr. Delgado and Mr. Chase graciously offered me an office at the hotel so I can oversee our work there over the next few weeks. Tell anyone who needs to get a hold of me that I have my cell phone and my computer."

Nancy jotted the note on the paper pad beside her.

She waved as Cecelia turned and went out the front door with her things.

By the time Cecelia arrived at The Bellamy, work was in full swing for the day. She spied her painting team's truck, which meant that they were already laying a coat of steely-gray paint on the walls of every suite. By the time they were done, the wallpaper should have arrived and be ready to go on the accent walls and in the bathrooms.

She gathered up her things and started up the walkway into the back of the hotel, passing landscapers as they planted trees and bushes nearby. Inside she found an organized-looking woman in a headset and asked for directions. She pointed her down a hallway to the business suite of the hotel. There, she found one office designated for each of the owners, one for the hotel manager, one for the reservations manager, one for the catering manager and one empty office that had yet to be assigned. She assumed that would be hers for now.

She opened the door and turned on the light, finding a nicely appointed office space. She hadn't been contracted to decorate the interior management rooms, but it wouldn't be necessary. There was a desk, a rolling chair and a bookshelf. That was more than she would need while she was here. She busied herself unpacking her things and getting ready to dig into her work.

Once she was up and running, she started her day by making important calls. All of her suppliers needed to know that she had won the project bid and the pending orders needed to go forward as planned. Fabric, furniture and wallpaper were just the beginning. She had orders for paintings to go up in every single room, 250 matching small lamps to go on each nightstand, along with another 250 torch lamps for the corner behind the reading chair. Thousands of feet of carpeting needed to be ordered, in addition to ceramic tiles for the bathroom floors.

And all that needed to get here as soon as possible. As in yesterday.

Cecelia was lost in the minutiae of managing her inventory and orders when her cell phone rang. She looked down and noticed it was Naomi calling from California. She picked up the phone and answered it. "Hey, girl, how's California?"

"It's beautiful here," she said. "The weather is unreal. It makes me never want to come back to Texas, but of course I will, because you and Simone would kill me if I didn't."

"Is everything set up for the fashion show?"

Naomi just groaned. "I really don't want to talk about it. There's always last-minute chaos at these things. I didn't call to talk about all that anyway. I called because I got a text about you and Chip breaking up yesterday. Is that true?"

Cecelia had been hoping it would take longer for the news to get out, but apparently it was already making Royal's gossip rounds. "Yes, we've broken up, but really it's for the best. I think we just had different ideas of what our future was going to be."

"Hmm. So it didn't have anything to do with a *certain someone* coming back to town?"

Cecelia rolled her eyes. Simone must've told her about her run-in with Deacon. "No, it had nothing to do with him. I honestly doubt Chip even knows he's here yet. I didn't mention it."

"So what set all this off?"

She hesitated. She knew that she would eventually tell Naomi and Simone about her little blackmail problem, but now wasn't the time. "It was bound to happen eventually. Things just boiled over at dinner last night, so we called off the engagement. I'll tell you and Simone more about it when you get home. I wish you two were here."

"I'm so sorry that all this happened while we were gone, Cece. You've broken off your engagement and your two best friends aren't there to commiserate with you. That really sucks. I promise that when we get back, we will get together for some wine, a couple cartons of Ben & Jerry's and some good girl time. You'll put this whole thing behind you before you know it."

That sounded great. Cecelia really needed her friends to talk to. Had they been in town last night, perhaps she wouldn't have found herself in Deacon's bed.

"Good luck with the show," Cecelia said.

"Thank you. Hang in there. Oh, and don't forget that Wes and Isabelle's engagement party is coming up. You're not getting out of it, you know."

Oh, she knew. Cecelia said goodbye and got off the

phone. She needed to remember to pick up a gift for that. Frankly, she had been surprised to receive the invitation, but Isabelle was the kind of woman who wanted to be friends with everybody, even the girl who had spilled the beans about her secret daughter and upended her whole life.

She had RSVP'd two weeks ago, but now she was regretting it. She didn't really want to stroll into the Texas Cattleman's Club and have to face everybody after the breakup. More than a few people there would get a sick amount of pleasure from her misfortune. But she said she would go, so she would go.

Cecelia had just turned back to her computer when she heard a tap at the door. She looked up and immediately felt a surge of panic run through her. Deacon was standing in her doorway, a look of expectation and irritation on his face. She'd been hoping, in vain, apparently, that he would be too busy to come looking for her this morning. "Good morning, Mr. Chase. What can I do for you?"

Deacon arched a curious brow at her and just shook his head. "So this is how it's going to be, huh? It never happened?"

Cecelia smiled, putting on her most businesslike face as she tried to ignore the rough stubble on his jaw that she'd brushed her lips across only hours earlier. Her fingers tingled with the memory of running through his golden-blond hair and pulling him close to her. "I always like to keep things professional in the workplace."

"And later, when we're not in the workplace?" he asked.

"There's not much to say about last night, now or later, except that I apologize for the way I acted. It was inappropriate of me to burden you with my problems. After Chip broke off the engagement, I wasn't sure where to go or what to do. I made the wrong choice, and I'm sorry."

Deacon's green-gold gaze flickered over her face, studying her as though he could see the truth there. His jaw tightened, and finally he looked away. "The head of your painting crew is looking for you. He's waiting in the lobby."

Cecelia watched as Deacon turned and disappeared from her doorway without another word. The warm, attentive Deacon from last night was gone, leaving only the cold businessman behind. She hated that it had to be that way, and she wished he could understand. Now, more than ever, she needed his warmth and his compassion. All too soon, the rest of Royal would be turning their backs on her. But there was too much history between them, too many memories and emotions to cloud the present. She knew she had to put up a wall to protect her business and her reputation.

And her heart.

# Five

He was a damn fool for thinking that their night together would go down any differently than it had.

Deacon knew better. He knew better than to just fall in the bed with Cecelia and think that things had changed. Just as before, he was good enough when they were alone, but not in public. He had thought that perhaps he had proved his worth, and that maybe things would go differently between them this time. Not so.

It had been a week since she'd shown up on his doorstep. They'd danced around each other at the hotel each day, both seemingly drawn to, and repelled by, each other. Cecelia avoided eye contact and stuck strictly to topics about work. But as hard as she tried to play it cool, it didn't change the underlying energy that ran through all of their interactions.

He wasn't about to give her the satisfaction of him chasing after her, however. The teenager whose heart she'd broken would've chased her anywhere if he thought he could have another chance. Real estate billionaire Deacon Chase didn't follow women around like a lost puppy dog.

But if there was one thing Deacon had learned in the past week, it was that she didn't regret that night. Not even one teensy, tiny, little bit. He'd seen the way her cheeks flushed when she'd looked up and seen him standing nearby. She had been hungry for the pleasure he happily gave her. That kind of hunger was nothing to be remorseful about. She'd come to him that night because she wanted to forget what a mess her life was for a little while, and he'd delivered in spades. More than likely, she regretted that she didn't regret their encounter.

Deacon hadn't lost too much sleep over it. They'd had sex. Amazing, mind-blowing sex, but just sex. It'd been thirteen years since they'd gotten together. They weren't in love with one another, and it was ridiculous to think that they ever would be. It would've been nice if she had said goodbye as she crept naked from his bedroom, but he supposed it had saved them from an awkward morning together.

No, what had bothered him the most during the past week was seeing who Cecelia had become over the years. Despite his feelings about her and their breakup, he had still loved the girl Cecelia had been. She'd been the sweetest, most caring person he had ever known outside of his own family. When the rest of the school, and the rest of the town, had turned their back on Deacon, Cecelia had been there.

The woman he watched stomping back and forth through the lobby of his hotel in high heels and a tight hair bun was not the Cecelia he remembered. She was driven, focused, almost to the point of being emotionless. What happened to her? When they had shared their dreams for the future as teenagers, being a hard-nosed CEO had not been on Cecelia's list of ambitions.

If he looked closely, every now and then Deacon could see a flicker of the girl he used to know. It was usually near the end of the day, when the stress and the worries started to wear her down. That was when her facade would start to crumble and he could see the real Cecelia underneath.

He was watching her like that when Shane approached him. "She's quite a piece of work, isn't she?"

Deacon turned to him, startled out of his thoughts. "What do you mean?"

"I've always thought that Cecelia was a victim of a contradictory modern society. If she were a man, everyone would applaud her for her success and uncompromising attitude in the boardroom. Since she's a woman, she's seen as cold and bitchy. Heck, I see her that way after the way she treated Brandee. But there's no way she could've gotten this far in business if she wasn't hard."

"You make it sound like nobody likes her." That surprised Deacon, since she'd been the most popular, outgoing person in high school. Everyone had loved her.

"Well, she has earned quite the reputation in Royal over the years. Aside from her few close friends, I'm not sure that anybody really likes her, especially inside the Texas Cattleman's Club. Tell you what, though, it's not for their lack of trying. She's just not interested in being friends with most people. She and the rest of the mean girl trio tried to sabotage my relationship with Brandee. They thought it was a big joke. I don't know if folks are just not good enough to be her friends or what."

Deacon flinched. "That doesn't sound like her at all. What the hell happened after I left town?"

"I don't know, man." Shane shrugged. "Maybe you broke her heart."

Deacon swallowed a bitter chuckle. "Don't you mean the other way around? She's the one who broke up with me."

"Yeah, well, maybe she regrets it. I certainly would rather date you over Chip Ashford any day."

"Aw, that's sweet of you, Shane."

"You know what I mean," Shane snapped. "I'd be a bitter, miserable woman if I were dating him, too. I'm curious as to what will happen to her socially, now that she's broken it off with Chip, though. A lot of people in town tolerated her and her attitude just because she was his fiancée."

The discussion of her broken engagement caught Deacon's attention. "So do you know exactly what happened between her and Chip?"

Shane just shook his head. "I haven't heard anything about it, aside from the fact that it's over. It seems both of them are keeping fairly tight-lipped about the whole thing, which is unusual. I have heard that her parents are beside themselves about the breakup. They've been kissing the Ashfords' asses for years to get in their good graces, and I'm sure they think Cecelia has ruined it for them."

It grated on Deacon's nerves that Cecelia's parents were always more worried about appearances than they were about their own daughter. Couldn't they see that she was miserable with Chip? Probably so. They just didn't care. Deacon had never thought much of their family. They acted like they were better than everyone else. "Who cares about the Ashfords?" he asked.

"Everybody," Shane said before turning and wandering off, disappearing as suddenly as he had arrived.

Deacon watched him go, and then he turned back to where Cecelia had been standing a moment before. She was barking orders at a crew of men hauling in rolls of carpeting. When she was finished, she turned and headed in his direction with her tablet clutched in her arms. He braced himself for a potentially tense conversation, but she didn't even make eye contact. She breezed past him as though he were invisible and disappeared down the hallway.

A cold and indifferent bitch, indeed.

Looking down at his watch, Deacon realized he couldn't spend all of his time staring at Cecelia. The hotel opening was in a little more than three weeks, and they had a ton of work ahead of them. That was why he had returned to Royal after all—well, the official reason anyway. He turned on his heel and headed back toward his office to get some work done before the end of the day arrived.

When he looked up from his computer next it was after seven. It was amazing how time could get away from him while he was working. He couldn't imagine doing this job and having a family to go home to every night. He imagined he would have a very angry wife and very cold dinners. He stood up, stretched and reached over to turn off his laptop.

He switched off the light as he stepped out of his office, noticing the business suite was dark except for one other space. Cecelia's office. As quietly as he could, he crept down the hallway to peer in and see what she was doing here this late.

Cecelia was sitting in her chair with her back to him, but she wasn't working. She was looking at something in her hand. Deacon took a few steps closer so he could make out what it was. Finally, he could tell it was an old, worn photograph. One that he recognized.

She'd shown him the photo the night she confessed her biggest secret: that she was adopted. It was of a young woman, weary and worn but happy, holding a new baby. It was a picture of Cecelia's birth mother on the day she brought her daughter home from the hospital. Deacon hadn't given much thought to the photo back then. He had been more interested in Cecelia and the way she talked about it. She had always seemed conflicted about her birth mother. It was as though she wanted to know her, wanted to learn more about who she had been and why she had gotten so lost, and yet she was embarrassed by where she had come from. Deacon had no doubt that she had the Morgans to thank for that.

There was a lot going on with Cecelia. More than just regret over their one-night stand. More than just missing her mother. More than just being upset over her broken engagement. There was something else going on that she wasn't telling him. The whole town was convinced she was just a stuck-up mean girl, but he'd bet not one of them had looked hard enough to see that she was hurting. Of course, she had no reason to confide in him. While he'd proved himself trustworthy in the past, they weren't exactly close anymore. In that moment it bothered him more than in the thirteen years they'd been apart.

He wanted to go into her office and scoop her up into his arms. Not to kiss her. Not to carry her away and ravish her somewhere, but just to hold her. He got the feeling that it was a luxury Cecelia could barely afford. Chip didn't seem like a supportive, hold-his-woman kind of guy, and that was exactly what she needed right now.

But did he dare?

She had done nothing but avoid him since their night together. She'd made it crystal clear that she didn't want any sort of relationship with Deacon, sexual or otherwise. She just wanted to do her job, and so he would let her. The last thing he needed was to leave Royal for the second time with a broken heart and a bruised ego.

As quietly as he could, Deacon took a few steps back and disappeared down the hallway so he didn't disturb her. As he stepped out into the parking lot, there were only two cars remaining—his Corvette and her BMW. He stopped beside her car and stared down at it for a moment, thinking. Finally, he fished a blank piece of scrap paper out of his pocket and scribbled a note on it before placing it under her windshield wiper.

"I'm here if you need to talk—Deacon," it read.

Whether or not she would take him up on it, he had no idea. But he hoped so.

Things had been hard for Cecelia the past couple of weeks. She tried to lose herself in her work and forget about everything that was going wrong in her life, but in the evenings at the hotel, when it was calm and quiet, she had nothing to distract her from the mess of her own making.

Earlier that night, she'd gotten another message from Maverick. As she'd expected, the original payment was just that, and not nearly enough to keep him quiet. Another twenty-five thousand had to be wired by the end of the week, or her secret would be out and her family would be humiliated. Staring at the photo of her mother, she'd quietly decided that she wasn't giving him any more money. She felt a pang of guilt where her parents were concerned—surely they would face an uphill battle in restoring the trust of those they lied to—but it was time for her to take control of her life. Come what may.

Now, sitting in her car in the long-empty parking lot of the hotel, she clutched what might be her only lifeline. Finding the note on her windshield from Deacon had been a surprise. They hadn't really spoken since the morning she ran out on him, aside from the occasional discussion about the hotel. She thought she was doing a good job at keeping her worries inside, but Deacon had seen through it somehow. He'd always had that ability. In some ways, that made him someone she needed to avoid more than ever. In other ways, he was just the person she needed to talk to. The only person she could talk to.

But could she take him up on his offer?

At this point, she didn't have much to lose. Before she could second-guess herself, she put her car in Drive and found herself back on the highway that led to Deacon's place. Her heart was pounding in her chest with anxiety as she drove up the gravel path through the trees. His car was there, and the lights were on inside. Hopefully he was there alone.

She bit anxiously at her lip as she rang the doorbell and waited. This time, when Deacon answered the door, he was fully dressed in the suit he'd worn to the hotel that day, and she was able to control herself. Barely. "Hi," she said. It seemed a simple, silly way to start such a heavy conversation, but she didn't know what else to say.

Deacon seemed to sense how hard it was for her to accept his olive branch. Instead of gloating, he just took a step back and opened the door wider to let her inside.

"You said you were here if I needed to talk. Is this a good time?"

Deacon shut the door and turned to her with a serious expression lining his face. His green-gold eyes reflected nothing but sincerity as he looked at her and said, "Whenever you need to talk to me, I will make the time."

Cecelia was taken aback by the intensity of his words and their impact on her. She never felt like she was anybody's priority, especially Chip's. He always had an important meeting, a campaign to run, a fundraiser to plan, hands to shake and babies to kiss. Cecelia had been an accessory to him, like a nice suit or pair of cuff links. "Thank you," was all she could say.

Deacon led her through the foyer and into his sunken great room. The space was two stories high with a fireplace on the far end that went all the way to the ceiling with stacked gray-and-brown flagstone. He gestured for her to sit in the comfortable-looking brown leather sectional that was arranged around a coffee table made of reclaimed wood and glass. It was very much a cowboy's living room, reminding her of the clubhouse.

"Are you renting this place?" she asked.

"No, I actually went ahead and bought it. It was a good deal, and it came furnished. That made it easier for me to settle in and gave me a real home to come to each night. Despite the fact that I build hotels for a living, I don't exactly relish living in one. When the hotel is finished, I'll return to France, but I'll probably keep this place. Shane will be overseeing the business operations, but I'll also need to come back from time to time."

Deacon walked to a wet bar in the corner. "Can I get you something to drink?"

"Yes, please. I don't really care what it is, but make it a double."

She watched as Deacon poured them both a drink over ice and carried them over to the coffee table. Cecelia immediately picked up her glass and took a large sip. The amber liquid burned on the way down, distracting her from her nerves and eventually warming her blood. "I want to start by apologizing for that morning I ran out on you. I panicked and handled it poorly, and I haven't done any better since then."

Deacon didn't respond. He just sat patiently listening and taking the occasional sip of his own drink. She wasn't used to having someone's undivided attention, so she knew she needed to make the most of it.

"Everything in my life is falling apart," she said. "I don't know if you've been in town long enough to hear about Maverick, but he's been targeting members of the club since the beginning of the year. No one is sure who he is, or how he got the information, but he's been blackmailing people and spilling their secrets. I'm his latest victim."

That finally compelled Deacon to break his silence. "What could you have possibly done to be blackmailed for? Your parents always kept such a tight leash on you, I can't imagine you got into too much trouble over the years."

"He's not blackmailing me about something that I did. He's blackmailing me because of who I really am. Somehow Maverick has gotten a hold of my original birth certificate. He's threatening to tell everyone about my mother and her deadly drug habit. Up until now, no one has known the truth except for me, you and my parents."

Deacon frowned. "I don't see how anybody could hold something like that against you. Why don't you just tell people the truth and take his power away?"

Cecelia sighed. "I thought about doing that, but my parents were very strongly against it. They don't want to ruin the image of the picture-perfect family they've created over the years. I paid the blackmailer, but he still went ahead and started sending out messages to club members that alluded to me. I got another one from him today demanding another payment. There's no way out of this trap. I tried to confide in Chip, thinking that he could help me somehow, but he accused me of living a lie and broke off our engagement instead."

When Cecelia turned to look at Deacon, his jaw was tight and his skin was flushed with anger. "What a bastard! I can't believe you were going to marry a man who could be so careless with your heart. You deserve better than him, Cecelia, not the other way around. By the time he figures that out, I hope it's too late for him to win you back."

Once again, she was stunned by his words. She just couldn't understand how he could say things like that to her after everything that she had done to him.

"Why are you being so nice to me, Deacon? I don't deserve it."

Deacon reached out and took her hand in his. His warm touch sent a surge of awareness through her whole body, bringing back to mind memories of their recent night together. She pushed all of that aside and tried to focus on the here and now.

"What are you talking about? You've already apologized twice for the other night, unnecessarily I might add."

Cecelia met his gaze with her own. "I'm talking about high school. We were in love, we had made plans to run away and live this amazing life together, and I threw it all away. Don't you hate me for that?"

"I was angry for a while, but I have to admit that it fueled me to make more of myself. I couldn't hate you, Cecelia. I tried to, but I just couldn't. The girl I loved wasn't the one who broke up with me that day."

Cecelia felt a sense of relief wash over her. At least that was one thing she hadn't completely ruined. "I've never been strong enough, despite all my successes, to stand up to my parents. I made the mistake of telling them that after graduation, I was leaving with you. They had a fit and laid down the law. I wasn't going anywhere, they insisted. It broke my heart to break up with you, but I didn't know what else to do. And now, when they told me to keep my mouth shut and pay the blackmailer, I did it even though I didn't want to. I dated Chip for years because that's what they wanted. I probably would've married him to make them happy if he hadn't broken up with me. They've never really allowed me to be myself. I've always had to be this perfect daughter, striving to prove to them that I'm better than my mother was.

"I've only ever done two things in my life just because it made me happy. One was starting my business. Marriage and family didn't come as quickly as I'd hoped, so designing and decorating nurseries for a living was the next best thing."

Deacon stroked his thumb gently across the back of her hand as she spoke. "What was the other thing?"

She looked at him, a soft smile curling her lips. "Falling in love with you. You made me happy. You never asked me to be anybody other than who I was. You knew the truth about my mother, and it never seemed to bother you."

"That's because you were perfect just the way you were, Cecelia. Why would I ask you to change?"

No one had ever spoken to her the way Deacon did. His sincere words easily melted her defenses, cracking the cold businesswoman facade that she worked so hard to maintain. She'd always felt so alone, and she didn't want to be alone anymore.

Unwelcome tears started to well up in her eyes. Cecelia hated to cry, especially in front of other people. She wasn't raised to show that kind of vulnerability to anybody. In the Morgan household, she learned at a very young age that emotions made one appear weak, and that wasn't tolerated. Her birth mother had been weak, they'd told her, and look where she had ended up.

"I'm sorry," she said, pulling away from him to wipe her tears away.

"Stop apologizing," he said. He reached for her and pulled her into the protective cocoon of his strong embrace. Cecelia gave in to it, collapsing against him and letting her tears flow freely at last. He held her for what felt like an hour, although it was probably just a few minutes. When she was all out of tears, she sat up and looked at him.

Deacon's face was so familiar and yet so different after all these years. He still had the same kind eyes and charming smile she'd fallen in love with, there was just more maturity behind his gaze now. She found that wisdom made him more handsome than ever before.

In that moment, she didn't want him to just hold her. She wanted to surrender to him and offer him anything she had to give. Slowly, she leaned in and pressed her lips against his. This kiss was different from the one they'd shared before. There was no desperation or anger fueling it this time, just a swelling of emotion and her slow-burning desire for him.

Deacon didn't push her away, nor did he press the kiss any further. It was firm and sweet, soft and tender, reminding her of warm summer nights spent lying in the back of his pickup truck. It was a kiss of potential, of promise.

Cecelia wanted more, but as she leaned farther into Deacon, she felt his hands press softly but insistently against her shoulders. When their lips parted, they sat together inches apart for a moment without speaking.

Finally Deacon said, "That's probably where we should end tonight. I don't want you to have any more regrets where I'm concerned. Or expectations."

Cecelia didn't regret a thing about what had happened between them, but she understood what he meant. What future could they possibly have together? She was still picking up the pieces from her broken engagement, and he'd be back in France in mere weeks. She nodded and sat back, feeling the chill rush in as the warmth of his body left her.

Setting her drink on the coffee table, Cecelia stood up. "I'd probably better get going, then. Thank you for listening and being so supportive. You don't know how rare that is in my life."

Deacon walked her to the door, giving her a firm but chaste hug before she left. It felt good just to be in his arms. She felt safe there, as though Maverick—and Chip and her parents and the gossipmongers of Royal—couldn't hurt her while Deacon was around.

"I'll see you at work tomorrow," he said.

Cecelia waved at him over her shoulder, feeling an unusual surge of optimism run through her as she climbed into her car. For the first time in a long time, she couldn't wait to see what life had in store for her.

# Six

"The chef has put together the tasting menu for the grand opening celebration. I didn't realize it was happening today, and I promised Brandee that I would go with her to shop for some things for the ranch. Can you handle it without me?"

Deacon looked up from his desk and frowned at his business partner. "I may have lived in Europe for the last few years, but I don't exactly have the most refined tastes. I am a meat-and-potatoes kind of guy. Are you sure you want to leave the menu up to me? That's a pretty important element of the party, considering we're trying to lure customers into the new tapas restaurant."

"I wouldn't worry about it. We hired the best Spanish chef in all of Texas to run the restaurant.

I'm pretty sure that anything Chef Eduardo makes is going to be amazing. If you're worried about it," Shane said with a wicked grin, "you could always ask Cecelia to join you. She's known for having excellent taste, in design and event planning."

Deacon sat back in his chair and considered Shane's suggestion. Since their kiss a few days ago, he had been considering his next move where she was concerned. He knew that he should back off before they both ended up in over their heads. The past had proven that his and Cecelia's relationship was doomed. They weren't the same people they were back in high school. Even so, he found his thoughts circling back to her again and again.

So what now? He wanted to spend some time with her. A date seemed too formal, especially since she might not want to be seen out with another man so soon after her engagement was called off. But this would be an interesting alternative if she had the time. "Okay, fine. You're off the hook. Get out of here and go buy some barbed wire or a horse or something."

Shane waved and disappeared down the hall. Deacon got up from his desk and went in search of Cecelia. He found her in the lobby directing the hanging of a large oil painting. It was a Western landscape, one of the few nods to Texas in her otherwise modern design.

"Perfect!" she declared after the level showed the frame was aligned just right.

"Well, thank you, I try," Deacon said from over her shoulder.

Cecelia spun on her heel and turned to look at him. "Very funny. Can I help you with something, Mr. Chase?"

Even now, always business first. Thankfully, he truly had a business proposition for her, even if his motivation was less than pure. "Actually, I was wondering if I could borrow you for an hour to help me with something."

"An hour? It's almost lunchtime."

"Which means...all your guys will be out in search of a taco truck and you will have nothing better to do than to join me for a private tasting at the new restaurant here in the hotel."

She arched an eyebrow at him, but she didn't say no. "Is the chef still working on the menu?"

"No, that's already set for both restaurants. What Chef Eduardo has put together for today is the menu for the grand opening gala. It features some of the items that will be on the restaurant's menu, but also some more finger-food-type selections that can be passed around by waiters. Shane was supposed to do this with me, but he's gotten roped into a shopping excursion with Brandee. That just leaves me, and I'm afraid I don't have the palate for this. I could use a second opinion."

Cecelia's gaze flicked over him for a moment, and then she nodded. She turned back to her crew. "Why don't you guys go ahead and take lunch? We'll finish up the rest of the paintings this afternoon."

She didn't have to tell them twice. The men immediately put down their tools and slipped out of the back of the hotel. Once they were gone, Cecelia turned back to Deacon with a smile. "Lead the way, Mr. Chase."

Technically, it wasn't a date, but Deacon felt inclined to offer her his arm and escort her down the hallway anyway. The Bellamy was designed with two dining options. The Silver Saddle was the more casual of the two, offering an upscale bar environment and featuring a selection of Spanish tapas in lieu of the typical appetizer selection. The other restaurant was the Glass House, a high-end farm-to-table restaurant, featuring all the freshest organic produce and responsibly sourced game available. The executive chef was even working on a rooftop garden where he intended to grow his own herbs and a selection of seasonable vegetables.

Normally, the Glass House would've been the appropriate venue for the grand opening, but Deacon had had other ideas. It wouldn't take much to lure the residents of Royal to the Glass House. That was right up their snooty, rich alley. Spanish tapas were another matter. Deacon had suggested that the food for the event be catered by the Silver Saddle instead, so they could introduce the town to what he and Shane hoped would be the newest hot spot in Royal.

When they arrived at the bar they found the executive chef waiting for them. Eduardo welcomed them with a wide smile. "Mr. Chase, I hope that you and your guest are very hungry."

"We are," Deacon replied. He'd seen a mock-up of the menu and knew they were in for a treat. He didn't actually expect to make many, if any, changes. Eduardo knew what he was doing. It was just good for him to know in advance what his guests had in store for them. "I can't wait to see what you put together."

Eduardo directed them to a corner booth. The decor of the bar was still a work in progress, but the majority of the key elements were in place. Along the edge of the room, the space was lined with burgundy leather booths and worn wooden tables. In the center was a rectangular bar that was accessible to guests on all sides. On the far side of the room from where they were seated, there was a stage for live music and a dance floor. Overhead, instead of a disco ball, Deacon had custom ordered a mirrored saddle, the bar's namesake.

They had gone for a cowboy atmosphere with a modern edge, much like Cecelia's room design, and Deacon was pretty sure they'd nailed it. In two months' time, he had no doubt that this place would be hopping on a Saturday night.

He helped Cecelia into the booth and then sat opposite of her. Before they could place their napkins in their laps, Eduardo called the first waiter to the table with a tray of four different beverages. He set them down and disappeared back into the kitchen.

"First, I wanted to start with the beverage selection for the evening. Of course we will have an open bar that will provide whatever beverages the guests would like. However, we will be showcasing the Silver Saddle's four featured drinks, as well." He pointed to the two wineglasses. "Here are our two signature sangrias. The first is a traditional red wine sangria, and this here is a strawberry rosé sangria.

"Next is our take on an Arnold Palmer, but instead of sweet tea, we use sweet-tea-flavored vodka and a sprig of rosemary in the lemonade. Last is the Viva Bellamy, designed exclusively for the hotel, with aged rye whiskey, sweet vermouth, blood-orange liqueur and orange bitters. Please enjoy, and we'll be out with the first round of tapas momentarily." Eduardo turned and disappeared into the kitchen.

"I have to say the best part of my job might be that I get to drink without ending up in the HR office," Deacon quipped with a grin as he picked up the old-fashioned glass containing the Viva Bellamy.

Cecelia opted for the rosé sangria. She took a sip and then smiled. "This is wonderful. It might be the best sangria I have ever had, actually. Try it."

She held the wineglass up to his lips and tipped it until the sweet concoction flowed into his mouth. It was a lovely beverage, but that wasn't what caught his attention. He was far more focused on Cecelia as she watched him. Perhaps Shane was smarter than Deacon gave him credit for. Feeding each other tapas could be quite the unexpectedly sensual experience for a weekday lunch at work.

Eduardo and the waiter returned a moment later with a selection of small plates. "Here we have stuffed piquillo peppers with goat cheese and seasonal mushrooms, seared scallops with English pea puree, chicken skewers with ajillo sauce, and black garlic and grilled lamb with rosemary sauce. Enjoy."

"Wow," Cecelia said. "This all looks amazing, and not at all what I was expecting from a place with a disco saddle hanging over the dance floor. I'd wager there's no place like this within a hundred miles of here. People are going to trip over themselves to get to your restaurant, Deacon."

He certainly hoped so. The array of food was both heavenly scented and visually impressive. He could just picture it being passed around on silver platters and arranged artfully along a buffet display. "Shall we?" he asked.

Cecelia nodded and looked around, considering where to start. "Do we share everything? I've never done tapas before, but this kind of reminds me of dim sum."

"Yes, it's similar. *Tapas* means small plates, so it's just tiny selections of many different, shareable dishes instead of large entrée. Just try whatever you like."

She started by reaching out and pulling a chicken skewer onto one of the empty plates they'd each been given to make the tasting easier. Deacon opted for the lamb.

Cecelia closed her eyes and made a moaning sound of pure pleasure that Deacon recognized from their night together. His body stirred at the memory of that sound echoing in his bedroom.

"Wow," she said as she swallowed her bite and opened her eyes. "I mean, I know I said that already, but it's true, this is so good. You have to try it." She slid a piece of the chicken off the wooden skewer, stabbed it with her fork and held it out to him.

Deacon took a bite and chewed thoughtfully. The flavors were excellent. Her feeding him wasn't bad, either, but he would much prefer to feed her. "That's good. Do you like lamb?"

She nodded. He took the opportunity to stab a small cube of lamb and feed it to her. She closed her eyes again as she chewed, thoroughly enjoying the food in a way he hadn't expected. She'd become quite the foodie since the last time they were together. He suddenly lost interest in trying the food himself, and wanted only to feed Cecelia.

He picked up one of the small stuffed peppers with his fingers and held it up to her. She leaned in, looking into his eyes as she took a bite. Her lips softly brushed his fingertips, sending a shiver through his whole body. When she finished, she took the second bite from his fingers. He tried to pull his hand away but she grabbed his wrist and held it steady.

"Don't you dare waste that sauce," she said. Without hesitation she drew his thumb into her mouth and sucked the spicy cream sauce from his skin.

Deacon almost came up out of his seat. The suction on this thumb combined with the swirl of her tongue against his skin made every muscle in his body tense up and his blood rush to his groin. She seemed unaffected. Cecelia pulled away with a sly smile, releasing his wrist. As though she hadn't just given him oral pleasure, albeit to his hand, she turned back to the selection on the table and chose one of the scallops.

She was just messing with him now. And he liked it.

\*\*\*

The plates just kept coming out of the kitchen, and Cecelia found herself in food heaven. Her roommate in college had been the daughter of a famous Manhattan chef, and she'd exposed Cecelia to cuisines she hadn't tried back home in Texas. She'd developed a brave palate and high expectations by the time she'd graduated. The little diner in Royal had been fine before she left, but when she returned, she found herself trekking to Houston for cuisine with more flair and spice.

Now she'd have access to world-class dining right here in Royal. At that moment, Eduardo and his waiter brought out fried chorizo wrapped in thin slices of potato, a selection of imported jamón ibérico and Spanish cheeses, marinated and grilled vegetables in a Romanesco sauce, garlic shrimp and salmon tartare in salmon roe cones. By the time they got to the dessert selections, Cecelia wasn't sure she could eat much more. She loved her sweets, but she was far more interested in the tall, handsome dish across from her at the moment.

Cecelia would be lying if she said that she hadn't been thinking about Deacon since they shared that kiss Monday night. Part of her wondered if that had been his plan all along—to kiss her, send her home and leave her wanting more.

Cecelia did want more. There was no question of it. She just wasn't sure if indulging her desires was the best idea. There was certainly plenty of sexual attraction flowing between them, and their night of passion would be one she would never forget. But could she risk giving herself to Deacon when she knew she might fall for him again?

It happened so quickly the first time, Cecelia had hardly known what hit her. For a while after they'd broken up, she had thought that perhaps falling in love was easy to do. The years that followed would prove otherwise. No one, not even her ex-fiancé, had captured her heart the way Deacon had. She feared he still had that power over her.

The hotel opened in a little more than two weeks. Deacon had told her that once things were up and running, he would return to Cannes. She couldn't risk his taking her heart with him when he left. A few weeks didn't seem like much time to be together, but Deacon was a well-known commodity to Cecelia. She knew the kind soul she once loved was still there, so even that short time was enough for her to fall miserably in love with him again, just to have him disappear from her life like before.

Cecelia wouldn't let herself believe that this was a second chance to put things right between them. They could make peace, and already had, really, but a relationship between them seemed impossible. Even if he weren't returning to the French Riviera in a few weeks, they both knew she was in no position to start something promising with anyone. Not with Maverick's threat hanging overhead.

She wouldn't blame him for indulging while he was here and not getting attached. Hell, if *he* broke *her* heart this time, it would be some sort of karmic retribution somehow. She deserved it.

Maybe she was just a masochist, but she couldn't walk away from him. Not twice in a lifetime.

"I've got to sample dessert," Deacon said, oblivious to her train of thought. "I might explode or spend this afternoon napping in my office, but I told Shane that I would try everything." He eyed the selection of desserts on the table with dismay.

"I think you've still got room," she said. She reached out and picked up a berry tartlet, bringing it up to his lips. "Take a bite."

He didn't resist. Deacon bit down into the sweet treat, taking half of it into his mouth. Chewing, he watched as she brought the rest of it up to her mouth and finished it off with a satisfied sound.

"Yummy," she said and picked up another treat. This one was a small brownie with whipped cream and a dusting of what looked like chili powder. That would be interesting.

As they made their way through the rest of the desserts, Cecelia could feel them building toward something more. If it wasn't the middle of the afternoon, she was certain he would take her home and make love to her. As it was, she wouldn't be surprised if he escorted her into his office and locked the door. The entire meal had been the tastiest foreplay she'd ever had. It made her want to spend the weekend in bed with him, and she would if it wasn't for that pesky engagement party she had to go to tomorrow night.

It occurred to her that there might be one way to

get through the evening after all. "Deacon, can I ask you for a favor?"

He leaned in, causing the most delicious tingles as he smoothed his palm down her arm. "Anything."

"Would you go with me to Wes and Isabelle's engagement party at the club?" She had no doubt that the gossip would be flying about her breakup with Chip, and it would be so much easier if she had Deacon there with her to soften the blow.

Deacon narrowed his gaze at her. "The club? The Texas Cattleman's Club? Are you serious?"

Cecelia frowned. "Of course I'm serious. Why wouldn't I be serious? I'm a member. Everyone in town practically is a member now. What's the big deal?"

With a sigh, Deacon sat back against the leather of the booth. "The big deal is that I'm not a member. They would never *let* me be a member. I don't exactly relish hanging out someplace where I'm not wanted."

Sometimes Cecelia forgot how hard it was for Deacon to live in Royal back when they were kids. He had never fit in with the others driving the BMWs they got for their sweet sixteenth and going home to their mansions at night. She never really thought about it, because none of it ever mattered to her. He had simply been the most wonderful boy she'd ever known. The fact that he'd driven a beat-up pickup truck and lived in a small, unimpressive house on the edge of town hadn't been important.

But it had been important to him both then and now, gauging by his reaction. Even though he was successful, even though he could buy and sell half the people in this town, he still had a chip on his shoulder.

"You're not seventeen and broke anymore, Deacon. Stop worrying about all those other people and what they might or might not think. Actually, most of them are so self-centered that they won't be nearly as concerned with your being at the club as they will be about a million other things."

She leaned into him and took his hand. The touch of his skin against hers made her long for the night they'd spent together with his hands gliding over her naked body. Cecelia really did want him to go to the party with her, and not just as a buffer from the ire of the town. She wanted to go back to his place afterward and spend all night relishing the feel of him against her.

Cecelia looked in his eyes, hoping they reflected her intentions and thoughts. She stroked the back of his hand with her thumb in the slow, lazy circles guaranteed to drive him wild and get her exactly what she wanted. "Come with me. Please."

Jaw tight, his gaze dropped to his hand. With a soft shake of his head, he sighed. "Okay, you win. When is this engagement party?"

"Tomorrow night. Seven o'clock. Will that work for you?"

Deacon nodded. "I suppose. Will I get some sort of special reward for being your escort for the evening?" he asked with a grin lighting his eyes.

"You absolutely will," she promised. "Do you have anything in mind?"

"I do." Deacon took her hand and scooped it up in his own. He pressed his fingertips into the palm of her hand and stroked gently but firmly, turning her own trick on her. It was easy to imagine those hands on her body, those fingers stroking the fires that burned deep inside her. "What are you doing after work today?" he asked.

Her gaze met his, a small smile curling her lips even as he continued to tease her with his fingertips. "Nothing much," she said coyly. "What do you plan to do tonight?"

Deacon leaned into her, burying his fingers in the loose hair at the nape of her neck and bringing her lips a fraction of an inch from his own. She wanted to close the gap between them and lose herself in his kiss. It was all she wanted, all she could think of when they were this close. She could feel the warmth of his breath on her lips. Her tongue snaked across her bottom lip to wet it in anticipation of his kiss.

Instead he smiled and let his fingers trace along the line of her jaw. "Why, I plan to be doing *you*, Miss Morgan."

# Seven

"So, are you friends with Wes or Isabelle?" Deacon asked as they slipped into the crowd mingling at the clubhouse.

Cecelia twisted her lips as she tried to come up with a good answer. "Neither, really. Wes and I are business rivals. We dated a while back, but that's it. I don't really know Isabelle that well, either."

"Why would he invite his ex to his engagement party?"

That was a good question, considering she was also the reason he'd gone years without knowing he had a daughter. She still felt bad about misjudging that whole situation. She'd helped to correct it in the end, but Wes would never get that time back, and that was her fault. "Well, in a roundabout way, I did help bring him and Isabelle back together after they broke up a few years ago."

"How's that?"

She shook her head and reached out for a flute of champagne being passed on a tray by a waiter in the standard black-and-white uniform of the club. Cecelia hesitated to tell Deacon what she'd done. He still saw her as the sweet girl he'd dated in school, and she didn't want him to see her any differently. "You don't want to know."

"Not good?" Deacon asked.

She shrugged. "Let's just say it wasn't my finest moment. But it all turned out well in the end, and since Isabelle invited me despite it all, I knew I needed to come and work on mending those bridges." Leaning into him, she spoke quieter so others nearby couldn't hear her. "I fear that before too long, I'll need all the friends I can get."

Deacon slipped a protective arm around her waist. "If anyone so much as says an ugly word to you tonight, I'll punch them in the jaw."

Cecelia smiled and leaned into his embrace. She wouldn't mind seeing Chip sprawled across the worn hardwood floor of the club, but that would cause more trouble than it was worth. And she probably deserved some of those ugly words. "That won't be necessary, but thank you."

As they turned back toward the crowd, the people parted and Isabelle rushed forward to give Cecelia a hug. She looked radiant tonight in a shimmering bronze cocktail dress that brought out the copper in her hazel eyes. "Cecelia, you made it! I'm so glad."

Cecelia accepted the hug and smiled as warmly as she could. Once she realized she'd been wrong about Isabelle's gold-digging ways, she found she really did like her. Now she just had to fight off the pangs of envy where Wes's fiancée was concerned. Soon, Isabelle would have the family that Cecelia had always wanted. She shouldn't hold that against her, though. It was a long time coming, raising Caroline as a single mother, in part because of Cecelia's meddling.

Turning to her date, Cecelia introduced them. "Isabelle, this is Deacon Chase. He's building The Bellamy with Shane Delgado."

Isabelle smiled and shook his hand. "I'm so excited for the hotel to open. It looks amazing from the outside."

Cecelia could tell Deacon was nervous, but he was handling it well. "Thank you," he said politely. "It looks amazing on the inside, too, thanks to Cecelia's great designs. Congratulations on your engagement."

"Thank you."

"It looks like a great turnout," Cecelia noted. "Even Teddy Bradford is here." That was a surprise to everyone, she was certain. She knew the CEO of Playco had been in merger negotiations with Wes before Maverick outed him as a deadbeat dad. Teddy espoused family values and had dropped Wes's Texas Toy Company like a rock when he found out about Isabelle and Caroline.

"I actually invited him," Isabelle confided. "I

haven't given up on the Playco merger, even if Wes thinks all is lost. I'm hoping that when he sees us together he'll reconsider the deal."

Cecelia could only nod blankly at Isabelle's machinations. The merger of Playco and Texas Toy Company wouldn't be good news for To the Moon and its bottom line, which is why Cecelia had kept her mouth shut where that was concerned. Wes was her biggest business rival. However, the success of Luna Fine Furnishings would make her untouchable if she could compete in both the adult and child luxury design markets. At the moment, things were going well enough that she didn't care if Teddy took Wes back.

"Good luck with that," she managed politely. "And congratulations on the engagement."

Isabelle crossed her fingers and said her goodbyes, slipping away to find Wes in the crowd. Once she was gone, Cecelia and Deacon continued to make their way through the room, saying hello and mingling appropriately. When they found the food, they each made a small plate and had a seat among some of the other guests. A long buffet had been set up for the party, with the centerpiece being a cake shaped like two hearts side by side with a third, smaller heart piped in pastel pink icing on top to represent their daughter. It was sweet.

They were perhaps an hour into the party, with no sign of Chip, and Cecelia was finally starting to relax. Maybe this event wouldn't be such a nightmare. Being there with Deacon had changed everything. She felt confident on his arm, which was a far cry from the times she'd gone to events with Chip. She was always on edge with him, wondering if she looked good enough, if she was saying the right thing… Now that it was over, she couldn't imagine a lifetime of being his wife. All she would have ever been was a prop he'd haul out at campaign rallies and fund-raisers. A Stepford wife in a tasteful linen suit with helmet hair and a single strand of pearls.

No way. Those days were behind her, and she'd never make that mistake again.

"I would like to propose a toast," Teddy Bradford said as he took position center stage with the microphone to draw everyone's attention. Cecelia noted that the boisterous old man was wearing his best bolo tie for the occasion. The crowd gathered around the stage to hear what he had to say. "Wesley, Isabelle, get on up here!"

The happy couple walked hand in hand to the stage and to stand beside Teddy.

"No one here is happier to see these two lovebirds tie the knot than I am. To me, and to the employees of Playco, family is everything. I had thought that perhaps Wesley felt differently, but I'm pleased—for once—to be proven wrong. Not only do I want to wish the couple all the happiness in the world, I want to wish it as Wesley's new business partner."

His words were followed by a roar of applause from the crowd. Wes turned to Isabelle with a look of shock on his face before he turned and shook Teddy's hand. Cecelia could only smile. Isabelle seemed sweet, but she was shrewd, as well. She had managed to accomplish tonight what Wes had been unable to over the past three months. Bravo. Perhaps she had more competition in the Texas Toy Company than she thought with Isabelle behind the scenes.

Wes turned back to Isabelle, they kissed and everyone in the club went wild. Deacon held Cecelia tighter to his side as though he sensed tension in her.

"Is this bad news for your company?" he whispered in her ear. Clearly, he knew it was or he wouldn't be asking.

"Perhaps, but I'm trying not to look at it that way. Those kinds of thoughts were what landed me such a miserable reputation in town. That's a worry for another day. Tonight I'd rather focus on the happy couple."

He nodded and pressed a kiss into her temple. "Then that's what we're going to do."

Cecelia sighed contentedly in his arms while Isabelle and Wes cut the cake and pieces started circulating around the room. "They cut the cake," she noted. "Cake is the universal sign at parties that it's finally okay to take your leave."

"Are you ready to go so soon?" Deacon asked. "I thought you were having a good time. And it looks like strawberry cake. We should probably at least stick around to have some. I love strawberry cake."

"When did you get such a sweet tooth?" Cecelia asked.

"It started back in high school when I couldn't get enough of your sugar."

Cecelia laughed aloud and leaned close. "You

don't need any cake, then. You're getting plenty of sugar once we get out of here. You've made it through the night with no complaints, and you should be rewarded."

Deacon smiled. "I'm glad you agree. It wasn't that bad, though." His glance moved around the room at the club and the people who frequented it. "I think I'd made more of this place in my mind because I couldn't be a part of it."

"No one would dare keep you out now."

Cecelia felt her phone vibrate in her purse, but she wasn't going to get it out just yet. As they waited on cake, she noticed quite a few people pulling theirs out.

"Oh, my God, honey." Simone ran up to her and clapped her hand over her mouth to hold back a sob.

Cecelia looked at her and again around the room in sudden panic. One person after another seemed to be looking down at his or her phone. The feeling of dread was hard for Cecelia to suppress. Especially when those same people immediately sought out Cecelia when they looked up.

Had Maverick's deadline already come and gone so soon? She had consciously decided not to pay the blackmail money again, but she never dreamed it would come out tonight, while she was at the club with everyone else.

"What is it?" she asked as innocently as she could, although she already knew the answer.

Simone held up her phone, showing the screen to her and Deacon. An old newspaper article about the drug overdose of Nicole Wood was there. It even featured the photo of Nicole and her infant daughter, the same one Cecelia carried in her purse. The section was circled in red and accompanied by a note:

Cecelia Morgan? More like Cecelia Wood—a liar and the daughter of a junkie and her dealer. No wonder the Morgans hid the truth. The homecoming queen isn't so perfect now, is she?

Deacon's arms tightened around Cecelia as she felt her knees start to buckle beneath her. It was only his support that kept her upright. She looked around the room, and it seemed like everyone was looking at her as though she smelled like horse manure.

Her head started to swim as she heard the voices in the room combine together into a low rumble. She could pick out only pieces of it.

*"Who knew she was so low class?"*

*"I should've known she wasn't really a Morgan. But it looks like she's not Maverick, either."*

*"Her mother probably used drugs during her pregnancy, too. I wonder if that's why Cecelia is so incapable of empathy."*

*"Have they ever revoked someone's club membership for fraud?"*

*"You can see the resemblance between her and this Nicole woman. She never had Tilly's classically beautiful features."*

Cecelia covered her ears with her hands to smother the voices. Her face flushed red, and tears started pouring from her eyes. Deacon said something to her, but she couldn't hear him. All she could feel was her world crumbling around her. She should've made the second blackmail payment. What was she thinking? That he would decide maybe that first payment was enough? That people wouldn't judge her the way she would've judged them not long ago?

It was a huge mistake, and yet, she knew this was a moment that couldn't be avoided no matter how much cash she shelled out. It wasn't about the money, she knew that much. He probably didn't care if he made a dime in the process. Maverick was set on ruining people's lives.

He would be a happy man tonight.

Deacon didn't know who Maverick was, but he sure as hell was going to find out. Why did this sick bastard get pleasure out of hurting people in the club? Deacon would be the first to admit this wasn't his favorite crowd of people, but who would stoop that low? If he could get his hands on Maverick right now, the coward would have bigger concerns than whose life he could make miserable next.

First things first, however. He could see Cecelia breaking down, and it made his chest ache. He had to get her away from this. With every eye in the room on them, he wrapped his arm around Cecelia and tried to guide her to the exit. She stumbled a few times, as though her legs were useless beneath her, so he stopped long enough to scoop her into his arms and carry her out. She didn't fight his heroics. Instead, she clung desperately to him, burying her face in the lapel of his suit.

The crowd parted as they made their way to the door. Half the people in the room looked disgusted. Some were in shock. A few more looked worried, probably concerned that their dark secret might be the next exposed by Maverick. There were only a few people in the room who looked at all concerned about Cecelia herself, and that made him almost as angry as he was with the blackmailing bastard that started this mess.

That was the problem with this town—the cliquish bullshit was ridiculous. It was just as bad in high school as it was now. It made him glad that he'd decided to leave Royal instead of staying in this toxic environment.

The problem was that most of the people in the town were in the clique, so they didn't see the issue. It was only the outsiders who suffered by their viper-pit mentality. Deacon had always been an outsider, and money and prestige hadn't changed that, not really. He'd gotten through the doors of the club tonight, but he still didn't fit in. And he didn't want to.

Yet if he had to bet money on Maverick's identity, he'd put it on another outsider. Whoever it was was just kicking the hornet's nest for fun, watching TCC members turn on each other so they would know what it felt like to be him.

Cecelia didn't need to be around for the fallout. This entire situation was out of her control, and she would be the one to suffer unnecessarily for it. Brent and Tilly should be here, taking on their share of the club's disgust for forcing her to live this lie to begin with. If they'd been honest about adopting Cecelia, there would've been nothing for Maverick to hold over her head.

He shoved the heavy oak door open with his foot and carried her out to the end of the portico. There, he settled her back on her feet. "Are you okay to stand?" he asked.

"Yes," she said, sniffing and wiping the streams of mascara from her flush cheeks.

"I'm going to go get my car. Will you be okay?"

She nodded. Deacon reached into his pocket to get his keys, but before he could step into the parking lot, a figure stumbled out of the dark bushes nearby. He didn't recognize the man, but he didn't like the looks of him, either. He was thin with stringy hair and bugged-out eyes. Even without the stink of alcohol and the stumble in his steps, Deacon could tell this was a guy on the edge. Maybe even the kind of guy who would blackmail the whole town.

"Cecelia *Wood*?" he asked, with a lopsided smile that revealed a mess of teeth inside. "Shoulda seen that one coming, right? Nobody is that perfect. Even a princess like you needs to be knocked off their high horse every now and then, right?"

Deacon stepped protectively between him and Cecelia. "Who the hell is this guy?" he asked.

"Adam Haskell," she whispered over his shoulder. "He has a small ranch on the edge of town. I'm surprised he hasn't lost it to the banks yet. All he does is drink anymore."

The name sounded familiar from Deacon's childhood, but the man in front of him had lived too many rough years to be recognizable. "Why don't you call a cab and sleep that booze off, Adam?"

The drunk didn't even seem to hear him. He was focused entirely on Cecelia. "You had it coming, you know. You can only go through life treating people like dirt for so long before karma comes back and slaps you across the face. Now you're getting a taste of your own medicine."

"Now, that's enough," Deacon said more forcefully. This time he got Adam's attention.

"Look at Deacon Chase all grow-w-wn up," he slurred. "You should hate her as much as I do. She treated you worse than anyone else. Used you and spit you out when she didn't need you anymore."

"Adam!" A man's sharp voice came from the doorway of the club. A lanky but solid man with short blond hair stepped outside with a redhead at his side.

"Mac and Violet McCallum!" Adam said as he turned his attention to them, nearly losing his drunken footing and falling over. "You're just in time. I was telling Deacon here how he's made a mistake trying to protect her. She's made her bed, it's time for her to lie in it, don't you think?"

Deacon's hands curled into fists of rage at his sides. He was getting tired of this guy's mouth. If he couldn't get his hands on Maverick, Mr. Haskell would do in a pinch.

"All right, Adam, you know you're not supposed to be here on the property if you're not a member of the club. They'll call the sheriff on you again. You can't afford the bail."

"Best sleep I ever get is in the drunk tank," he declared proudly, then belched.

"Even then." Mac came up to Adam and put an arm around his shoulder. "How about we give you a ride home, Adam? You don't need to be driving."

Adam pouted in disappointment, but he didn't fight Mac off. "Aw, I'm just having a little fun with her. Right, Cecelia? No harm done."

Mac just shook his head. "Well, tonight's not a good night for it. I'm pretty sure the party is over. If you stay around here any longer, it might be a fist and not the vodka that knocks you out tonight."

Mac was right. Deacon was glad the couple had intervened when they had or he might've had to get physical with the scrawny drunk.

"I can take anyone," Adam muttered.

"I'm sure you can," Mac agreed and rolled his eyes. "But let's not risk it tonight and ruin Isabelle's party any more than it already has been."

Mac led Adam toward his truck while Violet stayed behind with Deacon and Cecelia. "I'm so sorry, Cecelia," she said. "This whole thing with Maverick is getting out of hand. I can't imagine who would want to hurt everyone so badly. And the way people reacted…it's not right."

Cecelia came out from behind Deacon, still clinging to his arm. "Thank you, Violet."

The redhead just nodded sadly and followed Mac and Adam out into the parking lot. Cecelia watched her go with a heavy sigh. "There goes one of the five people in town who hasn't turned on me."

He hated hearing that kind of defeat from her. Cecelia was his fighter. He wasn't about to let Maverick beat her down. "You know what you need?" Deacon asked. "You need to get away from here."

She nodded. "Yeah, I'd like to go home if you don't mind."

Home wouldn't help. Word about her would just spread through town like wildfire, and soon everyone would know. Her parents would show up lamenting how embarrassing this was for them and making Cecelia feel even worse. Her friends would drop in to commiserate and reopen the wounds she was struggling to heal. No, she needed to get the hell out of Royal for a few days.

"I have another idea." Deacon took her hand and led her to his car. After the scene with Adam, he was too worried to leave her alone in case a partygoer came out of the club and had something nasty to say. When they got to his car, he opened the door and helped her in. "You're not going home."

She looked at him in surprise. "I'm not? Where are we going, then? To your place?"

Deacon shook his head and closed her door. He climbed into his side and revved the engine. He had bigger, better plans than just hiding her away at his wood-and-stone sanctuary. "I guess you could look at it that way."

He pulled out of the parking lot and picked up his phone. He dialed his private jet service and made all the necessary arrangements while Cecelia sat looking confused and beat down in the seat beside him.

Finally, he hung up and put the phone down. "It's all handled."

Cecelia turned in her seat to look at him. "You said we were going to your place, but that's back the other way. Then you have some vague conversation about going home for a few days. That doesn't make any sense. Where are we going, Deacon?"

He smiled, hoping this little mystery was enough to distract her from the miserable night. "Well, first we're stopping at your place so you can pack a bag and grab your passport."

He turned in time to see her silvery, gray eyes widen. "My passport? Why on earth…?"

Deacon grinned. This was a turn of events he hadn't expected, but it was the perfect escape. She needed to get away, he wanted to show her his crown jewel…it all worked out. By the time they returned to Royal, perhaps some new gossip from Maverick would crop up and make everyone forget about Cecelia's birth mother.

"Yes, and once you're packed, we're going to the airport where a private jet is waiting to take the two of us to one of my other properties, the Hotel de Rêve."

Cecelia sat in shock beside him. It took a few moments before she could respond. "Deacon, your other hotel is in *France*."

He pulled into her driveway and put the Corvette

into Park. "Yes. Hence the need for your passport. Pack for the French Riviera in the spring."

She shook her head, making her blond waves dance around her shoulders. Cecelia had really looked lovely tonight, in a beautiful and clingy gray lace dress that brought out the gray in her eyes, but he'd barely had time to appreciate it between the mingling and the drama.

"No, Deacon, this is crazy talk. I can't go to France tonight even if I wanted to. The Bellamy opens in two weeks. I have so much to do—"

"*Your staff* has things to do," he interrupted, "and they know what those things are. You're not carrying furniture and wiring lamps into the wall. You're the designer, and most of your work is handled. Shane will oversee everything else, I promise. You and I are getting out of this town for a few days to let this whole mess blow over. End of discussion."

The way Cecelia looked at him, he could tell it wasn't the end of the discussion yet. "Couldn't we just go to Houston or something to get away? Maybe New Orleans? No one would know where we were. We don't have to go all the way to France, do we?"

Deacon disagreed. He turned off the car and got out, opening her door. "Yes, we do."

"Why?" she persisted as she stood to look at him.

"Because I don't own a hotel in New Orleans. Now get inside and pack that bag. The plane leaves for Cannes in an hour."

# Eight

Cecelia woke up in a nest of soft, luxury linens with bright light streaming through the panoramic hotel room windows. Wincing from the light, she pushed herself up in bed and looked around the suite for Deacon. She could see him on the balcony reading a newspaper and drinking his café au lait at a tiny bistro table there.

She wrapped the blanket around her naked body and padded barefoot to the sliding glass door. The view from the owner's suite of the Hotel de Rêve was spectacular. The hotel was almost directly on the beach, with only the famous Boulevard de la Croisette separating his property from the golden sands that lined the Mediterranean Sea. To the left of the hotel was a marina filled with some the largest and most luxurious yachts she'd ever seen. To the right, beautiful, tan tourists had already taken up residence on the beach.

The sea was a deep turquoise against the bright robin's-egg blue of the sky. There wasn't a cloud, a blemish, a single thing to ruin the perfection. It was almost as if the place wasn't real. When they'd first arrived the day before, Cecelia wasn't entirely certain that this wasn't a delusion brought on by jet lag. But after a quick nap, Cannes was just as pretty as it had been earlier. Of course, enjoying it with the handsome—and partially clothed—hotel owner hadn't hurt, either.

"*Bonjour, belle*," he greeted her. He was sitting in a pair of black silk pajama pants, and thankfully, he seemed to have misplaced the top. His golden tan and chiseled chest and arms were on display, and now she knew how he had gotten that dark. If she spent every morning enjoying the sun here, she might actually get a little color for her porcelain complexion, as well.

Cecelia didn't know why she was surprised to find that he was fluent in French, considering Deacon had lived here for several years and had to interact with guests, locals and staff, alike. She supposed it just didn't align with the Deacon she had once known—covered in motor oil or rinsing cafeteria trays—although it suited Deacon perfectly as he was now.

It made her wish she had kept up with her French studies after high school. She'd quickly lost most of her vocabulary and conjugation, really being able to function now only as a tourist asking for directions to the nearest restroom. "*Bonjour*," she replied in her most practiced accent. "That's about all the French I have for today."

Deacon laughed and folded his paper, which was also in French. "That's okay," he said, leaning forward to give her a good-morning kiss. "Perhaps later we can crawl back into bed and practice a little more French."

Cecelia couldn't suppress the girlish giggle at his innuendo. Deacon was smart to bring her to Cannes. There was just something about being here, thousands of miles away from Royal and all her worries, that made her feel like a completely different person. She liked this person a hell of a lot more than the woman who had very nearly married Chip Ashford. Apparently most of Royal hadn't liked her, either, judging by their reaction to her being knocked down a peg or two by Maverick's gossip.

Cecelia sat down at the table next to him, and he poured her a cup of coffee, passing her the pitcher of milk to add as much as she would like. He followed it with a plate of flaky, fresh croissants and preserves.

"Do you have anything in mind that you would like to do today?" he asked. "Yesterday we were too exhausted to do much more than change time zones, but I thought you might like to see a little bit of the town this afternoon. You haven't been to Cannes if you haven't strolled along la Croisette, sipped a beautiful rosé and watched the sunset. We could even take my yacht out for a spin."

She took a large sip of her coffee and nodded into her delicate china teacup. "That sounds lovely. I've never been to the French Riviera, so I would be happy to see anything that you would like to show me. I mean," she continued, "it's not like this is a trip that I've planned for a long time. I basically just let you sweep me off my feet and I woke up in France. I would be perfectly content to just sit on this balcony and look out at the sea if that was all we had time to do."

Deacon smiled. "Well, I figure there is no place on earth better suited to relax and forget about all your problems than the French Riviera. I've seen more than one tightly wound businessman completely transform in only a few days. After everything that has happened recently, I think it's just what the doctor ordered, Miss Morgan."

She couldn't argue with that. He was absolutely right. Here, the drama of Maverick and the fallout of her exposed secret felt like a distant memory, or a dream that she'd nearly forgotten about as she'd awakened. She had gotten a couple texts from Simone and her mother yesterday morning after they'd landed, but Deacon had insisted she turn off her phone. Overage charges for international roaming were a good excuse, he'd said, and once again he had been right. She didn't want talk to her mother or anyone else right now.

She just wanted to soak in the glorious rays of the sun, enjoy the beauty around her and relish her time alone with Deacon. They would return home soon enough to open the hotel, and she'd finally face everything she had been running from her whole life.

"I took the liberty of scheduling an appointment for you at our spa today. My talented ladies have been told to give you the works, so a massage, a mud bath, a facial... Whatever your little heart desires. That should take up a good chunk of your day, and then we can hit the shore later this afternoon, once you've been properly pampered."

Cecelia could only shake her head and thank her lucky stars that she had Deacon here with her through all of this. How would she have coped alone? Just having him by her side would've been enough, but he always had to go the extra mile, and she appreciated it. She just wasn't sure how she could ever repay him.

She idly slathered a bit of orange marmalade on a piece of croissant and popped it into her mouth. "You're too good to me, Deacon," she said as she chewed thoughtfully. "I don't deserve any of this VIP treatment. I'm beginning to think that maybe Adam Haskell was right, and all the negativity I've been breeding all these years was just coming back to haunt me. It had to eventually, right?"

"You're too hard on yourself," Deacon said. "The girl I fell in love with was sweet and caring and saw things in me that no one else saw. You might pretend now that you are a cold-as-ice businesswoman set to crush your competitors and anybody who gets in your way, but I don't believe it for a second. That girl I know is still in there somewhere."

Cecelia appreciated that he had so much faith in her, but she wasn't the innocent girl he knew from back in school. That girl had been smothered the day her parents forced her to break up with Deacon and put her life back on track to the future that they wanted for her. She had become an unfortunate mix of both her parents—a cutthroat business owner, a perfection-seeking elitist and, more often than she would have liked, a plain old bitch. He hadn't been around to see the changes in her, but she knew it was true. She was absolutely certain that most of the people in town were thrilled to see her taken down a notch. Maybe even a few of the people whom she'd once considered her friends.

"I'm glad you think so highly of me, Deacon, but I can't help but wonder if you're actually seeing me as I am, or as you want to see me."

"I see you as you are, beneath the designer clothes, fancy makeup and social facade you've crafted. That girl hasn't changed. She's still in there, you just haven't let her out in a long time."

Cecelia felt tears start to well in her eyes as her cheeks burned with emotion. She really hoped that he was right, and that the good person he remembered was still here. It seemed like over the past decade she had lost touch with herself, if she had ever really known who she truly was. She'd spent her whole life trying to live up to her parents' expectations, then Chip's expectations...

Who *was* Cecelia Morgan anyway?

She wiped her damp cheek with the back of her hand and reached for her coffee cup to give her something to focus on instead of the emotions raging just beneath the surface. "I don't know who I am anymore."

Deacon leaned forward, resting his elbows on the knees of his pajama pants. "That's the beauty of being in charge of your own life and not trying to live up to anybody else's standards. You can do whatever you want to do. If I had just sat back and accepted the life that everyone expected of me, we wouldn't be sitting on the balcony of my five-star hotel in France. I wanted to be more, so I made myself more. You can be whoever you want to be, Cecelia, and if that means putting aside the mean-girl persona you've had all these years, and being the girl I used to know, you can do that, too."

"Can I?" she asked. "I'm not entirely sure that girl knew who she was, either. I was so easily manipulated at that age. I mean, all those plans we made, all those dreams we had for the future…that was important to me and I threw it all away. For what? Because my parents threatened to cut me off and throw me out of the house if I didn't."

Deacon's head turned sharply toward her. "What?"

Cecelia winced. "You didn't know that?"

His expression softened. "I suppose I knew they were ultimately behind your change of heart, but I thought you just wanted to please them as you always did."

"I did want to please them, but not about this. I loved, Deacon. I didn't want to break up with you. It broke my heart to do it, but I felt like I didn't have any choice. They were my parents. The only people in the world who had wanted me when no one else did. I couldn't bear for them to turn their backs on me."

"I wanted you."

Cecelia looked into Deacon's serious green eyes and realized she had made a monumental mistake that day all those years ago. Yes, she had a booming business and he had been successful on his own, but what could they have built together? They'd never know.

"I was a fool," she admitted. "I don't want to make the same mistake again. I want to make the right choice for my life this time."

Cecelia sipped her coffee and tried to think of who she wanted to be. Not who her parents wanted her to be. Not who Chip expected her to be. The answer came to her faster than she anticipated. She wanted to be the woman she was when she was with Deacon. When she was with him she felt strong and brave and beautiful. She never felt like she wasn't good enough. That was how she wanted to feel: loved.

But could she feel that way without him? Their time together had been exciting and romantic, but she had no doubt there was a time limit. Deacon had no interest in staying in Royal. He didn't like the town and he didn't like the people, and for a good reason. When The Bellamy was opened and running, he would return here to France, and she didn't blame him. This may very well be the most beautiful place she'd ever seen. She would be eager to return, as well.

She might feel like a superhero when she was with him, but once she was alone, could she be her own kryptonite?

"Dinner was wonderful," Cecelia said.

Deacon took her hand and they strolled along la Croisette together. The sun had already set, leaving the sky a golden color that was quickly being overtaken by the inky purple of early evening. The lights from the shops and restaurants along the walkway lighted their path and the crests of the ocean waves beyond them.

"I'm glad you enjoyed it. There's no such thing as bad food in France. They wouldn't allow it."

Cecelia laughed and Deacon found himself trying to memorize the sound. He hadn't heard her laughter nearly enough when they were in Royal. He missed it. In their carefree younger days, she'd laughed freely and often. He wanted her to laugh more even if he wasn't around to hear it. That was part of the reason he'd brought her here—to get her away from the drama of home in the hopes he might catch a fleeting glimpse of the girl he'd once loved.

Not that he didn't appreciate the woman she'd become. The older, wiser, sexier Cecelia certainly had its benefits. Looking at her now, he could hardly keep his hands to himself. She was wearing a cream lace fitted sheath dress. It plunged deep, highlighting her ample cleavage, and clung to every womanly curve she'd developed while they were apart. Falling for Cecelia was the last thing on his mind when he arrived in Royal, but it was virtually impossible for him to keep his distance from her when she looked like that.

"Can we walk in the water?" she asked, surprising him.

"If you want to."

They both slipped out of their shoes, and Deacon rolled up his suit pants. He hadn't thought she would want to walk along the shore and let the sand ruin her new pedicure. Yet with her crystal embellished stilettos in her free hand, she tugged him off the stone path toward the water.

The cold water that washed over them was a shocking contrast to the warm sand on his bare feet. He expected Cecelia to bolt the moment the chill hit her, but instead, her eyes got big with excitement and she laughed again.

"It's a little chilly," he said.

"It's April. It feels good, though. I can't remember the last time I put my toes in the sand and walked through the surf. Too long."

Deacon felt momentarily sheepish. He couldn't remember the last time he'd done it, either, and it was right outside his window the majority of the year.

"I understand why you'd rather be here than Royal," she said after they walked a good bit down the shoreline. "It's beautiful. And so different. I don't know that I want to go back, either." She chuckled and shook her head. "I will, but I don't want to."

Deacon felt the sudden urge to ask her why she couldn't stay. "Why go back?" he asked. "You don't have to do anything you don't want to do."

She looked at him through narrowed eyes. "Well, for one thing, I haven't finished your hotel yet. It opens in just a week and a half, if you'll recall. Plus, my company is in Royal. My employees. My friends and family."

"You could have all that here," he offered. "And me, too." Deacon surprised himself with the words, but he couldn't stop them from coming out. What would it be like to have her here with him all the time? Away from her parents' sphere of influence and the society nonsense she'd fallen prey to. He wanted to know.

Cecelia stopped walking, pulling him to a stop beside her. "You're not going to stay in Royal, are you?"

He shook his head. "You know I'm not."

Cecelia's gaze drifted into the distance. "I know. I guess a part of me was just hoping."

Deacon's heart sped in his chest. He hadn't given much thought to this fling with Cecelia lasting beyond the grand opening. He just couldn't disappoint himself that way. But it sounded like she was open to the possibility. "Hoping what?" he pressed.

"Hoping that you'd change your mind and stay awhile."

Deacon sighed. There were a lot of things he would do for her, but stay in Royal? He couldn't even imagine it. He didn't know why she'd ask him to, either. Didn't she realize how everyone treated him? How miserable it was for him? She didn't seem very happy there, either. "Royal, Texas, and I parted ways a long time ago."

Cecelia looked at him. "We parted ways, too, and yet here we are. Anything can happen."

He didn't want to argue about this and ruin their night. They were together now, and that was the most important thing. "You're right," he conceded. "Anything can happen. We'll see what the future brings."

Taking her hand into his, they started back down the beach. They were only a hundred yards or so from his hotel when he saw a child chasing after a dog on the beach. The little boy must've dropped the leash, and the large, wooly mutt seemed quite pleased with his newfound freedom.

In fact, the dog was heading right toward them. Before Deacon could react, the dog made a beeline for Cecelia. It jumped up, placing two dirty paw prints on her chest and knocking her off balance. Her hand slipped from his as she stumbled back and fell into the waves that were rushing up around their feet. She yelled as she tried—and failed—to find her footing in the icy water, soaking her dress and hair.

Deacon was in a panic and so was the little boy. They both lunged to pull the dog off her as it enthusiastically licked her face. It wasn't until the dog was yanked away that he realized Cecelia's shrieks were actually laughter. He stood, stunned for a moment by her reaction. Then he offered her his hand to lift her up out of the water, but she didn't take it. She was laughing too hard to care.

It was the damnedest thing he'd ever seen. The people back in Royal wouldn't believe it if Maverick circulated a picture of it. The perfect and poised Cecelia Morgan lying in the ocean fully clothed and covered in mud. The cream lace dress was absolutely ruined with dirty paw prints rubbed down the front. Her makeup was smeared across her skin, and her blond hair hung in damp tendrils around her face. She was a mess. But she didn't seem to care. And she couldn't have been more beautiful.

"*Je m'excuse, mademoiselle,*" the little boy said as he fought with the dog that weighed a good ten pounds more than he did. "*Mauvais chien!*" he chastised the pup, who finally sat down looking smug about the whole thing.

"Cecelia, are you okay?" Deacon asked. He wasn't sure what to do.

She struggled to catch her breath, then nodded. Her face was flushed bright red beneath the smears of her foundation and mascara. "I'm fine." She reached up for Deacon, and when he took her hand, she tugged hard, catching him off guard and jerking him down into the water with her.

"What the—" he complained as he pushed up from the water, soaked, but the joyful expression on her face stopped him. He rolled up to a seated position beside her. "Was that really necessary?" he asked.

She didn't answer him. Instead, she wrapped her arms around his neck and pulled him into a kiss. Deacon instantly forgot about the water, the dog, the cost of his ruined suit... All that mattered was the taste of Cecelia on his lips and the press of her body against his. She was uninhibited and free in his arms, kissing him with the same abandon she had that first night after her breakup with Chip. There was no desperation this time, however. Just excitement and need.

He couldn't help but respond to it. This side of Cecelia was one he thought he might never see again. It was the side that had made out with him in the back of his truck, letting him get her hair and makeup all disheveled. It was the side that had sprayed him with the hose while he was detailing one of his restored cars and led to them getting covered in mud and grass as they wrestled on his front lawn.

Deacon had missed this Cecelia. Perfectly imperfect. Dirty. Joyful. Hot as hell. He realized that they weren't alone in the back of his truck, however. The little French boy and his dog were still standing there. He forced himself to pull away, looking over the mess she'd become.

The dress had been tight before, but wet, it was clingy and damn near see-through. He could see the hardened peaks of her nipples pressing through the fabric. He would have to give her his coat to cover her when they walked home.

"*Américains fous*," the little boy said with a dismayed shake of his head. He tugged on the dog's leash and headed back in the direction he'd come from.

"What did he say?" Cecelia asked.

"He called us crazy Americans." Deacon wiped the water from his face and slicked back his hair. "I have to say I agree."

Cecelia giggled into her hand and looked down at her dress. Her fingers traced over some of the sand and mud embedded in the delicate lace and silk. "My mother just bought me this dress for Christmas. It was the first time I'd worn it. Oh, well."

"I'll buy you ten new dresses," he said. Deacon pushed himself up out of the water and helped her up, too. He slipped out of his suit coat, wringing out the water before placing it over her shoulders.

"I don't want more dresses," she said, pressing her body to his seductively with the little boy long gone. A wicked glint lit her eyes as her lips curled into a deceptively sweet smile. "I just want you. Right now."

Deacon swallowed hard. "I think this walk along the beach is over, don't you?"

# Nine

"Where are we going?" Cecelia asked.

Deacon smiled from the driver's seat of his silver Renault Laguna. In France he drove a French car. It seemed appropriate. They were only about ten minutes outside the city, and she was already keen to know everything. "It's a surprise."

Cecelia pouted. "Isn't it enough of a surprise to bring me to France on a whim in the first place?"

Perhaps. But last night, he'd gotten a sneak peek at the Cecelia he'd fallen in love with. There, lying in the surf, covered in muddy paw prints and soaked to the bone with seawater, he'd seen a glimpse of her. The radiant smile, the flushed cheeks, the weight of the world lifted from her shoulders in that moment... He wanted to capture that feeling in a bottle for her so she could keep it forever and pull it out whenever she needed to.

It also helped him realize he was on the right track with her. Getting her away from Royal was the best thing he could've done. It wasn't enough, though. Now Deacon wanted to get her even farther from the city, farther from people, to see what she could be like if she could truly let loose. There was nothing like the fields of Provence for that.

It was the perfect day for a picnic. The skies were clear and a brilliant shade of blue. It was a warm spring day, with a light breeze that would keep them from getting overheated in the sun. It was the kind of day that beckoned him outside, and the chance to make love to Cecelia in a field of wildflowers under this same sky was an opportunity he couldn't pass up.

The hotel's kitchen had put together a picnic basket for them, and he'd hustled her into the car without a word. Cecelia hadn't seen him put the basket and blanket in the trunk, so she was stewing in her seat, wondering what they were up to. He liked torturing her just a little bit. She was always in charge of everything at her company. Today, he wanted her to just let him take care of her and enjoy herself for once.

Of course, if he'd told her they were going to Grasse, she wouldn't know what that was. It was a tiny, historic French town surrounded by lavender fields that fueled their local perfumeries. It was too early for the lavender to bloom—that wouldn't happen until late summer—but there would still be fields of grasses and wildflowers for them to sit in and enjoy with a lovely bottle of Provençal rosé.

He found a tiny gravel road that turned off into a field about a mile before they reached Grasse. He followed it, finding the perfect picnic spot beneath an old, weathered tree. He turned off the car and smiled at Cecelia's puzzled expression.

"Where are we?"

Deacon got out of the car and walked around to let her out. "Provence. It's the perfect afternoon for a picnic in the French countryside with a lovely lady such as yourself."

Cecelia smiled and took the hand he offered to climb out of the Renault. She was looking so beautiful today. Her long blond hair was loose in waves around her shoulders. It was never like that in Texas. She always kept it up in a bun or twist of some kind that was all business, no pleasure. He liked it down, where he could run his fingers through the golden silk of it.

She was also wearing a breezy sundress with a sweater that tugged just over her shoulders. The dress had a floral pattern of yellows and greens that pulled out the mossy tones in her eyes. It clung to her figure in a seductive but not overtly sexual way that made him want to slip the sweater off her shoulders and kiss the skin as he revealed it, inch by inch.

"It's beautiful here," she said as she tilted her face to the sun and let the breeze flutter her hair.

Deacon shut the door and opened the trunk. He handed her a blanket and pulled out the picnic basket. "Let's go over by the tree," he suggested.

They spread the blanket out and settled down onto it together. "In the summertime," he explained, "these fields will be overflowing with purple lavender. The scent is heavenly."

She looked around them, presumably trying to picture what it would look like in only a few months. "I can see why you choose to live here, Deacon. I mean, who wouldn't want to live in France if they had the chance? It's beautiful."

"The scenery is nice," he admitted, "but it can't hold a candle to your beauty. Texas seems to have the market on that, unfortunately."

Cecelia blushed and wrinkled her nose. She shook her head, dismissing his compliment. "You're sweet, but I don't believe a word of it. Not compared to something like this." She looked away from him to admire the landscape and avoid his gaze.

There were days when Deacon wished he could throttle her parents. She was one of the most perfect creatures he'd ever had the pleasure of meeting, and she didn't believe him because the Morgans were always pushing her to be better. That was impossible in his eyes. "You don't believe me? Why not? Am I prone to hollow compliments?"

"No, of course not. It's just because," she began, looking down at her hands instead of staring him in the eye, "this is one of the most beautiful places in the world. People dream their whole lives of visiting a place like this one day. I'm just a pretty girl."

"You're more than just a pretty girl, Cecelia." Deacon leaned in and dipped a finger beneath her chin to tilt her face up to his. He wanted to tell her how smart and talented and amazing she was, but he could tell by the hard glint in her eye that she wouldn't believe him. Could she not tell by the way he responded to her touch? How he looked at her like she was the most delectable pastry in the window of Ladurée?

"What do we have to eat?" she asked, pulling away from his touch and focusing on the picnic basket.

"I'm not entirely sure," he admitted, letting the conversation drop for now. "The head chef put this together for me, so it's a surprise for us both."

Deacon opened the lid and reached inside, pulling out one container after the next. There was niçoise salad with hard-boiled eggs, olives, tuna, potatoes and green beans. Another contained carrot slaw with Dijon mustard and chives. Brown parchment paper was wrapped around a bundle of savory puff pastries stuffed with multicolored grape tomatoes, goat cheese and drizzled with a reduction of balsamic vinegar and honey. Another bundle of crostini was paired with a ramekin of chicken pâté.

Finally, he pulled out a little box with a variety of French macarons for dessert. It was quite the feast, and very much the kind of picnic she'd likely never experienced back in Texas. There was more to food than barbecue, although you could never convince a Texan of that.

They spent the next hour enjoying their lunch. Together, they devoured almost every crumb. They laughed and talked as they ate, feeding each other bites and reminding him of that afternoon they shared at the Silver Saddle. Their second chance had truly started that afternoon with a tableful of tapas between them.

Now, a week later, here they were. This was not at all what Deacon had expected when he agreed to build The Bellamy with Shane and return to Royal. Sure, he knew he would see Cecelia. He figured they would converse politely and briefly over the course of their work together at the hotel, but never did he think he would touch her. Kiss her. Lose himself inside her.

He hadn't let himself fantasize about something like that because it hadn't seemed possible when he left Royal behind all those years ago. Then she'd shown up on his doorstep, devastated and suddenly single, and everything changed. Was it possible that he'd succeeded in being good enough for a woman like her? A part of him still couldn't believe it.

"What is it?" Cecelia asked. "You're staring at me. Do I have something on my face?"

Deacon shook his head. "Not at all. I was just thinking about how lucky I am to be here today with a woman as amazing as you are."

He expected the same reaction as before, but this time, when she looked into his eyes, the hard resistance there was gone. Did she finally believe him? He hoped so.

Cecelia thanked him by leaning close and pressing her lips to his. He drank her in, enjoying the taste of her, even as he slipped the sweater from her shoulders as he'd fantasized doing earlier. He tore his mouth from hers so he could kiss a path on the line of her jaw, down her throat and across the bare shoulder he'd exposed. She sighed and leaned into his touch.

"I was such a stupid little girl back then," she said with a wistful sigh. "All this time I could've had you, and I ruined everything. I don't know if I can ever forgive myself for that. Can you?"

Deacon's gaze met hers. "Yes," he said without wavering. It was true. As long as they ended up right here, right now, who cared about the past anymore?

Reaching out, Deacon swiped all the containers and food wrappers out of his way, leaving a bare expanse of blanket to lay Cecelia down on. Her blond hair fanned across the pale blue wool as she laid back and looked up at him with her mossy, gray-green eyes and soft smile.

"What are you doing?" she asked as he hooked a finger beneath the strap of her dress and pulled it down her arm.

Her right breast was on the verge of being exposed, and his mouth watered at the sight of her pink nipple just peeking out from the edge of her dress. He didn't answer her. Instead, he leaned down and tugged the fabric until he could draw that same nipple into his mouth. Cecelia gasped and arched her back, pressing her flesh closer to him.

"Someone could see us out here," Cecelia said halfheartedly. She certainly wasn't pushing him away.

"Do you want me to stop?" he asked, ceasing the pleasurable nibbling of her flesh.

"No," she whispered, excitement brightening her eyes.

"Good. Let them see us. I'm about to make love to you, Cecelia, and I don't care who knows about it."

It had been a long time since Cecelia had made love in a public place, and even then, it had been in the back of Deacon's old pickup truck while they parked in a secluded area by the lake on a Friday night. This wasn't quite as private, and it was broad daylight, but there was no way she would tell him no. Not when he looked at her the way he did and said things that made her resistance as weak as her knees.

If she were being honest with herself, she couldn't say no to Deacon, no matter what he asked of her. He was her knight in shining armor; the prince who swooped in and saved her when she felt like the walls of her life were tumbling down around her. She would give him anything he asked of her, even her heart.

She looked up at Deacon as he smiled mischievously at her and returned to feasting on her sensitive breasts. He still looked so much like the boy she remembered, even if he had grown into such a handsome and successful man. It made her think of the days and nights she'd spent in his arms and the future they'd planned together all those years ago. They'd both accomplished more than they'd ever dared to dream, but they'd both done it alone.

Cecelia didn't want to do it alone anymore. She wanted to live her life and chase her dreams with Deacon by her side. She felt her chest tighten as she realized that Deacon didn't need to ask for her heart. He already had it, even if he didn't know it. She was head over heels in love with him, even after such a short time together. It made her wonder if she had ever truly stopped loving him.

Her parents had been behind the breakup. She had done what she had to do, putting her feelings for Deacon on a shelf to protect her heart, but they'd never truly gone away. She hadn't loved anyone else. How could she? Cecelia had given her heart to him back in high school.

Deacon looked down at her, bringing her focus back to the here and now. She ran her fingers through the dark blond waves of his hair and then tugged him to her. He didn't resist, dipping his head to kiss her. Cecelia felt the last of her resolve dissipate. She wasn't strong enough to keep fighting her feelings and denying what they had. She was out of reasons not to love him. Out of reasons to push him away. She had to travel to the other side of the earth to feel like she was in control of her own life, but she wasn't going back to the way she was before they left Royal.

She was in love with Deacon, and she didn't care who knew it. It was really none of their damn business. Just as her birth mother's identity, and the challenges she'd had to face, was none of their business. Considering all the dirt Maverick was digging up on people in Royal, the residents of her small town really needed to tend to their own gardens and stop worrying about hers.

They broke the kiss, and a sly grin curled his lips. She could feel his hand gliding up her bare leg, pushing the hem of her long cotton dress higher and higher.

"Yes," she encouraged when his fingertips brushed along the edge of her lace panties. "I don't want to wait any longer."

Not to have him inside her. Not to have him in her life. Not to love him with all her heart and soul. She'd spent her whole life waiting for this.

Deacon removed her panties and flung them unceremoniously into the picnic basket. With his green-gold eyes solely focused on her, he traveled down her body, pressing kisses against her exposed breasts, her cotton-clad stomach and down where her panties had once been.

He parted her thighs and continued to look right at her as he leaned down to take a quick taste of her. Cecelia gasped as the bolt of pleasure shot straight through her. She was both thrilled and horrified by the idea of doing something like this outdoors in broad daylight. She wasn't a prude, but there was something so intimate about the contact that it seemed like the kind of thing that should be done in the semi-darkness of her bedroom.

Deacon didn't seem to care where they were. His tongue flicked across her flesh again before he began stroking her sensitive center with abandon. There was nothing Cecelia could do to stop the roller coaster she found herself on. She gripped the blanket tightly in her fists, hoping it was strong enough to hold her to the earth.

Deacon was relentless. His fingers and his tongue

stroked, probed, teased and tortured her until her breath was passing through her lips in strangled sobs. Her whole body was tense from the buildup inside her. She tried to hold back, to prolong the feeling as long as she could, but she couldn't. He stroked hard and slipped a finger inside her at the perfect moment, and she came undone. Deacon held her hips, tightly gripping them to continue his pleasurable assault even as she writhed and trembled beneath him.

"Please," she gasped at last when she couldn't take any more. "I can't."

Only then did he pull away, allowing her to finally relax into the blanket. She closed her eyes and reveled in the way her body felt fluid, almost boneless, as she lay there. Her climax had seemingly stripped her of the capacity to move. The sun was warm on her bare skin, heating the outside of her even as her insides were near the boiling point.

She was barely cognizant of Deacon hovering near her, and she pried open her eyes. He was propped on his elbow, looking down at her with mild concern.

"Are you okay?" he asked.

"I'll be better when you're inside me," she replied, her voice a hoarse whisper after her earlier shouts.

"I thought you might need a minute." Deacon grinned.

"All I need is you," Cecelia said, and she'd never meant words more in her life. He was all she wanted. In her bed, in her life, in her heart.

"If you say so."

Cecelia shifted her hips and pulled her dress out

of the way so he could position himself between her thighs. He fumbled with his pants for a moment, and then she got what she wanted. He filled her hard and fast, freezing in place once he was as deep as he could go.

She watched as he closed his eyes and gritted his teeth, savoring the feeling of being inside her.

"Do you know," Deacon began without moving an inch, "you feel exactly the same way you did when you were seventeen? It takes damn near everything I have not to spill into you right now, you're so tight."

Instead of responding, she drew her knees up to cradle his hips and tightened her muscles around him.

"Damn," he groaned and made an almost pained expression as he fought to keep control.

She didn't care. He'd certainly shown no mercy when she was resisting her release, and she wasn't about to, either. She lifted her hips, allowing him in a fraction of an inch farther.

He blew air hard through his nose and shook his head in defiance. "Not yet, Cecelia. Not yet. When I go, you're coming with me." Deacon bent down and pressed his lips against hers. She wrapped her arms around his neck and held him tight enough that her breasts flattened against the starched cotton of his green button-down shirt.

His tongue slipped over her bottom lip and into her mouth. Slowly, he stroked her tongue with his own. Cecelia expected him to mirror the rhythm with his hips, but he was frustratingly still from the waist down.

Unable to take any more of his slow torture, she pulled away from his kiss, leaving only the tiniest fraction of an inch between his lips and hers. "If you want me, Deacon, take me. I'm yours. I always have been."

That was as close to "I love you" as she was willing to go. At least for now. It was early to confess her feelings, and if he took the news poorly, she'd be stranded in a foreign country. No, that was a revelation best left to her hometown. He'd be more likely to believe her there as opposed to it being some kind of vacation-fling confession. Hell, she'd be more likely to believe herself there, too.

Her words had the intended reaction. Deacon buried his face in the small of her neck, planted a kiss just below her ear, then began to move inside her. It was slow and sweet at first, but before long, he was thrusting hard. The small break they'd taken allowed him to continue on, but she could tell by the tense muscles of his neck and the pinched expression on his face that it wouldn't be long.

She wouldn't be long, either. Despite just recovering from her orgasm only minutes earlier, she could feel another release building. She clutched Deacon's broad back and lifted her hips for the greatest impact. That was enough to make both of them groan with renewed pleasure.

"Yes, please, Deacon," she whispered into the summer breeze.

He didn't need the encouragement to act. Deacon reached between them and stroked her center as he continued to thrust into her. His fingers quickly brought her to the edge, making her scream.

Cecelia quickly buried her face in his shoulder to smother the cries before they drew someone's attention. Yet there was no way to smother the sensations running through her body. An intense wave of pleasure pulsated through every inch of her, curling her toes and making her fingertips tingle. Her heart tightened in her chest, reminding her just how different it was to make love instead of just having sex. It had been so long that she forgot there was a difference.

Her flutter of release sent Deacon over the edge. With a roar, he spilled himself into her and collapsed, pressing her into the blanket.

Cecelia held him against her bare bosom as their breathing returned to normal and their heart rates slowed together. As she held him, she looked up at the brilliant blue sky and wished this moment could last forever.

Unfortunately, the time together in France was coming to an end. It was time to fly back to Royal, debut The Bellamy and face the music.

# Ten

Everything was perfect.

The hotel was flawless for its big debut. The black-tie-attired crowd filled the lobby of The Bellamy, flowing into the ballroom and out to the courtyard surrounding the pool. Even then it was almost elbow to elbow. It seemed as though the whole town had shown up to get their first peek at the resort. Unfazed by the crowd, the waiters moved expertly through guests with trays of delicious tapas and signature cocktails.

Shane and Brandee were beaming, and rightfully so. Deacon had heard nothing but compliments on the hotel so far. People loved the design, loved the food and couldn't wait to have guests stay at The Bellamy. Even people who at one time might've given Deacon dirty looks as they passed on the sidewalk stopped to congratulate him.

It was exactly what Royal needed, he was told. He certainly hoped so. He and Shane had a lot of money tied up in this place, and he hoped to get it back. If he could finally coexist with the upper-class circles of Royal, that would be even better. Maybe he'd be willing to stay a little longer than he'd planned after all. Deacon wasn't ready to make any big decisions, but the more time he spent in Royal, the easier it became. Cecelia might just talk him into becoming a Texan again before too long.

The only wrong tonight was the fact that he couldn't find Cecelia anywhere. Things had been crazy the minute they'd touched down in Texas. Their relaxing, romantic vacation came to a quick end with the final week of preparations that needed to be made for the opening of the resort.

He'd gotten used to having her in his bed and by his side, so it pained him to have her suddenly ripped away. He didn't even know what she was wearing tonight or if she was even here yet. He thought he saw her blonde head in the crowd, but he hadn't managed to get his hands on her with everyone wanting to congratulate him on the hotel.

"Mr. Chase?"

Deacon turned and found Brent and Tilly Morgan, of all people, waiting to speak to him. He made a poor attempt to mask his surprise, smiling and shaking Brent's hand although he had no idea why they wanted to talk to him. They never wanted anything to do with him before, and they certainly had never wanted him anywhere near their daughter.

"Mr. and Mrs. Morgan, so glad you could make it. How do you like the hotel?"

"It really is lovely," Tilly said. "Cecelia refused to give us any hints about her design, but I can see her refined aesthetic here in the lobby. I would love to see one of the guest rooms. Are any of them open to view?"

Deacon nodded, ignoring the fact that all of Tilly's compliments about the hotel were focused on their daughter's work and not on anything that had to do with him. "There's a gentleman near the elevators who is escorting guests to one of her suites on the second floor if you would like to take a tour. Cecelia really did an amazing job. Shane and I had no doubts in her ability to execute our vision here for The Bellamy. You should be very proud of her."

"Oh, we are," a man said from over Tilly's shoulder.

It'd been quite a few years since Deacon had laid eyes on Chip Ashford, but he instantly recognized him. Tall, blond...the perfect golden boy with an arrogant smirk and a spray-on tan. The people in Royal saw him as some sort of god, but he just looked like a game show host to Deacon—all smiles and no authenticity.

Deacon wasn't about to let Chip's treatment of Cecelia go unnoted after he stood there gloating about her as though they were still engaged. "I'm surprised to hear you say that, Chip. From what Cecelia tells me, you two didn't part very well. Something about her being an imposter."

"That was just a little misunderstanding," Chip said dismissively. "Wasn't it, Brent?"

Cecelia's father immediately nodded, as though he'd almost been coached with his response. "A little bit of nothing. Cecelia tends to get upset about the silliest things and make them into a bigger deal than they are. Nothing more than a little lover's spat."

Tilly nodded enthusiastically. Deacon was disgusted by how they sucked up to the Ashfords. The Morgans were a fine family on their own, and frankly, it was embarrassing.

"Brent, why don't you take Tilly upstairs to see one of Cecelia's rooms? I'd like to have a private chat with Deacon, if you don't mind."

"Not at all, not at all. Come on, Tilly." Brent put his arm around his wife and escorted her through the crowd to the wall of brass elevator doors that led upstairs.

Deacon watched them disappear, curious about what Chip had to say to him in private. The two of them had probably shared less than a dozen words between them. He imagined there was only one thing that Chip wanted to talk about: Cecelia. She was the only thing they had ever had in common.

The friendly expression on Chip's face vanished the moment the Morgans disappeared. When he turned back to look at Deacon, a scowl lined his forehead and drew down the corners of his mouth. "I've heard that you've been taking up with Cecelia."

Deacon did his best to maintain a neutral expression. He didn't want to give Chip any ammunition. "Have you? Good news travels fast."

"I wouldn't consider you making moves on my fiancée to be good news. Because of that whole dustup about the adoption, I am willing to be a gentleman and overlook the whole thing between you two. Especially since Cecelia has come to her senses."

Deacon tensed up and frowned at Chip's statement. "Come to her senses and realized marrying you was an epic mistake?"

Chip snorted in derision. "Hardly. You see, Chase, while you were busy getting ready to open this hotel, I was busy reconciling with my fiancée. I'll admit I reacted poorly to her news, but I apologized to her and she's accepted my apology. I presume, now that the hotel is open and the engagement is back on, that you'll crawl back into whatever European hole you climbed out of."

Deacon could hardly believe his ears. Chip couldn't be serious. There was no way that Cecelia would take him back after the way he had treated her. Deacon had been the one who'd comforted her when Chip broke their engagement. Deacon had been the one who'd whisked her away to France to avoid the cutting gossip after Maverick's revelation about her adoption. Deacon was the one who had held her in his arms, worshipped her body and accepted her for who she really was.

Would she really go back to the man who had shunned her after nothing more than a simple apology?

"You look surprised, Chase. I take it Cecelia hasn't gotten a chance to break the bad news to you yet. I would imagine the truth smarts a little, but you can't really be surprised. We all know who gets the girl in this scenario. I don't care how much money you've made over the years or who you've conned to get it. She wants a man from a good family with the connections and the power that only someone like I can give her. You might be a fun diversion in the sack, but you'll never be enough of a man in her eyes for anything more serious than that."

Deacon tried not to flinch at Chip's expertly aimed barb. Without fail, it hit him right in his most tender spot. He had worked hard to make more of himself, to be the man Cecelia always thought he could be. But he had always wondered if that was enough. It hadn't been enough back in high school when she broke up with him. She hadn't given him any reason to doubt her, but what really made him think that anything had changed?

Chip was right. He had money. But there were some things that money couldn't buy, things that Chip had been born with. If that really was the most important thing to her, Deacon would never be good enough.

"Besides, I've been doing a lot of thinking and talking to my campaign manager, and we've decided that her past isn't the career bombshell I thought it might be. In fact, it might even be an advantage. I'm not polling well with the working-class demographic. Having a fiancée with a tragic backstory like hers—

adopted with a drug-addicted mother and humble origins—might give me an edge come election time. It makes me more relatable to the masses."

Deacon looked at Chip's smug expression and felt his hands curl into fists at his side. Cecelia was nothing more than a campaign prop to him. Chip might be more connected than him, but he wasn't stronger. He had no doubt that he could lay Chip out on the floor without much effort. It would be amazingly gratifying to feel his knuckles pound into the man's jaw. He could just imagine the stunned looks on the faces of everyone around them as Chip lay bleeding on the newly laid marble floor.

But he wouldn't do that. He liked to think that he'd gained some class along with his money over the years. Starting a brawl at the opening gala of his five-star resort wouldn't earn him any new friends in this town. He wouldn't ruin this night for Shane and Brandee, or any of the hotel's employees. They had all worked too hard to make tonight a success, and he didn't want to undo their efforts with his brash behavior. Chip wasn't worth it.

Besides, if Chip *was* telling the truth and Cecelia had chosen to return to him after everything he'd done to her…she wasn't the woman he loved. The Cecelia he wanted was the one he'd fallen for again in Cannes. There, she had been happy and free of all the pressures this damned town put on her. That woman wouldn't have returned to Chip after his cold betrayal. But perhaps that woman had stayed behind in France.

Deacon eyed Chip coolly before swallowing his

pride and holding out his hand like a gentleman would. "Well, congratulations on your engagement. You two certainly deserve each other."

Chip narrowed his gaze at Deacon's backhanded compliment, but chose to grin and accept it anyway.

"If you'll excuse me," Deacon said, walking away before Chip could respond. He had to get away from him before he reconsidered punching him in the face. Instead, he sought out Shane and Brandee. He knew this was his party, too, but he couldn't stand to be here another moment. He certainly didn't want to be a witness to Cecelia and Chip's reconciliation. Seeing her on that bastard's arm was more than he could take. It was better that he leave now than risk causing a scene and ruining the whole night.

When he found Shane, he leaned in and whispered a few things to him. Shane turned to him with a surprised look on his face but knew better than to start a discussion about it right now. He simply nodded and clapped Deacon on the shoulder.

Deacon turned and disappeared into the bowels of the hotel where only staff were allowed to go. He wasn't entirely sure where he was headed, he just knew that he had to put some distance between himself and the woman he had been foolish enough to fall in love with the second time.

Shame on him.

Cecelia circled the ballroom for the third time, still unsuccessful in locating Deacon. She had been anxious about tonight—her first public appearance since Maverick spilled her secrets—but as she maneuvered through the crowd, everyone had carried on as if nothing had happened.

She was glad because she refused to have tonight ruined by old drama that was out of her control. She had more important things to tend to. She was bubbling over with nerves and excitement, eager to find Deacon, but so far she was having no luck. She was certain he was here—she had seen him earlier, and his car was still in the lot—but now he had vanished into thin air.

Arriving late to the party had not been a part of her plan for the evening, but it had been unavoidable. She'd had to make an unplanned stop to confirm something she had suspected since they got back from Cannes. Now that she knew for certain, she couldn't wait to find Deacon, but he was lost in a sea of tuxedos and cocktail dresses.

She was on the way to the office suites to see if he was hiding out and working instead of enjoying the party. That was when she found herself face-to-face with her ex-fiancé in a secluded hallway.

Chip was wearing his favorite Armani tuxedo, showing off his good looks the way he'd always liked to do. There had been a time when Cecelia could have been swayed by his handsome appearance, but that was in the past. There was no comparison between him and Deacon, and she couldn't understand how she let herself waste so much time on a man with few redeeming qualities outside of his social standing.

"There you are, kitten. I have been looking all over for you, tonight."

Cecelia folded her arms over her chest and narrowed her gaze at him. "I can't imagine why. And please don't use pet names, Chip. I'm not your kitten. I'm not your anything, if you recall us breaking up a few weeks ago."

Chip smiled, oozing all the practiced charm that he used on women and constituents alike. "Listen, I'm sorry about how all that went down. It was wrong of me, and I reacted poorly."

Cecelia was stunned by his apology, although it meant very little to her now. She didn't understand why he was bothering her, much less cornering her at the opening, when she had more important things to be doing. What was he after? "Thank you. Now if you'll excuse me I—"

Chip reached out and caught her arm, stopping her from pushing past him and returning to the party. "What's the rush, kitten? We really need to talk about some things. I've been doing a lot of thinking about us."

"Us? We don't have anything to talk about, Chip, but especially not about *us*." Cecelia was desperate to escape, jerking away from his grasp. She glanced over his shoulder, hoping to catch the eye of anybody who could come and rescue her, but there was no one in sight. The party was carrying on at the other end of the hallway. "I would rather have a root canal than talk to you right now."

Chip just smiled. "My favorite part of my kitten is

her claws. Now just relax and give me five minutes. We were together a long time, certainly you can spare a moment or two. That's all I ask."

Cecelia sighed. "Okay, fine. Five minutes, that's it. And stop calling me kitten. Do it one more time and I walk."

He held up his hands defensively. "Okay, okay. No more pet names. Cecelia, I came here looking for you tonight because the last few weeks apart have helped me realize that I was a fool. My feelings for you are stronger than I thought, even stronger than my concerns about your background. I've realized they're unfounded. I need you by my side going into this next reelection."

Cecelia could hardly believe her ears. When she was a liability, he couldn't dump her fast enough. Now that he decided she could be an asset to his campaign, he was crawling back. He was delusional to think she would go along with nonsense like this. "Chip, you've lost your mind."

"No, hear me out. You and I are good together. We always have been. We make the perfect American couple. Voters are just going to eat up the classic, traditional values we represent. This is a win-win for us both, Cecelia."

She could only shake her head. "You never wanted *me*, Chip. You just wanted some trophy wife you can parade around at fund-raisers and rallies. That's not what I want out of my marriage."

Chip didn't look dissuaded. He was well versed in debate, and she could tell that he wasn't going to give up until he won. "It wasn't so long ago that I was everything you wanted, Cecelia. You were so anxious to plan our wedding and start our life together. What about the children we were going to have? The future we planned? Are you willing to just throw all that away?"

"You threw it away, Chip, not me. And yes, I am willing to walk away from what you've offered me. I have found something infinitely better."

Chip chuckled bitterly. "You mean Deacon? Seriously? I'm offering you the chance to be the first lady of the United States, Cecelia. I'm going all the way to the White House one day, and I want to take you with me." He reached into his pocket and pulled out the engagement ring she'd returned the afternoon they broke up. He held it up like a gaudy offering to the diamond gods. "You're going to turn this down and walk away from the amazing life that we have ahead of us because you've got feelings for that loser?"

"As a matter of fact I am, Chip. Your five minutes are up." Cecelia brushed past him and the engagement ring she'd once worn and pushed into the crowd, hoping he didn't follow her. How she ever could've agreed to marry a man like that was beyond her. What was she thinking? She knew. It was what her parents wanted for her. She was tired of that. Now she wanted what she wanted for herself, whether they liked it or not.

She was about to start a new phase in her life, and she wanted to start it with Deacon. *If* she could find him. Finally, she spotted Shane and went up to him, hoping he could help her track Deacon down.

Shane spotted her and smiled in a polite, yet oddly cold fashion. "Good evening, Cecelia."

"Evening, Shane. Have you seen Deacon anywhere? I've been looking for him all night, and I haven't managed to find him."

Shane nodded. "Deacon had to leave, but he told me to tell you congratulations on your engagement."

Cecelia's blood went ice-cold in her veins. "What engagement?" she asked.

"You and Chip. Both he and your parents have been telling everybody at the party that you two have reconciled and the wedding is back on. It's all anyone can talk about tonight. Quite a shrewd tactic to suppress the other scandal, I have to say."

Her jaw dropped. She couldn't even believe what she was hearing. Chip was such an arrogant bastard that he'd gone around announcing their engagement before he'd even talked to her about it. How dare he tell people that they got back together without even consulting her! "I can't believe this," she said. And then she realized the depth of what this meant.

Deacon thought that she had taken Chip back. How could he believe such a thing? He hadn't even asked her if it were true. No wonder he had left the party early. She dropped her head into her hands and groaned.

"What's the matter?" Shane asked.

She couldn't even answer him. She didn't want to waste another minute talking to him when she could be tracking down Deacon and clearing up this whole mess. She turned and ran as fast as she could, weaving through the crowd to find the nearest exit and get to her car.

Cecelia was almost out of the ballroom when she heard her father's sharp, demanding voice say her name. She stopped and turned, seeing her parents standing a few feet away with a typically disappointed expression on their faces. "I can't talk right now, Dad."

"You can and you will, young lady. Chip tells us that you turned your nose up at his apology and proposal. What are you thinking? Do you know how hard we had to work to stay in the Ashfords' good graces after all this blew up? After Maverick released your information, you were nowhere to be found. Your mother and I had to deal with the backlash."

"Please reconsider, dear," her mother said in a less authoritative tone. "I really do think Chip is a good choice for you. He has so much potential, and he's from such a good family. We should be thankful that they're willing to reconsider the engagement after the truth about your lineage came to light. What are they going to think when Chip tells them that you've rejected him for the son of a mechanic?"

Cecelia's hands curled into fists at her side. If she'd gotten nothing else from her time in Cannes, it was that she wasn't going to let her life be dictated by her parents anymore. "Honestly, I really don't care what they think of me. I don't want anything to do with them, much less become one of them. I am not marrying Chip Ashford. If he hasn't ruined it for me tonight, I intend to marry Deacon Chase."

Both her parents looked at her with an expression of shock and dismay, but she didn't care. She cut her father off before he could start telling her why she was wrong. "I am tired of working so hard to meet your approval. If you truly love me, you will love and accept me for who I am, not for who you want me to be, and certainly not for whom I do or do not marry. If you can't agree to that, then I don't want you in my life any longer."

She didn't wait for their response. Right now, all that mattered was finding Deacon. Outside the ballroom, Cecelia slipped out of her high heels and ran through the back door of the hotel with them clutched in her hand.

She scanned the parking lot, but she didn't see his Corvette anywhere now. She rushed over to her own car and headed straight for his place. When she pulled up the gravel driveway, she was disappointed to find his car wasn't there, either, and all the lights were out. He'd told Shane he was leaving. Cecelia thought he had meant he was leaving the party, but now she had a sick ache in her stomach that made her think that perhaps he meant he was leaving Royal altogether.

She whipped her car back out onto the highway and rushed to the small executive airport where he had chartered the private jet to take them to France. If he was really, truly leaving, his car would be there.

At the airport, she found only more disappointment. The airport was mostly empty, with only one other car in the parking lot, and it wasn't Deacon's. She put her car in Park and sat there, unsure of what to do next. She didn't know where else to look for him.

Frustrated, she leaned back into her seat and let her tears flow freely down her cheeks. This was not the way she envisioned tonight going. Tonight was supposed to be happy. She was supposed to be sharing the most amazing and exciting news with the man she loved, and instead she was sitting in an empty parking lot alone, feeling as though everything she had ever wanted in life was slipping through her fingers.

Her whole life, all she ever wanted was her own family. Blood, love and a bond that nothing could split apart. Today, when she'd gotten home from the drugstore, she had looked at the two lines on the pregnancy test and thought that her dream was finally coming true. She had rushed to The Bellamy, anxious to share the good news with Deacon, only to have her dream intercepted by her delusional, lying ex.

And now, if she didn't find a way to clear things up with Deacon, she was going to find herself in a position she never expected: a single mother.

# Eleven

Deacon was nowhere to be found.

It'd been three days since the grand opening of The Bellamy, and no one, not even Shane, had seen him. Or at least that's what he'd said. He wasn't likely to roll on his friend if his friend didn't want to be found. Deacon hadn't shown up at the hotel offices to work. His laptop was missing from his docking station. He hadn't been seen at his house. It was like he had simply vanished off the face of the earth.

Cecelia had tried contacting him on his cell phone, but he wasn't responding to her calls or texts. She didn't even think his phone was turned on because it immediately rolled to voice mail. That or he'd blocked her. She supposed that if she dropped the news on him in a text, he would respond. However, it just seemed wrong to tell a man he's going to be a father that way.

She caught herself constantly checking her phone for a missed message, each time frowning in disappointment and putting the phone back down. When her phone did ring, it was people she didn't want to talk to. Her father was too stubborn to reach out, but her mother had called three times and left messages. Still, Cecelia wasn't quite ready to speak to them. They had sold her out to get back in the Ashfords' good graces, and it would be a long time before Cecelia would be calm enough to sit down with them and have an adult conversation about how she planned to live her life from now on. If they ever wanted to see their grandchild, they'd adjust to the new Cecelia pretty quickly.

She was even ignoring calls from Naomi and Simone. She knew if she spoke to them she would spill the news about the baby, and Deacon needed to be the first to know, no question.

She was starting to get desperate. With the job at The Bellamy complete, Cecelia had moved back into her business offices. Now was the time that she was supposed to leverage her high-profile job at The Bellamy and launch her adult furniture line, but she found her heart just wasn't in it. It required a level of dedication and focus that she simply didn't have at the moment. Perhaps it was pregnancy brain. She'd heard that it could cause difficulty concentrating.

Or maybe it was simply the fact that Chip had potentially ruined the future she'd always wanted with

Deacon. That made everything, including the success of Luna Fine Furnishings, seem insignificant in comparison.

Sitting back in her office chair, Cecelia gently stroked her flat belly. Her doctor, Janine Fetter, had calculated her to be four weeks along, but she would be showing before she knew it. How was it that her life had changed so drastically in such a short period of time? It seemed like only yesterday that she was getting ready to pitch her designs for The Bellamy to Shane, planning her wedding with Chip and paying off Maverick with blackmail money.

Now the job at the hotel was over, her engagement was broken, her secrets were public knowledge and she was pregnant with the child of a man who seemingly didn't want her any longer. She supposed she could blame the entire situation on Maverick. If he hadn't started meddling in her life, she wouldn't have had to confess to Chip and break their engagement. She wouldn't have thrown herself at Deacon because he was the only one who knew the truth and wouldn't judge her. She wouldn't have hopped on a flight to France with him to avoid the backlash of her secret being exposed to the entire town. She wouldn't have fallen in love with him again in a lavender field.

She also wouldn't be pregnant. It was a little ironic that the one thing she'd always wanted, the baby she'd dreamed of since she was a teenager, had come to be through the complicated machinations of the town blackmailer. If she ever found out who was behind it all, she supposed she should send him an invitation to the baby shower.

Cecelia's stomach started to sour. She reached for the roll of antacids in her desk drawer only to find she'd chewed the last one an hour ago. She didn't know whether it was thinking about Maverick or the latest in her constant bouts of morning sickness, but the Rolaids and saltine crackers she'd been eating lately weren't cutting it. At this rate, she'd be the first pregnant woman in history to lose weight.

With a sigh, she slammed the drawer shut and eyed the clock on her computer monitor. It was almost lunchtime. Time to run a few errands. She needed to go in search of something nausea friendly like chicken noodle soup and maybe a big glass of ginger ale to go with it. Her next stop would be the drugstore to restock her medicinal supplies before heading back to the office.

Pushing away from her desk, Cecelia picked up her purse and swung it over her shoulder. The offices of To the Moon were fairly close to downtown Royal, so she was able to walk the two blocks to the Royal Diner.

The Royal Diner was one of the few places in the town proper to eat, or at least it had been before The Bellamy opened with their high-class offerings. The diner was far more informal, complete with a retro '50s style. As Cecelia stepped in, the sheriff's wife and owner, Amanda Battle, waved at her from behind the counter. She opted for one of the unoccupied red leather booths. Sitting at the counter would invite too much conversation, and her heart just wasn't in it today.

There was chicken and wild rice soup on the menu. She ordered a bowl of that with crackers and a ginger ale. Amanda wrote down the order and eyed her critically, but didn't ask whatever questions were on the tip of her tongue.

Amanda returned with a tray a few minutes later and started unloading everything. "I brought extra crackers," she said, her tone pointed. "You look like you need them."

Cecelia looked up at her, wondering if she looked that awful. "Thank you."

"When I was pregnant," Amanda began, "I had the worst morning sickness you can imagine. Do you know what helped?"

Cecelia tried not to stiffen in her seat. Why was Amanda telling her this? It was one thing for her to look green around the gills, another for the woman to know she was pregnant.

"Those bracelets they give you when you go on a cruise. It puts pressure on some part of your wrist that makes the nausea go away. You can get them at the drugstore. If it wasn't for those and ginger ale, I might've never made it to the second trimester. That one is a lot more fun."

"Thank you," Cecelia repeated. "I'll look into that."

Amanda smiled, seemingly content to help and not at all concerned about the juiciness of the information she had inadvertently unearthed. "I'm glad you've got some new joy coming into your life. I felt so bad over those posts about your birth mother. That stupid Maverick can't ruin everything, no matter how hard he might try."

At that, Amanda turned and walked away, leaving Cecelia with her soup and her thoughts. She was right. Everything was a mess at the moment, but she knew things would work out.

Perking up in her seat, Cecelia had a thought. Maverick had managed to spread gossip to damn near everyone in town with hardly any effort at all. Maybe she could use his tricks to get Deacon back, as well. The power of social media had worked well for him, so why wouldn't it work for her?

Cecelia quickly finished her lunch, left money for the tab on the table and headed down the street to the drugstore. The morning sickness that had dominated her thoughts faded to the back of her mind as she formulated her plan with each step. She quickly restocked her supply of antacids, grabbed a bottle of prenatal vitamins and, on Amanda's recommendation, picked up a special nausea wristband designed for pregnant women.

After checking out, she rushed back to the office and immediately started drafting a message. She kept it short and sweet, using Maverick's hashtag. Plenty of people in town were following it, so the news should spread like wildfire. And, if Maverick himself was a little perturbed that he hadn't managed to ruin her life by exposing her latest tidbit of gossip, all the better.

She started with Snapchat and a photo of her bare ring finger. She followed it up with Instagram and

Twitter. Finally, she posted to Facebook. Everyone in town, including her parents, the Ashfords and Deacon himself, should be using one or more of those platforms.

*"Despite persistent rumors to the contrary, I am not, and never will be, engaged to Chip Ashford ever again. I would much rather be Mrs. Deacon Chase, and I hope that after everything that has happened between us, he will believe that and know how much I love him."*

That done, she sat back in her chair and hoped for the best. There was a new flutter of butterflies in her stomach, but this time it had nothing to do with morning sickness and everything to do with putting her heart on the line. Every word of the post was true. Even if Deacon never looked in her direction after what happened, she wasn't about to go back to the life she'd escaped with the Ashfords. Being with Deacon had helped her to realize that there was more to a relationship than arm candy and photo ops.

She wanted a real, loving relationship with a man who respected and appreciated her no matter what. And she knew now, more than ever, that she wanted that relationship with Deacon. Their baby would be the icing on the cake, completing the family she'd always wanted.

Surely Deacon didn't really believe that she would take Chip back after everything he had done to her? He'd torn off, taking Chip at his word. She couldn't imagine what Chip had said to him to send him into hiding without even asking her first. If she knew,

Chip would probably be earning a well-deserved black eye. Let Maverick tweet about that.

Cecelia had done her part to put things right between them. The message was traveling through the interwebs, hopefully on its way to Deacon's inbox. She could already hear her cell phone buzzing in her purse, so the message was spreading at the speed of Royal gossip. Her father was probably having a heart attack on the imported living room rug at that exact moment, and her mother was calling to chastise and disown her. That was fine by her. She was more interested in being a Chase than a Morgan anyway.

If everyone else was seeing it, Deacon should, too. Surely when he read the message he could come out of hiding and seek her out. She couldn't very well locate him, if the last few days were any indication. No, she'd left a digital breadcrumb trail for Deacon to follow, and all she could do was to sit back, wait for the love of her life to sweep her off her feet and brace herself for her world to change forever.

Deacon was used to being invisible in Royal. As a kid, most people had paid him no mind, and not much had changed over the years, despite his Cinderella moment at The Bellamy grand opening. He'd considered bailing on the town entirely after the fiasco with Chip, but something had kept him here. Whether it was his obligation to Shane or his misguided feelings for Cecelia, he wasn't sure. Either way, he knew he wasn't staying long, but in the meantime, the most effective course was for him to hide in plain sight—at The Bellamy itself.

He pulled the laptop out of his bag and set it up at the modern glass-and-chrome desk that was a feature of the penthouse suite. He could go downstairs to his office, but he ran the risk of running into someone and having to answer questions. Shane knew he was up here, but he had respected his space so far and promised he wouldn't reveal his whereabouts.

He'd never actually left the hotel that night. He'd marched through the bowels of the building trying to burn off his anger, then he'd had the front desk code him a key for the unoccupied penthouse suite, and he'd been there ever since. He'd left only to move his car from the employee lot to the virtually empty parking garage for guests.

He'd returned to the lobby just long enough to see Chip holding Cecelia's hand as they spoke to one another in a dark, quiet corridor near their offices. Hearing Chip boast had been bad enough, but it was like a knife to his gut to see them together like that.

He doubted anyone missed him, or was even looking for him, but if they were, they wouldn't expect him here. Why would he stay in a hotel with a perfectly lovely and secluded home only a few miles away?

To avoid Cecelia.

It was childish, he knew that. And perhaps she didn't give a damn where he was or what he was doing. She might be off making lavish wedding plans with Ashford for the social event of the year. If she *was* looking for him, it might just be to apologize for leading him on or to thank him for the lovely trip to France. Thanks, bye.

Either way, he didn't want to know what she had to say to him. He'd heard plenty that night from Chip. She'd made her decision, wrong as it might be, and he would live with it. He just didn't have to stick around so they could rub it in his face. He was going to make sure the hotel was running smoothly, hand over the reins to Shane, put his rustic lodge up for sale and return to his role as The Bellamy's silent, and invisible, partner.

Hell, if Shane could buy him out, he'd let him. Then he'd have no reason or need to ever set foot in the state of Texas again.

Maybe once he returned to Cannes, he could wipe Chip's smug face from his memory. Deacon hadn't even known they were competing for the same woman until Chip announced that he had won. Of course he'd won. Chip didn't believe for a moment that Deacon was his competition. And despite the strides he'd made over the years, Deacon wasn't sure he was Ashford's competition, either.

They offered Cecelia different things. They both had money and good looks, so with that canceling out, Chip had things Deacon simply couldn't give her. Could never give her. Like a good family name, political connections and peace at home with her parents. That couldn't be bought, no matter how much money he made.

Then again, Chip didn't deserve a woman like Cecelia in his life. Not even with all that he could offer her, because he just wasn't a good person. He wasn't nice to Cecelia, much less to the little people whose votes he was constantly chasing. The only question was whether Cecelia knew that and appreciated what that meant for her future. If she even cared.

In France, away from her parents and the pressures of Royal, she had been free to be the person she wanted to be. That was the person he loved. But apparently those two Cecelias couldn't coexist back home. Within days of returning to Texas, she'd not only changed her mind about Deacon…changed her mind about who she wanted to be and how she wanted to live…but she'd decided to take Chip back. Never mind how cruel he'd been, or how he'd kicked her when she was down. Once he was willing to "overlook" her shortcomings and take her back, she'd fallen into his arms.

Apparently she preferred being the good robot her parents wanted her to be than the happy, free spirit he saw inside her. And if that was the case, Deacon was fine moving on without her in his life. He didn't want *that* Cecelia anyway.

The suite doorbell rang, pulling Deacon from his thoughts. He didn't know who it could be. He hadn't ordered room service, and housekeeping had already visited for the day. With a frown, he got up and went to the door. Through the peephole, he spotted Shane. Reluctantly, he opened the door. If something was wrong at the hotel, he needed to man up and deal with it, not barricade himself in the penthouse, even if it meant he might see Cecelia downstairs. "Hey," he said casually, trying to act as though they didn't both know he was hiding up here after getting his heart trampled.

"Hey." Shane had a strange expression on his face. It was a weird mix of excitement and apprehension, which made Deacon even more curious about this unexpected visit. "Have you been online?" Shane asked.

Deacon took a step back to let his business partner into the suite. "No," he admitted. "I've done some work, read some emails, but I haven't really felt like seeing what the rest of the world was up to the last few days." He certainly didn't want to see a new engagement announcement for Cecelia and Chip, or run across any type of society buzz about their upcoming wedding being back on despite her tragic, secret past. He intended to be far, far away from Royal, Texas, by the time that event took place.

Shane charged in, nearly buzzing with nervous excitement. "So you really haven't seen it?"

Deacon closed the door, slightly irritated at the intrusion. "Seen what, Shane? I told you, I've been living in a cave for the last few days."

"Wow. I'm so glad I came up here, then. You need to see this." Shane turned his back on him without elaborating further, ratcheting Deacon's irritation up a notch, and walked over to the computer. He sat down at the desk, silently typing information into the web browser.

"Can't you just tell me?" Deacon asked as he came up behind him.

"No," Shane said. "You have to see this for yourself."

Deacon tried not to roll his eyes. He crossed his arms over his chest and waited impatiently for Shane to pull up whatever important news had to be seen firsthand. At the moment, all he could see was that he'd pulled up Facebook. Deacon didn't even have a Facebook account. He didn't need a social site to remind him that he didn't really have any friends to keep up with online.

"Here," Shane said at last. He pointed to the screen as he got up from the chair. "Sit down and read this."

Deacon didn't argue. He sat down and looked at the post Shane had pointed out. It was a post from Cecelia's Facebook account. Her screen icon was a selfie that the two of them had taken when they were walking on the beach in Cannes. That was an odd choice for a woman who was engaged to another man, he thought. Then he read the words, and his heart stopped in his chest.

*"Despite persistent rumors to the contrary, I am not, and never will be, engaged to Chip Ashford ever again. I would much rather be Mrs. Deacon Chase, and I hope that after everything that has happened between us, he will believe that and know how much I love him."*

Deacon sat back against the plush leather of his computer chair and tried to absorb everything he'd read. She wasn't engaged to Chip? Had the smug bastard lied to Deacon's face about the whole thing? Was he so arrogant that he'd assumed she'd take him back if he only asked? That was a bold bluff, he had to give Chip that. From the sound of that post, it was a bluff that hadn't succeeded. If they really weren't together, that meant she still wanted to be with him.

Judging by her words, she wanted to be more than just with him. She wanted to spend the rest of her life with him.

She loved him.

It was a damn good thing Shane had made him sit down.

"Can you believe it?" Shane asked. "When I saw her that night at the party after you left, she seemed really confused by my congratulations on her engagement. I thought maybe she was just annoyed that the news got out before they could make an official announcement, but now it looks like it was because she didn't know what the hell I was talking about."

Deacon almost didn't believe what he was reading. He had been jerked around so many times where Cecelia was concerned that he was afraid to think it could really be true. He wanted it to be true, though. He'd made the mistake of letting himself fall in love with her again these past few weeks. He'd never intended on it, but after that afternoon in Provence, he couldn't help himself. He was madly in love with Cecelia Morgan. Could she really, truly be in love with him, as well?

"What are you going to do?" Shane pressed.

"I have no earthly idea," he answered. And that was the truth. He didn't want to screw this up. If he and Cecelia got back together, that was it. It was for life. He was going to marry her, make it official and never let that sweet creature out of his sight again. Even if that meant living in Royal for the rest of his life. It was the sacrifice he was willing to make to have her as his wife.

"Well, are you just going to sit here? Why aren't you rushing out the door to sweep her off her feet? She wants to marry you, Deacon. Stop hiding in this damn penthouse suite and do something about it."

Deacon closed his laptop screen and turned to face Shane. "I want to do this right. I can't half ass it on a whim. She deserves better than that. I don't think the little jewelry store in town is going to have what I need. Care to join me for a trip to Florida to get the perfect engagement ring?"

Shane grinned. "Florida? Just for a ring? There're some great places in Houston."

Deacon shook his head. "There's only one ring in the world for Cecelia, and it's in Florida."

"Okay," Shane agreed. "Do we need to have my assistant book some first-class tickets?"

"First class?" Deacon smirked, then shook his head as he reached for his phone. "Nope. We're taking a private jet."

# Twelve

Cecelia slipped the key card into the elevator panel, allowing her to go to the restricted top floor of The Bellamy. When her message went out into the universe and everyone but Deacon seemed to receive it, she decided it was time to take some drastic measures. Someone had known where he was. Her money had been on Shane, but she'd opted to approach his fiancé instead. It was a risk, considering how Brandee probably felt about her, but she was her only hope. Brandee would likely have had the information without that pesky sense of loyalty to a friend.

It turned out she was right. Brandee not only gave her Deacon's location, but the access card to get her there. She had seen the posts online and, despite everything, was all too happy to help Cecelia reunite with Deacon.

The elevator chimed and the doors opened. Cecelia stepped out onto a small, elegant landing. There were doors at each end of the hallway. One was labeled the Lone Star Suite and the other the Rio Grande Suite. Brandee said that Deacon was in the former, so she took a deep breath to steel her courage and turned left toward his room and, hopefully, her future.

Facing the massive oak door, she raised her hand to knock but was surprised when the door whipped open before she could make contact.

Deacon was standing there, looking just as startled to find Cecelia on his doorstep. He was wearing an immaculately tailored dark gray suit with a sapphire-blue shirt that reminded her of the color of the ocean in Cannes. It clung to every angle and line of his body, making him look impossibly tall and more handsome than she could even remember.

Their sudden face-to-face stole the words from Cecelia's lips.

"Cecelia? What are you doing here?" he asked.

She bit anxiously at her lip. "Brandee told me where you were. I'm sorry, but I had to talk to you about something. It looks like you're headed out the door, though, so I guess I'll come back."

"No!" Deacon shouted, catching her upper arm before she could turn away to leave. "No, I was going to find you."

Cecelia felt a bit of the pressure crushing her rib cage lift. "You were?"

"Yes, please come in." Deacon stepped back and held out his arm for her to follow him into the suite.

She made her way into the room and over to the seating area with the modern couches she'd designed and had manufactured. It felt a little weird to be sitting on them as a guest. "You're a hard man to find," she admitted.

Deacon sat down on the sofa beside her, angling his shoulders and hips to face her. "I didn't want to be found. Especially by you."

The words were like a kick to her gut, but she had to understand where he was coming from. He didn't know the truth. "You know that Chip is a boastful liar, right? I hadn't seen or spoken to him since we broke up, and I certainly hadn't agreed to marry him before you two had your run-in at the party."

Deacon nodded. "I know. Shane showed me your post yesterday."

"Yesterday?" He'd seen it and done nothing. Why had he waited? She'd put her heart on the line, and he'd sat back and thought about it overnight. She'd been in misery, on pins and needles, waiting to hear from him. That was the only reason she'd come after him. If he wasn't swayed by her declaration of love and desire to marry, he at least needed to know he was going to be a father.

"I had a lot to think about after I saw that."

"Well, I came here today because I have more to say to you than can fit in one hundred and forty characters. I also need to say things that don't need to be posted for the whole world to read. Not because I'm ashamed of them or you, but because some things are meant to be private, and between two people."

She closed her eyes for a moment to gather her thoughts. She had a lot to say, and she wanted to say it just right. "First, I wanted to thank you."

"Thank me?" Deacon looked surprised.

"Yes. You've taught me how to feel again. To love again. After we broke up, it hurt so badly to lose you that I shut down inside. I couldn't bear the pain, and I didn't want to fall in love with someone else and lose them, too. I decided I was done with love and I was going to focus on my career instead. I built baby furniture because a part of me thought it would be as close as I would ever get to having children. At least with a loving partner. I convinced myself that a loveless marriage that made good business sense was the right choice.

"I was wrong about everything. I didn't know I was starving until you gave me a taste of what I'd been missing. Then I knew I was wrong to close off my heart, wrong to think Chip was the kind of person I needed in my life... But most of all, I was wrong to think that I could ever stop loving you, no matter how hard I tried to suppress it."

She hesitated for a moment and turned to look at him so he would be able to sense and feel how much she meant the words she was about to say. "You are the only person I've ever known who loved me just the way I was. No restrictions, no requirements. So I wanted to thank you for that."

Deacon stared at her silently for a moment, and

then he reached out to take Cecelia's hand in his own. "I've never stopped loving you, Cecelia. Even when I was angry or hurt, I still loved you. You're the reason I haven't left Royal yet. There was no reason to stay, but a part of me just couldn't leave you behind, even if you'd chosen that greasy politician over me."

"I would never do that. He doesn't hold a candle to you. I don't understand why my parents can't see what kind of man he really is, but in the end it doesn't matter. In France, I decided I was going to live my own life on my own terms, and that hasn't changed. If my parents come around, they can be in my life, but if they don't, I'm okay with that. I'm never choosing them over you again."

Deacon squeezed her hand as she spoke. "You have no idea how happy I am to hear you say that. I've got a few things I need to tell you, as well."

"I wasn't finished," Cecelia said, but he raised his hand to shush her. She hadn't gotten to the critical news yet.

"I've been doing a lot of thinking while I've been holed up in his hotel suite. Your message and your arrival here today made things easier, but I was determined to change things between us before that happened. I walked away that night when I was faced with Chip's challenge, and I shouldn't have. Suddenly, I was eighteen again and not good enough for you. I walked away that night all those years ago, and I walked away again, instead of fighting for your love the way I should have. I'm not making that mistake again because you are worth fighting for.

"When I ran into you at the door just now, I was coming to tell you how much I loved you. Even if Chip had convinced you to take him back, I was going to steal you away, and I knew I could because he could never give you what you really needed. I'm the only one who can love you the way you need to be loved. I want to give you that life you've dreamed of, the family you've always wanted. I am determined to give you everything your heart desires. Starting with this."

Deacon reached into his coat pocket and pulled out a black velvet box. "I was on my way to find you and give you this. You said you wanted to be Mrs. Deacon Chase, and I didn't want to make you wait a moment longer. I didn't immediately come running to you because I wanted to have the right ring, the right words, the right suit...I wanted this moment to be perfect."

Cecelia shook her head with tears glistening in her eyes. "It is perfect, Deacon. You could be in jeans with a grape ring pop and I would say yes because you're the best thing that's ever happened to me."

Deacon smiled. "This is a little better than a grape ring pop."

He opened the box, revealing the prettiest vintage ring she'd ever seen. It had a round diamond set in a thin rose-gold band. A circle of small diamonds set in rose gold surrounded the center stone, and intricate scrolls were cut into the setting and along the sides. Cecelia had never seen anything like it.

"I didn't want to compete with Chip to get you the

biggest, gaudiest diamond I could. Instead, I wanted to get you the most meaningful ring I could. This one belonged to my grandmother. Shane and I flew to Florida yesterday to get it from my parents."

Deacon plucked the ring from its velvet bed and held it up to her. "Cecelia, this question has been a long time coming, but will you be my wife?"

Cecelia had been asked that question one time before, but this was completely different. There were butterflies in her stomach, her heart was racing and she couldn't take her eyes off the beautiful ring. When Chip proposed, she didn't know what it should feel like. Accepting his proposal had been like signing the paperwork to buy a new car—nice and satisfying, but not exactly a moment to cherish for a lifetime. This blew everything out of the water.

"Yes!" she said, bubbling over with love and enthusiasm. "I've been waiting to be Mrs. Deacon Chase since I was seventeen years old."

Deacon slipped the ring on her finger. It fit perfectly. The minute he read the message from Cecelia online, he knew this was the ring for her. His grandmother had told him as a child that her ring was to be kept so he could give it to the love of his life one day. Her marriage had been full of love and laughter, and she wanted the same for him. Even in their hardest financial times, his parents refused to sell the ring. He would need it one day, they insisted.

And based on the light in her eyes and the smile on her face, she liked it. The anxious muscles in his neck and shoulders started to relax now that she'd said yes. He snaked his arms around Cecelia's waist and tugged her to him. Their lips met, and suddenly it felt as though all was right with the world. Cecelia was going to be his wife. Nothing else mattered.

When their lips finally parted, Deacon studied Cecelia's face for a moment. "You've been waiting a while to be married to me. How much longer do you want to wait to make it official? We can be on a jet to Las Vegas in an hour."

Her nose wrinkled as she considered his offer. The idea of her being his wife before the sun went down was intriguing. Their relationship had come apart so many times, he was keen to make it legal once and for all before she could slip through his fingers again.

"No," she said at last. "I want to be your wife more than anything, but I don't want to elope. I want this whole town to put on their best cowboy boots, go down to the church and witness you and me making vows to love one another until the end of time. I want my parents to see it. The Ashfords to see it. I even hope Maverick will be sitting in those pews, so he'll know that he didn't win this time, not with me."

Deacon couldn't have been more proud of his fiancée than he was in that moment. Even if he had come to terms with this town and what people thought of him, it made him happy to see that she was proud to be his wife. "They'd better get used to having me around anyway."

Cecelia perked up beside him. "Does that mean you're willing to move here?"

He hadn't given it a lot of thought, but yes, if that was what she wanted. "I'd live on the moon if that's where you were. I'll have to travel quite a bit to my various hotels, but if you want Royal to be home, that's fine with me."

"Can we spend the summers in France?"

Deacon grinned. "You bet. I can't say no to you. If you want to live here, we'll live here. If you want a big church wedding with four hundred guests, let's do it. I happen to know the guy who owns the big new hotel in town, if you want to have a reception there. Anything you want, you'll have it. The white dress, the church, the flowers, the whole thing. Go buck wild, baby."

"I won't go too crazy," she said, although he could already see the wheels turning in her head with wedding plans. "I still want to marry you as soon as possible. Maybe not tonight, but soon."

That was fine by him. All he wanted was to be married. Cake, flowers and all the other trappings of the ceremony were unnecessary distractions to him, but he understood their importance to her. "Okay. We'll get the engagement announcement in the Sunday paper. Or shall we go post the good news online before Maverick can beat us to the punch?" Deacon asked in a joking tone.

Cecelia shook her head. "Not yet. I want to keep this just between us for a day or two. And besides that, Maverick doesn't know everything. I've got another little secret of my own."

Deacon's brow raised in curiosity. What other big news could she possibly have to share? "What's that?"

She untangled her fingers from his and placed his hand across her stomach. "I'm having Deacon Chase's baby."

Deacon didn't think that he could be stunned speechless, but she'd just done it. His baby? She was pregnant with his baby? He looked down at his hand and the still-flat belly beneath it. "You're pregnant?"

"Yes. You're happy, aren't you? Please say you're happy."

He pinned her with his gaze so there were no doubts in her mind about how he felt. "I'm thrilled beyond belief. I'm just not sure how it happened. We were careful, weren't we? How far along are you?"

"Four weeks. I think it happened that first night we were together, when I threw myself at you."

Deacon arched an eyebrow. "The day you sneaked out on me?"

"Yes," she admitted with a sheepish grin. "I guess I would've been back no matter what."

Deacon couldn't even imagine how he would've taken the news if she had shown up after her disappearing act and announced she was having his baby. He was nearly blown off his feet as it was. "How long have you known?" he asked.

"I started feeling poorly on the flight back from Cannes. I thought I was just airsick, but when it persisted a few days, I realized there might be more to it. I bought a pregnancy test the night of The Bellamy's grand opening. That's why I was late to the party. When I did arrive, I was looking all over for you to tell you the news, but you'd already left after arguing with Chip. When I realized what had happened, I was heartbroken, but I couldn't find you to tell you the truth."

Deacon squeezed his eyes shut to keep from getting angry. Not at her, but with himself. He'd ruined that moment they would've shared together because he thought so little of himself that he let Chip scare him off. There she'd been, searching the crowd to tell him they were having a baby, and he was licking his wounds in the penthouse.

"I am so sorry," he said. "I let Chip ruin that night for us. We should've spent this week together picking out baby names and planning our future together."

"I don't care about that," Cecelia insisted. "It's just a few days in the scheme of things, and it gave us both some time to figure out what we really wanted, baby or no baby. What matters is that you and I love each other, we're getting married and we're having a baby. I've always wanted a family of my own, and now I'm going to have it. With you."

Deacon pulled Cecelia close again, this time tugging her all the way into his lap. He cradled her in his arms, capturing her lips in the kind of kiss he'd fantasized about since they got back to Texas. She melted into him, reminding him just how much he'd missed her touch these last few days.

"If you're having my baby, maybe we should reconsider the Vegas option and get married tonight."

Cecelia shook her head. "This isn't a shotgun wed-

# TRIPLETS FOR THE TEXAN

JANICE MAYNARD

For Charles Griemsman, editor extraordinaire.
Thanks for all your hard work and your
commitment to making stories shine.
The Texas Cattleman's Club
wouldn't be the same without you!

# One

Royal, Texas, was a great place to call home. Running her own ad agency, being a member of the esteemed Texas Cattleman's Club and maintaining a hectic social life kept Simone Parker plenty busy. Busy enough not to worry about the ghosts of lost loves.

Today, her luck had run out. Five years. It had been five long years since she'd last laid eyes on Troy Hutchinson. Now here she sat in a freezing exam room at Royal Memorial, naked but for a thin paper hospital gown, and in walked the man who broke her heart. Pressing her knees together instinctively, she gripped the edge of the exam table and blurted out the first thing that came to her mind.

"Where's Dr. Markman?"

Hutch—almost nobody called him Troy—stared at her impassively. "He took a position in Houston. I'm the new head of the maternal-fetal medicine department."

Made sense. Royal's state-of-the-art hospital hired only the best.

It occurred to her that Hutch didn't look at all surprised to see her. But then again, he'd obviously glanced at her chart before entering the room. He was as gorgeous as ever—chocolate eyes, closely cropped black hair and mocha skin. The only thing missing was his killer smile.

Tall and lean, in his physical prime, the man was impressive even without the lab coat. Wearing it, he exuded authority and masculinity. Making Simone feel small and stupid.

Her stomach curled with nausea. Today's situation was volatile enough without having to confront old lovers. As if the term applied. She'd been a twenty-two-year-old virgin when she and Hutch first hooked up. She'd had only one relationship after that, and it had been brief and unexceptional.

For most of her life she'd chosen to hide behind her reputation as a shallow party girl. Even Hutch had believed it in the beginning. Until he'd realized he was the first. Then there had been hell to pay.

Her palms started to sweat. "You can't be my doctor."

"Of course not," he said. "Dr. Markman left rather abruptly. We've been in the process of notifying his patients. Somehow, your appointment fell through the cracks. Dr. Janine Fetter has agreed to take over your case...with your permission, of course."

"That's fine," Simone said impatiently. "But that doesn't explain why *you're* here."

A faint smile lightened his face. "Don't shoot the messenger. Scheduling should have postponed your ultrasound until next week. Dr. Fetter doesn't have any openings until then. She's not even here today."

*Great, just great.* Hutch knew every inch of her body. Even so, no way in heck was she going to calmly put her feet in those stirrups and let him examine her. That was too icky for words. "What are my options?"

"You can make an appointment for next week and go home..."

"Or?"

"Or if you don't want to wait, I can go over the ultrasound with you. But no exam," he said quickly.

"Ah." Simone had badgered the tech to explain all the grainy images on the screen, but the woman had been well trained. She'd done her job, escorted Simone to yet another exam room and left her to worry for forty-five minutes. Plenty of time for a single woman to regret the impulsive decision that had led her to this moment.

"So tell me," she snapped, her nerves getting the best of her. "I'm not pregnant, am I? Don't worry. I won't fall apart. I knew the odds when I went into this."

Pursuing fertility treatments and intrauterine insemination had been more involved than she had ever imagined. Even now, she wouldn't be entirely unhappy if it hadn't worked. Picking out a sperm donor and dealing with hormone shots had been stressful, expensive and time-consuming. It had also given her plenty of opportunity to rethink her hasty decision.

Her late grandfather had left instructions with the executors of his will that she would be entitled to half of his vast estate—five million dollars cash and the family homestead, worth infinitely more—if, and only if, she produced an heir to continue the family bloodline. With no plans to settle down anytime soon, she'd decided to go the route of single motherhood.

Trying to live up to the terms of her grandfather's will—without weighing the cost—was, in retrospect, probably a stupid decision.

She must have had gut-level doubts from the beginning, because she hadn't even told her two best friends, Naomi and Cecelia. Naomi had seemed distracted and tense ever since she got back from Europe, and Cecelia had been on cloud nine after reuniting with former flame Deacon Chase. So Simone had kept her plans to herself.

For the first time, Hutch's facade cracked. His jaw firmed, and his eyes were bleak. "No one told me you had gotten married, Simone. Though, knowing you, I'm not surprised you kept your maiden name. Don't you want the baby's father to be here when we talk about these results? Can you contact him? We could reschedule for later this afternoon."

She stared at Hutch. "Have you read through my file?"

"Not yet. But I will, of course. All I've seen is the ultrasound report. I only came on board officially yesterday. To be honest, I'm still a little jet-lagged."

And no wonder. He'd spent the past half decade in Sudan with Doctors Without Borders. The man was almost too good to be true, strong, sensitive and—when he unleashed that boy-next-door charm—virtually irresistible.

Though they had no longer been a couple when he left Royal, Texas, in the intervening months and years, she had worried about him. Malaria. Viral hemorrhagic fever. Political uprisings. He had thrust himself into a hotbed of danger and never looked back. Even without being there, Simone knew he had saved untold numbers of mothers and babies.

Hutch had completed not one but two stints in Sudan. When he hadn't returned after the first one, she knew for sure he was no longer interested in resurrecting their relationship—although that was possibly too mature a word for the affair. She and Hutch together had been like fireworks, burning hot and bright and beautiful, but over too soon.

While she mentally rehashed the painful past, Hutch waited patiently, his expression guarded. Having him eye her with the impassivity of a medical professional hurt. A lot.

Whipping up a batch of righteous indignation helped. It was none of Hutch's concern what she did with her life. "There is no father in the picture," she said bluntly. "Go ahead and tell me what you have to say."

For a split second, something flickered across his face. Shock? Probably. Relief? Unlikely.

"I'm sorry to hear that," he said, his tone so formal it

could have frozen the air itself. "Are you divorced? Widowed?"

"I don't think you're supposed to ask me that, Dr. Hutchinson." She was furious suddenly—at herself for making such a mess of things, at Hutch for having the audacity to come home looking wonderful and completely unapproachable, if a bit tired, and at life in general.

He swallowed. "My apologies. You're right. That was out of line."

Despite her best intentions, she couldn't stay mad. Not today. And besides, what did it matter if she told him? Not the whole truth, of course. But he had her file at his disposal. Sooner or later, he would know. She might as well put a good spin on it.

"I wanted to have a baby," she said bluntly. *Maybe for all the wrong reasons, but still...* "I chose to use an anonymous sperm donor, because I had no significant other in the picture. This baby will be mine and mine alone. There are plenty of single mothers out there doing very well. I have a good job, financial resources and plenty of friends. I'll be able to handle motherhood, Hutch. You don't have to look at me like that."

Her decisions about parenthood and her grandfather's bequest were her own. She didn't want to be judged, and in truth, the facts could very easily be misinterpreted, leaving her in a bad light.

It was a real worry, particularly since the mysterious Maverick had somehow found out about her fertility treatments and threatened to expose her secrets. She pushed that situation to the back of her mind. Dealing with Hutch was enough drama for one day.

He stared at her with such intensity she felt oddly faint. Her heart beat loudly in her ears. Hutch's expression was a mixture of incredulity, pity and disapproval. Or at least that was how she interpreted it. At one time, she could guess what he was thinking. That was long ago, though.

Tossing the manila folder on the counter beside the computer, he shoved his hands in his pockets. "I have no doubts about your ability to care for a baby," he said.

She frowned. "Then why all the mystery? Why do you look like you're about to deliver words of doom? Is it something else? A tumor? Some weird cancer? Am I dying? That would suck."

His lips twitched. "Not at all, Simone. You're having triplets."

Hutch cursed when Simone went milk pale and keeled over. He caught her before she hit the floor, but just barely. Hell, he knew better. It wasn't the kind of news one delivered with a baseball bat. As usual, though, she rattled him. Even now.

Cradling her in his arms, he turned back to the exam table. His instinct was to hold her until she woke up. But that was all kinds of unethical. Instead, he laid her gently on her back and reached into the cabinet for a soft, mesh-weave blanket. Covering her all the way up to her neck, he tried not to notice the way she smelled. He could have identified her scent with his eyes closed. A mix of floral and spicy that was uniquely Simone.

She roused slowly, those incredibly long lashes fluttering as she came back to him. "What happened?"

When she tried to rise up onto her elbows, he put a hand on her shoulder to keep her down. "Give yourself a minute to recover. You've had a shock."

Even befuddled and wrapped in a generic blanket, she was striking. Her blue eyes were electric, somewhere between royal and aquamarine. Her hair made as much of an impact as her eyes. The smooth, silky fall was the black of a raven's wing…shot through with blue in the sunlight. He tried not to remember what it felt like to wrap his hands in all that thick, glorious hair. At one time, it had reached almost to her waist. The style was shorter now, but still a couple of inches below her shoulders.

Her gaze cleared gradually. "So I wasn't dreaming." The words were not really a question.

"No."

"I want to sit up."

He helped her, though it was difficult to touch her. She made him feel like a gawky adolescent. That was bloody uncomfortable for a man supposed to be in charge of Royal, Texas's world-class obstetrics department.

"I apologize for springing it on you, Simone. There's no easy way to drop that bomb. I have to tell you I'm surprised and concerned that you've chosen this option."

"I'm not getting any younger." The set of her jaw was mulish.

He remembered all too well what Simone was like when she made up her mind about something. "You're not even thirty. Couldn't you have waited and taken the traditional route?" he asked.

The wash of color that had returned to her face leached away again. Her eyes glittered with something that might have been pain or anger. "I tried that once or twice. I'm not a fan. Men complicate things."

The blunt retort was a direct shot at him. It found its mark. Clearly, Simone still blamed him for their breakup. He wanted to fight back, but it was pointless after all this time. His job wasn't to be her friend, or even her boyfriend. He was charged with overseeing her medical care.

"I suppose it's a moot point now," he said, feeling weary and discouraged. "Unless you've changed your mind. Do you want to terminate the pregnancy? If that's your decision, hospital staff would of course preserve your privacy."

Simone blinked. "Is that what *you* think I should do?"

He weighed his words carefully. "Having triplets is an enormous commitment, even for a two-parent family. You would be doing this alone."

She stared at him. Her restless fingers pleated the edges of the blanket. "I want these babies."

He cocked his head, trying to read her emotions. "You wanted *one* baby, Simone. I think you need to weigh the situation seriously. While it's still very early."

"There's nothing to consider. I made a choice. I have to live with the consequences."

"For the rest of your life."

Hot color streaked her cheekbones. "I know you think I'm flighty and impulsive and a lightweight. What you don't realize is that I've grown up a lot in the time you've been gone. I can do this."

"But why?" That's what confused him. It wasn't as if she was running out of time. Besides, she had never particularly struck him as the maternal type.

"My reasons are my business, Dr. Hutchinson. Am I free to go now?"

There were secrets in her eyes and in her heart. He knew it. The two of them might have been separated by time and distance for the past few years, but there had been a moment when he had known everything about her. Every thought. Every feeling. Every beat of her energetic, enthusiastic, passionate heart.

The Simone he knew jumped into life with both feet, usually via the deep end. She had her naysayers—Royal was a relatively small town with a long memory. Her youthful missteps had cost her. A reputation was a hard thing to shake. But he knew she had a good heart.

"Just hear me out. You should know, Simone, that a multiple pregnancy immediately puts you in the high-risk category. The hospital hired me for my expertise. I'll be overseeing your case indirectly. Dr. Fetter will alert me if any problems arise. Will that be a problem?"

Simone blinked. "Do you have any crackers?"

"Excuse me?" Had his hearing taken a hit in Sudan?

"I need saltines. I'm about to puke."

Oh, lord. "Hold on," he said. Opening the door to the hallway, he bellowed for a nurse. The poor woman must have sprinted, because she was back in two minutes with the crackers and a cup of ice chips.

He took them with muttered thanks, closed the door firmly and turned to Simone. She wasn't white anymore. More like a transparent shade of green. Grabbing a plastic basin from the cabinet, he put it in her lap and unwrapped the crackers. "Slowly," he said.

"Don't worry," she muttered. "I'm afraid to move."

"Poor baby." He'd seen pregnant women almost every day of his professional life, but none had ever touched him as deeply as this one. Without overthinking it, he put an arm behind her back to support her. "I'll hold the cracker," he said. "You nibble."

It was a measure of how miserable she was that she didn't fight him. No snappy comeback. No insistence she could feed herself. When she leaned into him, his heart actually skipped a beat. A huge neon sign flashed in his brain. *Warning! Warning!*

Even though he knew he couldn't get close to her again, his body betrayed him. She was so familiar, so delightfully feminine. Every caveman instinct he possessed told him to fight for her, to protect her. Women were tough, far tougher than men at times. Still, this Simone who had come to him today was at a low spot. He wanted to make it all right for her.

Yet he was the last person she needed. He'd suffered too much heartache, witnessed too much heartbreak to offer Simone anything resembling the love they had once shared.

She managed the first cracker and started on the second. In between bites, he offered the ice chips. Four crackers in each pack, eight in all. Eventually, she finished them.

"Thank you," she said. "I'm okay now."

It was patently untrue, but he took her words at face value. He handed her what was left of the cup of ice. "I have other patients to see," he said, wondering why the thought of leaving this room was so unappealing.

"I know," she said. "Go. I'm fine. I'm glad you didn't die in Africa."

He chuckled. "Is that all you have to say?"

"I don't want to add to your ego. I won't be surprised if the town makes you the patron saint of Royal. Saint Hutch. It has a ring to it, don't you think?"

"You're such a brat."

"Some things never change." Her teeth dug into her bottom lip.

Gradually, her color was returning to normal. The doctor in him approved. "That's not true, Simone. Neither of us is who we were five years ago. I know I'm not."

She tucked a wayward strand of hair behind her ear. "Is that a polite warning? You're telling me not to get any ideas?" Her sidelong glance held a touch of wry mischief.

Even now, she had the power to shock him. While he'd been willing to dance around their painful past, Simone plunged right into the murky depths. Maybe she knew him better than he realized.

"I wasn't, but I probably should have."

"You're not my doctor."

"No. Not technically." He paused, weighing his words. "Perhaps this is presumptuous on my part, but you opened this can of worms. I knew we would see each other again, Simone. It was inevitable if I came home. But…"

"But you've moved on."

"Yes. I have." He didn't tell her the rest. He couldn't.

Simone nodded. "I understand, Hutch. I think it's obvious I have my hands full, too. Maybe we can be friends, though."

"Maybe." He let the lie roll off his lips. As much as he wanted to help her, he couldn't get close. Not again. "Are you okay now? The nausea's better?"

She handed him the basin. "False alarm. You're good at this. Maybe you should be a doctor."

His smile was genuine. Simone had always been able to make him laugh, even when he took himself too seriously. He reached in his pocket for a business card and scrawled his cell number on the back. "I need you to promise," he said, handing it to her.

"Promise what?" She handled the little rectangle as if it were a poisonous snake.

"I want you to promise that you'll call me immediately if you have any problems."

"What about Dr. Fetter?"

He shoved his hands in the pockets of his lab coat. "She's a busy doctor with a lot of patients."

"And you're not?"

They stared at each other in silence. "Hell, Simone. You're not making this easy."

"I don't understand you."

"We share a past. I want to make sure you and these babies are okay."

"Saint Hutch."

If that's what she wanted to think, he might as well let her. It was far better than the truth. "I care about you," he said quietly. "I mean it. Any hour. Night or day. This isn't a typical pregnancy. I want to hear you say it."

She lifted one shoulder in an elegant gesture he remembered well. "Fine. I promise. Are you happy now?"

He hadn't been happy for a very long time. "It will do. I'll be in touch, Simone. Take care of yourself."

# Two

After the run-in with Hutch, the actual appointment with Dr. Fetter a week later was anticlimactic. The rules for a multiple pregnancy were pretty much the same as any pregnancy. Take vitamins. Sleep and rest the appropriate amount. Exercise every day. Report any spotting or bleeding.

That last bit was scary. Simone stared at the obstetrician as the woman entered notes on a laptop. "How often does that happen? Bleeding, I mean."

Dr. Fetter looked up over the top of her glasses. "Ten to twenty percent of all pregnancies end in miscarriage, Simone. With multiples, the risk is higher. Nevertheless, you shouldn't waste time worrying about it. Your ultrasound looks good, and we'll monitor you closely, much more so than a typical pregnancy warrants."

"I see." It was easy for the doctor to say *don't worry*. She wasn't the one carrying three brand-new lives.

Soon after that sobering conversation, Simone was back outside staring around in a daze at the nicely landscaped grounds of the hospital. *Triplets*. No matter how many times she repeated the word in her head, it didn't seem real. She'd had daydreams about pushing a stylish stroller with a tiny infant dressed in pink or blue. It was hard to fathom the reality of taking three babies out on the town.

She sat in her car for the longest time, telling herself everything was going to be okay. Her initial motives in getting pregnant had been less than pure. Was the universe punishing her for playing around with motherhood?

Despite evidence to the contrary, she was stunned to realize that she *wanted* these babies desperately. Not one of them, or two…but all three. Placing her palm flat on her abdomen, she tried to imagine what she was going to look like in a few months. With triplets, she could be huge.

Oddly, the thought wasn't as alarming as it should have been. For a woman who wore haute couture as a matter of course and worked hard to keep her body in shape, the fact that she was able to imagine herself as big as a blimp without hyperventilating showed personal growth.

At least that's what she told herself.

It was getting late. She was supposed to be at Naomi's condo in less than an hour. Naomi and Cecelia were making their signature jalapeño and shredded beef pizza. Normally, Simone gobbled down at least three pieces. How was she going to make it through the evening when the thought of food made her want to barf?

As she drove to the other side of town, she practiced what she was going to say. *By the way, I haven't had sex in months, but I'm pregnant with triplets.* Or how about *I ran into Hutch last week. I don't think I ever got over him.*

Already she was reconsidering her decision to keep Naomi and Cecelia in the dark. This was too hard to do alone. She needed someone to talk to…someone who would have her back. If she couldn't confide in her two best friends, she couldn't confide in anybody. Naomi and Cecelia had been her closest companions and confidantes since grade school. Still, she wasn't ready to spill *all* her secrets at once. She needed time to wrap her head around things. It was happening too fast.

As Simone entered her code on a keypad and rolled

through the elegant gate, she noted the perfectly manicured grounds of the luxury condo complex. Naomi's privacy was protected here. Naomi Price was famous in Royal for any number of reasons. Her cable television show had been picked up nationally, so now she was dispensing style advice to women—and men—coast to coast.

Simone parked and walked up the path. When she rang the buzzer, Cecelia answered the door. "It's about time. Where have you been?"

Clearly, the question was rhetorical, because Cecelia disappeared into the kitchen, leaving Simone to put a hand over her mouth and gag at the smell of cooking meat. *Oh, lordy.* She fished a water bottle from the depths of her leather tote and took a cautious sip. If she wasn't ready to talk about the babies, she had to get her stomach under control. Otherwise, her secret wasn't going to be a secret for very long.

Gingerly, she rounded the corner and entered the kitchen. The room wasn't huge, but it was as stylish as the woman who hovered over the stove. Naomi had brown eyes and long copper-brown hair. She was charming and extremely pretty, but Simone knew her friend didn't understand how beautiful she was.

Cecelia, on the other hand, had bombshell looks and knew how to use them. Her platinum hair and long legs drew men in droves. Her company, To the Moon, produced high-end children's merchandise but had recently branched out to the adult furniture realm with the launch of Luna Fine Furnishings. Simone and her ad agency were currently producing a hard-hitting campaign designed to take Cecelia's company to the next level.

The other two women barely said hello at first. They were squabbling over the correct ratio of peppers to meat. At last, Naomi looked up. "Hey, hon. What's the matter with you? I've seen ghosts with more color."

That was the thing about good friends. They didn't sugarcoat things. "Just an upset stomach," Simone said. "I think I ate too much at lunch." Fortunately, meal prep took precedence and no one called her on the lie.

Normally, Simone would have offered to help, but right now she stayed as far away from the food as possible. When the large pizza was in the oven, the three women adjourned to the living room. Simone envied Naomi's innate sense of style. Her home was stunning but extremely comfortable.

Simone claimed a comfy chair and sat down gingerly. She'd always heard about morning sickness, but she had never imagined how wretched it could be. Tucking her legs beneath her, she tried to get comfortable.

Cecelia, on the other hand, hovered by the window. She was always a high-energy person. Today she practically vibrated with excitement.

Naomi took a sip of her Chardonnay and waved a hand. "What's up, Cecelia? You said we had to wait for Simone. She's here now. Don't keep us in suspense."

The tall blonde spun around, fumbled in her pocket and held out her hand. "Deacon proposed! And I'm pregnant."

After that dual announcement, much squealing ensued. Simone and Naomi hugged their friend and admired the ring. Deacon Chase was quite a catch. He'd lived in Europe for a decade, but had returned to Royal and purchased a beautiful country lodge on the outskirts of town. The gorgeous, self-made billionaire hotelier had confidence and charisma and a dimpled smile that broke hearts everywhere. As far as Simone was concerned, he was one of the few men alive who could handle Cecelia and not be intimidated by her looks and personality.

Clearly, now was not the time for Simone to share her own news. For one, she didn't want to steal Cecelia's thunder.

When the furor died down, they adjourned to the kitchen

and dug into the freshly baked pizza. Simone's stomach cooperated enough for her to get down most of one piece, though she surreptitiously removed the jalapeños and wrapped them in a paper napkin. No point in tempting fate.

"So who's your doctor?" Simone asked. *Please don't let it be Hutch.*

"I'm seeing Janine Fetter. She's not real chatty or friendly, but I don't need that in a doctor. I want someone I can trust to take care of me and my baby. Dr. Fetter fits the bill."

Naomi shook her head. "I still can't believe it. This means we'll have to plan a baby shower."

Cecelia laughed. "Give it time. I'm still in my first trimester. Plenty of opportunity for that. Deacon and I are going to keep the news to ourselves for a while, but he knew I would have to tell you two."

"Well, I should think so," Naomi said. "We've never kept secrets from each other."

Simone grimaced inwardly. The trio's tight friendship had backfired in Royal at times. Some people referred to them as the mean girls. The label wasn't fair. They weren't mean. But when three women were extremely successful, attractive and high-profile, there were bound to be those who took potshots. The criticism had sharpened after Naomi, Cecelia and Simone had been admitted into the Texas Cattleman's Club.

Some diehards still thought women should be kept out. And *somebody* had started the rumor that Naomi, Cecelia and Simone could be behind the malicious blackmail messages various residents of Royal had been receiving via social media.

It wasn't true. Even Cecelia had received one of the blackmailer's threats. Simone, too, though she hadn't told anyone.

Later that evening as Simone drove home, she struggled with feelings of envy. Cecelia had a baby on the way and a wedding to plan. That meant Cecelia's situation was cause for celebration. Simone, on the other hand, was pregnant with triplets whose biological father was an unknown sperm donor.

Lots of people used sperm donors in situations of infertility. But those were loving couples who made a joint decision and were excited about the chance to bring a child into their home.

Simone had done it selfishly because of her grandfather's stupid, archaic will. Blinking back tears, she clutched the steering wheel and apologized to the three tiny sparks of life in her womb. "I swear I'll be a good mom," she whispered. "I would take it all back if I could, but now you're on the way, and I want to keep you. You'll find out soon enough that grown-ups make mistakes. Me, in particular."

It would have been nice to have someone say, "There, there, Simone. Don't be so hard on yourself. Everything will work out for the best. You'll see." Unfortunately, unless she confided in Naomi and Cecelia, no one in Royal was likely to fulfill the role of pep squad. She'd have to be her own cheerleader. First order of business would be enjoying a relaxing evening at home.

Her house was welcoming and warm, but in a whole different way than Naomi's. After the ad agency landed its third big client, Simone had moved out of her bland apartment and purchased a five-acre estate in Pine Valley. The place was ridiculously large for one person, but she loved it.

At least she would have plenty of room for a live-in nanny. Or maybe two. *Triplets!* How would she ever manage?

When she made the turn from the main road onto her property, she noted with pride the way the flowering cherry trees lined the driveway. When the wind blew, tiny white petals fluttered down like snow. Spring in Royal, Texas, was her favorite time of year.

It was a surprise to see a black SUV parked on the curving flagstone apron at her front door. An even bigger shock was the man who stepped out to face her. Not bothering to put her small sports car in the garage, she slammed on the brakes and slid out from behind the wheel. "What are you doing here, Hutch?"

She hated the way her heart jumped when she saw him. Even without three babies on the way, she shouldn't get involved again. Given the current situation, it would be emotional suicide to think she had any kind of chance with the good doctor.

In his muscular arms he held a medium-sized box. "I brought you some books from my medical library. I remembered how you like to research things on your own, so I thought you could take a look at these. Plenty of stuff here about multiple births, both from a medical standpoint and from a practical parenting aspect."

"That's thoughtful of you," Simone said. "Do you offer this kind of service to all your patients?"

His lips quirked in a reluctant smile. "You're not my patient, remember?"

"True." She wasn't exactly sure what the protocol was here. In any case, she couldn't leave the man standing outside. "Would you like to come in for some iced tea or a cola?"

"Decaf coffee?" he asked hopefully.

"That, too."

"I'm in."

She unlocked the front door and tossed her keys on a table in the foyer. Hutch set the box on a chair and looked around with interest. "I like your house," he said. "It looks like you."

Simone made her way to the kitchen, painfully aware

that he followed closely at her heels. "How so?" She opened the refrigerator to cool her hot face and to hide for a moment. Her heart raced at a crazy tempo.

"Modern. Stylish. Simple. Sophisticated."

Wow. Was that really how he saw her? While she put the coffee on to brew, Hutch perched on a stool at the bar. "Thank you," she muttered. Was he thinking about all the money she had spent while he was caring for sick babies in terrible poverty? Was his compliment actually a veiled criticism?

Maybe she was reading too much into a casual comment.

"Where will you live now that you're back?" she asked. "Somewhere near the hospital?"

"Actually," he said with a weary grin, "I'm going to be your neighbor. I'll be closing on the brick colonial down the road soon."

"Oh." She knew the house well. It was less than half a mile from her place. Was that a coincidence?

Hutch shrugged. "I'm too old for bachelor digs. I wanted to put down roots."

"No more Doctors Without Borders?"

"I don't think so. It's a young man's game. I gave it more than five years of my life. It's the best thing I've ever done, but it was time to come home."

"I'm sure your parents are delighted." Hutch's mother and father were both lawyers. They had raised their son to believe he could be or do anything he wanted. Hutch had excelled all the way through school, despite the occasional run-ins with bullies.

"They were over the moon when they heard."

"Must be nice. My mom and dad drop by only when they want to lecture me about something. Of course, you probably remember that." Her parents had been none too thrilled about their only daughter dating someone they hadn't hand-picked for her. Neither Hutch nor Simone had let the veiled disapproval dissuade them.

Remembering the passionate affair and its inevitable end was something Simone managed to avoid. Mostly. But with Hutch in her kitchen, the memories came crashing back.

The two of them had met at a party at the Cattleman's Club. Simone had been barely twenty-two and ready to fall in love. The town had thought she was promiscuous—still did—but that was a facade she hid behind. If people wanted to look down their noses at her, she wasn't going to stop them.

Being introduced to Troy Hutchinson by a mutual acquaintance had been kismet. The moment she laid eyes on him, she knew he was the one. Though he was ridiculously handsome, it was his quiet, steady intelligence that drew her in. Hutch was no callow boy looking for an easy lay.

He had talked to her, listened to her opinions. Danced with her. Laughed at her jokes. And in a secluded corner outside the club, he had kissed her. Even now she could remember everything about that magical moment. The way he smelled of lime and starched cotton. The sensation of feeling small and protected, though she was more than capable of taking care of herself. He was taller than she was and extremely fit, which made sense, of course, for someone who had devoted himself to the pursuit of medicine.

"Simone? Hello in there…"

Suddenly he was standing in front of her, his smile quizzical. "You've been stirring that cup of coffee for a long time."

Heat flooded her cheeks. Did he know what she was thinking? Could he read her mind?

"Here," she said. "I fixed it the way you like it. Strong enough to peel paint and enough sugar to give you cavities."

He took the cup and sipped slowly, his eyes closing in

bliss. "Now *this* is good coffee. Might even compete with the real stuff in Africa."

"I'm sure not everything was great. As I recall, you were a meat-and-potatoes guy, too. Not much prime beef where you were, I'd say."

"You're right, of course. I lost twenty pounds after I arrived in Sudan and never quite gained it back."

"Let's take our drinks into the den." She grabbed a package of cookies out of the cabinet and led the way. Hutch chose a wing-backed chair near the dormant fireplace. Simone claimed one end of the sofa.

He sat back with a sigh, balancing his cup on his flat abdomen. "You've done well for yourself, Simone. I'm proud of you. Everyone in town sings your praises—well, your ad agency's praises," he clarified.

"That might be a stretch, but thanks. Hard work and a dollop of luck."

"I always knew you'd make your mark in Royal."

She frowned. Her ambition had been partly the cause of their breakup, but not from her perspective. She hadn't wanted to stand in the way of Hutch's dreams. When he'd offered to wait on Africa until her agency was established, she had insisted he should go. Hutch read that as a rejection. He thought she cared more about her business and money than about him. Stupid man.

Still, that was a long time ago.

For several long minutes they drank their coffee in silence. She was tired and queasy and sad. Seeing Hutch again was a painful reminder of how many times in her life she had made mistakes.

Would she ever learn?

At last, the silence became unbearable. She set her cup on a side table. "I think you should go now," she said. "I don't feel very well. I'd like to rest. And if I'm being honest, I'd rather not have people see your car in front of my house."

# Three

Hutch grimaced. Her words stung, even though they gave him an easy out.

He had told himself he was indifferent to Simone now, but in his gut he knew the truth. The first moment he laid eyes on her in that exam room a week ago, he'd felt the same dizzying punch of desire he'd always experienced when he was with her.

Panic swept through him like a sickening deluge. He couldn't do that again. Not after what had happened in Sudan. It was better that Simone knew the score.

She lost patience with his lack of verbal response. "If you have something to say, say it. I've had a long, stressful day, and I want to take a bath and get into bed."

*I'd like to join you...* His subconscious was honest and uncomfortable.

The dark shadows beneath her beautiful eyes reminded him she was in a fragile state, both mentally and physically.

The fact that he wanted so badly to hold her told him he had to protect himself.

He stood and paced, his hands jammed in his pockets. "I understand why you want me to move my car. Now that I'm back in town and we're both still single, the gossip mill will undoubtedly have us hooking up any day now. People may even say your triplets are mine."

Simone swallowed visibly. "Gossip isn't reality."

"Maybe not. But I have to be up front with you. I'm not willing to get involved in a relationship."

She was pale and silent, her sapphire-eyed stare judging him. "I don't recall asking you to. But to clarify, is your distaste for romance because of our past?"

"Not entirely. I fell in love with a fellow doctor while I was in Sudan. Her name was Bethany."

For a split second, he could swear he saw anguish in Simone's eyes. But if it was there, she recovered quickly.

"You said *was*? Past tense?"

He nodded jerkily. "She died two years ago. Cut her foot on a rock. Doctors make the worst patients, you know. She didn't tell any of us how serious it was. Ended up with sepsis. I couldn't save her." Even now the memory sickened him.

Simone leaned forward. "I am so sorry, Hutch."

Her sympathy should have soothed him. Instead, it made him feel guilty. "I'll always be fond of you, Simone…and I'll care about you. But I need you to know that's all it will be."

She blinked. "I see."

"I suppose you think I'm assuming a hell of a lot to think you would even be interested after all this time."

"Not at all. You're a gorgeous man. With a kind heart. I'm sure I won't be the only woman in Royal who appreciates your sterling qualities."

"Aw, hell. You're making fun of me, aren't you?"

"Maybe a little." She smiled gently. "Six months ago your virtue might have been in danger. But now I have three babies to consider. Their welfare has to come before anything else in my life."

"Even romance?"

"Especially romance."

"Then I guess we've cleared the air."

"I guess we have."

"I should go," he said. But he didn't move.

Simone stood up, swaying a bit before she steadied herself with a hand on the back of the chair. "Yes, you should."

Squaring his shoulders, he nodded. The urge to kiss her was overpowering.

She kept a hand on the chair, either because she felt faint or because she intended to use it as a shield. Either way, it didn't matter. He wanted to taste her more than he wanted his next breath.

He put his hands on her shoulders, noting the tension there. She wasn't wearing shoes, so the difference in their heights was magnified. Winnowing his fingers through her hair, he sighed. "I should have come home a year ago. Then maybe I could have talked you out of this single-mom idea."

"Not your business, Doc."

It was as easy as falling into a dream. He had loved Bethany, deeply and truly. And grieved her passing. But this thing with Simone was something else. Did he dare explore the possibilities?

Slowly, he moved his lips over hers, waiting for the protest that never came. She tasted of coffee and wonderful familiarity. But not comfort. Never comfort. There was too much heat. Too much yearning. When she went up on her tiptoes and wrapped her arms around his neck, he groaned. Five years. Almost six. Gone in a flash.

He ran his hands over her back and landed on her bottom. She was thinner, but every bit as soft and appealing as she had ever been. Before he left for Sudan, when they were alone together, Simone had been unguarded…innocent. A far cry from the woman who tilted her chin and dared the world to disrespect her.

Every beat of his heart was magnified. He kissed the

sensitive spot behind her ear...nipped her earlobe with his teeth. Simone did nothing to stop him. In fact, she didn't even try to hide the fact that she wanted him. Temptation sank its teeth into his gut and didn't let go. He was hard as a pike. The sofa was close by. Damn. How could he still want her so badly? No. This had to stop. Now.

Dragging in great gulps of air, he broke free of the embrace, stumbled backward and wiped a hand over his mouth. "Does it make you happy to know I still want you?" he snarled. He felt like a fool.

Simone's expression was gaunt and defeated. "Not happy at all, Hutch. But message received. You have nothing to fear from me. I'd appreciate it if you would let yourself out."

She waited until she heard the front door slam before bursting into tears. Sliding down the wall and curling up in a knot of misery on the hallway floor, she cried ugly, wretched sobs that left her throat raw and her chest hollow.

She knew her hormones were all over the map, but it was more than that. Hutch might as well still be in Africa. The gulf between them was so deep and so wide, it was doubtful they could ever even manage to be friends. Yet the same incendiary attraction that had drawn them to each other in the beginning still existed.

The sensation of being wrapped in his strong arms...of feeling his steady heartbeat beneath her cheek...of knowing he wanted her as much as she wanted him brought back such crazy joy. Never in her life had she felt as happy or free as she had when she and Hutch were a couple.

What he said was true. If he had come home six months ago, she would never have embarked on this path of insanity. She'd been angry at her dead grandfather and determined to prove she was worthy of carrying on the family name. It had never been about the money, but more about legitimacy, a sense of belonging.

Now it was too late for second thoughts. The babies were a reality.

Stumbling to her bathroom, she washed her face and sprawled on the bed. She was hungry again, but it was a weird hunger. Beneath the pangs of an empty stomach rolled a sensation of nausea in the offing.

Finally, at midnight, she dragged herself out of bed and went to the kitchen in search of a snack. Milk seemed like a bad idea. Ditto for cheese or yogurt. Craving something salty, she found half a bag of stale, plain potato chips. She gobbled two handfuls and washed them down with ginger ale.

Her hunger appeased, she went back to bed only to jump up twenty minutes later and rush for the bathroom. She threw up violently, so hard that her ribs ached. Even rinsing out her mouth made her stomach heave.

Groaning, she found a damp cloth and pressed it to her forehead. The notion that she might have to endure weeks of this misery pointed out once again how foolish she had been. *I'm sorry*, she said silently to the three lives she carried.

No matter what sacrifices it demanded, she would make sure this was a healthy pregnancy.

The following morning was no better. Dry cereal and water came right back up as soon as they went down. Her hands began to cramp, signaling possible dehydration. Doggedly, she sipped from a water bottle and forced herself to put on the same dress pants from the day before but with a different top. She couldn't simply stay home because she felt bad. She had a business to run…a business that would soon support three tiny infants.

Driving was doable, but only because she never pushed the speedometer over thirty miles an hour. When she reached her office, the receptionist, Candace, gave her a wide-eyed stare. Simone didn't engage. She made a beeline for her private suite, closed the door and put her head on the desk. The sharp corner of a business card poked her stomach through her pocket.

She pulled the rectangle out and laid it on the desk. Hutch. Dr. Hutch. Saint Hutch. It would be a cold day in hell before she called him for *anything*.

With nothing more than dogged determination and the inherent stubbornness that got her into trouble more often than not, she made it through an entire workday. The campaign for Luna Fine Furnishings, a subsidiary of Cecelia's company, To the Moon, was coming along nicely. Phase one had already been rolled out. In two weeks, an intensive social media blitz would back up the initial print ads and billboards.

The noon lunch hour came and went. Simone didn't even attempt to eat. At five o'clock, she closed her laptop, packed up her things and took a deep breath before heading out to her car. Once there, she had to spend another chunk of time convincing herself she could make the drive home. She was shaky, light-headed and so very sick.

She must have dozed when she got home, because suddenly it was seven o'clock. Naomi would bring her food if she called, but then Simone would have to explain what was going on. Even if it was time to share her secret with her friends, she'd rather do it with both women present.

Carryout pizza sounded revolting. Canvassing the pantry in her kitchen was an exercise in futility. She knew *how* to cook but seldom spared the time. Most days she had lunch with clients and grabbed a salad for dinner.

In the end, the only available choice was peanut butter. That was protein—right? Even her crackers were stale. But smeared with peanut butter, they were edible. At first, Simone thought she had landed on a miracle. The peanut butter was comfort food, its smell and taste appealing.

Sadly, no matter the enjoyment going down, everything she consumed came back up in a matter of minutes.

The night passed slowly. She alternated between lying on top of the covers covered in a cold sweat and hunching over the toilet. No matter how slowly she sipped water, it wouldn't stay down. Nor would anything else.

Once she almost fell, so dizzy the room spun around her. Finally, at 4:00 a.m., she collapsed into an exhausted slumber.

When her alarm went off, she muttered an incredulous protest. How did working mothers do this?

Dragging herself into the shower, she held on to the towel bar as she washed her hair. Blow-drying it took everything she had. At last she was dressed and ready to go. By now the thought of trying to eat was beyond her. Maybe she'd be able to attempt some lunch.

The ride to work was a blur. This time she barely noticed the receptionist's look of consternation. Simone's mouth was dry and fuzzy. How could she risk taking a drink when she might have to rush for the bathroom? No one in Royal knew she was pregnant. Well, aside from Hutch and Dr. Fetter. It was far too early to let that cat out of the bag.

As she sat in a stupor at her desk, the buzzer on her phone sounded. "Line two, Ms. Parker. It's your accountant."

Later, Simone couldn't remember the exact details of that conversation. For all she knew, she might have agreed to transfer her personal and business funds to illegal offshore accounts.

Thankfully, her two full-time employees—including her exceptional right hand, Tess—were out of town at a conference. The receptionist was fairly new and wouldn't have the temerity to invade her office uninvited.

So the hours passed.

At one, Simone knew she had to eat something. Her headache had reached monumental proportions. Maybe she would send Candace out to get chicken noodle soup. Not only would that guarantee Simone a few minutes of privacy to test her stomach with a sip of water, but the soup might actually be good for her.

She stood up on trembling legs. Rarely did she ask an employee to carry out a personal errand, but she was literally incapable of walking down the block. Carefully, she opened her door. "Candace, can you come in here?"

Candace looked up and blanched. Apparently Simone looked even worse than she felt. Her receptionist rushed into the office. "Can I help you, Ms. Parker?" she asked.

Simone nodded, wincing when the motion sent shock waves through her skull. "Would you mind grabbing me some chicken soup from the diner?"

"I'd be happy to," Candace said.

"Let me get my billfold."

"No worries. We can settle up later. Do you want something to drink? Lemonade? Iced tea?"

Oh, wow. Tea sounded wonderful. "Tea would be great." Her mouth was so dry. "Hurry, Candace. I don't think I can—" She stopped dead, nausea rising in her throat. "Oh, damn. I'm going to—"

It might have been hours or days later when she woke up completely. She had vague memories of an ambulance and several people in white coats. Now she was in her own bed.

When she shifted on the mattress, Hutch's voice sounded nearby. "Take it easy, Simone. You're going to be okay."

"My head hurts," she groaned, trying to recreate her spotty memory.

"No wonder." Hutch crouched beside her bed, his smile quizzical. "You whacked it pretty hard on the edge of your desk when you fainted. The ER doc put in three stitches, but there's no concussion."

Panicked, she tried to sit up. "The babies?"

"Steady, woman. They're fine."

"What happened to me?"

"Hyperemesis gravidarum."

"Oh, God. Is that as bad as it sounds?"

"Yes and no. You were badly dehydrated, Simone, and disoriented. One of the unlucky women who suffer from severe nausea and vomiting when pregnant. Women with multiples are more prone to it."

"Well, that's just peachy," she muttered.

"Dr. Fetter wanted to admit you, but you pitched a fit and demanded to go home. She only agreed because I promised to stay with you."

For the first time, Simone realized she was hooked up to an IV. "You did this?"

He looked at her strangely. "Yes. But if you've changed your mind, I'll take you back to the hospital."

Now that her head was clearer, she did remember most of what he was saying. It didn't paint her in a good light.

"How did you hear I had passed out? Why were you there with the EMTs? Candace doesn't even know you."

"She was trying to call 911 and saw my card on your desk."

"I knew I should have thrown that away."

Hutch had the audacity to laugh. When he did, she caught a glimpse of the carefree young doctor she had fallen in love with so many years ago. Heaven help her. With the shadows gone from his eyes—chased away by genuine humor—he was irresistible.

He fiddled with a setting on the monitor. "It will take at least twenty-four hours to get your electrolyte levels balanced again. After that, we'll have to see if you are able eat or drink at all. Otherwise, you'll have to get nutrition intravenously."

"How long will this last?"

"Well..." It was clear he didn't want to upset her.

"Go ahead, Hutch. I can handle it."

"Days. Weeks." He grimaced. "For some it's all the way till the end. But you're in the earliest moments of this pregnancy. Your body is adapting to the flood of hormones. With any luck, things will settle down soon."

"Thanks for the pep talk," she said drily. She watched as he moved around the bedroom. "You can't stay here. You have a job."

"I was going to talk to you about that. I have a friend, a nurse, who does in-home care. She's expensive, but it's cheaper than being hospitalized and a lot more comfortable."

"She would stay overnight?"

Hutch rubbed two fingers in the center of his forehead. "No. I would be here when I get off work in the evenings."

Simone closed her eyes and told herself not to get upset. That wouldn't be good for the babies. "You know that's impossible," she whispered.

He sat down on the edge of the bed and took her hand, the one with the needle taped into it. "My job is to protect high-risk infants. What happened to you is serious, but there's no reason to take up a hospital bed."

"What about staying away from each other?"

"You're all hooked up. How bad could we be?"

The droll comment startled a laugh from her when she could have sworn she didn't have it in her. "I have friends," she said. "And parents."

"Don't be coy, Simone. I happen to know that Cecelia is newly engaged and pregnant and Naomi flits all over the country. Your parents wouldn't begin to know how to be nurturing. I've met them, remember? I'm your best shot if you want to stay out of the hospital."

Well, damn. The idea of checking into a hospital for something like this gave her the hives. "You could teach me about the IV," she said, giving him a hopeful glance.

"Nice try, kiddo. Even Kate Middleton had to stay in the hospital a few nights when she struggled with this condition. Despite the fact that she had castles and servants at her disposal. Count yourself lucky that Dr. Fetter trusts me."

"She should. You're her boss."

"You know what I mean."

"I'm sorry Candace dragged you into this."

He leaned over and brushed a strand of hair from her cheek. "I'm not. You gave everyone a real scare. I'd just as soon be the one keeping an eye on you."

# Four

Hutch kept his easy smile with effort. Never had he imagined seeing Simone in the state she'd been in when she collapsed. Severe dehydration could even affect the heart. When he'd first seen her, he had actually feared for her pregnancy.

Not only that, he had flashed back to losing Beth. Even though he didn't want a romantic relationship with Simone again, there was no way in hell he was going to let anything happen to her on his watch.

The stubborn woman had to have been in misery. Yet she'd been determined to power through on her own. She looked a little better now, but not much. He estimated that she had already lost six or seven pounds. Her cheekbones stood out sharply, as did her collarbone.

He touched the spot beneath her ear. "They put motion-sickness patches on you in the hospital. I'll change those out as necessary."

"Is it safe?" Her fingers moved restlessly, pleating the sheet.

He frowned. "A hell of a lot safer than collapsing from dehydration. You were in a bad way, Simone."

"I thought I could handle it."

"You hate depending on other people for help, don't you?"

"I don't like to take help from *you*." Tears welled in her beautiful eyes, making them sparkle.

He sat down again, telling himself he had to be the professional in this situation. "I owe you this much, don't you think?"

"For what?" She couldn't quite meet his eyes.

"For taking your advice and going to Africa." He couldn't help the fact that the words sounded accusatory. When it had become clear that he and Simone were crazy about each other, he had offered to linger in Royal for a few years until she got her ad agency off the ground. He'd assumed she would jump at the offer. Instead, she had broken up with him. She'd insisted she didn't want to stand in the way of his doing something so important.

Bitter and disillusioned, he had realized that Simone didn't love him the way he loved her. While he couldn't bear the thought of leaving her behind, she had cut him loose and bid him a cheerful farewell.

"I did the right thing," she said stubbornly. "You had a mission to fulfill."

"And what did *you* have, Simone?" Suddenly, he felt like a beast for harassing her. She looked fragile enough to shatter. "Forget I said that," he muttered. "I'm sorry. It's not important."

Without warning, a noise from the front of the house had his head jerking up. Surely no one would barge in uninvited. But he had forgotten about Naomi. The style guru/TV star was as much a force of nature as Simone, though in a different package.

Naomi burst into the bedroom, wild-eyed. She barely glanced at Hutch. "Good lord, Simone. What the heck is going on? I just saw you a few days ago. What happened?"

Hutch moved toward the door. "I'll leave you two ladies alone."

Simone held up the hand that wasn't tethered to an IV.

"No. Don't go, Hutch. You might as well both hear this at once."

Naomi turned to frown at him. "I didn't know you were back in town. Made yourself at home, didn't you? I fail to see why you're in this house. You hurt her enough the first time around. I'm here now. You can leave."

Simone tried to sit up. "Hush, Naomi. You don't know what you're talking about. Ignore her, Hutch. You know how dramatic she can be."

Naomi's teeth-clenched smile promised retribution. She sat down on the side of the bed, careful not to jostle Simone. "Fine. What don't I know?"

Hutch positioned himself at Simone's elbow. "You don't have to do this now, Simone. You're weak and sick." He worried about her state of mind.

She shot him a look that held a soupçon of her usual fire. "I'm not an invalid." Reaching for Naomi's hand, she twined their fingers. "Don't be mad. I didn't want to steal Cecelia's thunder the other night. I'm pregnant, too. And apparently not handling it nearly as well as our newly engaged friend."

The self-derision on her face hurt Hutch. "It's not a contest," he said.

Naomi gaped. "You're pregnant?" She glared at Hutch.

He held up his hands. "Don't look at me."

"Then who?" Naomi seemed genuinely befuddled.

Maybe Simone had been telling the truth about not having a man in her life. That shouldn't have pleased him so much. Simone tried to sit up again, and again, he shook his head. "Too soon. Stay put."

"Fine. Anyone ever tell you you worry too much?" She transferred her attention to her shell-shocked friend. "I wanted to have a baby, Naomi. And I didn't want to wait. So I used a sperm donor."

"A sperm donor..." Naomi repeated the words slowly.

"Don't look so stunned," Simone pleaded. "It's a perfectly acceptable thing to do."

"But it's not something the Simone *I* know would do."

Hutch saw Simone's bottom lip tremble. "That's enough, Naomi," he said. "This has been a rough day for her."

"Sorry," she groaned. "What's the matter with her?"

"She's suffering from extreme morning sickness."

"I'm right here," Simone snapped. "And I don't know why they call it morning sickness. It lasts the whole damn day."

He and Naomi looked at each other, trying not to laugh. Hutch lifted a shoulder, edging toward the door. "I really do have some phone calls to make." He looked at Naomi. "Shout if you need me."

In the kitchen, he prowled restlessly. Neither of the phone calls was urgent, but he had needed some space to clear his head. He already regretted his impulsive decision to take on Simone's crisis. The odd thing was, *she* was the one who usually jumped without looking. There was a time when he had admired her joie de vivre and her impulsive spirit.

He'd been the older one, the stick-in-the-mud. He'd often wondered if that was why she broke up with him. Perhaps his overly conscientious approach to life had struck her as boring and pedantic.

It didn't matter now. If they hadn't had anything in common five years ago, that was even more true now. Hopefully, her nausea would soon settle down and he could go back to pretending she was just another pregnant woman.

Simone looked at Naomi. "Help me sit up, please."

Naomi frowned. "Hutch said that wasn't a good idea."

"Are you kidding me? Since when are you in the Troy Hutchinson fan club?"

"I didn't say I was a fan, but the man's a brilliant doctor, and you, my girl, look like something out of a zombie movie."

"Gee, thanks."

Despite her protests, Naomi stood up and grabbed extra pillows to put behind Simone. "Satisfied?"

Simone closed her eyes. "I'll be satisfied when I can eat a milk shake and a cheeseburger without puking."

"Can I get you anything?" Naomi hovered.

"No. Thank you." Unexpected tears stung her eyes. "I feel so stupid."

Naomi chuckled. "Well, you should. If anybody was going to knock you up, it should have been that Greek god doctor of yours."

"He's not my doctor," Simone said automatically. "And besides, we're not anything to each other."

"Which explains why I found him in bed with you."

"Don't be dramatic. He wasn't *in* my bed. He was *sitting* on my bed. There's a big difference."

"Not from where I'm standing."

"For God's sake, let it go, Naomi. Hutch and I were over a long time ago. And besides, even if I had the slightest interest in rekindling that flame—which I don't—what man wants to be father to some other guy's triplets?"

Naomi gaped. The look of total consternation on her face might have been funny if Simone hadn't felt so wretched. "Triplets?" she said, her eyes round.

"Um, yeah. I guess I forgot to mention that part. I'm having three babies. At least I hope so."

"What does that mean?"

"It's still early. Too early to know if all the fetuses are viable."

Naomi sprang to her feet and paced. "How can you be so damned calm? This is huge. What were you thinking, Simone? You own and manage a thriving ad agency. You have no husband. Why on earth would you do something so crazy?"

Sadly, Simone couldn't tell the whole truth. Not to Naomi or Cecelia, and certainly not to Hutch. "I wanted a baby," she said stubbornly. "By the time I got in the midst of everything, I began to have my doubts, but I didn't back out. I should have, I suppose."

"Ya think?" Naomi seemed more indignant than flat-out angry. Simone understood, really, she did. If the situations had been reversed, surely she would have expressed doubts about Naomi's decision.

"I screwed up, Naomi. I know that now. But I didn't know how sick I could get. And besides…"

"Besides, what?"

"I want them," Simone whispered. "The babies. All of them. Hutch said it wasn't too late from a medical standpoint to rethink my position, but I could never do that. I started this, and I'll finish it."

Naomi pursed her lips. "I hope it doesn't finish *you*."

Hutch returned in time to hear that last comment. He frowned when he saw Simone upright, but he didn't say anything.

Simone looked at him. "May I have a drink of water, please?"

"It's up to you. It would be good if you can manage it."

With both of them watching, Simone didn't want to make a scene, but she knew she couldn't avoid drinking indefinitely. There was a pitcher and disposable cups on the bedside table. Hutch poured one glass half-full and offered it to her. She took it from him, wincing. "Bottoms up."

With her two observers looking on eagle-eyed, she sipped tentatively. At first, the water tasted amazing. Her lips were partially chapped. The cool liquid felt wonderful in her parched throat. But moments later, her stomach cramped sharply. "Hutch!" She panicked.

He was there immediately, holding a small basin as the water came back up and she retched helplessly. Hutch held her hair. Naomi produced a damp cloth for her forehead. *Oh, God.* If she had ever felt so humiliated and miserable, she couldn't remember it.

Hutch didn't wait for permission. He removed the pillows and helped her lie flat again. "Okay now?" he asked.

She nodded, unable to look at either of them. "I'm sorry to drag you both into this."

Naomi forced a laugh that sounded almost natural. "C'mon, girl. We've been through a lot of rough patches together over the years. Cecelia and I will help. And you're not poor. That's a plus."

Even Hutch thought that was funny, though he quickly turned his chuckle into a cough. It was probably not acceptable bedside manner to make jokes at the patient's expense.

"Hilarious." Suddenly, it struck her. "Well, crud. I'll never fit into a slinky bridesmaid dress."

Even Naomi didn't have the chutzpah to pretend that wasn't true. But she tried to put a spin on it. "Maybe they'll elope. You never know."

Hutch spoke up, for the first time sounding more like a doctor than an interested party. "I'm glad you came by, Naomi. I'll keep you posted if anything changes. Simone needs to rest now."

Simone wanted to argue that he was being high-handed, but it was the truth. "I should tell Cecelia the news in person," she said.

"No worries." Naomi gathered up her car keys and cell phone. "I'll take care of it. She'll understand."

That wasn't the problem. *No one* was going to understand unless Simone's original motive was revealed. Then she was in big trouble. "Thank you, Naomi."

"Anything for a friend." With a wave and a smile, she was gone.

In the silence that followed Naomi's departure, Simone tried to pretend Hutch had left, as well. Unfortunately, he was impossible to ignore.

Simone loved her bedroom, as a rule. She had always found it soothing with its color scheme of pale lemon yellow and navy. It wasn't too girly.

Today, though, with Hutch in residence, the charming space felt claustrophobic. "How long do I have to have the IV?"

"Until you can take nourishment of some kind. I'll show you how to unhook and stop the monitor from beeping when you need to go to the bathroom. You'll have to promise me, though, that you'll hold on to something and sit down the moment you feel dizzy. Otherwise, I'm going in there with you."

"Over my dead body." Her whole body flushed.

He didn't bother arguing that one.

"You look tired," she said impulsively.

Hutch half turned, his striking face in profile. "It's been a tough day," he said.

"Surely not as tough as Sudan."

"Tough in a different way. You need to sleep now, Simone."

"It's only seven o'clock. Have you eaten?"

"I'll get something later."

"Go now," she urged. "I swear I won't move until you get back."

He shook his head, his expression wry. "I'm not sure I trust you. For the next seventy-two hours, you're my responsibility."

"What am I supposed to do if I can't eat or drink or get out of bed?"

"How about a movie?"

"Will you watch it with me?"

His dark gaze made her shiver, despite her weakened

state. He closed his eyes, took a deep breath and dropped his chin to his chest. After a moment, he lifted his shoulders and let them fall, then looked at her with a carefully blank expression. "If that's what you want. I'll go make myself a sandwich. Here's the remote. You pick something out and I'll be back shortly."

She channel surfed halfheartedly, feeling almost normal for the moment. The pregnancy didn't seem entirely real. Was that odd? Shouldn't she feel a rush of maternal devotion? She did have a connection already. She knew life was growing in her womb even now. But those little blips on the screen didn't have faces and personalities. What if they grew up to be like her?

Eventually, she found a Tom Hanks romantic comedy from the '80s in the on-demand section. That would do the trick. She and Hutch could make fun of the sappy dialogue. At least that's what she told herself. Never in a million years would she let him know how much she loved that story.

When he came back from the kitchen, he had his hands full. He stopped in the doorway as if expecting to find her flouting his orders. She smiled innocently. "I've been good as gold."

"That'll be the day."

Her bed was a king, so when Hutch parked himself on the opposite side, there was an entire stretch of mattress protecting her virtue. Not that it mattered. Who was she kidding? She'd seen herself in the mirror.

Hutch got comfortable and began to wolf down his meal. Suddenly he looked at her in dismay. "Will the smell bother you? I can eat in the kitchen."

"No. I'm fine. If you were eating Thai food, it might be different. That ham sandwich is nausea neutral."

She started the movie, trying not to notice the way Hutch seemed entirely comfortable in her bed. When they had been a couple, she had lived in an upscale apartment downtown, as had Hutch. They'd split their time between locations, some nights in his bed, some nights in hers.

The sex had been incredible, but even more than that was the feeling of rightness... She didn't know how else to explain it. In the beginning, they had talked for hours. She learned that Hutch decided to go into medicine after an older cousin had a difficult pregnancy when he was in high school. The mother and baby both died. Thus, maternal-fetal medicine became his focus when it was time to specialize.

Simone had been out of college barely a year when she met Hutch. She'd worked for a high-end clothing store as a buyer. Marketing was her passion, though, and she'd spent many hours telling Hutch about her intent to open an advertising agency of her own.

Aside from that, they had, of course, talked about their families. Simone was an only child. Hutch had a younger brother who was studying abroad and hoped to go into the diplomatic corps.

Hutch's parents were warm and nurturing, whereas Simone's were strict and cold. Though it was a sad cliché, her father had wanted a boy. But complications during her mother's pregnancy meant no more children after Simone. No matter how hard Simone tried, she never seemed to measure up to a list of invisible standards.

Perhaps that was why she reveled in Hutch's attention. Not that she saw him as a father figure. Far from it. The age difference was too narrow for that. But when she spoke, he took her seriously. It was heady stuff.

In her peripheral vision, she could see that Hutch's attention was focused on the television. Was he really engrossed in the movie? She doubted it. More likely, he was thinking about important doctor stuff.

Unlike Simone's endeavors, Hutch's work actually involved life-and-death situations. She teased him about being a saint, but she had never met another man who impressed her so deeply with his work ethic and his compassion.

If he had stayed, they might have ended up married, and Hutch's involvement with DWB might never have materialized. In Simone's twenty-eight years, many people in her life had characterized her as self-centered. Sadly, that had probably been true at one time. But at least she had the comfort of knowing that in this instance she had done the right thing.

She had loved Hutch madly, deeply, desperately...but she had let him go.

When the memories stung too sharply, she hit the mute button on the remote and silenced the TV. "I've seen this one a dozen times," she said. "What I'd really like is for you to tell me about Bethany. And about Sudan."

# Five

Hutch froze. He'd been a million miles away. Simone's question caused him to flinch inwardly. Unfortunately, he couldn't think of an excuse to deflect it quickly enough.

"Why?" he asked bluntly.

Simone turned on her side and tucked her hands beneath her cheek. She was drowsy. He could hear it in her voice and see it in her eyes. "You were gone for a long time. Two tours of service. Why didn't you come home after the first one?"

It was a logical question. That had been the assumption all along. Still, when the time came, the thought of returning to Royal and confronting Simone had seemed far more dangerous than anything he would face abroad. So he had stayed.

A month later, he'd met Bethany.

Sensing that Simone wouldn't be dissuaded, he steeled himself for the pain and remorse that choked him when he allowed himself to remember. "I was introduced to Bethany just as I signed up for a second rotation. All the medical staff I had worked with were headed home. Bethany was one of the newbies."

"A nurse?"

"No. A doctor. A pediatrician. Bethany was the daughter of medical missionaries in Central America. She had never lived in the United States full-time until she went to college and med school. She adored children. Wanted five or six of her own one day. In the meantime, her goal was to save as many as she could in Sudan, specifically West Darfur, the state where we were stationed."

"Admirable."

"You would have liked her, I think. She was only five foot one, but somehow you never noticed that about her, because her personality was so compelling. She was passionate about her work and truly believed she was fulfilling her destiny."

"You said you fell in love," Simone prompted him with an expression that was difficult to read.

He stretched his arms over his head, feeling the fatigue of a long day. The last thing he wanted to do was rehash his past with Simone. Especially when it came to talking about another woman. But Simone was relentless when she wanted something.

"I fell in love," he said flatly. "It was slow. At first we were only friends. But I was lonely. I had been in Sudan for a long time."

"And Bethany?"

"I don't know what she saw in me," he said. "It certainly wasn't a romantic situation. Sometimes I think we were just two people doing the best we could."

Simone shifted restlessly. "You don't have to tell me any more, Hutch. She sounds like a lovely person. I'm sorry you lost her. Another day I'd like to hear about your work, but not tonight. I'm tired. I think I can sleep now."

He nodded. "I'll bunk on the sofa. I've programmed my cell number in your phone. Just buzz me when you need to get up."

"I have four perfectly lovely guest rooms, Hutch. You're way too big for the sofa."

He grimaced. "After the past five-plus years, I can sleep pretty much anywhere, trust me."

"But why would you?" Simone frowned.

It seemed cruel to be blunt when she was so sick, but it was better for him to draw the line in the sand. Better, and necessary. "You said it yourself, Simone—you know the way gossip spreads in Royal. It's important to me not to create the impression that I've moved in with you, even for the short-term."

"I see."

When her bottom lip trembled, he felt like a jerk and a bully. She looked small and defenseless in the big bed, though he knew that was only an illusion.

He sighed. "I don't want to hurt you." Hell, he didn't want to hurt himself.

She smiled, though her eyes glistened with tears. "I can handle honesty, Dr. Hutchinson. Let me get my stomach under control, and after that I doubt our paths will cross very often."

It didn't take a medical degree to know when a woman was hurt and fighting back. Rolling to his feet, he straightened the covers on his side of the bed. There was probably some kind of comment that would smooth this situation, but he hadn't a clue what it was.

"Do you want to try some water again?" he asked.

"Absolutely not." She shuddered.

"You'll have to eventually."

"Thanks, Dr. Obvious."

"I forgot what a smart mouth you have." His neck heated.

"And I forgot what a pompous, holier-than-thou hypocrite you are."

"Hypocrite? Seriously? How so?" His temper had a long, slow fuse. But Simone knew how to pour gasoline on any argument.

"You may be done with love and romance for now because Bethany broke your heart. I'll leave you to your crusty bachelorhood, believe me. But I wasn't the only one in the middle of that kiss the other day. I know when a man wants me."

"Damn it, Simone."

"Are you denying it?"

He'd taken an oath to heal and to protect. At the moment, he wanted to strangle his erstwhile patient. "Good night, brat. I'll be in to check on you several times, but use the phone if you need to. I'm close by."

She smirked at him. "Saint Hutch."

He didn't bother turning on lights in the house. During his rural rotations there had been many nights when he and his team only had enough fuel for two hours of lantern light. After that, he'd learned to maneuver in the dark under any circumstances.

He found a new toothbrush in one of the guest bathrooms. Since he always kept a change of clothes in the trunk of his car, he was able to put on a clean shirt and pants after a quick shower.

In the living room, he surveyed the sofa. Actually, it wasn't as small as Simone had intimated. If he bent his knees or propped his feet on the arm, he'd be fine. The couch was leather and cool to the touch. He settled down and pulled an afghan over his lower body.

Fatigue could be measured in degrees. There had been times in Sudan when he worked sixteen hours straight. In the blistering heat. On those nights, he had stumbled to bed and collapsed, asleep in seconds.

Now he was definitely tired. But it was different. Though his body wanted rest, his brain spun like a hamster wheel. Going nowhere.

Simone made him ache—not only physically, though that was certainly true, but emotionally, as well. If he could go back and undo the past, he would never have asked her to dance. That one misstep had led them down a narrow, treacherous road that petered out into nothing.

Time was supposed to heal all wounds. By rights, he should be able to look at his past and acknowledge that things had worked out for the best. But the opposite was true. He felt empty. Even in Africa, when he knew he was saving lives and improving the quality of other lives, he'd learned a painful truth. His being there had been a lie, in part.

Unlike Bethany, who had been so very confident and sure of herself and her life's goals, Hutch had gone to Sudan a broken man. He had utilized his training. He had contributed to the greater good. Still, it hadn't been enough.

He'd been adrift…lost. Losing Simone had made him doubt himself and his place in the world. Eventually, falling in love with Bethany had helped heal the rough places and ease his loneliness. But even before she died, he'd wondered fleetingly if he was using her as a stand-in for the woman he really wanted.

Closing his eyes, he practiced the relaxation techniques he'd used in med school. One muscle group at a time. He dozed on and off, never fully comatose. Many doctors were light sleepers, ready to spring into action when the situation demanded. Which reminded him of the real reason he was here.

He had set the alarm on his phone for three-hour intervals. At one o'clock, he walked quietly down the hall and peeked into the patient's room. If she was resting well, he didn't want to bother her. "Simone?" He whispered her name. She wouldn't hear him unless she was awake.

"Come on in." Her voice was soft, but alert.

"Why aren't you sleeping?"

"I did sleep. For a little while."

"And now?"

"I'm hungry."

"But still nauseated?"

"Oh, yeah…"

He hesitated. "Simone…"

"What?"

"I've seen acupressure really help in these situations. One of the doctors I worked with in West Darfur was Chinese. He taught me the technique, and I actually used it on half a dozen women in my care."

"Is there a downside?"

"I'd have to hold your hand for three minutes. Each one."

A long silence ensued.

Finally, Simone spoke. "Sounds pretty risqué."

He choked out a laugh and sat on the end of the bed. Even at her lowest points, Simone was still able to manufacture humor. That ability boded well for a difficult pregnancy.

"Well," he said, "what do you think?"

"I'd dance with the devil if I thought it would make me feel better."

"Gee, thanks," he said drily. "Your enthusiasm is duly noted."

He stood up and moved closer. "We can do this with you sitting up or lying down, whichever feels the most comfortable." The bizarre situation somehow seemed more acceptable, because it was the middle of the night.

"I'll stay put," she said. "Don't want to make any sudden moves that might tip the balance."

It made more sense to sit on the bed, but instead he grabbed the small chair from the vanity and positioned it at Simone's elbow. He wanted the illusion of distance. For the same reason, he didn't turn on the lamp. The faint illumination from the night-light in the bathroom was all he needed.

Most of this procedure was by touch, anyway. He had

learned where to apply pressure. It wasn't an exact science, but he had practiced enough to feel comfortable doing it.

Now if he could be equally at ease with his beautiful guinea pig, he might come out of this next half hour unscathed. "Let's do the easiest one first," he said. Her left hand rested at the edge of the mattress. He picked up her arm, noting that her fingers were cold.

"Will it hurt?" she asked.

He had a hunch that the nervous question was more about him touching her than any real fear of acupressure. "It shouldn't. But if I press too hard, tell me."

Over the years, he had learned that speaking to a patient in steady, reassuring tones while in the midst of a difficult or painful procedure was helpful. In Simone's case, the distraction might prove useful for *both* of them.

Turning her hand palm up, he pressed his thumb to her soft skin. "The spot for this is P6," he said. "About three fingers above the crease of your wrist and in between two tendons." He applied pressure. "Okay so far?"

She nodded.

Three minutes was a hell of a long time when a man held a woman in a dark bedroom and knew every one of the reasons he couldn't or wouldn't let himself be drawn in again. He counted off the seconds in his head, trying to ignore the fact that she trembled.

After an eternity, he cleared his throat. "Other hand," he said.

He hoped this was going to help, because it was tearing him apart. Her hair fanned out across the pillow. The thin, silky nightgown she wore was cut low in the front. Though at first she clutched the sheet in a death grip, when she shifted slightly and gave him her right arm, he could see the shadow of her cleavage and the outline of her breasts.

God help him. He kept the pressure firm, resisting the urge to stroke upward to the crease of her elbow. Kissing her there had been a game he played in the past, a teasing caress she always swore tickled. But it also made her sigh and melt into his embrace.

"Hasn't it been long enough?"

Simone's timid question snapped him out of his reverie. He'd lost count of the seconds. "I think so," he muttered. He released her and sat back. "How do you feel?"

She rubbed her wrists together and flexed her fingers. "Better. I think. Is this honestly a valid treatment?"

"Been around for thousands of years."

"I hesitate to tempt fate, but I think I could eat something."

"Good. That's usually the case. The effects aren't permanent, of course, but you can take advantage in the interim. What can I get for you?"

"Let's start small. Dry toast with a tiny bit of apple jelly? Do you mind?"

"Of course not."

In the kitchen, he rested his forehead against the cool stainless steel of the refrigerator door. This wasn't going to work. He'd find someone else to help out, but it couldn't be him.

Desire was a steady ache in his gut. And it wasn't even entirely about sex. He wanted to crawl into that bed and hold her. Too many nights in the last few years he had summoned Simone's image to get through the hot, lonely hours. He'd missed home. He had missed his friends and colleagues. He had even missed the unpredictable Texas weather.

Now he had returned home, and almost everything was back to normal. Almost, but not quite.

On autopilot, he retrieved the bread and prepared a single piece of toast. Simone had to start slow. Her stomach had suffered significant trauma in the past few days.

In the end, he was gone maybe twenty minutes. When

he returned, she was sitting up. He frowned. "You should have let me help you."

Simone's smile was sunny. "I think I can eat," she said. "You're a miracle worker, Dr. Hutchinson."

"Don't get too excited," he cautioned. "The nausea will likely come back."

"I can handle that," she said. "At least if I can have some normalcy in between."

He offered her the small plate. "One bite at a time. We're in no rush."

She nodded. Carefully, she took one dainty bite. Clearly, she was so excited about eating that she had forgotten her state of dress. He tried not to stare. Instead, he prowled her bedroom, studying the things with which she had surrounded herself.

Between two large windows, a tall set of antique barrister bookshelves held a collection of travel books, popular novels and childhood favorites. In another corner, an overstuffed armchair and matching ottoman provided a cozy reading spot. Books were only one of many passions he and Simone had shared.

He remembered a summer picnic in the country long ago when they had laughed and enjoyed playful sex and finally rested in the shade of a giant oak. While he had drowsed with his head in Simone's lap, she had read aloud to him from a book of poetry. That might have been the moment he knew he was in love with her. She was so much more than a beautiful woman or a wealthy debutante or a Texas Cattleman's Club darling.

Simone Parker was a free spirit, a lover of life. She was warm and intelligent and effortlessly charming. Other men had looked at him with envious eyes when he and Simone were out together in public. She was the kind of woman some guys considered a trophy girlfriend.

To Hutch, she had simply been his life. When they met,

he'd been twenty-eight. Plenty old enough to have sown his proverbial wild oats. About the time he'd been rethinking his plans to head off to Africa, Simone had cut him loose. She'd insisted that he was a gifted doctor and that she wouldn't stand in his way.

"Hutch!"

Pushing the painful thoughts away, he spun around, alarmed. "What is it?"

Simone beamed. "I ate it. And I think it's going to stay down. Will you pour me some water?"

He did so immediately and handed her the glass. "Tiny sips," he cautioned.

She scrunched up her face as she drank the water one tablespoon at a time. "That's enough," she said finally.

"How do you feel?"

"Tired. Weird. But not pregnant. Is that bad?" She bit her bottom lip, a telltale sign she was agitated.

He took the glass and set it back on the table. "Of course not. It will be a long time before you start to show, especially because you've lost weight already. As far as actually feeling the babies kick, I'd guess that will be weeks from now. So it's no surprise you don't feel pregnant. That's why Mother Nature gives you three trimesters to get used to the idea."

"I suppose…"

"Can you go back to sleep now?"

She slid back down in the bed and straightened the covers. "I think so."

"And the nausea?"

"Hardly any right now. Thank you, Hutch."

He shrugged. "I'm glad the acupressure worked. Sometimes modern medicine looks for answers when they're right at hand."

"Right at hand." She giggled. "Dr. Hutch made a funny. Get it? You held my hands?"

"If I didn't know better, I'd think you'd been drinking," he said ruefully.

"I would never do anything so foolish. I'm just giddy with relief that you made the nausea go away, even for an hour. Are there other people in Royal who might know how to do what you did?"

The intent behind her question was obvious. Neither of them thought Hutch should be the one to help her through the terrible sickness produced by her pregnancy. Nevertheless, he spoke the truth. "I doubt it, Simone. Maybe in one of the big cities. But Royal is not exactly a hotbed of ancient Asian medical practice."

"I see."

It was impossible to miss the layers of frustration and unease she gave off. "We'll figure something out," he promised. "One day at a time."

She moved restlessly. "I shouldn't have let you kiss me the other day. That was wrong of me. I'm sorry."

"Forget about it. I could have stopped."

"Why didn't you?" she asked softly.

It was a very good question. One he had asked himself a dozen times since. He was a grown-ass man. He knew better than to show weakness to Simone.

"I guess part of me wanted to remember," he muttered. "But now all I want to do is forget."

# Six

When Simone awoke next, she realized she had slept for six hours straight. Her head was clear, and although she did indeed feel sick again, it wasn't at the intense level she had experienced recently.

As she stretched and tried to convince herself she could get up and go to the bathroom without incident, a woman in navy scrubs peeked her head around the door. "Ms. Parker? Good, you're awake. I'm Barb Kellum. Dr. Hutchinson called me and said you needed some help."

"That would be great," Simone said. "I'd love to get a shower."

The nurse smiled. "First things first, young lady. Let's eat a bit of breakfast and go from there. I brought over some of my homemade chicken broth. Warmed it in the microwave. How does that sound?"

The nurse with the salt-and-pepper hair was midfiftyish, tall and sturdily built. Her eyes were kind, but her tone of voice was more drill sergeant than nanny.

Simone smiled hesitantly. "I'll give it a try. But I make no promises."

While Simone sat up in bed, the nurse bustled about, straightening the covers and carefully placing a white wooden tray over Simone's lap. The serving piece must have come with Barb as well, because Simone had never seen it. Although the china, glass and silverware were arranged artistically, Simone's stomach rebelled at the aroma of the chicken broth.

Barbara picked up the bowl and held it under Simone's nose. "Don't let your brain overrule your stomach. You're hungry, even if you don't know it. Breathe in and tell yourself you're about to have a treat."

Amazingly, it worked. Mostly. Inhaling the scent of the thin soup sent a sharp hunger pang through Simone's stomach. She picked up the spoon and scooped up the first bite. "What if this doesn't work?"

Barbara pointed at the floor beside the bed. "Basin and plastic ready. Nothing to worry about."

It took half an hour, but Simone finished every spoonful. Afterward, she scooted down onto the mattress and lay there frozen, afraid to move. "How long before you think it's safe to get up?"

The nurse shook her head. "Sorry, love, but you can't play that game. It might help the nausea, but your muscles will start to atrophy if we don't keep you on your feet. Exercise can actually help nausea."

The following few hours were a lesson in patience. Barb unhooked the IV and hovered as Simone visited the bathroom. After that, the two of them managed a modified shower for Simone. She threw up twice in the process, but it wasn't as violent as the episodes earlier in the week.

Once she was clean and dry, she felt as weak as a baby.

Barb beamed at her. "I'd say we did well, Ms. Parker."

"Please call me Simone."

"And I answer to Barb. Now sit in that chair for half a shake while I remake the bed. Nothing feels better after a shower than clean sheets."

By the time Simone was tucked back into bed and the IV

was reattached, she felt embarrassingly exhausted. "How long do I have to be hooked up?"

Barbara checked her blood pressure and pulse before answering. "That all depends on how much you can eat on your own. I'll draw blood after lunch and send it off to the lab. Then again before dinner. Tomorrow, Dr. Hutchinson will read the results and assess how you're doing."

The nurse was right about clean sheets. Simone's eyes were heavy. "Is it okay if I nap?"

"Definitely. Later, we'll try a walk around the house. Don't worry, Ms. Parker. You'll survive this, I promise."

Simone dozed on and off during the next hour, watching the patterns of light and shadow on the ceiling. All her problems hovered just offstage, but for now, she was content to drift. She vaguely remembered Hutch checking on her a couple of times last night after the acupressure incident, but they hadn't spoken since. Beneath the sheet, she laced her fingers over her abdomen. Her stomach was flat and smooth, the muscles taut and firm. Though she had friends and acquaintances who had already become mothers, she had never thought much about the process. At least not until her grandfather died.

Suddenly, she realized she hadn't looked at her email in over forty-eight hours. Stealthily, not wanting to incur Barb's wrath, she reached into the bottom drawer of the bedside table and retrieved her laptop. Leaning on one elbow, she opened it up and turned it on. Fortunately, her battery charge was at 50 percent. She could do a few things quickly without asking for help.

Email was not a problem. She deleted the junk and replied to a couple of queries that needed an immediate answer. Then, with shaky fingers, she logged on to Facebook and checked the message box. A tiny numeral one appeared on the icon. Damn. Most of her friends texted her. The only recent Facebook message she had received was one from the mysterious Maverick. Maverick—the anonymous, eerie, dark presence who had threatened many of the citizens of Royal, one after another.

Simone's first message had appeared two weeks ago. Since nothing bad had happened in the interim, she'd hoped the blackmailer had moved on to someone else. Apparently not.

The message was brief and vindictive.

Simone Parker, you're a money-grubbing bitch. Enjoy life now, because soon everyone in town will know what you have done and why. Maverick.

She shut the computer quickly and tucked it under a pillow. This time, the nausea roiling in her belly had more to do with fear and disgust than it did with pregnancy. All she could think about was the look on Hutch's face if he ever learned the truth.

Unfortunately, Barb returned about that time and frowned. "You're flushed. What's wrong?"

Simone didn't bother answering. She was afraid she would cry. The thought that someone in Royal hated her enough to blackmail her was distressing. She wasn't a saint—far from it. But she tried to learn from her mistakes.

The nurse took her pulse and frowned. "You need to calm down, young lady. Stress isn't good for the babies. What brought this on?"

Simone scrambled for a convincing lie. "I have so much to do at work. Each day I get farther behind. I need to make plans…to decide how I'll manage three babies. It's a lot, you know."

Barb nodded sympathetically. "I understand, I do. But you can't climb a mountain in bare feet. Baby steps, remember. First we have to get you stabilized and healthy. Then you'll have plenty of time to plan for the future."

"Easy for you to say," Simone muttered in a whisper. Did no one understand what a colossal mess she had made of her life? It wasn't as if she could wave a magic wand and get a do-over.

Lunch was not as successful as breakfast. Two bites of lemon gelatin came right back up. But Simone waited an hour and tried again with better results. Afterward, Barb brought in her tray of torture implements. Having blood drawn was no fun, but Simone knew she had to get used to it.

Next was another nap, and after that, Barb came in to say it was time for a walk around the house. Simone leaned on the older woman unashamedly as they made a circuit from room to room. Clearly, this was necessary, because already her muscles were quivering.

Finally, she was allowed to collapse into bed again. Meanwhile, Barb changed out the IV bag, straightened the room and drew more blood. As she packed up the vials, she eyed Simone with an assessing gaze. "Will you be okay for the next few hours? I hate to leave you alone, but I promised a friend I'd sit with her mother at the nursing home this evening."

"I'll be fine," Simone said. "Dr. Hutchinson showed me how to unhook things so I can go the bathroom, and I'm feeling much stronger. Don't worry about me."

"There's more gelatin and broth in the fridge. And I brought you a fresh box of saltines this morning."

"You've been wonderful. Will you be here tomorrow?"

Barb nodded. "Dr. Hutchinson said at least three days."

"Okay then. I'll see you in the morning."

"Should I bring the meal before I go?"

"It's still early. I'd rather wait."

"All right then." She gave a little wave. "I'll let myself out."

With the nurse gone and Hutch still presumably at the

hospital, the house was desperately quiet. As the sunlight faded, Simone felt the weight of her situation drag her down. Whatever lay ahead, she would take care of these innocent babies. If she decided she was incapable of functioning as a single mother, she could give them up for adoption when they were born. There were likely dozens of couples in Royal with fertility issues who would be overjoyed at the chance to give three little babies a home.

The thought left Simone feeling hollow. Not only had she rushed into this situation with less than pure motives, she had given little or no thought to the future. Now that she was pregnant, the situation was painfully real.

At six thirty, she actually felt hungry...in a normal way. Hutch had said he'd be back, but who knew what kind of emergencies might have come up.

Mindful of her promises to Barb, she sat on the side of the bed for a full three minutes before attempting to get up. Unhooking the IV was not hard once she'd learned what to do. Walking slowly, she made her way to the kitchen and opened the refrigerator. After eating a few bites of the gelatin, she drank half a glass of ginger ale. The calories she had consumed today were helping. She felt steadier and stronger already.

Darkness closed in, and with it, her uneasiness returned. Hutch had given her his phone number. Should she simply text him and tell him not to come?

When she saw headlights flash as a car turned into her driveway, she scurried back to the bedroom, reattached the IV and settled into bed. She didn't want Hutch to think she was being reckless. It was important to her that he knew she was taking this pregnancy seriously.

When he finally appeared at her door, he looked tired, but wonderful.

"Hey there," he said, his lips curving in a half smile. "Barb said you had a pretty good day."

Simone nodded. "I'd give it a seven and a half. Thank you for suggesting her. She's very kind and competent."

"How's your stomach?" He sat on the foot of the bed and ran his hands over his face. He had obviously showered before leaving the hospital, because he smelled like the outdoors, all fresh and masculine.

She sat up and scooped her hair away from her face. Barb had taken the time to blow-dry it after Simone's shower. Now it fell straight and silky around her shoulders. "We're on speaking terms again. Barely."

"Good."

"Have *you* eaten?"

"I grabbed a burger in the cafeteria."

"That's not entirely healthy. Physician, heal thyself."

"You let me worry about me. What did you have for dinner?"

"Some gelatin. I was contemplating Barb's homemade chicken broth, but I'm feeling pretty normal at the moment, and I'd hate to tempt fate."

"You look better."

His steady regard made her blush. "Thank you."

"How 'bout I warm the broth and bring it to you?"

"Okay," she said reluctantly. "If you insist."

Hutch grinned. "I do."

While he was gone, she grabbed a small mirror out of her purse and examined her reflection. Other than having cheekbones that were too sharp, she didn't look half bad. Pinching her cheeks added color to her face.

Hutch must have found the bed tray in the kitchen. When he returned with her modest meal, he had poured a serving of broth into a crockery bowl and added a glass of ice water, along with some soda crackers.

Simone scooted up in bed. "Barb is a good cook."

"Her specialty is invalid food."

She wrinkled her nose. "That's a terrible way to describe it."

"Sorry."

The stilted conversation was awkward, to say the least. "You don't have to watch me eat, Hutch. And you don't need to spend the night. I'm much better. I appreciate all you've done."

He shrugged, his expression impassive. "One more night won't hurt. I'll have the results of your blood work in the morning. If everything looks sound, you can follow up next week with Dr. Fetter at a regular appointment."

"And you'll ride off into the sunset to rescue another damsel in distress."

His eyes narrowed. His jaw tightened. "Are you pissed that I went to Africa? Is that it, Simone? If you'll recall, I offered to stay here until you got your agency off the ground. But you were pretty emphatic that I should go. So don't blame me for the mess you've made of your life."

She swallowed hard. Already, her stomach cramped with nerves and nausea, and she hadn't even taken a bite yet. The old Hutch would never have been so blunt. There was a time he'd humored her every whim and thought her biting sarcasm was funny.

Not so much anymore.

She lifted her chin, striving for dignity. "You're right. I apologize. Now if you don't mind, I think I'll have a better chance of getting this to go down successfully if I don't have an audience. And to be clear, I don't blame you for anything. You're an easy target, and I'm at the end of my rope. But don't worry, Hutch. I'll be just fine."

Hutch cursed softly, striding rapidly out of the room. How was it possible for one small woman to make him feel like a complete and utter failure? No one in his entire adult life had caused him as many sleepless nights as Simone Parker. Not even Bethany.

He prowled the house, pacing from room to room, feeling his bitterness and frustration grow. Though he finally managed to sleep for a few hours, at 3:00 a.m. he was up again. In the darkest moments of the night, he at last admitted to himself why he was so angry.

In some foolish, illogical corner of his brain, he had entertained the hope that he and Simone might mend fences. Despite his utter despair at losing Bethany, seeing Simone that first day in the exam room at the hospital had given him hope.

But the feeling was a lie. He was a bloody idiot. He and Simone were no more compatible than they had ever been. She had a chip on her shoulder so big it was a wonder it didn't crush her. Surely she didn't expect him to sit at her feet like a puppy dog begging for scraps. Those babies she carried weren't his. She didn't want to be married. Not to him, not to anyone. With this unconventional pregnancy, she was thumbing her nose at the world.

He might not understand why, but he knew it was true.

At last, sheer exhaustion trumped his fury. He went to Simone's bedroom to check the IV, more for something to do than any real expectation that the bag was empty. Barb had changed it late that afternoon.

What he heard as he stood in the hallway put a knot in his chest.

Simone was crying...not just crying, but sobbing. Plucky, confident, decisive Simone sounded as if her heart was completely broken.

He backed away quietly, not wanting to embarrass her. Then he stopped. Not even the most coldhearted of bastards could leave her in that condition.

Though he suffered misgivings on a massive scale, he

padded over to the bed in his sock feet and crouched beside her. She lay on her back with one arm flung over her eyes.

"Simone," he whispered, not wanting to alarm her. "Stop crying, honey. It only makes things worse."

Without waiting for permission, he unhooked the IV, scooped her up and sat down with her in his lap. Leaning against the headboard, he stroked her hair. "Talk to me, little mama. Tell me what's going on in that head of yours."

Though she huffed and protested and struggled briefly, he felt the moment she went limp in his embrace. She burrowed into his chest like a frightened child. Tears wet his shirt. The sobs were less ferocious, but the crying didn't stop.

It worried him. Simone was not one to give up on any challenge. He'd never seen her like this. Gently, he held her close, telling himself the position was for her benefit. He didn't even flinch at the lie. That's how easy it was for his libido to seize the wheel.

Minutes ticked away on the clock. Simone was a welcome weight against his body. Though she was too thin, and arguably not at her best, to him, she was as stunningly beautiful as she had ever been. Imagining her round belly in the advanced stages of pregnancy flooded him with an entirely inappropriate rush of arousal.

At one time, he had envisioned that scenario with pride and anticipation. Now everything was wrong. And he felt powerless to make it right.

# Seven

"Enough, Simone," he said firmly. "That's enough."

Gradually, she calmed. Except for the occasional tiny, hiccupping sob, the storm was over.

He played with her hair, plaiting it between his fingers. He didn't touch her breasts. He wanted to... God knows he wanted to. But that would be too much temptation. He wasn't prepared to throw all caution to the wind.

Pregnancy was the most natural thing in the world, and yet complicated. From teenagers who didn't mean to get pregnant to full-grown women who craved a child and couldn't conceive, the process was messy and fraught with pitfalls. He couldn't imagine the toll this was taking on Simone emotionally.

He smoothed his palm over her back. "Better now?" he asked.

She nodded, sitting up and sniffling. Her damp eyes were sapphires framed in coal-black lashes. "Hutch."

His name was a caress on her lips, a sweet, irresistible invitation. God help him. He slid his hands beneath her hair and steadied her head, tipping her mouth up for his kiss. He wanted her to stop him. He needed her to be alarmed and outraged. Instead, she leaned into him.

Their lips clung, mated. She tasted like toothpaste.

"Sweet Simone," he muttered, easing her onto her back. He moved half on top of her, his leg wedged between her thighs. She sighed and welcomed him, though her thin nightgown hampered her movements.

He kissed her forehead, her eyelids, her slender throat. Simone arched against him, her breathing ragged. When he made his way down to the place where the neckline of her gown covered her breasts, Simone stiffened for the first time.

Instinctively, he drew back. He was half out of his mind, but not so far gone he didn't know when a woman said no. Verbal or body language, it didn't matter.

She frowned. "Why did you stop?"

"I felt you tense up."

"Not because of you."

"Then why?"

"I don't want to hurt the babies."

He smiled, though it took an effort. "Nothing a man and a woman do in this situation is cause for alarm. I swear to you."

She kept one hand on his shoulder, the other free to comb through his hair. The feel of her fingertips on his scalp made him shiver. "Hutch?"

"Yes?"

"I guess it's obvious we both need this. But it won't mean anything beyond tonight. It can't."

"Is that an ultimatum?" Why couldn't the damn woman live in the moment? That was a lesson he had learned in Sudan when life was so very fragile and joy came only in fleeting snatches.

She rubbed her thumb across his cheekbone. "No ultimatum." She sighed.

"Do you want me?"

"So much it hurts. Is that normal?"

"Many pregnant women find themselves with increased libido."

Simone laughed at him. "You're funny when you get all serious and medical."

"Most people respect my position and my expertise."

"Most people haven't seen you naked."

His lips twisted in a wry grin. He would never develop too much of an inflated ego with Simone around. "Are you feeling ill? At all?"

She wrapped one slender, toned thigh around his leg. "I'm good to go."

Hutch knew he was making a mistake. Simone must have known it, too. But the heat and yearning between them was too powerful to ignore. "I've been tested recently," he said. "I'm clean."

"I'm in the clear also. And it's not like you're going to knock me up." The line should have been funny, but neither of them laughed.

Very deliberately—to give them both a chance to change their minds—he stood and stripped off his clothes. Simone tracked his every move. Afterward, he helped her sit up, and they both managed to raise her gown over her head. She wasn't wearing any underwear, so now she was completely nude.

He reclined beside her and put a tentative hand on her belly. "Odd, isn't it…that you can't really feel anything when so much is going on?"

She leaned against him, her hand on top of his. "I'm scared, Hutch."

"Of which part?" He kissed her softly, almost lightheaded because every bit of blood had rushed south to his sex.

"All of it. Labor. Delivery. Bringing home three newborns. Trying to breastfeed."

"Women have been doing this since the dawn of time.

You're smart and organized. I have no doubt you'll conquer motherhood like you do every other hurdle in your life."

"Make love to me, Hutch."

Her eyes were damp. She seemed more sad than amorous. But he couldn't tell her no. Not anymore.

Carefully, he spread her legs and tested her readiness with two fingers. Her sex was moist and swollen. "Simone," he groaned. He slid into her with one steady push. The sensation was indescribable. Pausing to let her adjust to his size, he rested his forehead on her shoulder. Her fingernails scored his back.

"More," she demanded. "More, Hutch."

He lost his mind. There was no other way to describe it. His fantasies from endless dark, hot, uncomfortable nights in West Darfur burst into life with a euphoric explosion that took him to the brink of a powerful orgasm in seconds. He could tell Simone wasn't far behind.

Deliberately, he reached between their sweat-slickened bodies and found the little spot that made her tumble over the edge. They clung to each other like survivors in the aftermath of a killer wave.

The room was dark and silent. At last, he pushed up onto one elbow and cupped her cheek with his hand. "Again?" he asked hoarsely.

"Yes," she whispered. "Again…"

Simone spent the waning hours of the night wrapped in Hutch's arms. He spooned her, her back pressed to his chest. Though she felt his sex flex against her bottom, stiff and ready, they didn't make love again.

It was the most restful sleep she'd experienced in the last two weeks. If she tried really hard, she could pretend the past five years never happened.

Toward morning, the nausea returned. Hutch held her hair and washed her face after she retched helplessly. He helped put her nightgown back on and sat with her, coaxing her bite by bite until she finished several crackers.

Then Barb arrived and Hutch transformed into Dr. Hutchinson. "I'll call with the lab results," he said, his expression distant and remote.

"Thank you," Simone said, her heart shredding in agony.

Barb bustled about, oblivious to the tension in the room.

Hutch nodded. "You ladies have a good day. I need to get to the hospital."

When Simone didn't reply, he spun on his heel and walked out.

After that, the day was an endurance test. Eat. Get sick. Eat again. But the episodes were coming further apart, and she was actually managing to keep food down long enough to reap the benefits.

When Hutch called the landline with Simone's test results, Barb answered and jotted down some numbers. She hung up the phone and gave Simone a thumbs-up. "Your electrolytes and other blood levels are right where they need to be, young lady. Let's take that needle out of your hand and allow you to get back to normal."

Barb stayed for the remainder of the day, but it was clear that Simone was learning to manage the nausea on her own. The efficient nurse said her goodbyes just before five o'clock, about the time Cecelia showed up with a huge pan of lasagna and a crusty loaf of French bread.

Cecelia blanched when Simone got teary-eyed. "What did I do?" she asked urgently. "Are you in pain?"

Simone hugged her tightly. "I'm just so glad to see you."

Her beautiful blonde friend carried everything through to the kitchen. "No garlic on the bread and no heavy spices in the lasagna. I'm determined to fatten you up. You look awful, hon."

Simone simply shook her head. Was there no one who would lie to her and tell her she looked great? "I feel like I could eat the whole pan. But I won't," she said hastily. "My poor stomach is barely speaking to me as it is."

Cecelia nodded. "It should keep in the fridge for several days. When will you be able to go back to work?"

"I know you're worried about your campaign, but I'm not going to drop the ball, I promise. I'm planning to go in tomorrow, even if I have to cut the day short."

The other woman raised one perfect eyebrow. "Please give me some credit. I'm not worried about the campaign, I'm worried about *you*, Simone. Would you mind telling me why in the world you had to get pregnant right now? It doesn't make sense."

"I thought Naomi filled you in." Simone perched on a stool at the granite counter. She didn't really want to go through the whole explanation again, especially when it wasn't all that believable the first time.

Cecelia waved a hand, the one not showcasing her amazing engagement ring. "Naomi tried to put a positive spin on it, but I wasn't buying it. Since when do *you* want to be a mother?"

Cecelia's skepticism stung. "Is that really so hard to imagine?"

"You've poured your heart and soul into the agency. You've dated one or two…not more than three guys since Hutch headed off to Africa. And never once have you given any indication that your biological clock is ticking any louder than mine or Naomi's. I know you, girl. Something strange is going on." Cecelia broke off a warm piece of bread, wrapped it in a paper napkin and handed it to Simone. "Tell Auntie Cee Cee what's up, or I'll be forced to resort to blackmail."

It was a poor choice of words. When Simone flinched, Cecelia frowned. "What did I say? You know I was only kidding. But seriously, Simone. Tell me what the heck is going on."

Sooner or later the truth would come out. Sooner or later Simone would have to confide in her two best friends. But she still felt raw and guilty about her decision. She needed time to come to terms with what she had done before she came clean completely.

"It's true," she muttered. "There's more to this than you know. I won't keep it a secret forever. But in the meantime, I need you to be my friend and tell me everything is going to work out fine."

"Is that because the gorgeous doctor is going to step in and make an honest woman out of you?"

"Don't even joke about that," Simone snapped. "Hutch doesn't deserve to be dragged into my mess."

"Well, maybe he'll at least stick around this time." Cecelia's dour comment made Simone want to rush to Hutch's defense. The man had simply followed his dreams and his calling. While she appreciated her friend's wholehearted support, it really wasn't fair to paint Hutch as the villain.

"Let's eat," Simone said. "The lasagna smells amazing. And if you don't mind, let's not talk about Hutch or babies or my sordid secrets. Dr. Fetter says stress can make my nausea worse."

"Sordid?" Cecelia perked up. "I'm intrigued."

"You're also wildly happy, aren't you?" Simone said, trying to change the subject as she piled a small dollop of lasagna on her plate. "Deacon must be good for you. I'm pretty sure you're glowing."

Cecelia's smile was smug. "He's amazing. And we're both thrilled about the baby."

"I'm very happy for you."

Cecelia sobered for a moment. "Is it true you're having triplets?"

Simone nodded. "As long as nothing goes wrong. Sometimes one fetus doesn't develop. It's too soon to know."

"Would you be relieved if you only had one or two?"

Trust Cecelia to cut to the heart of the matter. "You'd think so, wouldn't you? Lord knows how I'll manage. But now that I know there are three, I want them all so badly. It doesn't make any sense. I can't really explain it. All I know is that I would be heartbroken if anything happened to even one of them. I feel like their mother already."

Cecelia leaned over to hug her. "I get it, hon. This whole pregnancy thing turns the world upside down." She hesitated, clearly looking for a tactful way to phrase her question. "So how does the good doctor figure into all of this? Naomi said he was here the other night when she came over."

"He's the new head of the maternal-fetal department at the hospital. Not *my* doctor," Simone said hastily. "I'm Dr. Fetter's patient. But I'm considered high-risk because of the multiples. Hutch oversees and keep tabs on all the cases."

"And does he make house calls to each of those pregnant women?"

"Of course not."

Cecelia rolled her eyes. "Fine. Live in the land of denial while you can."

Simone felt her face get hot. What would Cecelia and Naomi think if they knew about last night? "I doubt I'll see much of him. The only reason he was here is that I chose to have my IV at home instead of taking up a hospital bed. He wanted to make sure I was okay. That's all."

"Whatever you say, little chick. I won't harass you when you're so sick. Still, the day of reckoning will come. Don't think you can avoid this subject forever."

That was the problem, Simone thought bleakly. With this Maverick person threatening her, she was always going to have the sword of Damocles hanging over her head. Telling her parents was going to be bad. She knew she had to do it soon. If they got wind of her pregnancy any other way, they might pressure her into marrying the baby's father. How was she going to explain that the mystery man was no more to her than a control number on a test tube?

Cecelia waved a hand in front of Simone's face. "Hello, in there. Anybody home?"

Simone took a bite of lasagna and washed it down with tea. "Sorry. I was thinking."

"About what?" Cecelia said. Clearly, *her* pregnancy was going well. She ate an astonishing amount of lasagna with no consequences as far as Simone could see.

"I don't want to make a big deal about this pregnancy. Especially not this early, not when there's a chance I could miscarry."

"Lots of people wait until after the first trimester to make any kind of announcement."

"True. But you know how gossip flies in this town. The fact that I was taken from my office on a stretcher is not a secret."

"You'll figure something out," Cecelia said breezily. She grabbed her sweater and purse. "I've gotta run. I'm meeting Deacon for a late dessert."

"Oh, Cecelia. Why didn't you tell me? You should have dropped off the lasagna and had dinner with your brand-new fiancé."

Cecelia's grin was cheeky. "Don't be silly. That lucky man gets to eat dinner with me the rest of his life. He won't begrudge me one evening with a sick friend."

"I'm doing better, honestly."

"Good. 'Cause to tell you the truth, Naomi had me worried after she saw you the other night."

"Let her know I'm fine."

"I will." Cecelia hugged her. "I'll call you tomorrow.

Don't worry about the campaign. You're the most important thing to me. Love you, hon."

And with that, Simone's gorgeous friend blew out the door.

Simone stood at the living room window and watched the car fly down the driveway and onto the main road. Suddenly, she was aware of the crushing silence in the house. No Cecelia or Naomi. No Barb. No Hutch.

He had talked about staying three nights, but she was better now. All her tests had come back with good results. The nurse had removed the IV and packed up all the paraphernalia to take back to the hospital. There was absolutely no reason for Hutch to return.

Life was back to normal. Almost.

Telling herself she wasn't depressed, Simone took a shower and changed into an old pair of yoga pants and an oversize T-shirt. She'd spent far too much time in bed. She wanted to get outside and breathe the fresh spring air.

Not bothering to put on shoes, she opened the back door and made her way down the steps. Dr. Fetter had said moderate exercise was helpful, so Simone had no qualms about risking the babies. The healthier she was, the healthier they were.

Outside, she perked up instantly. Her gardener was a genius. Flowers and ornamental shrubs and fruit trees met and mingled in a display that was appealing without being too formal. In the center of it all lay a deep, verdant lawn. It reminded her of the quad at college where this time of year she and her friends would toss Frisbees and sunbathe and study when they absolutely had to…

All of that seemed like a lifetime ago.

The evening air was cooler than usual. She wrapped her arms around her waist and meandered aimlessly. There in the corner might be a good spot for a play structure. Swings and a slide and maybe even a tiny house with real windows and miniature furniture inside.

It was fun to daydream, because she wanted to be a good mother. She wanted her children to grow up feeling loved and supported. If she had a boy who aspired to be a ballet dancer or a girl who loved fire engines, she would nurture them and help them follow their dreams.

But what happened when the babies grew old enough to ask about their father? What would she say? Stricken by her own selfishness and shortsightedness, she fell to her knees and covered her face with her hands. The scope and ramifications of her mistake were crushing. How could she ever make this right?

She blamed the cry fest on hormones. The tears leaked between her fingers and spotted the front of her shirt. In the spacious yard surrounded by a tall privacy fence, she faced the enormity of what she had done. There was no one to see her break down…no one to witness the moment she hit bottom.

Later, she wasn't sure how long she'd been kneeling there in the grass. She only knew that her knees were sore and her skin covered in gooseflesh when a very familiar voice said her name.

"Simone?"

# Eight

Hutch hadn't meant to come. He'd had a hell of a long day. He was exhausted, and he needed seven or eight straight hours of uninterrupted sleep.

Despite all that, here he was at Simone's house. Again.

He crouched beside her in the grass, touching her shoulder briefly. "What's wrong, Simone? Are you hurt?" Her hair shielded her expression.

She jumped to her feet and backed away from him, rubbing the tears from her face with two hands. Her smile didn't reach her eyes. "Hormones," she said lightly. "You should know all about that. Crazy pregnant women."

After last night, he'd wondered if Simone might want more from him than medical advice. Apparently not.

He took a moment to absorb the breath-stealing realization that she was not happy to see him. Her response was painful and unexpected. It was just as well. Hadn't he come tonight for the express purpose of telling her there was nothing between them? He wasn't prepared to risk his heart a third time. He had an important new job and little opportunity for a social life, much less a love affair.

"Barb told me you're improving slightly," he said.

"Yes. Especially in the evenings. Cecelia brought me lasagna. I managed some of that. And bread."

"Good." Fourteen hours ago they had been naked together in her bed. Now she could barely look at him. "I won't stay tonight," he said. It was a statement, but it came out sounding like a question. Would she ask him to change his mind?

"I know," she said, her gaze wary. "No need."

He cursed beneath his breath. She was far too pale. "Simone, I—"

She held up her hand. "I think we both know what last night was," she said. "Curiosity. Echoes of the past. Let's not beat ourselves up over it. Even if you wanted a repeat, I would have to say no. I need to start planning for my new family. If I hang around with you, the temptation will always be there to lean on you for help. I can't afford to do that."

"Everybody needs a hand at times."

"You know what I mean."

He did. All too well. She was putting up walls. Shutting him out.

He should be relieved. "If you go back to work, please pace yourself. Otherwise, you'll wind up in the same situation as before."

"I understand. You can trust me, Hutch. I want these babies to be safe and healthy. I won't be stupid, I promise."

He nodded. "I should go."

"One more thing." She seemed to hesitate, as if searching for the right words. "I appreciate all you've done for me, Hutch. Later on, when I'm stronger, I'd like to make dinner for you. No strings attached," she said quickly. "Just friends."

"Okay. But you know it's not necessary."

"I want to."

"Just let me know." For some reason, he couldn't get his feet to move. "You still have my card? My phone number?" There was so much they weren't saying.

"I do." She seemed lonely and forlorn.

"Good luck, Simone."

"Thank you."

Simone watched him walk around the side of the house and disappear. The hollow feeling in her chest would get better. It had to. She was done with tears for now.

As she headed back inside, she didn't feel sleepy yet. Watching television wasn't appealing. Instead, she decided to measure one of the guest rooms. Upstairs, she had three guest rooms. The main level of the house included her master suite and a fourth guest room. That might make the best nursery.

She made a few notes and pursed her lips. How did one handle triplets? Did all three babies share? Three cribs in one space? What if one kid woke up in the middle of the night and started crying? Wouldn't that bother the other two?

Abandoning her architectural conundrum, she went in search of the box of books Hutch had dropped by earlier in the week. She planned to start with something simple, perhaps one of the parenting guides. The medical books would be too scary. She didn't want to think about complications, even in a theoretical sense.

With a cup of decaf coffee and a cozy lap blanket, she curled up in her favorite chair in the bedroom and started to read. It wasn't only the advice about being a mom of multiples she needed, it was advice about *everything*. She felt woefully unprepared for motherhood.

At the end of a chapter, she closed the book and stared out the window. It was dark now, that time when problems grew bigger and optimism winnowed away. What would have happened if Hutch had come home a year sooner? Would she have pursued the same course? Her grandfather's death had rattled her...that and his will.

For now, the circumstances of the will were private, but Maverick seemed to know something about it. Perhaps she should go to the police. A cybercrimes expert might be able to use her laptop and trace the blackmailer's IP address.

Still, that would involve exposing her secrets, and she was scared. How would Hutch look at Simone if he learned the truth? It wasn't about the money, not really. She wanted to be recognized as a full-fledged member of the Parker family. Her father had made no secret of his disappointment that he had no son. Her grandfather had felt the same way about having only a granddaughter. Simone, as successful and ambitious as she was, was a poor substitute for two men who should have known better.

It was a skirmish she had fought her entire life. Unfortunately, in the heat of battle sometimes a person made mistakes. Simone's was a whopper. Only time would tell if she could survive the fallout.

The following morning, she made it to work more or less on time. She had set her alarm earlier than usual in order to give herself time to be sick. It was a ghastly way to start the day. Still, she counted it a victory that she had to dash to the bathroom only twice. Maybe she would be one of the lucky ones and this nausea business would eventually subside.

Her two key employees were back from the conference, so the three of them dug into the campaign for Cecelia's business. Candace must have given them some kind of report on her health, but Simone's associates were too professional and kind to grill her. Until she started showing, she hoped to be able to conceal her pregnancy and carry on as usual.

Unfortunately, even though the nausea was no longer as severe, her energy level was nonexistent. She had many, many months to go, but already these babies were impacting her life. It must have been sheer naïveté that made her think the adjustments would happen only *after* the birth.

For ten days, she had no contact with Hutch at all. Even when she visited Dr. Fetter's office at the hospital, there was no sign of the man who had returned from Africa...the man who recently shared her bed for one incredible night. Even at her lowest point, being intimate with Hutch again had made her feel like a desirable woman.

She told herself his absence from her life was for the best, and she almost believed it.

Fortunately, she was able to roll out the last of the campaign for Luna Fine Furnishings without incident and right on time. Cecelia was ecstatic. Deacon treated the three friends to dinner to celebrate. He probably enjoyed being out on the town with a trio of attractive women, but in truth, he had eyes only for Cecelia.

Simone laughed and talked during the meal, but it was hard to keep up a celebratory front. Though she was thrilled for Cecelia, it hurt to see the way Deacon looked at his bride-to-be. Simone had practically guaranteed that she would never have that kind of relationship. What kind of man would want to take on an instant family, including babies that weren't his?

She picked at her salmon, pushing the meal around on her plate so her friends would think she was eating. Unfortunately, no matter how hard she tried, she was still losing weight rather than gaining. Many pregnant women would love to have her problem, but it wasn't good for the babies.

April came to an end. May dawned with blue skies and balmy temperatures. Simone missed Hutch terribly. Knowing he was living in Royal was somehow worse than when he had been on the other side of the world.

Work became her salvation. She managed to keep her pregnancy under wraps from most of Royal, but she decided to tell her parents, come what may. She spent an uncomfortable afternoon at their house trying to explain convincingly why she'd taken the route she did.

She suspected that both her mother *and* her father knew she was going out of her way to fulfill the conditions of her grandfather's will, but they didn't press her. Perhaps her father was willing to overlook an indiscretion or poor judgment if he finally got the boy he'd always wanted.

What if all three babies were girls? What then? In that situation, Simone would have satisfied the letter of the law, but would her father still be disappointed? That would be hard to bear.

After the first few days of the month, spring began to feel like summer. The higher temperatures made Simone's nausea worse. She lived off decaf iced tea and fresh-squeezed lemonade. On the hottest days, even the mention of food was enough to make her ill.

Though she tried her best to eat, she wasn't keeping up. She grew weak and listless, and one morning she couldn't convince herself to crawl out of bed. Naomi was at a convention on the West Coast. Cecelia and Deacon had flown off to Bermuda for a quick holiday.

Simone was alone in her misery.

Around noon she knew she had to eat something. When she sat up on the side of the bed, the room spun around her. Hutch's number was programmed into her phone. All she had to do was call him.

Did he really care? Was it the doctor in him who had made the offer, or the lover? Had Simone alienated him? She never had issued the official thank-you dinner invitation, mostly because she hadn't been well enough to cook.

Stumbling to the kitchen, she held on to the walls for support. She felt terrible. This was more than simple nausea. She had a pain in her left side, and a terrible sense of foreboding. When the cramping started low in her abdomen, she panicked.

She had forgotten to bring her phone to the kitchen. It was an agonizing trip back to the bedroom to retrieve it. With fumbling fingers, she found Hutch's name and hit the call button.

One ring. Two. *Please, God, let him pick up.*

On the fourth ring, he answered. "Simone. It's nice to hear from you." Obviously the caller ID let him know it was her. The sound of his voice was enough to calm her a fraction.

"I'm sorry to bother you, Hutch. Can you stop by after work? I'm not feeling very well."

His voice sharpened. "Can you drive yourself to the hospital?"

"No…I…" Her throat clogged with tears. "Never mind," she whispered. "Never mind…"

Hutch heard a noise on the other end of the line as if the phone had been dropped. His heart plummeted to his stomach. He shoved the stack of charts he was holding into a nearby nurse's hands and grimaced. "I have to leave. Get Dr. Henry to cover my appointments. I'll let you know when I'll be back."

"Is everything okay, Doctor?"

"I don't know," he said grimly.

He jumped in his car and headed across town. On the way, he called Janine Fetter and explained the situation. Today was her day off. Fortunately, they were old friends. She agreed to meet him at Simone's house.

Hutch arrived first by minutes only. Simone always hid her extra key in the same place, even at a new address. He tipped over the flowerpot, retrieved the key and burst through the door, leaving it ajar for Janine.

The steps from the front door to Simone's bedroom seemed to happen in slow motion. He found her in a heap on the carpet, her face ashen. Her pulse was sluggish. She was clammy and barely responsive.

"Simone!" He said her name sharply, trying to cut through the fog.

Her eyelids fluttered. "Hutch? You came?"

"Of course I did," he said, cradling her in his arms. "Why are you so damned hardheaded?"

Janine arrived right about then and assessed the situation in a glance. Hutch didn't even care. The other doctor smiled at him gently. "Put her in bed and I'll examine her. You wait in the other room."

He bristled. "But I—"

She touched his arm lightly, with sympathy in her eyes. "I don't think you can be impartial about this one. Let me see what's going on. You need to take a few minutes to pull yourself together. Are the babies yours?"

The question caught him off guard. He wanted them to be. But they weren't. "Of course not," he muttered. "You know she had IUI with a sperm donor."

Janine shrugged. "I've seen doctors falsify charts for a friend. I'm not judging."

"Well, they're not mine," he growled. "You'll see that soon enough when you deliver them." Standing awkwardly, he carried Simone to the bed. "Do we need an ambulance?"

"What do you think?" Janine's grin was wry. He was acting like a total basket case.

"Sorry," he said. "She's stable. So, no."

"Go on, Hutch. Get yourself a stiff drink. I'll yell for you in a few minutes."

He paced from the bedroom down the hall to the kitchen. There he saw that Simone had tried to fix herself a sandwich. The jar of mustard was still open, and a grilled chicken breast languished on a plate.

The situation was unacceptable. He should have known from the beginning that she was going to need a babysitter. This kind of pregnancy was tricky. Simone was too inexperienced to know what she was facing.

It seemed like hours before Janine summoned him, but according to his watch, only twenty minutes had elapsed. He found Simone awake but chastened. Janine sat on the end of the bed. "I've given our patient a stern talking-to," she said.

"It's about time somebody did," he grumbled.

"I can't stay home for weeks and months," Simone wailed.

"Actually, you can." Janine's bark was worse than her bite, but the other doctor meant business. "Think about it, Simone. You're more fortunate than most. You own your own business. You have capable employees. Not only that, but you can keep tabs on things via your laptop. Now all we need is someone to play watchdog."

Hutch folded his arms across his chest. "That would be me," he said bluntly. At this point, he didn't care what Janine thought. Simone was still too damn pale. Her inky hair emphasized her pallor.

"No way," Simone said. She still had a bit of spunk left. "You have an important job."

"So I'll take some time off."

"You just got back from Africa," she cried. "You don't *have* any time off."

"Then I'll quit my job." His priorities were crystal clear. A sense of calm fatalism swept through him. He and Simone were bound by invisible threads. Maybe she didn't want him here, and maybe he shouldn't be here. But there it was. Some things defied explanation.

Janine watched both of them with speculation in her gaze. "Do you still want me to be her doctor?"

Hutch grimaced. "Of course." Then he looked at Simone. "Right?"

She glared at him. "Why ask now? It looks like you're prepared to take charge of my whole life."

Her sarcasm didn't faze him. "Damned straight."

Janine put her bag back together and checked Simone's pulse one more time. She smoothed a hand over Simone's flushed forehead. "Listen to the man. He may be arrogant, but he knows what he's doing. I'll feel a lot better knowing you're not living here on your own."

Simone's eyebrows shot to her hairline. "He can't move in here."

"Oh, yes, I can," Hutch said.

Janine grinned and stayed quiet.

The patient simmered. "What about gossip?" she said. Her gorgeous blue eyes were damp with tears.

Her vulnerability caught something in his chest and gave it a sharp squeeze. "I don't give a damn about gossip," he said. "What we do is our own business. My job is to take care of mothers and babies. For the foreseeable future, you're at the top of my list."

Janine nodded. "Sounds good to me. You have my number, Hutch. If you need me outside office hours, don't hesitate to call."

He kissed her cheek, overwhelmed with gratitude. "Thanks," he said gruffly.

Janine motioned toward the hall. Hutch followed her, closing the door most of the way so they wouldn't be overheard. "Honestly, how is she doing?" he asked.

"I'm concerned that Simone is still losing weight, by her own admission. Even in cases of hyperemesis, we need to see her belly growing. She's as tiny as the first day I examined her. Force-feed her if you have to…little bits around the clock. But if those babies are going to have a chance, we need to strengthen their mother."

Hutch nodded. "When is her next ultrasound scheduled?"

"Not for another month. But under the circumstances, I think I'll bump it up. I want to make sure things are progressing."

"And if they're not?"

Janine shrugged. "You know the statistics. Don't alarm her more than necessary. But make her eat."

"You can count on it."

"I'll let myself out," Janine said. "Unless you want me to stay while you run home to pack a bag."

"It can wait until tomorrow. I'm sure one of her friends will come over if I call."

"I'm guessing she's been putting on a brave front."

He grimaced. "That would be Simone. Never let them see you sweat."

"Or in this case, barf."

Hutch chuckled. "Thank you for coming."

She cocked her head and stared at him. "Are you sure you know what you're doing?"

Janine had known him a long time. And she knew the history. "Not at all," he said. "But I don't really have a choice."

# Nine

Simone overheard the last thing Hutch said to Dr. Fetter, and it cut her to the bone. *I don't really have a choice.* He was stuck with Simone because of some kind of moral obligation. Saint Hutch.

She bit her lip to keep from crying when he came back into the room. He still wore his white coat with Dr. Troy Hutchinson neatly embroidered on the chest. "Why are you doing this?" she asked wearily. "We can get Barb."

"Barb is overbooked as it is. Besides, I know you, Simone. You wouldn't be comfortable with a stranger in your house."

"*You're* practically a stranger," she shot back. "You've been gone for almost six years. Neither of us is the same person we used to be."

He didn't let her bait him. "That's a good thing, isn't it? Surely we've both grown up by now. I hope I have."

When Simone closed her eyes and didn't answer, he knew she was trying to shut him out. It didn't matter. Whatever the current relationship between them, he was going to protect her and her babies, God willing.

Shrugging out of his lab coat, he unbuttoned his blue dress shirt and rolled up the sleeves. The house was hot. Simone could use some fresh air. But the heat and humidity outside would only make her feel worse. He found the thermostat and made the AC click on. Soon, cool air began to blow out of the vents.

When he returned to the bedroom, Simone still had her eyes closed. He didn't know if she was resting or pouting. Grinning inwardly, he sat down on the edge of the bed and stroked her arm. "What if I fix scrambled eggs and bacon? That used to be your favorite." On the weekends in the old days, they would often spend most of their time in bed. When they were sated and content, they ended up in the kitchen eating breakfast for dinner.

Simone opened one eye. "With cinnamon toast?"

"Whatever you want, brave girl. All you have to do is ask."

Finally, he coaxed a smile from her. "That would be lovely," she whispered.

"And you'll stay in bed in the meantime?"

She nodded. "I will."

Fortunately, he found the kitchen stocked with basics. Soon, he had bacon sizzling as he worked on the toast. The eggs turned out fluffy and perfect. He hoped having the comfort food on hand would coax Simone into eating something, at least.

When he carried the tray to the bedroom, he realized that she had dozed off again. He wondered if she'd had trouble sleeping at night, or if it was her weakness making her drowsy. He set the tray on the bedside table and touched her arm. "Wake up, sleepyhead. Dinner is served." He guessed she had missed lunch entirely.

Simone struggled to sit up in bed. "That was fast."

Once she was settled, he sat down beside her. "I'm going to feed you," he said.

"I'm not a baby."

"No, but you're not a hundred percent. We'll take this slow. If we need to stop, we will."

She was visibly hesitant, but she eyed the plate longingly. "I want to gobble it up," she said glumly. "But that would be a disaster."

"I'm sure your stomach has shrunk. You won't be able to eat a normal meal yet. We'll get there gradually over the next few weeks. What do you want first?"

She wrinkled her nose. "Eggs, I think. I need the protein."

He offered her a forkful and nodded approvingly when she opened her mouth, chewed and swallowed. "So far, so good?"

Simone nodded. "You always were a better cook than me."

"Doesn't matter. You have other talents."

Her cheeks turned pink. She shot him a look from beneath her lashes, a look that made his blood run hot. "Naughty, naughty, Dr. Hutchinson. Are you trying to raise my blood pressure?"

"Whatever it takes, honey. Whatever it takes."

The gentle flirting reassured him. Simone looked a hell of a lot better now than when he'd first arrived and found her on the floor. He shuddered inwardly at the memory. If he had any say in the matter, she would never get to that point again.

His patient managed to eat half of the eggs, one piece of bacon and an entire slice of cinnamon toast. It was probably too much, but he didn't have the heart to refuse her when she was clearly starving.

She wiped her mouth with a napkin. "That was wonderful, Hutch. It seems to help when I don't have to be the one to fix it. Yesterday, I took one look at a raw egg and had to dash to the bathroom."

"Understandable. Let me clean up the kitchen, and then I have an idea."

The chore didn't take long, but once again, Simone was

asleep when he returned. He decided to let her rest for a little bit. He needed to deal with a few urgent work situations if he was going to stay here semipermanently.

After half an hour of answering emails and texts, he was done, for the moment. Like Simone, part of his responsibilities could be dealt with remotely. His patient list was very small so far. Most of what he had been doing in these first few weeks was consulting on cases. Since he had access to the electronic records in his department, some things could go forward unchanged.

When he entered her bedroom this time, she was awake. Her color was better, and her eyes were brighter. "More dinner?" he asked.

"No. But so far, so good with what I ate."

"Excellent. I know you're exhausted, but what if we take one short stroll around the backyard? The exercise will do you good, and it will help you sleep more deeply. I'll be right beside you."

"Okay." She climbed out of bed on her own, waving him off when he tried to take her arm. "If this is going to work, you can't treat me like an invalid. I can go to the bathroom by myself."

He didn't like it, but he had to tread carefully with Simone. Her fierce independence was going to be at odds with his need to cosset her.

When they made it outdoors, the heat of the day had abated. The air was fresh and sweet. Simone's backyard was a rainbow of color, flowers blooming everywhere.

He put an arm around her waist. "Lean on me," he said. "And tell me if you need to stop."

They didn't speak as they made a lazy circuit of the premises. Simone's legs were shaky…that was easy to tell. But she powered on. By the time they made it back to the starting point, she was leaning on him heavily, and her breathing was rapid. He scooped her up in his arms and climbed the shallow steps.

"Good girl," he said softly. "I'm proud of you. Food and exercise. You'll make it yet."

"My hero," she smirked.

His lips twitching in amusement, he managed the knob and bumped the door open with his hip. "Do you want to go ahead and take a shower now? Or do you need to rest first?"

Simone looked up at him with big eyes. "Are you offering to join me, Doctor?"

"Do you need medical assistance?"

"I'm sure I do."

The little brat was taunting him, but there wasn't a chance in hell he was going to make love to her tonight. She knew the power she had over him, and she wasn't afraid to use it.

He deposited her on the bed and inspected the bathroom. If he put the tiny vanity stool in the shower, Simone wouldn't have to stand the whole time. "Okay," he said. "Let's do this."

She raised up on one elbow. "Don't you still keep a change of clothes in the car?"

Actually, he did, but he'd forgotten. Finding Simone semiconscious had thrown him off his game. "Why do you ask?"

"Well, if you're going to help me shower, you'll get soaked. You should go get what you need before we start."

"True."

She watched him intently.

"What are you thinking, Simone?" he asked. "I don't like that look."

"You know it makes sense for you to be naked, too."

Immediately and urgently, he was hard…painfully so. He schooled his expression not to reveal his physical turmoil. "I can take off my wet clothes when we're done. Stay put. I'll be back."

Outside, he put his hands on top of the car and banged his head softly against the metal door frame. He and Simone were playing a dangerous game of chicken, and he was losing. Grabbing the gym bag that held a clean pair of jeans, a knit shirt and underwear, he told himself he could be a gentleman.

Despite her propensity for suggestive repartee, Simone was in a fragile state. Even if she *wanted* to make love to him, she was in no condition to do so. He would help her with the shower and tuck her into bed. Period.

Their first argument was over who would undress her. She stood at the bathroom counter, eyes blazing. "I can take off my own clothes, Hutch."

"If you get dizzy and fall, you'll hit something hard and smash your skull. You don't want that to happen, do you?"

"What I want is for you to treat me like an adult. Take off your own clothes, big boy." No man with an ounce of testosterone could resist such an all-out dare. He wasn't a teenager. He could control himself.

They stripped down side by side. Hutch tried not to look in the mirror. It was bad enough seeing Simone in the flesh. He didn't need to be surrounded with multiple images.

When he saw her completely naked for the first time, he cursed. The one and only time they had made love since he came home from Sudan, the room had been mostly dark. Now, in the bright light from the bathroom fixture, he took note of each feminine detail.

She crossed her arms over her breasts. "What's wrong?"

"I can see every one of your ribs, damn it. I can't believe how much weight you've lost."

"It's a new technique. I call it the triplet diet."

Even now, she was a smart-ass. "That's not funny." He couldn't decide if he wanted to spank her or kiss her.

Ignoring the urge to do either, he stepped past her to turn on the water and adjust the faucet. When he was satisfied the temperature was just right, he put the small stool in the large granite shower stall and took Simone's arm. "In you go."

She sat down with a small sigh. Closing her eyes, she leaned her head against his hip. "Thank you, Hutch," she whispered. "For everything."

Tenderness came, overwhelming him and muting his physical need for her. "You're very welcome. Close your eyes and let me take care of you."

He started with shampoo, lathering Simone's long, dark tresses and rinsing with the handheld sprayer. Afterward, he grabbed the bottle of shower gel and soaped up a washcloth. Moving it over her shoulders and back, he made himself recite multiplication tables in his head to keep from going insane.

Her breasts were full and firm. When he soaped them lazily, the rosy nipples perked up. Eventually, he had washed everything he could reach. "Do you think you can stand for a minute?" he asked gruffly.

She nodded but didn't move.

"Do you want to do the rest yourself?"

Simone looked up at him with drowsy eyes. Her pupils were dilated; only a ring of deep azure remained. Her eyelashes were spiky and wet. "You're doing fine. Don't stop now." She put her hands on his forearms and drew herself upright.

Now her nose reached the center of his chest. He wanted to lift her and slide her down onto his rigid sex. He wanted to take her up against the wall of the shower and pound into her until the gnawing ache in his gut found release.

Instead, he did the honorable thing. He knelt and washed her feet and calves and thighs. Then, standing, with Simone embracing him, he rubbed between her legs.

Her breath caught audibly. "I want you," she whispered.

Hell. He shut his eyes and gritted his teeth. "We can't, sweet girl. Not today."

Their bodies were wet and slick and primed for action. But Simone was weak as a baby kitten. She fussed half-heartedly when he shut off the water and urged her out of the shower. As he dried her with a big fluffy towel, she murmured something he didn't quite catch. Afterward, he set her on the counter and grabbed another towel for himself.

Simone's back was to the mirror, her hair a tangled mess of black silk at her shoulders. "I'll have to dry your hair," he said. "It's too wet for you to get straight into bed."

He found a large-tooth comb and a hair dryer in one of the drawers. Simone seemed to be half asleep sitting up. Though he was clumsy at best, he managed to dry her hair until it was tangle-free.

She leaned into him. "You should do this for a living," she muttered, yawning.

"Only for you, kiddo." He picked her up and carried her to the bed. "Pajamas?"

Her smile was wicked. "Not tonight."

With shaking hands, he covered her all the way to the chin. "Go to sleep, Simone. I have some work to do, but I'll be in later. I'll take the other side of the bed."

"Will you be here when I wake up?" Her eyes had darkened, and for a moment, the impertinent facade slipped and he saw loneliness.

"I'm not going anywhere," he said firmly.

He pulled on the clean boxers and pants without the shirt. The house had cooled down some, but not enough. Or maybe he was the one who was overheated.

Firing up his laptop and dealing with a backlog of email occupied him for an hour. Simone had an exercise bike in the guest room, so he did ten miles there. After that, he prowled, trying to convince himself he could lie in that bed with Simone and not go stark, raving mad.

During the course of the evening he had managed to get his erection under control for brief periods of time. Still, every moment he allowed his attention to wander, his libido took over, telling him how damn good it would feel to be intimate with Simone again.

His head was messed up, no doubt about it. First, there was the ghost of Bethany. The guilt he felt about her death might be illogical, but it lingered. Then there was Simone's unorthodox pregnancy. She was hiding something.

There were any number of men in Royal who would have been happy to provide sperm the old-fashioned way. What reason had been compelling enough to send Simone down this path?

He prayed unashamedly for her three babies. If she lost any or all of them, it would destroy him. Even more harrowing was the prospect of losing Simone. Women still died in childbirth occasionally. It was rare, but it happened. She wasn't his to lose, but he was the one in her court for the moment.

Finally, at eleven, he decided he was tired enough to go to sleep, no matter the provocation. He moved through the house checking locks and turning off the lights. By now, he knew his way around the master bedroom. He brushed his teeth with the toothbrush from last time. Leaning his hands on the counter, he gave himself a pep talk.

"Don't be stupid, Hutch. She doesn't need any added stress, and you don't need the drama. She broke up with you the last time. Now she's in an even worse place to have a relationship with you. Get over it. Move on."

It was a good speech. Maybe even a great one. Despite that, when he stood beside the bed and studied the small lump under the covers, he rubbed his chest, trying to ease the ache there.

He'd always assumed he'd have a family one day, though not like this. Even if Simone had any residual feelings for him, he would have to wonder if she needed a father for her babies more than she needed a lover. It was a sobering thought.

Thankfully, he did sleep. And on his own side of the bed.

Once, toward dawn, he roused when Simone got up to go to the bathroom. He could see the outline of her nude body. "You okay?" he asked groggily.

"Yes."

She wasn't gone long. When she climbed back in bed, he could hear her breathing. "Hutch?" she said.

"Hmm?"

"Will you hold me?"

He inhaled sharply. "I don't think I can do that."

"Why not?"

Was she deliberately being obtuse, or did the woman truly not understand how badly he wanted her? "You're naked. I'm naked. Things will happen."

She chuckled. "Is that so terrible?"

Desperately, his better nature fought the good fight. "You're not one hundred percent."

"Then make love to what's left of me, please. And this time don't let go."

Simone knew she was being unfair. What was the penalty for tempting a saint? Eternal damnation? She had already tasted the depths of hell. When Hutch left for Sudan, she'd come close to falling apart completely. Only sheer force of will had enabled her to get out of bed and get dressed every day.

Eventually, the pain dulled. Work and friends and hobbies filled the hours. After a year, she dated again. Casually. Always, she wondered what would happen when Hutch came home. And then he didn't come home.

After the first three years, she had faced the bitter truth. By sending him off to fulfill his destiny, she had destroyed her chance at happiness with him. Even now, she was under no illusions. They had sexual attraction going for them, no question. But she was pregnant with another man's babies.

Lots of couples adopted children. This was different. Even if he could forgive her for the huge mistake she had made, surely he would want to father his own son or daughter.

What if she got pregnant again and it was as bad as this time? The thought of facing another nine months of misery was too wretched to contemplate. And four children? Simone didn't even know how to mother one or two or three, much less four.

The only thing left was hot sex with no strings attached. Even that would come to an end when she got embarrassingly huge.

With tears stinging her eyes, she met him in the middle of the mattress. "I'm not a very nice person," she whispered. "I should leave you alone."

He ran a hand down her flank, raising gooseflesh everywhere he touched. "I'm a big boy," he said. "I can handle it."

# Ten

She reached for him in the dark, finding his erection and wrapping her hand around it. Hutch shuddered. She stroked him firmly, remembering instinctively what he liked. In the space of a hushed breath, the years melted away and the two of them were the same young, wildly infatuated couple they had once been.

Her body wasn't cooperating. She felt weak and barely able to move. Still, she wanted Hutch desperately. With the empathy that marked everything he did, he held her close and winnowed his fingers though her hair. "You're not up to this, Simone. Admit it."

His body was warm and hard and masculine against hers. The light fuzz of hair on his broad chest tickled her breasts and reminded her that he was a man in his prime. The stark contrast of tough male to soft female sent a shiver of delight down her spine. Having him wrap his muscular arms around her in a firm hug made her feel secure and cherished. He was right. She didn't have the energy for sex. Yet everything she knew told her to bind Hutch any way she could. She didn't want to lose him again. And she didn't want only his tender care. She wanted his love.

*Dear God.* The truth left her breathless. She still loved Troy Hutchinson. Illogically. Inescapably. Which meant she was destined for even greater heartbreak than before. The yawning hole in her chest was terrifying. She couldn't survive a second time. Especially not with babies in the mix.

As she lay there trembling, her change in mood must have alerted Hutch that something was wrong. He eased her onto her back and reclined on one elbow. Placing his hand, palm flat, on her stomach, he sighed. "Talk to me, honey. I'm not a mind reader."

"I shouldn't have gotten pregnant." She wanted to tell him the truth. She wanted to tell him why. But she was afraid he would look at her in disgust and disappointment.

"Your timing could have been better, that's true. But there's nothing wrong with wanting to become a mother."

Except that Simone had taken something so sacred and wonderful and used it for her own ends. "Are you still in love with Bethany?" She blurted it out, her pain and confusion erasing all sense of boundaries.

Hutch went still. He removed his hand. "Bethany has nothing to do with you and me," he said, the words flat.

"You didn't answer my question, Hutch." Why was she torturing herself? "Do you still love her?"

She heard him curse beneath his breath. His reaction was so out of character it shocked her.

"I will always love Bethany," he said. "She was selfless and pure in her devotion to the hurt and needy. She gave her life doing the things she considered essential for the good of humanity. She made me a better doctor...a better man. So, yes, Simone. I love Bethany. But she's gone, and I'm still here. If that's a problem, tell me now."

Her throat was so tight she could barely breathe, much less speak. Why had she wanted so badly to know the truth? Now she would never be able to forget what he'd said.

She touched his arm. "I'm sorry. You're right. She has nothing to do with us." Moving carefully, she climbed on top of him and buried her face in the curve of his neck. He was still hard and ready.

Hutch didn't need any further invitation. He lifted her hips and joined their bodies with a firm thrust. She cried out, the small sound muffled against his shoulder. He made love to her with such tenderness she wanted to weep. He was a doctor, yes. So he had taken an oath to do no harm. But this was more than that. He was coaxing her into trusting him, one heartbeat at a time.

What he couldn't know was that she would trust him with her life...and the lives of her babies. That wasn't the issue at all. The problem was the way she had let herself get twisted in knots over her grandfather's will and her feelings of not being able to measure up to her family's expectations.

It was too late now.

Hutch was hot, his taut body damp. He held her hips in a grip that might bruise, though she didn't think he realized it. "Are you okay?" He ground out the words between clenched teeth.

She cupped his cheek with her hand, feeling the stubble on his face and chin. "I'm glad you came home, Hutch. I missed you." It wasn't an answer to his question. She wasn't okay...not at all. How could she tell him that she had been missing a part of herself for five long years?

At twenty-two, twenty-three, she hadn't understood how rare it was to find someone like Hutch. It shamed her to realize that if the situation arose now, she would beg him not to leave. In her youthful naïveté, she had assumed one of two things—either Hutch would come home after two and a half years and they would pick up where they left off, or she would eventually find someone else to love.

Neither scenario had been the case.

He rolled suddenly, taking her with him. She wrapped her legs around his waist and twined her arms around his neck. Hutch was wild now, his thrusts uncontrolled, his passion barely in check.

"Simone… Ah, hell…" He came with a groan that sounded more like pain than pleasure.

She wasn't even close. As much as she craved his touch, she was unable to summon the energy to climax. It was enough to know he wanted her.

In the aftermath, he moved them onto their sides and held her gently, stroking her hair and feathering kisses over her eyelids and cheekbones.

"I remembered this," he said quietly. "In Sudan. When things got bad. Sometimes we lost babies who should have lived. Mothers, too. It ate me up inside. When I couldn't sleep at night, I would imagine you in bed with me. It helped. It anchored me."

"But you didn't come home the first time." She heard the note of accusation in her own voice. "That sounded angry," she added quickly. "And I wasn't. I'm not." What she had been was devastated.

He sighed, his breath stirring the hair at her temple. "I was going to," he said. "I had every intention of coming back to Royal when my first tour was over. But…"

"But what?"

"You and I had ended things on a difficult note. I wasn't sure there was any reason to come home. And the need in West Darfur was overwhelming. You were so damn young when we broke up. It occurred to me that I was probably someone to experiment with…someone unsuitable you could toss in your parents' faces to prove you were a grown woman."

Simone flinched, incredibly hurt. "It wasn't that. It was never that, Hutch. I adored you."

"But not enough to beg me to stay."

"That's not fair."

"I knew you were ambitious. I knew you wanted to be

successful. You had life in the palm of your hand. It's not surprising that my life and yours didn't mesh."

"I was trying to do the right thing," she said bitterly. "For once in my life, I was being unselfish." *And look where it got me...*

He sighed. "Why don't we agree to let the past stay in the past? Neither of us handled the relationship well."

"And now?"

"What do you mean?" His question held a tinge of wariness.

"Are we handling *this* well?"

"How the hell should I know? I'm an obstetrician, not a shrink."

Simone was shocked when he rolled away from her and left the bed. "Where are you going? It's still dark out."

"I need to clear my head," he said gruffly. "Go back to sleep."

Hutch didn't wait to see if she obeyed his command. Her scent was on his skin. The sound of her voice echoed in his head. His heart pounded as adrenaline surged through his veins. He either wanted to run or to fight or to climb back into his lover's bed and stake a claim.

It was easy to pretend that Simone was the same woman he'd left behind. Easy, for now. When her pregnancy began to show, all bets were off. Every time he looked at her, he would be reminded that she had made a choice to be a single mom. It still made no sense. Simone was the quintessential career woman. Not only that, she was far too young to worry about her biological clock.

He let himself out of the house quietly and prowled the backyard. At this hour, the air was cool and sweet. Janine Fetter was no gossip, but sooner or later, word would filter around town. Simone Parker was pregnant. And Troy Hutchinson was living in her house.

Did he care? That was the million-dollar question. People would make assumptions about Simone's pregnancy. It was only natural. Undoubtedly, some folks around Royal would believe he had returned from Africa so that he and Simone could pick up where they left off.

If anybody did the math, they would know he wasn't the father of her triplets. But was anybody going to be following their situation that closely?

For one brief moment, he considered offering Simone a version of what they'd had in the past. Not his heart. That wasn't up for grabs. Something else instead. She was going to need help. He liked having regular sex with someone he cared about.

There were worse reasons to hook up.

Still, there was no rush. He was here to make sure she took care of herself. In the meantime, he could decide if they were actually compatible. Simone liked to jump in the deep end without pondering the consequences. He was a planner, a cautious man who preferred to calculate the risks.

Maybe it would work. Maybe it wouldn't. He had time to decide.

After that first night, their time together fell into a routine of sorts. The mornings were hardest for Simone. He was a decent cook, so he tempted her with light fare, anything he thought she would enjoy and be able to keep down.

Gradually, her color improved and she became stronger—strong enough to want to go back to work.

They argued ten times a day, it seemed. Him pointing out that she had a long way to go in this pregnancy, Simone insisting he was a worrywart. In the end, they compromised.

He'd been sleeping under her roof for seven nights when Simone revealed the real reason she was desperate to get back to work. While Hutch made grilled cheese sandwiches and tomato soup for both of them, Simone sat at the kitchen counter with her laptop and fretted.

"I'm in charge of this upcoming charity event," she said, waving her hands. "It was my idea. I can't let the preparations slide anymore or we'll never be ready."

He listened with half an ear, wondering if the rough weather that buffeted the windows would turn into a tornado watch. He'd been in Sudan when a killer storm leveled big chunks of Royal a few years ago. People were still antsy whenever the skies turned dark.

Simone tossed a paper wad at him. "Pay attention, Hutch. I'm trying to explain."

He shrugged with an unrepentant grin. Now that Simone was feeling slightly better, she talked his ear off. "I'm sorry," he said. "Go ahead. I'm listening. What's it called again?"

"Nothing yet," she grumbled. "That's part of the problem. The invitations need to go out by Monday, and I have everything ready but the name."

Royal's hardworking charity organization, Homes and Hearts, was slated to be the beneficiary of Simone's latest PR idea. When she fell ill recently, she'd been in the midst of planning a grand masquerade ball to raise money to build more houses for the homeless.

Instead of hosting at the Cattleman's Club, Simone and Cecelia had cooked up the idea of christening the grand ballroom at Deacon Chase's new five-star resort, The Bellamy. He and Shane Delgado had been inspired by the Biltmore House in Asheville, North Carolina, though their architectural baby here in Royal was hipper and more modern. Sitting amid fifty-plus acres of lush gardens, The Bellamy was lavish and expensive.

Simone had declared it the perfect location.

"How about Masks for Mortar?" he said. "Has a ring to it, don't you think?"

Simone squealed and jumped off the stool, rounding the

island to hug him enthusiastically. "That's perfect, Hutch. Let me insert that line in the file, and I'll get it off to the printer."

"Don't you need somebody else's approval? I don't want to be responsible if the idea bombs." He was only half kidding.

"It's exactly right," she insisted.

While she futzed with her email, he shoved a plate under her nose. "Here's your lunch, Simone."

She nodded absently. "Put it right there. I'll try a few bites."

Leaning over the counter, he closed her laptop. "Eat now. Doctor's orders."

He wasn't going to budge on this one. It pleased him to see her so happy, but she could easily get into trouble again if she didn't make sure to nibble when her stomach was actually cooperating.

She made a face at him. "Dictator."

"Shrew." He grinned. Gradually, they were becoming less cautious with each other. It was a good sign, but he was pretty sure the détente was only temporary.

For one thing, Simone never talked about the babies. She let Hutch check her blood pressure twice a day, and she ate as much as she was able to. Other than that, there was no outward indication that anything was going on beneath the surface.

One afternoon a week or so later, she seemed moodier than usual.

He tugged the end of her ponytail. "What's bugging you?"

"I'm almost three months along. When will I feel them move?"

Suddenly, he realized she was still fretting about the pregnancy. "Well..." He hesitated, trying to speak the truth without offering false promises. "Every day that passes brings you one day closer to a successful outcome. In a normal pregnancy, you'd likely start to notice the baby moving at five months."

"But with triplets?"

"Could be sooner. Could be later."

"And for that sound medical judgment you went to med school…"

Her snarkiness amused him. "Things are going well," he said gently.

Simone bit her bottom lip. "Dr. Fetter wants me to come in for the ultrasound tomorrow."

"I know."

"What if…"

He put his hand over her mouth and kissed her nose. "The ultrasound will make you feel better."

"Or maybe not," she mumbled against his fingers.

"Are we having the glass half-empty, half-full conversation?"

Her blue eyes glistened with tears. Like bluebonnets in the rain. He knew he was in trouble when he realized he was waxing poetic, even in his head.

Simone wriggled until he released her. She wrapped her arms around her waist. "You don't understand. As long as I'm standing here with you in this kitchen, those three babies are alive and developing normally. I don't want to go to the hospital and find out differently."

He wondered if any of the other people in her life knew that beneath Simone's facade of bravado and confidence lurked a sensitive, vulnerable woman. "I'll go with you," he said. "It will be fine. And if it's not, you can lean on me."

"I have to do this alone," she insisted, her chin set in stubborn mode.

"No, you don't. That's ridiculous."

"I'm serious, Hutch. It's one thing for you to stay here and make sure I eat. It's a whole other ball game for you to parade up to that hospital with me when everybody in the building knows who you are. I can't deal with that, too. You can drive me there if you insist, but I want you to drop me off at the door and leave."

His temper started to boil. "You're being absurd."

"Don't patronize me," she snapped. The tears spilled over now. "Leave me alone," she cried. "I'm going to my room."

He told himself pregnant women were at the mercy of roller-coaster hormones. Simone needed her space.

It made sense. The artificial situation in which they found themselves was beginning to fray at the seams. After the first night of his stay, he hadn't made love to her at all. He'd wanted to, God knew, but he had felt the need to back up and reassess. He'd been sleeping in the guest room ever since. Alone.

If Simone really cared about him as more than a doctor and a friend, she would make the first move. But she hadn't.

A crack of thunder right over the house made him jump. He was horny and frustrated and angry at himself for getting involved with a woman who had far too many issues at play.

The fact that she didn't want him in the room when she had the ultrasound done was a red flag. He wanted to protect her and keep her from any kind of pain, physical or mental.

What Simone wanted was a mystery.

Her sandwich and soup sat uneaten on the counter. He zapped the plate in the microwave and carried it down the hall as a peace offering.

He found the bedroom door ajar. Simone sat in the middle of the carpet with a strange look on her face. He set the tray on the dresser and squatted beside her. "Is this some new yoga pose I don't know about?" he asked lightly.

She raised the hem of her shirt, took his hand and placed it flat on her belly. "I have a baby bump, Hutch. I really do!"

# Eleven

She actually did. Only someone who had studied her body as much as he had would have been able to tell, but it was legit. He stroked her stomach. "You do, indeed. A real baby bump. Congratulations."

Simone rested her head against his knee. "I know it sounds stupid, but I was afraid nothing was there."

"And you were deathly ill because…" He raised an eyebrow.

"I said it didn't make sense."

Being so close to her after a week of strained celibacy filled his body with a fine tension. He rose to his feet. "You still haven't eaten lunch. I hate to beat a dead horse, but I'm not willing to see you back in the shape you were in before." He reached out a hand to help her to her feet.

"I'll eat, I swear. But Hutch…" She looked up at him, her eyes sparkling.

"What?"

"I'm feeling lots better."

The look on her face spelled trouble for him. Especially because he hadn't decided what he wanted from her or what Simone needed from him. "I'm glad," he said, pretending to misunderstand her artless invitation.

"Are you going to make me beg?" She wrapped her

arms around his waist and rested her cheek right over his heart—or what was left of it.

He'd spent hours wondering why this woman still had the power to move him. It was more than the past they shared, though that was part of it. It was also more than the fact that he felt protective of her as a mother-to-be in the midst of a high-risk pregnancy.

Even now, he was afraid to name the emotion that made him hold her close. He wouldn't cheapen it by calling it lust. But he couldn't say it was love. He'd loved two women in his life, and both relationships had ended badly. Maybe he was using Simone. Maybe she was using him. In the end, what did it matter? They were emotionally and physically entangled, for better or for worse.

"I assume you're talking about sex?"

She leaned back and scowled at him. "Don't be so stuffy, Doctor."

"You still haven't eaten your lunch." Though he tried to stave off the inevitable, he was hard and ready. And he was pretty sure Simone knew it.

"Bring me the damned sandwich," she said.

"And the soup."

"Oh. My. Gosh. You're going to drive me insane."

He scooped her up in his arms and dumped her on the bed. "I'd say that's a two-way street." He liked carrying her. Some people thought doctors had a God complex. Hutch didn't. At least, he didn't think so. However, he *would* cop to being an inveterate caretaker. It was in his blood.

When he grabbed the food and turned back around, he stumbled. Simone had stripped off her top and bra and was starting in on the rest of her clothes. "You said you would eat," he pointed out. It was hard to speak because his throat was so dry.

She crooked a finger. "I didn't say when."

Even a highly trained medical professional had his limits. He abandoned the meal tray so quickly it was a wonder he didn't spill tomato soup all over Simone's beautiful carpet. "Damn it, woman. Move over."

Simone was giddy. For the first time in days she felt almost like herself. Even more important, she saw tangible proof of her pregnancy. The change in her belly was infinitesimal, but it was real. Without Hutch's careful attention, she might have become so ill that she miscarried. Instead, he had watched over her day and night, despite the fact that she was pregnant under the worst of circumstances.

Her heart overflowed. Everything that had drawn her to him six years ago was still there: his patience, his sense of humor, his deep commitment to his calling. In some ways, *she* was the one who was different. And in the midst of that fresh perspective, she found herself falling more deeply in love with him than ever before.

In the years Hutch had been gone, Simone had grown and matured. Even in her misguided attempt to become a mother, she had found new meaning in her life. The babies she carried were a sacred responsibility.

If she could have her way, she would kneel beside the bed and propose to Hutch. *Marry me. Make a family with me.* But that would be so unfair. So she did the next best thing. She gave herself to him and demanded nothing in return.

She hadn't truly understood what it cost him to stay out of her bed the past few days. Not until now. He was flushed and desperate, his body pinning hers to the bed as his teeth raked the curve of her neck. His intensity didn't frighten her. She understood it in the marrow of her bones.

No force on earth could have kept them apart.

He handled her roughly, with little foreplay. They kissed wildly. She wrestled with him and taunted him, for nothing more than the pleasure of being subdued. He manacled her wrists in one big hand and tried to mount her. She eluded him but didn't get far. They rolled from one side of the mattress to the other, kicking the sheets aside in their frenzy. Hutch muttered her name along with a few choice expletives.

Laughing out loud, she bit his earlobe. "I love you this way," she whispered. "Take what you want. Make me submit. Do it, Hutch."

When he moved between her thighs and thrust all the way in with one deep push, she cried out. "Don't stop. Don't stop."

He took her at her word. She had waved a red flag in front of the bull, and now he was crazed. He rode her hard. Never had she seen him so greedy, so dangerously male. Maybe she had wanted to make him snap. Maybe she reveled in his physical need for her.

Even so, his total absorption was shocking. And thrilling.

Her climax hit hard. Hutch groaned, his face buried in her hair. She clenched him with her inner muscles, wresting from each of them the last ripples of pleasurable sensation. Then he shuddered, his body went rigid and he slumped on top of her.

Time ceased to have meaning. The Grecian shades at her bedroom windows were open, letting the harsh midday sun flood the room. Hutch might have been asleep. She wasn't sure. She didn't know whether to let out an exultant sigh or to burst into tears.

When he didn't move, she surmised that he really was out cold. It was no wonder. He'd spent the last week wandering the halls at night, making sure she was okay. The man had to be exhausted.

Silently, she eased out from under him and went to the bathroom to clean up. Afterward, she put her clothes back on and examined the cold sandwich and soup. The simple meal was a truce flag of sorts. Wrinkling her nose, she made herself eat three-fourths of it.

Perhaps it would have made more sense to go back to the kitchen and heat it up, but she wanted to be around when Hutch roused. She wasn't about to climb back into bed to eat. Though there were two chairs in the bedroom, she didn't like the idea of balancing the tray on her lap. In the end, she sat on the floor, legs crossed, and leaned back against the dresser.

He opened his eyes without drama. One minute he was dead to the world—the next he was completely alert.

"Did you eat?" he asked.

She shook her head at his single-mindedness and held out her hand, indicating what little was left of the meal. "As promised."

Hutch nodded. "Good." Without fanfare, he climbed out of bed, picked up his clothes and disappeared into the bathroom.

She was rapidly discovering that sex in the daytime was far different than sex at night. There was literally nowhere to hide. Not that Hutch had any apparent qualms about his nudity. Fortunately, she was completely clothed.

The urge to escape was humiliating, but she gave in to it, anyway. It was *her* house, her bedroom. Why did she feel the need to disappear?

In the kitchen, she rinsed her lunch dishes and put them in the dishwasher. Hutch still hadn't made an appearance. Chewing her lip, she sat down in front of her laptop. Remembering how he had shut it without her permission should have made her angry. Instead, it made her sad.

Deep in her heart she wanted Hutch to be her date at the masquerade ball. Assuming, of course, she was well enough to attend when the time came. Unfortunately, she sensed that the two of them were fast approaching a showdown. They couldn't go on as they were.

After giving the mock-up of the invitation one last edit, she hit Send. The card stock and envelopes had been selected days ago. The printer already had a list of the recipients and would take care of the mailing. After that, it was only a matter of how many invitees would RSVP with a yes.

Cecelia and Naomi were supposed to drop by tomorrow afternoon to finalize decorating plans, not only for the tables, but for the ballroom as a whole. Deacon had given them carte blanche to spend whatever necessary to make this a night Royal would never forget.

With that one pressing chore completed, Simone pulled up the Neiman Marcus website. She visited the flagship store in Dallas a couple of times a year, but hadn't been recently. Fortunately, even though she had been too sick to travel, her personal shopper several hundred miles away had dropped images of four exclusive ball gowns into Simone's shopping cart.

She clicked on them one at a time. Buying this kind of dress while pregnant might ordinarily have been a risky roll of the dice. But she had lost so much weight, she knew she would still be able to get into her regular size.

With the prospect of a late-stage pregnancy in her future, it seemed only natural to want to look her best on the special night that was rapidly approaching. Two of the dresses were black, another white and the last one was a vibrant red. Although the guests would be asked to wear masks, the evening was formal. No Tin Man and Dorothy or Darth Vader costumes for this crowd.

Royal's elite would be out in full force wearing tuxedos and couture fashion. Both of the black dresses on her computer screen were beautiful and undeniably suitable for the occasion. But she didn't feel a strong connection to either one. The white dress was sexy, but a little too bridal for an unwed mother-to-be.

That left only the red. With Simone's jet-black hair, the

vivid color would be dramatic in the extreme, and the style of the dress was perfect. The halter neckline would leave her shoulders bare. The back would plunge to the base of her spine. Though there were no adornments at all, the fabric was a slubbed-silk blend that would hopefully move and sway as she walked.

Only by trying them on could she decide for sure. She selected the red dress and added one of the black ones in case her first choice didn't work. With overnight express shipping, she would still have plenty of time to shop for other options if neither of these fit well.

She was reaching for her credit card in her purse when Hutch startled her.

"Retail therapy?" he asked casually, dropping a kiss on top of her head.

"How do you do that?" she said.

"Do what?"

"Walk like a ghost."

He shrugged. "Lots of night rounds. We learned not to wake the patients unless absolutely necessary."

"Ah."

He sat at the opposite side of the counter and stared at her. "We need to talk."

She nodded glumly. "I know."

"I would like to go with you to the ultrasound tomorrow."

That wasn't what Simone had expected him to say. She shook her head. "I've already explained why that's not a good idea."

"And I've already told you I want to be there."

"Please don't make this difficult."

His gaze narrowed. "You're the one who's throwing up barriers. Are you saying it's okay for us to sleep together but not to be seen in public?"

"Not at the hospital," she muttered. She was still holding

out hope that Hutch would be her date for the masquerade ball, although to be fair, they would all be wearing masks, so even then no one had to know Hutch and Simone were a couple. Sort of... Who was she kidding? The man had a serious presence and would be recognized—mask or no mask.

Usually in the wake of sexual satisfaction, men were relaxed and mellow. Hutch was livid. His jaw was carved from stone, and his brown eyes burned. "Okay then." He reached for his own laptop, unplugged it and tucked it into the sleek leather briefcase monogrammed with his initials.

Simone frowned. "What are you doing?"

"I'm leaving." He never even looked at her as he calmly gathered his pens and billfold and hospital ID.

Panic made her stomach cramp. "Why?"

"Don't be naive, Simone."

"Tell me," she said, distraught. "The ultrasound is no big deal."

"I'm a doctor," he said, the words colder than any she had ever heard him utter. "Of course it's a big deal. But this is about more than ultrasounds, isn't it? You're making sure that no one but Janine knows we have any kind of connection. I was prepared to be a friend to you and these babies, but you don't need any more friends, do you, Simone?"

She grabbed his arm as he started to walk out of the room. "I don't want you to go," she said. Her heart cracked along fault lines years in the making.

He shrugged her off. "You're eating a suitable amount now. The nausea has subsided to manageable levels. There is absolutely no reason for me to remain. Or am I wrong?"

His gaze was impassive. Yet beneath his icy calm, she understood that he was daring her to do something. Anything.

The trouble was, she had no clue how he felt about her. Could she bear to have a relationship with him knowing the sainted Bethany would always be a ghost in their bed? And even if she could make peace with being second best, would Hutch ever want to be more than her friend? Was he interested in any kind of permanent role as stepparent?

Why would he be? He had the world at his feet.

During a split second when time stood still, mocking her indecision, she imagined and discarded half a dozen scenarios for her future. In none of them was there any real possibility that Hutch would be included.

So she tamped down her terror and her desperation and lifted her chin. "No," she said quietly. "No reason at all."

She had honestly thought she couldn't sink any lower than the miserable days of severe nausea and collapse. But it turned out she was wrong. Watching a stern-faced Troy Hutchinson walk out of her house without a backward glance sent a knife through her chest.

The pain was so intense, she thought she might pass out. She clung to the counter, her breathing shallow and rapid, and tried to stop shaking. Life was so unfair. Why had Troy come back to her at such an inauspicious moment? Why did she still love him when he had left his heart in Africa?

Why had she ever thought her grandfather's will was such a big deal?

In the space of a few weeks, all of her priorities had changed. It was a sobering realization to understand that every single one of her heartaches and heartbreaks was of her own creation.

She wasn't able to sleep in her bed that night. Instead, she went to the guest room and curled up in a ball where Troy had lain. The sheets still smelled like him. She cried for an hour and then made herself stop. It was no longer possible to be the same self-centered, ego-driven woman she had once been.

By this time next year, she would have three infants living under her roof. Hutch or no Hutch, that was her reality. It would have been easy to blame the babies for her situation. Without them, perhaps she and Hutch might have found their way back together for good.

Even reeling from the afternoon's trauma, she had to face the truth. Hutch was gone. The babies were here to stay. And she was their mama. Bless their hearts. Already, she knew they deserved better.

Somehow, she would pick herself up and go on. Somehow…but not tonight. Tonight, she would grieve, and if she was lucky, perhaps she wouldn't dream about the good doctor at all.

# Twelve

When morning came, she tried to avoid looking in the mirror. She knew she was haggard and pale. At least she was strong enough to drive. Her stomach was a little queasy, but that had more to do with heartbreak and a sleepless night than her pregnancy.

She showered and styled her hair on autopilot. Choosing something to wear, once a pivotal point in her daily routine as a young twentysomething, now barely merited a moment's thought. The only reason she cared at all was that she didn't want anyone to feel sorry for her.

With that in mind, she chose a sunshine-yellow dress, sleeveless with white trim, and paired it with cork-heeled sandals. Normally, she used foundation only for special occasions. She'd been blessed with good skin.

Today, though, she needed help covering up the deep shadows beneath her dull eyes. Mascara and brightly colored lip gloss gave her a semblance of health, but if anyone looked closely enough, they wouldn't be fooled.

Frankly, she was terrified. She knew the ultrasound itself was painless, but what the test would reveal was a mystery. If she had asked either Naomi or Cecelia, both would have volunteered to come with her. Was it pride or a need to lick her wounds that kept her from contacting her two best friends?

She would see them later today. If the news she received at the hospital was bad, she wouldn't be able to hide her grief. Maybe that was for the best. They were the only people who would be able to help, the only ones who knew her inside and out.

Much like before, the ultrasound tech was professional but frustratingly uncommunicative when it came to explaining the images on the screen. Simone lay on the table with her eyes closed and prayed.

At last it was over. She dressed again in her cheerful outfit and managed a smile when the tech escorted her to an exam room. Then came the usual pokes and prods. Her blood pressure was a tad low. The scale showed she had lost ten pounds since her last visit. The nurse's expression of consternation was quickly masked, but Simone knew she should be gaining.

The last hurdle was waiting for Dr. Fetter. There was no need for a pelvic exam today. The only reason Simone had come to the hospital was to discuss the ultrasound. So she clasped her hands in her lap and waited.

Twenty-seven-and-a-half minutes. Could have been worse. Janine Fetter burst through the door with a quick apology. "I've got two babies in progress, one about to deliver three weeks early. But we have a few hours yet. Let's take a look at these pictures so you can be on your way."

The other woman opened Simone's record on the laptop. The tech had already uploaded the images. The doctor studied them for interminable minutes, flipping from screen to screen, and finally looked up with a smile. "Congratulations, Simone. As far as I can tell, you have three extremely healthy fetuses. Barring any unforeseen circumstances, I think we're past the immediate danger point."

"But what about all the weight I've lost?" Simone asked, afraid to give in to relief too fast.

Dr. Fetter stood up and tucked her reading glasses in the pocket of her lab coat. "That's the wonderful thing about babies. They've been taking all the nutrition they need. You're the one who's fragile right now, not them. Since your nausea is easing to a great degree, I'm confident we'll see your weight bounce back in the coming weeks."

"Oh…"

The doctor cocked her head. "Simone?"

"Yes, ma'am?"

"You can drop the *ma'am*. I'm not that old."

"Sorry."

"My job is to take care of you and your babies, not to pry into your personal business. But…" She trailed off with a wince.

"But what? Go ahead. Say what you're thinking."

"I don't think you understand what you're facing."

The doctor's lack of faith hurt. "I'm doing my best," Simone said stiffly.

"It's not that. I'm talking about *after* the pregnancy. Having triplets is not a solo event. It requires coordinated teamwork. For quite some time."

"Naomi and Cecelia have promised to help me."

"That's lovely, and I'm sure they mean well, but neither of them knows babies, do they?"

"No. Isn't it a kind of learn-as-you-go thing?"

"Yes and no. Giving birth to triplets means having your life scheduled beyond belief. It means *at least* three adults holding, feeding and diapering three babies around the clock until they begin sleeping through the night. Are your parents physically capable of helping you?"

Simone shook her head. "Physically, maybe, but not emotionally. They won't be the warm, fuzzy kind of grandparents."

"Pardon me for asking, but what about Dr. Hutchinson?"

Simone froze inside. "What about him?"

The doctor clearly tried to choose her words with care. "If there is something between you—if he is willing to help—I think it would be in your best interests to let him."

"And that doesn't strike you as a poor bargain for Hutch?"

"Troy Hutchinson is a grown man. I'm sure he can make those decisions for himself."

Simone left the hospital in a daze. She was thrilled her pregnancy was not in danger. Even so, the confirmation that she would be giving birth to three babies was shockingly real.

She returned home just as Naomi and Cecelia pulled into her circular driveway. Hugging them both, she blinked away stupid tears. "Thanks for coming. I really want to finish all the details for the masquerade ball. The nausea is better for the moment, but it might come back again. I want all my ducks in a row before that happens."

"*If* it happens," Naomi insisted as she gathered up a stack of file folders and followed the other two up the steps.

Cecelia nodded. "Think positive."

Simone didn't shoot back with a sarcastic retort. Naomi was entitled to her optimism. After all, she was the only one not slated to be a parent in the near future. Cecelia, on the other hand, should know better. Even though she seemed to be sailing through her own pregnancy, surely she didn't think the rigors of childbirth and motherhood could be withstood using perky catchphrases.

Suddenly, the truth dawned on Simone. Cecelia wouldn't be any help at all with the triplets. She and Deacon would have their own bundle of joy. How had Simone ignored that glaring reality? Maybe because Cecelia seemed so normal.

Not to mention the fact that the three friends had barely seen each other in the past few weeks.

As the other two women spread all their work on the dining room table, Simone grabbed a handful of plain crackers. "You want anything?" she asked.

Naomi shook her head. "I'm good."

Cecelia declined, as well. "Let's get started," she said. "We have a lot to do."

Planning an event of this magnitude was fun but challenging. Cecelia had struggled at length with color-coded spreadsheets to work out the placement of tables in the large room. The final information would be transferred onto diagrams so the volunteers and hotel staff would have something to work from during decorating and setting the tables.

Naomi, a gifted amateur artist, had sketched out three different themes and color palettes for the event as a whole. "I like the silver and navy," she said. "But do we need an accent color?"

Simone and Cecelia studied the other two contenders. Cecelia pointed at the brightest of the lot. "These colors are great, but they remind me more of a beachy summer event."

"I agree," Simone said. "And I think the burgundy and gray is *too* dark."

Naomi nodded. "So we're going with the silver and navy?"

Cecelia nodded. "I do like it the best. We could always add some pops of crimson."

"Perfect," Naomi said.

Simone jotted notes in her phone. Pregnancy brain must be a real condition, because she was already having trouble remembering things. She hoped one of the dresses she had ordered would fit. With the color scheme they had selected, the red would work nicely.

After an hour, most of the urgent decisions had been made. Naomi yawned, still in the midst of jet lag. Cecelia excused herself to call Deacon about something. Simone nibbled the end of her fingernail.

"Naomi," she said quietly.

"Hmm…" Her friend blinked and sat up straight. "Sorry. I should have flown home yesterday. Early-morning flights are a killer."

"Do you still think me getting pregnant is a terrible idea?"

Naomi lifted an eyebrow. "Does it matter? That horse is out of the barn, if you'll pardon the expression."

"Well, duh. But yes, it does matter."

"Why?"

Simone jumped to her feet and took a glass out of the cabinet, keeping her back to Naomi so the other woman couldn't see her face. "I know you won't lie to me."

"Damn." Naomi sighed. "Nothing like being boxed into a corner. Look at me when I say this."

"That bad, is it?" Simone managed a smile.

Naomi drummed her fingers on the countertop. "I don't understand why you did it. I don't know how in the world you're going to manage. I'm worried about the risks of childbirth and a complicated pregnancy. I'm feeling like an outsider while you and Cecelia are in some special club I can't understand. I'm confused about why Troy Hutchinson is hanging around. I know I want to help you, but my on-camera schedule is not very flexible right now. The whole situation seems like a recipe for disaster."

"Wow…" A tear rolled down Simone's cheek.

"Let me finish." Naomi stood up and wrapped her arms around Simone. "I know you, Simone. I know your generous heart and your loyalty. I've seen you make big mistakes, but I've always noted how hard you work to overcome them. If you want babies, then by damn, I'm going to play the auntie role to the hilt. And if anybody in Royal has the guts to criticize you, they'll have to answer to me."

Simone sniffed. "I think I got snot on your shirt."

"No worries."

"It's a designer piece, isn't it?"

Naomi gave her one last hug and released her. "Gucci. But my dry cleaner is a miracle worker."

Cecelia returned right about then, all starry-eyed from her conversation with her fiancé. She stared at the two in the kitchen. "What did I miss?"

"Not a thing," Naomi said. "Simone was being stupid, but I straightened her out."

Cecelia sniffed. "You shouldn't be unkind to a pregnant woman. We need to be cosseted."

Simone shook her head ruefully. Cecelia—blonde, tall and gorgeous on any given day—was absolutely radiant right now. "I'm fine. Believe me."

Naomi changed the subject. "Have either of you heard any more about the mysterious Maverick?"

Simone felt her face freeze. She knew she should disclose the contents of her own threatening email, but she was afraid. "The rumor in town is that he or she has gone underground. Things have been suspiciously quiet."

Cecelia huffed. "Good riddance, I say. After the pain he caused me and some of the other members of the TCC, he should be prepared for backlash."

After that, the conversation drifted back to the upcoming masquerade ball. Simone ordered pizza for the three of them. When it arrived, they all sat in the backyard to enjoy the evening.

By eight o'clock Simone was drooping. "I hate to run you off, but I have an old-lady bedtime right now." The fatigue came in waves, threatening to squash her beneath its weight.

They walked back through the house and out onto the front porch. After exchanging hugs, Naomi slid behind the wheel of her car. She had picked up Cecelia on the way. "Call us if you need anything."

Cecelia nodded. "I don't like you being here alone. What happened to the yummy Dr. Hutchinson?"

"He has a job, you know." Simone managed a cheery smile. "I'm doing lots better. Don't worry about me."

As the car drove away, she bit her lip, hard enough to remind herself that she was a proud, strong, independent woman. She didn't need Naomi or Cecelia or even Hutch to hold her hand for the next six months.

After turning off the lights and locking up the house, she took a shower and curled up in her bed with the TV remote. She was too restless to read.

Hutch was gone. She might as well get used to it.

The trouble was, everywhere she looked, she saw him. Laughing at her in the kitchen…caring for her in the bedroom when she was too sick to stand…holding her up as he coaxed her through laps around the backyard.

The man was a healer. Looking after the needy was what made him tick. She couldn't and shouldn't read too much into the fact that he had made himself available as her round-the-clock personal physician.

Really personal. She moved restlessly in the bed. It was humiliating to realize that despite his disdain and their argument and his icy exit, she still wanted him.

Glancing at the clock, she saw that it was only nine forty-five. Earlier, she'd been exhausted. Now, with yearning and arousal pulsing through her veins, she had no desire to sleep. At all. With a mutter of ridicule for her own foolishness, she climbed out of bed. After putting on old jeans and a soft cotton sweater in blue and gray stripes, she shoved her feet into espadrilles and tossed her hair up in a ponytail.

She didn't have a clue about the location of Hutch's temporary apartment. But she did know which house he had bought. It was the only one for sale in her neighborhood. Suddenly, her curiosity overcame her good sense.

The pizza she had eaten earlier rolled suspiciously in her stomach, but she ignored it. She was on an investigative mission. Soon, Hutch was going to be living very close to her. What if he brought beautiful women home with him? What if Simone saw them arriving and departing in a steady stream? How was she going to handle that?

The For Sale sign was still up in the front yard, but the Realtor had tacked a Sold banner diagonally across the original notice. Simone parked in the driveway and got out. The landscaping looked scruffy. Nothing a master gardener couldn't take care of in a week or two.

Unlike Simone's more modern home, this was one of the last original structures on the street. It probably dated back to the earliest days of Royal. She remembered that the previous owner, or maybe the one before him, had gutted the inside and created a more open floor plan.

Of course, the front door was locked. Someone had left a single light burning somewhere down the hall. She had to be content with peering through a window. The hardwood floors gleamed. In the front foyer, a set of stairs led upward to the second floor. Did Hutch have plans to settle down and fill his new home with children and a wife?

A wide porch ran all the way around the main floor of the house. It would be perfect for swings and flowerpots and maybe even a hammock on the side facing away from the street. She sat on the back steps and propped her hands behind her. The night breeze picked up, raising gooseflesh on her arms beneath the light sweater.

Hutch had clearly come home to Royal planning to stay. He'd been awarded a prestigious job, and he had family nearby. Everything he could possibly want, Royal had to offer.

It would be up to Simone to learn how to be friendly

without betraying her secret. Hutch could never know she still loved him.

Moodily, she kicked at a cricket that hopped around her shoe. "Go away," she said. "I don't like pests."

"I hope that doesn't mean me."

The deep voice startled her. She jumped to her feet, and as she did so, her toe caught the edge of the top step. She pitched forward in slow motion, striking her knee hard on the wooden floor of the porch.

Hutch reached for her, but she went all the way down in an ungainly heap. Pain shot from her shin to her toe.

"Did you hit your head?" he asked urgently, squatting beside her as she struggled to sit up.

"No."

"Are you sure?"

She gaped at him. "Seriously? You don't even think I'm capable of assessing my own injuries?"

"Do you have a medical degree?" he asked mildly.

Refusing to admit that her leg hurt like hell, she shook her head. "No, Doctor, I don't. I can tell you with confidence, though, I'm fine."

He helped her to her feet. "What are you doing at my house?"

That was a tricky question. He didn't sound mad, but he didn't come across as friendly, either.

"I couldn't sleep."

"So you thought breaking and entering was the way to go?"

# Thirteen

Hutch was stunned at how glad he was to see her. The last twenty-four hours had been rough. He'd been forced to rethink his whole life's plan. And all because of an impetuous, contrary, completely frustrating woman who was pregnant with another man's babies.

Simone's grin was sheepish. "I was curious about your house."

"Would you like a tour?"

"Of course."

He unlocked the front door, feeling the same rush of satisfaction that had overwhelmed him when he signed his name on the sheaf of closing papers. This old house welcomed him. Though he wasn't a whimsical man, he had a healthy respect for the past. He liked feeling a part of something bigger than he was.

He led Simone from room to room, standing back and observing as she got to know his home.

In the dining room, she ran her hand along the chair rail. "It's beautiful, Hutch. The whole place. I can imagine Christmas dinners in this room."

The dining room was larger than most. It included a working fireplace that would be expensive to insure and maintain, but Hutch looked forward to using it the following winter. "I have some painting to do. And a few small repairs. Hopefully, I'll be able to move in a couple of weeks from now."

She stood at the window, looking out into the dark with her back to him. "Why such a big place, Hutch?"

The silence lasted for half a dozen beats. "The usual reasons. I want to have a family someday…a boring, normal life."

She glanced at him over her shoulder. "You'll never be boring, trust me. Arrogant, maybe. Bossy, infuriating and egotistical. But not boring."

"Careful, Simone. Too many compliments and I'll begin to think you might actually like me."

She whirled around. "Those *weren't* compliments, Dr. Hutchinson."

He chuckled. "Come on. I'll show you the kitchen." Actually, it was the kitchen that had sold him on the house. All the modern conveniences were included, but the hardwood floor remained, as well as the antique oak cabinets. During past renovations, granite countertops had been chosen to complement the color of the wood. Cream appliances, clearly special ordered, finished the cozy look.

Simone put her hands to her cheeks. "Oh, Hutch. This is gorgeous."

Her reaction pleased him more than it should. "I'm glad you like it. My parents raised me to appreciate the old with the new. I made an offer on this place the first time I saw it. I knew it was the one for me."

Without overthinking it, he put his hands on Simone's waist and lifted her to sit on the countertop. "I owe you an apology," he said.

"For what?" Her gaze was wary.

"For thinking it was my right to go with you to the ultrasound. You're a grown woman. Those babies you carry are your responsibility. I was out of line." He had realized his mistake after storming out of Simone's house. As much as he hated to admit it, she had been right to go alone.

"It went well," Simone said, her soft smile radiant. "Dr. Fetter says I have three viable fetuses. Three babies, Hutch. Can you imagine? Not one, but three. I don't know whether to be terrified or ecstatic."

"A little of both would be in order." He kissed her forehead. "I have a question to ask you."

Her eyes widened. "What is it?"

"Would you allow me the honor of escorting you to the masquerade ball?" He'd been thinking about it on and off. He realized there was no other man he'd want to see by her side. Even the thought of it left a bad taste in his mouth. In his gut, he knew he was cruising for a fall, yet he was helpless to stop himself.

Knowing the right thing and doing it were two entirely different realities.

Simone nodded slowly. "I like that idea. In fact, I was going to ask *you*, but you beat me to it." She hooked two fingers in the open neckline of his collar and pulled. "Let's seal the deal."

One thing he'd always loved about Simone was her confidence when it came to sex. She had a healthy self-image, and she didn't play coy games. "I could be persuaded," he muttered. Already, his body responded to her invitation. He was pretty sure all she had in mind was a kiss. Still, he was good at persuasion.

With a deep sigh that encompassed relief and inevitability, he slid his hands beneath her hair and cupped her face. "You are so damned beautiful, Simone Parker. I think pregnancy becomes you."

It was the hint of vulnerability in her blue eyes that did him in. It always had. He kissed her slowly, taking his time, demanding a response and receiving more than he asked in return.

Her arms wrapped around his neck in a stranglehold. "Let's declare a truce," she pleaded in between frantic kisses. "Until after the babies are born."

"On what grounds?" He nipped her bottom lip with his teeth. She had put him through hell over the years. It was only reasonable that he made her work for this.

"Neighbors. Friendship. Old times."

"I could live with that. Lift your hips, woman."

When she obeyed instantly, dangerous lust roared through his veins. He ripped her jeans down her legs and tossed them aside. Her white cotton undies struck him as ridiculously erotic. Pressing two fingertips to her center, he caressed her through the layer of fabric.

Simone gasped, arching her back. He lifted her sweater but didn't take the time to remove it completely. Then he went still. "You're not wearing a bra."

As statements went, that one was sophomoric at best. But his brain had gone all fuzzy. "You're not wearing a bra," he repeated, dumbfounded.

Simone cocked her head and gave him an impertinent smile. "It's late. I was all alone. I had no idea the master of the house was planning to seduce me."

"I wasn't planning *anything*," he insisted. "But when a man finds a gift on his porch, he isn't dumb enough to throw it away." Deliberately taking his time, he lowered the zipper on his pants.

Simone shivered. "Are there any beds upstairs?"

"Not even a measly cot. Don't worry, little mama. We'll make do."

"Hurry," she said.

When the tail of his shirt caught in his zipper, Simone laughed. "For a doctor, you're awfully clumsy."

She was taunting him deliberately. It was an old game they played, one guaranteed to drive him insane. At last he managed to free his erection. He was burning up, but a shiver snaked its way down his spine as he looked at his very first houseguest.

"We can do this," he muttered. Somehow.

Simone scooted closer to the edge of the counter. "That refrigerator seems awfully sturdy."

"Good point." He lifted her into his arms and groaned when she wrapped her legs around his waist and her arms around his neck.

"You won't be able to do this too much longer," Simone said.

"Couples can have sex until very late in the pregnancy." He was counting on it.

"I was talking about carrying me, silly man. But I like where you're headed."

Where he was headed was to a padded room if he didn't get inside her soon. "Hold on," he muttered. He pushed her up against the refrigerator and grinned when the cold metal against her bum made her squeak. "I hope you're not attached to this underwear." Panting from exertion, he kept one arm around his prize and used his free hand to shove aside the narrow strip of fabric that was the only thing standing in his way.

When he joined their bodies, Simone moaned and buried her face in his neck. "Oh, Hutch."

He loved the way she said his name, her bedroom voice drowsy with pleasure. Simone could be a firecracker, a sharp-edged combatant. But when he had her like this, she was an entirely different person.

"Hold on, darlin'," he said, barely able to form a coherent sentence. The position taxed his strength, but it also gave him a jolt of satisfaction. Slowly, steadily, he thrust upward, taking her again and again until there was nothing left to take.

In this position, Simone was helpless. He was the aggressor. If there had been anything on top of the fridge, it would have crashed to the floor. He thrust wildly, coming in a climax so powerful it blurred his vision.

Through it all, Simone clung to him and never let go.

At last, the storm passed. He thought he heard and felt her orgasm. He hoped so. In his own delirium, he hadn't been the most considerate of lovers.

He eased her to her feet and steadied her when her legs wobbled. The water had been turned on, so the kitchen tap worked. There was nothing in the house, though. No paper napkins, no cloth towels.

Simone wrinkled her nose. "I should go home now. I need a shower. And it's late."

He nodded. "You want some company?"

She looked up at him, smaller and less combative than in many of their confrontations. Her smile bloomed, her blue eyes clear and happy. "What a lovely idea, Dr. Hutchinson."

That first evening set the tone for days that followed. He and Simone, by unspoken agreement, tabled their arguments and their differences. Often, he slept at her place. Other nights he worked at his own home, unpacking boxes until his eyes crossed with exhaustion. Simone tried to help, but he'd been forced to exile her when he found her lifting a container of heavy glassware in the kitchen. She'd pouted at him, but she hadn't gotten mad.

They were living in a fantasy world, totally ignoring the fact that Simone's life was about to change radically. Not to mention his.

Once the triplets were born, he wouldn't see much of Simone anymore. She would have her hands full caring for three small infants.

The thought of losing her again made his stomach clench. He reminded himself that he hadn't been home from Sudan long. Royal had dozens of available women, one of whom might even be his soul mate if he believed in such a thing. He was a man in his prime. During med school, he hadn't sown many wild oats. He'd been focused on getting through and excelling. It was what his parents expected and what Hutch wanted.

Now was the perfect time in his life to see who was out there for him. Not that he was foolish enough to think that there was another woman who could set his blood on fire like Simone did—but a man could hope.

Fortunately, Simone was incredibly busy getting things ready for the masquerade ball. He didn't have to worry about neglecting her when things got crazy at the hospital. The advent of the full moon meant a rush of babies being born. Though he hadn't picked up many patients of his own yet, he'd been called in on several high-risk cases.

A breech birth. One drug-addicted newborn. A seven-month infant delivered prematurely as a result of a car accident. Thankfully, in that situation, mother and baby had stabilized, but it was touch and go for a while.

There were seventy-two straight hours where Hutch didn't make it home at all. He snatched a few hours of sleep in the doctors' lounge, but it was fragmented rest and unsatisfying. He lived off hospital food and bottled water. The only way he knew time had passed was that he changed into clean scrubs twice a day.

Several times he thought about texting Simone, but each moment he pulled out his phone, he ended up being summoned to one labor room or another.

His week went from bad to worse on Wednesday. A young woman, barely six months pregnant and a recent transplant to Royal, came in through the ER. Her vitals were all over the map and the monitors showed fetal distress. It took hours, but finally a team nailed down the cause. The woman was diagnosed with a previously undetected and very rare blood abnormality. She was hemorrhaging internally.

Despite every attempt to save them, the mother and baby both died.

Unfortunately, Hutch's on-call rotation ended on that note. What he desperately wanted was to stay at the hospital and lose himself in work, trying to get those images out of his head. But that choice would endanger the patients in his care because of his extreme exhaustion.

Instead, he would do the mature, responsible thing. He would go home and sleep.

Simone bounced from day to day on a bubble of pure happiness. All of her problems were still out there on the horizon, but for now, life was good.

The masquerade party appeared destined to be a smashing success. Over 95 percent of the invitees had responded with an enthusiastic yes.

Thanks to Simone and her staff, the event received unprecedented saturation in both traditional print media and radio as well as blogs, email blasts and social media. Naomi and Cecelia had coordinated an entire crew of volunteers to help transform the ballroom. Tomorrow, the actual decorations would start going up.

Every day, Simone tried on the red dress, almost superstitiously afraid to leave anything to chance. She'd heard some pregnant women say they'd had to resort to maternity clothes overnight. One day they were fine with their jeans unzipped, the next, nothing fit.

She didn't want that to happen to her.

Knowing that Hutch would be her date for the party was both exciting and alarming. Even with Hutch wearing a mask, everyone would know who he was. Then the speculation would begin.

It probably already had, but this would be the first and likely only time she and Hutch would make an official appearance as a couple. Simone was pregnant. Hutch was back from Africa. Lots of people would make educated guesses.

She hadn't heard a word from him in almost four days. Fortunately, she wasn't the kind of woman who needed constant attention from a man. Still, when he neither texted nor called, she began to wonder if she had done something to upset him.

Though she was feeling markedly more like herself, Dr. Fetter had been insistent that Simone not overdo it. Thus, even though Thursday would be the last full workday before the party, Simone closed the office at five sharp on Wednesday and drove herself home.

Now that she felt like eating again—at least most of the time—she was actually hungry. Would Hutch be up for dinner at a quiet restaurant? Honestly, that sounded wonderful to Simone. This pregnancy was taking more of a toll on her body than she had anticipated. Her usual fount of energy was nowhere to be seen. Unwinding with Hutch and a nice, juicy steak might perk her up.

On a whim, she texted him before getting in the shower. By the time she was clean and dry and dressed, he still hadn't answered. Frowning, she tried to recall his schedule. She was almost certain he'd said he'd be off on Thursday *and* Friday, which meant that his shift should have ended this afternoon.

Maybe she would pick up carryout Chinese and go over to his house. If he was tired, too, he might welcome the food and the company. At one time, she would have been reluctant to invade his privacy. They'd been on good terms lately, though.

She sent him another text.

Still, he did not answer.

Bit by bit, her confidence eroded. She and Hutch were temporary. They both acknowledged that. What if Hutch had met someone else? What if he regretted his offer to escort her to the masquerade ball?

Maybe he and the mystery woman were over at his house now christening Hutch's new bed. He'd been sleeping on a mattress on the floor, but she had met the furniture delivery truck day before yesterday and opened Hutch's house so the men could set up the massive cherry king-size bed in the master suite.

Even with misgivings swirling in her stomach, she grabbed her keys and climbed into the car. Unfortunately, the Chinese restaurant was in the wrong direction, but the detour gave her more time to think. The order took no time at all. When she arrived at Hutch's place, the house was dark, and his car was in the driveway.

Now, she began to get worried. What if he were ill?

That was dumb. The man was a doctor. He was more than capable of taking care of himself.

Again, she wondered if his sudden absence from her life was because he had realized he was wasting his time. The man had a strongly developed moral conscience. Perhaps it had finally occurred to him that Simone was not meant to be a part of his life.

Leaving the food in her car for the moment, she got out and walked up the front steps. Testing the door gingerly, she found it locked.

Maybe he had come home and gone to bed early. At six forty-five? Not likely. Then what was the explanation for the fact that the house was in total darkness? Again, her mind went to the other-woman theory. If Hutch had brought someone home with him, they could be upstairs.

With her chest tight, she took a deep breath and let it out. Hutch would never sleep with two women at the same time. If he met someone else, he would do the honorable thing and tell Simone face-to-face.

Even so, she had a bad feeling about this. Something

was definitely amiss. Had the blackmailer chosen now as the time to reveal Simone's secret? Was Hutch pondering how to boot her out of his life?

She had to *make* herself walk around the porch. The easy thing would be to run away. But she had to be sure Hutch was okay.

The end of her search was anticlimactic. She found him sitting on the top step, slumped over, his elbows on his knees, his head in his hand.

"Hutch?" She crouched beside him, alarmed. Something in his body language kept her from touching him. "Why didn't you answer my texts?"

"Go home, Simone."

She froze. His voice was monotone, gruff and raspy. "Have I done something to offend you, Hutch? Talk to me. I can't fix it if you don't let me know what it is."

He stood up, forcing her to do the same. His eyes were the dull brown of fallen leaves in the late fall. Yet somehow, a tiny flame in them seared her. His body language spoke volumes. "For God's sake, Simone. The whole damn world doesn't revolve around you. Not everything I do or don't do is about *you*. Grow up, damn it. I don't need you hovering every minute of every day."

# Fourteen

Simone gaped at him, her heart imploding in shock and bitter hurt. Never, even in their most painful days before he left for Sudan, had Hutch lashed out like this. He'd always possessed a maturity beyond his years. Hutch was never cruel.

Apparently, people changed.

She could do nothing about the tears that spilled down her cheeks. Stepping back awkwardly, unconsciously putting distance between herself and the furious, aggressive male, she held out a hand. "I shouldn't have come. My mistake."

Hutch only stared at her.

Everything crumbled in slow motion. The faux happiness that had helped her ignore their problems was a sham. She'd been living in a dream world.

One last time, she tried to get through to him. "I brought dinner. Chinese. Your favorite. I'll grab it from the car."

"I'm not hungry. And I'm not in the mood for company."

"I see." She didn't. Not at all. But she wasn't stupid. "Okay, then." Embarrassed, humiliated, hurt and angry, she gave him a curt nod. Without another word, she fled.

It took her three tries to put the car into gear. She was crying so hard, she couldn't see. At the end of Hutch's driveway, she stopped. She shouldn't operate a vehicle in her condition. Resting her head on the steering wheel, she wept.

Hutch had taken a bad day and made it worse. In the midst of his burning guilt and regret over what had happened at the hospital, he had added the poisonous taste of shame. The memory of Simone's face galvanized him into action.

Racing around the side of the house, he inhaled sharply when he saw her car still parked in his driveway. He jerked open the driver's-side door and felt like the lowest kind of scum when he realized she was crying too hard to make the short trip home.

"Oh, hell," he groaned. "Come here, baby. I'm a bastard. Let me hold you."

He scooped her out of the car without a struggle. Bumping the door closed with his hip, he strode back to the house.

Inside, he wasted no time. He carried her up the stairs and sat down with her on his bed. "I'm sorry, Simone. My bad temper had nothing to do with you. Please forgive me."

She had cried so hard her face was blotchy and red. And she couldn't stop. He held her tightly, unable to stem the flow of tears.

It was a hell of a time to figure out he was still in love with her.

The bolt of truth was a knife to his gut. Was this something new, or had his feelings for Simone lain dormant all those years in Sudan? Maybe deep down, his guilt over Bethany's death wasn't so much about not being able to save her as it was knowing he had never loved her the way he should have.

Bethany had given her heart and her trust to him. Had he unwittingly offered her far less in return?

He stroked Simone's hair. "Hush now. You'll make yourself sick again."

It took a long time, but finally, Simone wore herself out.

He wiped her face with the tail of his shirt. To explain would be to dump some of his anguish on her, but how else could he account for being so deliberately cruel? "I lost a mother and a baby today," he muttered. It embarrassed him that his voice broke on the word *baby*.

Simone struggled to sit up. She stared at him with big, wet eyes. "Oh, Hutch. What happened?"

He gave her an abbreviated version. "I don't think the patient ever really had a chance, but we tried. God, we tried. I kept seeing the nurses' faces. It's hard, you know. We're supposed to maintain that professional distance...so we can do what we have to do. Loss of life in any circumstance is difficult beyond words. This...this was devastating."

"The baby couldn't be saved?"

"No. She looked perfect. Tiny, but perfect. Still, it was far too soon. Sometimes, even with all our sophisticated equipment and technology, we can't overcome that. We save dozens of preemies, often against large odds. Today we lost. She lived for an hour."

Simone—generous, openhearted Simone—wrapped her arms around him and held him so tightly he could barely breathe. Or maybe that was his reaction to knowing he had the love of his life in his arms.

She shuddered. "I can't even imagine what it was like for all of you. I couldn't do what you do. How does anyone bear it?"

He *knew* what she was thinking. "You don't have to worry about your pregnancy, Simone. The woman today had a serious medical condition. You're healthy and strong and perfectly normal."

"I don't think anyone's ever called me normal." Her

smile was wry, her face still damp as she pulled back and stared at him.

He wanted to ease her down on the bed and make love to her to erase the memories of the day. But he felt raw and unsteady and light-headed. It was a time for caution. Simone didn't deserve to be used as tranquilizer. He needed to take stock of what was happening.

Carefully, he released her and stood up. "Did you mention something about food?" he asked, trying to lighten the mood.

Simone's face was hard to read. She rose as well, her posture defensive, arms wrapped tightly around her waist. And no wonder. He'd treated her like dirt. She shrugged. "It's hot outside. I don't know if we should risk it. Food poisoning is not fun."

He winced. "True." And in Simone's condition, it could be lethal. "What if we drive through somewhere and grab a milk shake and fries?"

She raised an eyebrow. "For a doctor, you don't seem to have a grasp of good nutrition."

He knew she was teasing him. "After today, I think we could both use some junk food, don't you? How about it?"

Simone hesitated. "I need to get home," she said.

"You're mad."

"No." She shook her head vehemently. "I forgive you. But the next two days are going to be tough. Dr. Fetter says I need to pace myself."

"Of course." He didn't want to eat alone. He sure as hell didn't want to sleep alone. But his outburst on the back porch had changed something. Maybe Simone was rethinking her relationship with him.

The awkward conversation ended there. Simone headed downstairs with him on her heels. Once she climbed into her car and started the engine, he leaned down, one hand on top of the car. "Are you sure you're okay to drive?"

Simone nodded. "I'm good."

He winced, remembering what else he had to tell her. "I'd hoped to do something fun with you tomorrow, but my dad needs me to help him in the garden. The man does love his fresh produce, but he overplanted his year."

"No worries, Hutch." Her gaze was guarded. "I'm going to be working flat out, too. I'll see you Friday evening."

"What time do you want me to pick you up?"

"Five thirty will work. I have to be there early. I could drive my own car, though," she said. "No need for you to hang around."

"I could help."

She pursed her lips. "Maybe. What if I let you know tomorrow?"

"I'm picking you up, Simone. End of discussion." His temper started a slow boil. Something had shifted. Was it the things he had said to her earlier? Had he damaged a relationship already on shaky ground? Or was something else going on?

"Fine." Simone revved the engine. "Good night, Hutch."

He was forced to step back or risk having her run over his foot. After his recent behavior, he couldn't blame her.

Simone refused to think about Dr. Troy Hutchinson. He could hurt her only if she allowed it. The new lives growing in her womb were all she needed. Even if Hutch wanted to hang around after the babies came, she wouldn't have time for him.

Tonight had exposed a valuable truth. Hutch didn't love her. It hurt to admit it. It hurt like hell. But she was better off accepting reality.

She didn't hold his bad temper against him. Anyone in a similar situation would be raw and grief stricken and likely to lash out. No, that wasn't the root of her sadness. What pained her was that Hutch, in his hour of need, hadn't turned to Simone for help and comfort. If she dug deep to the heart of their relationship, she saw the chasm between what she wanted and what he was willing to give her.

Friendship? Yes. They had mended fences over their earlier breakup and moved on. Sex? The sex was amazing… hot, intense and deeply satisfying. She and Hutch had no problems in the bedroom.

She could even see that the two of them had established a tentative relationship of trust. Certainly, she trusted him to look after her physical well-being. Not only that, but Hutch had been very honest with her about Bethany. There were very few secrets between them.

Though in Simone's case, the one she had omitted was gigantic.

Tonight's drama with Hutch had stolen her appetite, replacing it with the now-familiar nausea. Nursing a cup of hot tea, she curled up in the comfy chair in her bedroom and opened her laptop.

For some reason, she had never deleted the message from the mysterious Maverick. The cryptic note was evidence, in any case. Maybe he or she was not a threat anymore. Word of her pregnancy was slowly beginning to spread. The cat was out of the bag. Perhaps Maverick had wanted to extort money from her to keep her pregnancy quiet.

When she opened Facebook, she saw that she had received a new message. She clicked on it and read, "Your day of reckoning is near. Maverick."

That was odd. And menacing. She placed a hand on her stomach, instinctively alarmed. It was one thing to fear for her own safety. Now she carried the responsibility for three tiny humans.

The only secret she had kept from Hutch and her friends…from everyone, in fact, was private. This Maverick person would have no reason to know what Simone had done…or at least *why* she had done it.

She hated feeling helpless. Even more, she hated feeling powerless to track down the subpar person who held grudges against so many of Royal's upstanding citizens. She sure as heck wasn't going to engage in an online conversation with Maverick. The best thing to do was to go about her business, pretending that everything was normal.

Thursday morning dawned bright and clear and sunny. After a restless sleep, Simone was grateful for weather that lifted her spirits. Sometime around three the night before, she had turned on the light and made a list. She was a mother-to-be with a successful business to run.

This thing with Hutch, well, it was fun, but it was also painful. After tomorrow night, it was probably best if she put an end to it. At least that way, she would be the one calling the shots and not Hutch.

Beneath her surface calm, her heart was breaking. She wanted it all. The babies. The company she had built from the ground up. The respect of her parents. And last but not least, she wanted the man she had loved since she was twenty-two years old.

Fifty percent wasn't a bad average. In baseball, it was extraordinary. Too bad she had never been good at sports.

After showering and drying her hair, she put on a new black knit dress and topped it with a cheery hot-pink cardigan. The knit fabric and empire waistline were designed to grow along with her belly. Today, it simply looked liked a casual outfit suited to a pleasant spring day.

She had called Tess and told her she was coming in a little late. Tess was brilliant. Simone had hired the younger woman straight out of business school with a freshly minted MBA. At no time had Tess ever let her down or not been able to handle the work. Simone was counting on that.

When she made it in to her office, she asked Tess to come in and close the door. Tess might have been alarmed, but she didn't show it. "What's up, boss?"

Simone had insisted that Tess call her by her first name. But Tess had just as insistently refused. Simone eyed the girl on the other side of the desk. From her magenta-accented pixie cut to her triple-pierced right ear, Tess was an original.

For some reason, Simone was having a hard time getting this conversation off the ground. "Tess," she said, "are you happy working with me?"

Tess nodded. "Of course."

"And do you have plans to move up the ladder? To go somewhere else? Dallas, maybe? Or Houston?"

"None." A tiny frown appeared between Tess's brows. "Are you trying to get rid of me?"

"Not at all. Quite the opposite."

"I'm confused."

Simone realized she wasn't handling this well. "I suppose you know I'm pregnant."

Tess grimaced. "Yes, ma'am."

"What you may not know is that I'm having triplets."

"Good God." Tess's eyes rounded. "I hope it's not contagious." She shuddered. "I'm not antibaby, but three?"

"Yeah," Simone said wryly. "It's a lot to take in. But on the other hand, it's a done deal, so I'm trying to make plans."

"No offense, boss, but I'm not really a fan of little kids. They scare me. Probably comes from my dad dropping me on my head when I was six months old. I think it warped me."

Tess was talking a mile a minute, clearly rattled.

Simone sighed. "Stand down, Tess. I'm not asking you to babysit. I want to know if you're willing to be top dog of this company for a year. I'd still be involved in all major decisions, but you would be in charge. What do you think?"

"Where will you be?"

"At home. I'll have help with the triplets...out of necessity. There's no way I can do it alone. But I'll be their mother. Even saying that out loud sounds strange. I want these babies, Tess. I'm going to give this motherhood thing a hundred percent of my time when they're born, at least for a year. After that, if we've managed some kind of routine, I may consider day care. But that's a long time off, so I can't think about that now."

"You're awfully brave."

"Not brave. Just determined. If you need time to think about this, I understand."

"I don't have to think about it," Tess said with a huge grin. "I'm honored. And pumped. You can count on me, boss."

"When we get around to this new arrangement, do you think you could call me Simone?"

Tess shrugged sheepishly. "Maybe. I'll try."

"Good. And, Tess?"

"Yes, ma'am?"

"This is between you and me for the next few months. I don't want anyone to know I'm thinking about taking a sabbatical. It's my business."

"I get it." She mimed sealing her lips. "Your secrets will go to my grave."

"Thank you." Simone shooed her out and tackled the stack of paperwork overflowing her inbox. Between snail mail and email, she never caught up. The business was growing undeniably. Soon, she might have to consider adding another employee. But then again, with Simone gone for a year, they might lose ground. It would be a game of wait and see.

For the second day in a row, she closed the office at five. As someone accustomed to keeping late hours when in the midst of a project, it was not her usual behavior. She liked to think motherhood was going to be good for her. Keeping a healthier lifestyle...all of that.

She didn't call Hutch that evening. Or text him.

He didn't contact her, either. Maybe they were both ready to admit their relationship was never going to blossom into something permanent. Simone had known that from the beginning. Getting pregnant with an unknown man's sperm had erased virtually every chance she had to get married. No one she knew would be willing to take on a young mom with three babies, even if that man was madly in love with her.

Hutch wasn't madly in love. She didn't deceive herself there. He liked her. He enjoyed having regular sex. Neither of those things guaranteed a happily-ever-after. As she let herself into the house, she told herself she could handle this baby thing with or without Hutch.

Though she cooked oatmeal for dinner, she was barely able to eat half. Afterward, she read and watched TV until ten o'clock. Like a high school girl in the throes of a crush, she picked up her phone every ten seconds to check for messages.

The screen remained blank.

Uncertainty was painful and demoralizing. She was even more resolved to end things with Hutch after the ball. Never mind that her heart raced in panic at the thought. The two of them had enjoyed reuniting. Nothing that came afterward pointed to a rosy future. Even Hutch himself had never made any pretense of wanting to be a father to her babies. He was too honest to lead her astray.

More honest than she deserved.

When she finally turned out the light and curled up in a ball underneath the covers, her heart raced. Tomorrow night was big. Huge, in fact. A good turnout meant significant sums of money for the charity.

Unfortunately, all she cared about at the moment was seeing Hutch again and, hopefully, dancing the night away. Even if the bliss would only be temporary.

# Fifteen

Hutch had some big decisions to make. He knew it, but he couldn't quite wrap his head around what that would mean. Everyone thought he was so smart, so damned wise. The truth was, he was as clueless as the next guy.

It felt odd to put on a tux again. He'd been forced to buy a new one for the masquerade ball. His time in Africa had made him leaner, harder. Living life on the edge of civilization had taught him how to survive without many of the comforts of home. His physical stamina was greater than it had ever been.

He looked at himself in the mirror and straightened his bow tie with a grimace. All he had ever wanted in life was to make his parents proud of him. On a whim, he grabbed his keys and headed out to the car. It was too early to pick up Simone, but he had a sudden urge to see his father.

Both his parents were sitting outside on the porch enjoying a cold beer when Hutch arrived. His mother was her usual stately, put-together self. His dad was scruffy today. Apparently, he'd worked in the garden again.

Hutch took a wicker chair and sat across from them.

His mother cocked her head. "Did I forget it's my birthday? You look very handsome this evening, Hutch."

The senior Hutchinson nodded. "You clean up real nice. But I'm guessing you didn't come to pull more weeds."

"Should I leave you two boys alone?" his mother asked.

"No, ma'am." Hutch might be closing in on his midthirties, but his mother still ruled their family with an iron fist. "I want you both to hear this."

"So serious," she said, smiling. But he noted a trace of anxiety in her brown eyes that were so like his.

His father frowned. "Spit it out, son. Bad news never gets any better in the waiting."

"Who said I have bad news?" Hutch ran a hand over his head, aware that he was starting to sweat.

His mother leaned forward and patted his knee. "You look as somber as a judge. Tell us, son."

Hutch rubbed his damp palms on his pants legs. "Do you remember Simone Parker?"

Both of the older adults flinched. "We do," his father said. "Your grandmother never got over the way she treated you. Thank God she's passed on. I have a feeling she wouldn't like what you're about to tell us."

"You raised me to believe that people deserve second chances."

"Yes, we did," his mother said. "But that woman was wrong for you in many ways."

Hutch bristled. "Like what? I thought you were glad she convinced me to go to Sudan."

His dad drained his beer and set the bottle on the floor. "We were. We still are. Those years will make a huge difference in how you practice medicine. But this Simone… well, she's…" He trailed off.

"She's selfish and shallow," his mother said sharply. "She has a reputation around town as a bit of a snob. Only child. Wealthy parents."

"I'm an only child," Hutch pointed out mildly, though he felt anything but calm. "I'm surprised to hear both of you speak so negatively. Simone might have been a little self-centered in her youth, but she's changed."

His father shrugged. "If you've come to ask for our blessing, I don't think we can offer it. But you're a grown man and long past needing our approval. Give it some time, boy. Sleep with her, but don't marry her."

Hutch's mother punched her husband in the arm...hard. "Don't talk like that, Edward Hutchinson. What's gotten into you?"

"You don't like her, either."

"I don't know her," she conceded.

Hutch stood up. He wasn't sure what he had expected from his parents. Maybe he just wanted someone to tell him that what he was contemplating wouldn't make a damn fool out of him. "I haven't made any big decisions, so you can quit having heart attacks. I suppose I was hoping you'd tell me that true love lasts."

"Well, of course it does," his father said. "The trick is to marry the right person in the first place."

Hutch was not in a good frame of mind to go to a party. He was horny and agitated and completely confused. Just when he thought he had things figured out, something happened. Either Simone pulled back, or he did. And now his parents, thanks to him, had weighed in on the situation. With a big ol' negative.

He parked in Simone's driveway and stared up at the house. The structure was attractive and neatly kept. Exactly like its owner. The golden brick with the mahogany shutters at the windows was modern and, at the same time, classic.

Fumbling to slide his phone into his pocket, he told himself that tonight was not the time for grand gestures. Tonight was mostly business for Simone. He was only her escort, not her boyfriend. In fact, this wasn't some romantic date where the two of them would be all alone.

Two-thirds or more of Royal's movers and shakers would be out in force tonight. Maybe they would come to show off their jewels and their trophy wives. Perhaps they really cared about the charity. Either way, the word of the evening was *money*...and lots of it.

Simone answered the door as soon as he knocked. He took a step backward, feeling a mule kick to the chest. She looked incredible.

"Hi, Hutch," she said breathlessly. "Come on in. I'm almost ready. A phone call slowed me down."

She was fluttering, nervous, her eyes not quite meeting his.

Without overthinking it, Hutch captured her wrist and gently reeled her in. "You look stunning, Simone." He kissed her softly, keeping a tight check on his caveman instincts. Her lips were soft beneath his. Her hands landed on his shoulders. For a few breath-stealing moments, he lost himself in the kiss. He wanted to carry her up the stairs and lock the door.

His heart pounded, his entire body hard as iron. He wanted to take and take and take. The prospect of sharing her with hundreds of other people tonight was unappealing at best.

She wore a red dress designed to make a statement. Simone Parker was *in* the building. In his arms she felt fragile and small, though he knew she was anything but. Simone was smart and strong and determined. Having triplets would be extremely challenging, but he had no doubts about her ability to cope.

In the end, he had to force himself to release her and step back. Her silky black hair fell in soft waves about her shoulders. Her sapphire eyes, framed in dark lashes, sparkled.

Her grin was self-conscious. "I really do have to finish getting ready."

He waved a hand. "Go. I'll entertain myself down here."

He glanced at his watch. "You'd better hurry, though, if we're supposed to be getting there early."

Simone rolled her eyes. "I'm not the one who started that kiss."

She disappeared before he could retaliate. With a smile on his face, he prowled the downstairs restlessly. Anticipation flooded his veins. He and Simone had things to discuss. Big things. Life-changing things. Maybe this time, they could rewrite the ending.

After the talk with Tess, Simone had begun to feel as if she finally had a handle on the mess that was her life. Seeing Hutch at her door just now in black tie knocked the wind out of her. He was so handsome, so brilliant, so unbelievably sexy. Why would a man like that want to tie himself to a woman like Simone? Nevertheless, she was going to give it a shot.

She had built her business on taking calculated risks. Hutch cared about her. The fact that he wanted her physically was irrefutable. The only question that remained was how he would respond if Simone asked for more.

Earlier, she had decided to break things off with Hutch, but that was the coward's way out. Tonight, after the ball, she was going to lay her cards on the table. Love was a hard thing to offer outright, but maybe she owed him that. Above all, she was going to confess the truth. It would put her in a bad light, no doubt about it. Still, there was no hope for a future with Hutch unless she was completely honest.

After tweaking her hair one last time and applying a bold lipstick to match her dress, she eyed her reflection in the long mirror on the back of her closet door. Not too shabby. She placed her hand, palm flat, against her belly. Feeling the tiny bulge filled her with wonder and humility.

Despite everything she had done wrong in her life, here was a chance for a new start. More than anything else, she wanted to be a good mother to these three babies. Unlike her own upbringing, she was determined to be a hands-on parent. Though she would have to have help, professional or otherwise, she was going to be *present*.

A quick glance at the clock told her there was no time left to linger. Lifting her skirt in one hand, she made her way carefully down the stairs. Hutch stood at the bottom, waiting. She held up a hand. "No more kissing. I'm camera ready, as Naomi would say."

His smile was wicked. "I can wait. Maybe." He ran his thumb over her cheekbone. "Let's just say I'm really looking forward to removing that dress in a few hours."

"Hutch!" She gaped at him.

He shrugged. "If you don't want me to open the gift, you shouldn't wrap it so nicely."

They made it to the hotel in record time. Because they were early, traffic wasn't bad yet. In the parking lot, Simone handed Hutch the rectangular box that had come in the mail. "These are our masks. Will you hang on to them for the moment?"

He grimaced, exhibiting the usual male reluctance for such things. "Sure."

The following hour was taken up with a variety of last-minute responsibilities. While Hutch cooled his heels in the bar, Simone met with Naomi and Cecelia for one final, excited rundown. Everything had fallen into place perfectly.

At last, it was time to find Hutch and start enjoying the more personal portion of the evening. He had returned to the car in search of fresh air and his business card wallet. After a quick text to ascertain his whereabouts, she joined him there, relishing the moment of privacy inside the vehicle to catch her breath and collect her thoughts before the event began in earnest. "I missed you, my handsome doctor."

As masquerade parties went, this one was going to be

ultrasophisticated, no costumes or elaborate ensembles allowed. The men had been instructed to wear traditional tuxes. With so many of them in the room, anonymity would be upheld. The women, on the other hand, had been asked to choose a color. The masks for the female guests would complement their gowns. Simone's mask was scarlet trimmed with delicate black lace.

Her heart beat faster when Hutch put on his black mask. It made him look remote and dangerous. "Will you help me with mine?" she said. "So I won't mess up my hair?"

Hutch took the mask from her trembling fingers and carefully fitted it over her head, smoothing any strands of hair that were pushed out of place. Then he bared the side of her neck and pressed a kiss just below her ear. "I could eat you alive," he muttered.

His hot breath against her skin and the subtle rake of his teeth against her sensitive flesh flooded her body with heat and yearning. "I could say the same to you," she whispered. "I used to think your white lab coat was the sexiest piece of clothing you owned. But tonight you're seriously hot. I'll have my hands full keeping other women from stealing you away."

He cupped his hand around her breast, using his thumb to tease the nipple that beaded beneath the fabric. "Does that mean you want me all to yourself?"

Simone shuddered. Arousal stole through her veins and made her reckless. "I dare anyone to lay a hand on you, Troy Hutchinson. For tonight, you're mine."

He groaned, resting his forehead against hers. "What are we doing, damn it? I can't walk in there with an erection. Hell, Simone, you make me crazy."

For once, he didn't sound too happy about that. She sat back in her seat and tried to steady her breathing. "I'll go in alone," she said. "You can follow when you're ready."

Beneath the mask, his jaw was like iron. "I'm ready

now," he growled, deliberately misunderstanding her suggestion. The words were forced beneath clenched teeth.

Helpless to stem the tide of insanity that had overtaken them, she touched him lightly through his trousers. His erection was as hard as his jaw. "Oh, Hutch," she said. "What I wouldn't give to walk away from all of this. I don't know if I can wait."

"Maybe you don't have to." He leaned over her. The windows of his black SUV were tinted. No one was around to notice when he slid a hand beneath her skirt and ran his fingers from her ankle up her thigh to the edge of her satiny underpants.

"Um, Hutch…" She gripped the door handle with her right hand.

"Relax, Simone."

That was easy for him to say. Her entire body clenched in anticipation of what he was about to do. When he pressed two fingers against the very heart of her yearning, she gasped. Carefully, he pleasured her.

She should have made him stop. Cecelia and Naomi were expecting her inside. But none of that mattered. Hutch took her somewhere dark and visceral and so compelling, she lost everything except the feel of his hands on her body.

When she came, her fingernails left marks in the leather seat. Chest heaving, she opened one eye. "You're some kind of sorcerer," she said.

His grin was a slash of white teeth beneath his mask. "All the better to seduce you, my dear."

Heart pounding still, she hesitated. This was where her lack of experience failed her. "Do you want me to…"

"No." He said the word forcefully, though his body spoke otherwise. "When I have you in bed tonight, and I'm deep inside you with you crying out my name, *then* I'll get what I'm waiting for…but not before."

Simone nodded, unable to find the words to tell him

what she felt. With all her heart, she wanted to believe Hutch would forgive her when she told him the truth. Honestly, she wanted to tell him now and get it over with... end the suspense. That wasn't an option, though. She had a party to execute.

They barely spoke after that. Hutch brooded, gaze trained out his window as Simone fussed with her hair and makeup. When she was reasonably certain she was back to normal, she picked up her small clutch purse. "I'm ready."

The Bellamy was magnificent. From the vast, sophisticated lobby, down the wide hallways covered in luxurious Oriental rugs, to the entranceway into the ballroom, the place was awash in flowers and tiny white lights and golden gauze bows. Pale orchids in cream and lavender emitted a subtle fragrance. Cecelia's touch was on every bit of design and decor in the building. This new hotel was destined to become a centerpiece of Royal's social scene.

Hutch was deeply grateful he was wearing a mask. He felt raw and gutted. If he hadn't known he was in love with Simone before, he knew it tonight. She was incandescent. Pregnancy gave her a glow of contentment. His physical need for her was only outweighed by a gut-deep certainty that she was the only woman who could make him whole.

After his stunt in the car, which slowed Simone and him down, a crowd of guests already gathered in the lobby and moved toward the ballroom.

The Bellamy had hired ample staff for the big evening. In addition to its own roster of chefs and waiters, tonight's event demanded even more. Every guest would be expecting perfection.

Even with attendees wearing masks, it was easy to pick out a few here and there. He was almost certain he identified Harper Lake with one of the Tate brothers, though he couldn't tell the twins apart. Clay Everett limped in with his gorgeous secretary. That might raise a few eyebrows.

Thirty minutes after the official starting time of the masquerade ball, the room was packed. Old friends and new. Octogenarians whose history went way back in Royal. Young, hip entrepreneurs who had made their mark in reshaping the town. Everything in between.

After twenty minutes of mingling and chatting, Simone was flushed and sparkling with excitement. "Let's dance," she said.

"I thought you'd never ask."

Hutch led her onto the floor and tucked her against his chest. With Simone wearing heels, they could have kissed easily. He inhaled sharply, dizzy from the scent of delicate perfume and warm female skin.

He held her firmly, confidently. As they twirled around the room, he saw people watching them. All male eyes were on Simone. She would stand out in any crowd with her dark hair and sexy dress. His arms tightened around her. No man in the room was good enough for her, not even him.

Over the past few weeks, Simone had told him stories about the headaches involved in planning tonight's event. The committee had squabbled over which band to hire. A few people wanted a modern, trendy group. But in the end, given the stately atmosphere of the hotel and the knowledge that the crowd would include a variety of ages, the decision was made to go with a small orchestra. The playlist included songs from all decades, primarily the kind of romantic pieces that encouraged slow dancing cheek to cheek.

Hutch thought it was a brilliant strategy. When a man dressed up in a monkey suit and took a woman out on the town, he wanted to be able to hold her. Vertical foreplay. That's what it was. And he couldn't wait to get Simone horizontal.

Occasionally, the band would break into a fast, snappy

number so the folks who really knew how to dance had a chance to shine out on the floor. Simone was a good dancer, and Hutch was decent...but she begged off because of the babies. Her lengthy illness had sapped her stamina. Now she appeared to be slowing down. Instinctively, he wrapped his arms around her.

"I'm dying of thirst," she said, leaning into him. "And I wouldn't mind sampling that menu I've spent weeks planning."

# Sixteen

Hutch steered a path to the buffet with Simone in tow. The spread was amazing, even by Royal's standards. Prime rib, of course. After all, this was cattle country. But also chicken kebabs skewered with vegetables, crab puffs and enormous prawns iced down in a magnificent crystal bowl. Not to mention all the usual accoutrements.

"Well," he said. "Anything you want me to avoid?" He was keenly aware that even the sight of certain foods was enough to set off Simone's nausea. This was her special night. He didn't want to take any chances.

She leaned her head against his shoulder momentarily. "That's sweet of you, Hutch. I think I'm okay, though. I won't attempt the caviar, but everything else looks good to me right now."

They filled their plates to overflowing and sought out a table for two in a distant corner. Large potted plants provided cover for discreet trysts. "Was this your idea?" he asked as he held out her chair and helped her get seated. They were sheltered, although not completely private, of course.

She popped a carrot stick in her mouth and grinned. "Romance is alive and well in Royal…didn't you know?"

"I'll grab us a couple of drinks."

"Plain tap water, please."

When he returned moments later, Simone sat with her chin on her hand staring at a large stuffed mushroom with a frown. He handed a glass. "What's wrong?"

She shrugged. "I don't know about this one."

"Then for God's sake, don't take any chances," he said. He filched the mushroom and popped it into his mouth. Fortunately, the rest of her choices were winners.

The food was excellent, but he knew he was in trouble when just watching her eat made him hard again. Soft lips. Small white teeth. Lord help him. Simone was oblivious to his mood, her gaze tracking various couples on the dance floor. She named them off one by one.

"How do you do that?" he asked. "Isn't the whole point of a masquerade ball anonymity? I know I've been away a long time, but I only managed to spot a few people I could identify for sure."

"I cheated," she confessed. "I was the one who processed all the names and built the spreadsheet. Even with everyone wearing masks, I think I could name most of them."

"My hat's off to you. I'm guessing a few of those couples who responded were a surprise?"

"Oh, yes. Definitely. I *would* tell you, but then I'd have to kill you."

"Isn't that taking secret identities a step too far, Mata Hari?"

"You could always try to torture it out of me."

Her big blue eyes were wide and innocent. When she stuck out her tongue to catch a bit of cocktail sauce at the corner of her mouth, he sighed. "You're messing with me, aren't you?"

"Would *I* do that?"

"In a heartbeat."

He reached across the table and took her hands in his. "You think you're safe from retaliation because we're in a public place, but fair warning, my sweet. I could toss you over my shoulder, walk out of here to the front desk and get a room."

"You wouldn't..." She eyed him askance.

"Try me."

"Okay, Hutch," she said, her tone placating. "I'll behave from here on out. No flirting. No innuendo. No dancing."

"I didn't say no dancing. A man has to take what crumbs he can get."

She cocked her head. "I'm confused. Are you a barbarian laying down the law or a puppy begging for scraps?"

He stroked the backs of her hands with his thumbs. "What do you think?"

For a long second, their gazes locked. Her eyes were nothing so simple as blue. They were dark at the outer rim, like midnight, but lighter near the pupil. He was mesmerized studying them.

"Hutch?"

He heard her say his name, but he was lost in a fantasy where she was stark naked on his bed. "Hmm?"

"We probably should get back out there since we've finished eating. After all, I'm one of the ones in charge."

"Yes..." He whispered the word, still caught up in a vision he hoped like hell would come true in only a few hours.

Suddenly, his dream woman stood up. "Hurry," she said, excitement in her voice. "I think Deacon is about to make an announcement."

Hutch followed her, disgruntled. They found a spot near the front. The stage was set up just behind the orchestra. Deacon Chase stood at the microphone with a genial smile on his face and a raised hand. When the crowd at last fell silent, he spoke.

"First of all, friends and neighbors, Shane Delgado and I would like to welcome you to The Bellamy. This hotel and all it encompasses is a dream come true for us. We're delighted to have all of you here tonight. I hope you'll spend a lot of time at The Bellamy in the years to come, not only overnight for special occasions, but also dining with us on a regular basis at either the Silver Saddle or the Glass House. Our new spa, Pure, is open to the public. All you need to do is make a reservation." He paused and cleared his throat. "I know everyone is eager to get back to the dancing, but I hope you'll grant me a moment of personal privilege."

He held out his hand, and to Hutch's surprise, Simone's friend Cecelia took the stage. Deacon introduced her with a broad smile. "If you think we have a beautifully appointed hotel, this is the woman who gets the credit. I'm forever in her debt for helping us make The Bellamy a reality. Even more than that, I am beyond happy that she has agreed to be my wife."

The room erupted in shouts and cheers. Shocked, Hutch looked sideways at Simone. "Did you know about this?"

She nodded, beaming. "He gave her the ring several weeks ago, but they only told close friends and family before tonight. I guess this makes it official. Look how sweet they are together."

He did look, and Simone was right. Judging from the expressions on their faces, Cecelia and Deacon were ridiculously happy with their new status. Hutch continued to brood while Simone joined the crowd of friends who wanted to congratulate the bride-to-be and her groom.

Deacon Chase had chosen well. As far as Hutch could tell, the billionaire hotelier and the gorgeous platinum blonde had a lot in common. Case in point—the two of them, along with Delgado, had turned a dream into a reality. Deacon built hotels. Cecelia had the know-how to furnish them.

What did Hutch and Simone have in common? Not one damn thing.

Suddenly, his bow tie choked him, and the room was

far too hot. His heart beat out an unfamiliar cadence in his chest. Working his way over to Simone, he reached out and tapped her on the arm. The crowd was so noisy, he had to bend down so she could hear him.

"I'm going outside for some fresh air," he said. "Stay here and enjoy your friends."

Big blue eyes searched his face. "Are you okay?"

He dredged up a smile and brushed the back of his hand across her cheek. "Never better," he lied. "I'll be back shortly."

"How will you find me?"

Was she serious? "Honey, that red dress stands out in a crowd. Don't worry. I won't leave without you."

Desperately, he plowed his way to the other side of the room. Had the fire marshal okayed this crowd? Hell, the marshal had probably been invited for that very reason.

Outside, he jerked his bow tie off and stuffed it in his pocket. After that, he took a deep, cleansing breath and leaned against a marble statue of Pan in a clump of daisies. He wished he smoked. Since he didn't and never had, the next best thing was walking. He'd read the press packet about the new hotel. The grounds included several miles of wooded trails.

He didn't care where he went at this point. It wasn't like he could get lost. This was Royal, not the middle of a wilderness.

The night was perfect...too perfect. He walked with his head down, trying not to notice the moonlight or the sweet scent of flowers in the air. If he proposed to Simone and she accepted, there would be no going back. He wouldn't be able to return to Sudan to escape her hold on him.

Could he and would he be able to love three babies who weren't his biological offspring? That seemed the least of his worries at this point. He adored children. He always had.

Besides, the triplets carried half of their mother's DNA. If he loved Simone, he would love her babies, too.

But what if he proposed and she said no? Why had he purchased a house so near hers? He had to drive by Simone's house every day on the way to work. That would be unbearable if they broke up for a second time.

He'd never been good at games of chance. Knowing the odds were stacked against him meant he'd never had any real trouble staying away from gambling. He liked being in control.

Yet here he was, contemplating a course that was neither certain nor even advisable. On paper it seemed absurd. His parents clearly agreed. Why would he risk so much when he had no idea if Simone cared for him at all?

Again, he visited the possibility that she was using him. With triplets on the way, she might think she needed a second parent in the house above all else. Such a rationale made her seem cold and calculating. The Simone he knew was neither of those things.

When he regained a modicum of control over his emotions, he put on the bow tie again. It was time for him to go back inside to smile and to dance and to do whatever it took to make it through the remainder of the ball. After that, he'd get his reward. One whole night in Simone's bed. Or his. He wasn't too picky about locale.

As he turned around to head back the way he had come, a large man about Hutch's height stepped out of the shadows and blocked the path. Hutch froze, sensing danger. But the man was in formal attire and wore one of the masquerade masks. Surely this wasn't some gate-crasher come late to wreck the party.

"What can I do for you, sir?"

The man straightened. He was big and broad, but even in the moonlight Hutch could see that his face was gaunt. "It's what I can do for you, Dr. Hutchinson."

"Who are you? How do you know my name?"

"You can call me Maverick. It doesn't matter how I know your name. I'm here to give you fair warning about the woman in the red dress."

Hutch frowned. "Simone?"

"Of course, Simone. Who else? You don't have a clue what she's really up to, do you?"

"This conversation is over." Hutch was furious and perturbed underneath that. Why did the stranger even care? Hutch went to brush past him, but the old guy put a beefy hand smack in the middle of Hutch's chest. "Don't run off, young man. I'm here to save you from yourself."

"It sounds to me like you're here to bad-mouth Simone. And I don't care to listen anymore."

The man got up in his face. "That little slut in the red dress got pregnant on purpose so she could inherit half of her grandfather's estate. Did your precious Simone ever bother to tell you *that* twist in the story?"

"You're lying," Hutch said. Fury blurred his vision. He wanted to drag the man into the moonlight and see his face. With the mask and the shadows, he hadn't a clue who he was.

"It's no lie. You ask her. And ask her if she knows Maverick. I think you'll be unpleasantly surprised."

"Go to hell." Hutch shoved past him, determined to walk away without indulging in a fistfight. He knew how to fell an assailant, but he'd rather not in this setting.

The other man was older, but bulkier. Hutch never even saw the blow coming. It caught him in the temple. Something sharp, a ring perhaps, cut into his skin. Then he fell hard and hit his head.

Simone began to worry when Hutch didn't come back after half an hour. Fifteen minutes after that she decided to go in search of him. She didn't bother with looking inside the hotel. He had professed a need for fresh air.

Outside, she inhaled deeply, happy to be away from the crush of the party. It was, by every measure, a grand success. She and Naomi and Cecelia could be justifiably proud of what they had managed to pull off. The money raised for Homes and Hearts would be enough to build modest homes for three needy families.

Even knowing that her event was a smashing victory wasn't enough to erase her unease. She walked away from the building toward the parking area. "Hutch!" she called out, her voice fraught with worry. She noticed that the space in and around the cars had been landscaped beautifully. Plenty of places to hide if a person or a couple didn't want to be discovered.

"Hutch!" She stood by his car now, only a little relieved to see it was still there. At least he hadn't left the premises.

Still no answer. She followed a series of small signposts leading back into the trees. For a moment, she stood, irresolute. Normally, she would take more care with her personal safety. This was private property, though. She had seen at least a dozen uniformed security guards mingling with the crowd and monitoring the entrances and exits. No one was out here trying to mug unwary party guests.

At least she hoped not.

She continued to walk, half a mile at least. Her shoes were not meant for traipsing about in the woods. When the pain of a blister became too much to handle, she stopped and took off her expensive footwear. Chances were, the heels were a loss. When she looked back, she could see the hotel in the distance all lit up like a fairy-tale castle. "Hutch!"

A faint groan was her only answer. She almost tripped over him. "Hutch!" She knelt urgently, reassured in part when she heard him breathing. "Hutch, it's Simone. Wake up." Frustrated and scared, she removed his mask and her own. This was no time for pretense.

She had no water, no rag to put water *on*. No way to sponge his face and wake him up. Nevertheless, she got one arm around his shoulders and held him against her breast. "Hutch. Can you hear me? It's Simone. What happened to you?" Even in the shadowy woods, she could see something dark against his temple. When she tested it with a fingertip, she got woozy. Blood. Definitely blood.

Gently, she ran her fingers over his scalp and discovered a second injury, this one an enormous knot. He must have hit his head when he fell. But that didn't explain the wound at his temple.

Why hadn't she brought someone with her? This was the worst rescue attempt in the history of rescue attempts. She wished she remembered her first-aid training.

It seemed as if she held him forever, but in reality only five or ten minutes elapsed. She stroked his forehead carefully, speaking to him in a jumble of whispered words. Fear unlike any she had ever known paralyzed her. She couldn't lose Hutch. Not again. Not forever.

Part of her wanted to run for help. The other part was desperately afraid to leave him here alone in the dark. So she stayed…and she prayed.

At last, Hutch regained consciousness. Slowly, he stirred. She felt him stiffen as he realized where he was. With her help, he sat all the way up, putting his head in his hands, groaning and cursing beneath his breath.

"Tell me how this happened," she pleaded. "Who did this to you?"

"Would you believe I ran into a door?"

"That's not funny. Let me help you up."

He batted her hand away. "I can do it."

It took him two tries, but he managed. His truculent independence was a good thing, because Simone had no idea how she would have managed to stand with a two-hundred-pound man draped across her shoulder.

When he swayed, she reached for him. Again, he eluded her touch. Instead, he leaned on the nearest tree.

"Are you able to walk?" she asked calmly. Something bad had happened. She knew it in her gut. Something beyond Hutch's head wounds. His body language screamed at her to stay away.

He nodded. "I can do it."

They were farther from the hotel than Simone first realized. Hutch made it a quarter of a mile or so before he had to sit down and rest.

"This is stupid," she said. "You stay here. I'll go get help."

"No!" He shouted the word and then cursed again as his outburst clearly caused him agony.

"You might have a concussion."

"I'm a doctor. I don't need *you* to practice medicine."

Now she was certain something was wrong. The disdain in his voice, edged with fury, was a far cry from the Hutch who had wanted to make love to her in a tucked-away corner.

Her heart sank. She waited in silence until he was able to stand again. This time she knew better than to offer help.

They made it only as far as the parking lot. Beneath a streetlight, she caught her first glimpse of the wound at his temple. It was an angry red knot, sliced clean through with a cut that oozed significant amounts of blood.

"Tell me what happened, Hutch. Who did this to you?"

He leaned against his own vehicle. She saw his chest rise and fall as he struggled to speak. "Does the name Maverick mean anything to you, Simone?"

# Seventeen

Dread made her blood run cold. Her voice froze in her throat.

Hutch's gaze was bitter. "I see that it does. Your face gives you away."

Hot tears burned her eyes, but she didn't let them fall. "Maverick is the stranger who has been sending mysterious, threatening messages to people in Royal. I got two of his nasty notes, but so have others."

"I don't really care about anyone else but you, Simone. Why would an anonymous blackmailer have anything to hold over *your* head?" The words were icy and clipped. It appeared that Hutch was prepared to be judge and jury.

"How do you even know about this?"

Hutch shrugged, wincing as he did so. "I ran into him on the trail. He confronted me. We argued. I tried to leave. He punched me."

"You need X-rays, Hutch. Please go to the hospital."

"First things first, Simone. Tell me… Is it fair to say that you got pregnant only to satisfy the terms of your grandfather's will?"

Hutch watched her face. Every drop of color washed away. Her eyes welled with tears. He had his answer. "My

God," he said. "It's true." His heart shattered into sharp pieces that stabbed his chest. "You wanted money, so you decided to have a baby. Do you have any idea how incredibly selfish and immoral that is? I've spent my entire career protecting mothers and babies. What you did is unconscionable."

She stood proud and tall as he annihilated her. "I made a foolish mistake. I admit that. But it wasn't really about the money, I swear."

"Of course it wasn't," he sneered.

"I'm telling you the truth," she cried. "Let's go back inside so you can sit down. I'll explain everything."

He shook his head violently, almost welcoming the pain. "I don't need to hear your explanations. I see it all now. That's the real reason you sent me off to Africa, isn't it, Simone? You thought you were dating an up-and-coming surgeon, but then you found out I was more interested in offering my services to the poor than building a mansion in Royal and inviting you to be lady of the manor."

"Tonight isn't a good time to discuss this," she said quietly. "Come back inside with me. I'll get some ice for your head."

When she tried to take his arm, he jerked away. He saw the agony in her eyes, but he didn't care. He didn't care about anything at this moment. "I'm sure there are a number of people at the ball who will be glad to take you home, Simone. You and I are done here. In fact, we're done permanently."

"Hutch, please…" Tears spilled down her cheeks. "You're twisting the facts and coming up with the wrong answers. This isn't as bad as it seems."

He opened the car door and managed not to groan when he slid behind the wheel. "I don't want to hear it, Simone. Goodbye." Barely allowing her time to jump out of the way, he put the car in gear and screeched out of the parking lot.

Though he was cautious getting out of town, when he made it to the interstate, he pressed down on the accelerator and tried to outrun his demons.

Thank God he hadn't told her he loved her. That would have been the final indignity. He felt like a credulous fool. Hell, he *was* a fool. He had let hot sex blind him to Simone's real nature. She was a user and a manipulator.

He drove on into the night with no particular destination in mind. At last, though, his massive headache forced him to pull off and find a motel room for the night. The clerk gaped at him—he must have looked like something out of a horror movie—but handed over the key without protest.

Hutch parked in front of the door to 11C. He had no suitcase, no shaving kit, nothing. What did it matter?

Before he could collapse onto the bed, he had one phone call to make. He was scheduled to work Saturday and Sunday. Fortunately, he was able to get in touch with his second in command, who agreed to switch shifts for a couple of days.

That left Hutch totally unencumbered for the next forty-eight hours. He stumbled into the bathroom, took a quick shower and carefully washed the wound on his head. Then he went back into the other room, pulled back the hideous bedspread and fell facedown on the mattress.

The following morning, he awoke with the hangover from hell. Then he realized he hadn't been drinking. After that, he remembered that Simone was gone. He felt empty inside. Though he was hungry, no amount of food could fix what was wrong with him.

Even so, he couldn't sit around in his tux all weekend. He downed some acetaminophen and made it out to the car on shaky legs. Fortunately, there was a diner nearby… the ubiquitous staple of rural Texas. The waitress took one look at his face and didn't bother with chitchat.

After a hearty meal of bacon, eggs and toast, Hutch felt marginally better. Next on his list was a stop at a discount store. There he found a pair of jeans that fit his long, lanky body. He grabbed a couple of plain knit shirts, some underwear and socks, and cheap sneakers.

Back at the motel, he took another shower. It was hot as hell outside. Afterward, he put on his new duds and stretched out on the bed to watch TV. He rarely had time in his life for something so mindless and sedentary. Every day was filled with work and more work and, recently, Simone.

For the first time, he allowed himself to remember what had happened. There was plenty to be pissed about. The worst was that she had lied to him. By omission, but still. She told him she got pregnant because she wanted to be a mother.

Maybe that part was true, but it wasn't the whole truth. The real truth was money. Lots of it. People would do almost anything for money.

Eventually, his anger was replaced by a dull acceptance. Maybe he wasn't supposed to get married and have a family of his own. Maybe he was supposed to devote his life to helping other people have healthy babies.

By Sunday morning, both bumps on his head were healing nicely. In addition to his new clothes, he had bought a handheld mirror so he could look at the knot on the back of his skull. That was a mistake, because suddenly the memory of Simone stroking his brow and running her fingers over his head came back with a vengeance.

He had to check out of the room by eleven. After that task was accomplished, he sat in his car and clenched the steering wheel with two hands. One thing was certain. He was not returning to Royal in order to worm his way back into Simone's good graces. He probably wasn't even in love with her, not really. He'd been dazzled by good sex and his need to watch over triplets who needed him.

Slowly, he cruised the small town, which was little more than a wide space in the road. They had a fast-food place but little else. The only meal he had eaten was breakfast yesterday. His stomach had been rolling and pitching too much to think about food again. Now, though, he was hungry.

In the drive-through he ordered a double cheeseburger with fries and a Coke. His whole life was in ruins. Why not indulge in junk food, as well?

The calorie-laden meal filled the hole in his stomach. Unfortunately, the aching maw in his chest was not so easily appeased. It hurt. His whole body hurt. So be it.

He turned the vehicle around and headed for Royal. Monday morning would come bright and early. He'd taken far too much advantage of his flexible schedule lately. If he kept this up, the hospital board would decide they had made a mistake in hiring him.

Hutch was good at medicine. He was lousy at love. It made sense to concentrate on the one aspect of his life that had never disappointed him.

When he finally made it back to Royal, darkness had fallen. He deliberately avoided looking at Simone's house when he was forced to pass by it on the way to his. At home, he walked from room to room, pacing aimlessly. In the back bedroom there were still a few boxes he hadn't unpacked yet. Maybe he would list the place this week and move across town.

If he were honest, though, he didn't want to give Simone the satisfaction of knowing she had that kind of power over him. He'd been taken in by a pro, but he didn't have to let it happen again.

Monday morning, he showed up for work clean shaven and bright eyed. He'd slept reasonably well from sheer exhaustion. Despite that, the pain in his chest and his gut remained. Doggedly, he concentrated on the cases at hand. His own personal trauma would not be allowed to interfere with the quality of his performance.

The day lasted a thousand hours. It was all he could do to dispel the images of Simone from his mind. She was what she was. He needed to cut his losses and move on.

He was thirty minutes from finishing his shift when he ran into Janine.

She frowned at him. "You look like hell. Are you ill? Go home, Hutch. Get some rest."

"I'm not sick," he said. "Just tired. I was about to leave."

"I know you're glad Simone is doing better," she said.

Hutch went still. "Oh?"

Janine frowned. "I assumed you've been with her since she got out of the hospital. Isn't that why you look like you're running on four hours' sleep?"

"I haven't seen Simone recently," he said carefully. "What's wrong with her?"

The other doctor stared at him. "She collapsed at the party Friday night. One of the guests found her in the parking lot. No one could find you, so they called an ambulance."

Hutch felt his bones turn to water. "An ambulance?"

"Her blood pressure skyrocketed. She had some kind of panic attack. Because she was already weak from the battle with nausea, we had to give her IV fluids again. Simone told me you were meeting her at her house. That was the only reason I released her when I did."

"I wasn't there," Hutch said slowly. His heart slugged in his chest. "But I'm headed there now. Thank you, Janine."

This couldn't be happening again. Another woman he cared about slipping away, and him powerless to save her. Simone wasn't perfect. If he took a mental step backward, though, he could admit that the love she had demonstrated for her babies was real and fierce.

Maybe he had made too much of her original motives. God knows, he had screwed up at several major points in his own life. Was it fair to judge Simone for *her* missteps, when his had been equally egregious?

The truth dawned slowly, in tandem with incredulity. The reason he'd been so angry with her at the party was because he loved her. Her betrayal had cut straight through to his heart, leaving him bleeding in more ways than one.

He drove like a madman, half expecting to find Simone unconscious or worse. When she answered the door at his first knock, the moment was anticlimactic at best.

"Why did you lie to your doctor?" he demanded, going on the attack.

Simone gazed at him with blank eyes. "What are you doing here, Hutch?" She didn't back up, and she sure as hell didn't invite him in.

Suddenly, everything coalesced into one shining bubble of certainty. "We need to talk." He said the words quietly, trying not to spook her.

"I don't think so." She tried to shut the door, but he stuck his foot in the opening.

"Please, Simone. Let me speak my piece. Then if you want, I'll leave."

She lifted one shoulder in a careless shrug. "Whatever."

He closed the door behind him and followed her to the den. Simone chose a straight-back chair. Hutch decided to stand. "I'm in love with you," he said bluntly.

Her eyelids flickered, but the look on her face didn't change. "I see."

"I don't care if those babies aren't my biological children. I want to be their daddy."

"That's not going to happen." At last a spark of blue in those lovely eyes gave him hope. He couldn't get through to frozen Simone. Angry Simone was another story.

He ran a hand over the back of his neck. "I've done a

lot of thinking in the last seventy-two hours. I was a fool to think your motives for carrying those babies were anything but pure. It was a knee-jerk reaction. You'll never know how sorry I am for not trusting you."

"And that's supposed to make me feel better? You shut me out, Hutch, and not for the first time." Her anger made him wince.

"I know. My only excuse is that your Maverick guy got inside my head. As far as your inheritance goes, who am I to judge? Money isn't a bad thing in and of itself."

"Just people like me…" Her facade cracked. For a moment, he saw how deeply he had hurt her.

"Oh, God, Simone." He knelt at her feet. "I was an ass. I lost you once. I won't lose you again. I love you, and I'm pretty sure you love me, too. Marry me, sweetheart. Let's make a family together. Forgive me, little mama."

She lifted a hand to touch the scab at his temple. "People would talk."

"Let them. Nothing matters except you and me and those precious babies. I won't give up on us. I won't. This is too important."

Simone eluded his hold and stood, fleeing to the other side of the room. She had her back to him, so he couldn't read her expression. "There's something else you should know," she said.

His chest tightened. "Oh?"

After a long silence, she turned around. "You wouldn't be marrying an heiress."

"I don't understand."

"As soon as I deliver these babies, I receive five million dollars. That was the deal. I could only inherit my share of the estate if I produced an heir of my own. Otherwise, all of it went to my father. But my lawyer has drawn up papers to put three million in trust, one million for each of the children when they turn twenty-five."

"Two million is still a lot of money."

"That's how much I'm donating to Homes and Hearts. I didn't want to keep any of it. Not after the way you looked at me Friday night. I need you to understand why I did what I did."

"You don't have to explain. You're entitled to your own choices."

Her short laugh held little humor. "Don't you mean my own mistakes? Here's the thing, Hutch. I've been jockeying for my father's attention my whole life. He and my grandfather made no secret of the fact that I was a disappointment. They wanted a boy, another Parker male to carry on the family tradition. When I heard the terms of the will, I was hurt. And angry. I've never been good enough, you know?"

"Simone—"

She held up a hand, cutting him short. "I don't want you feeling sorry for me. It is what it is. But I'm keeping the land. Those acres of Texas are my birthright. Generations of Parkers have lived there and ranched and farmed and done whatever they had to do to survive. I won't apologize for wanting that legacy, not only for me, but for my children."

He exhaled, his shoulders tight. "Are you done?"

"What else is there to say?"

"You could tell me you love me." He managed to say the words jokingly, but the fear he had ruined something precious choked him. Simone's silence was frankly terrifying. "I'll grovel if need be, my sweet firecracker."

He saw the muscles in her throat work as she swallowed. "You'll want children of your own."

It wasn't a question. He frowned. "I think it would be more correct to say I will want *more* children of my own. I already cherish those three little lives you're carrying. I don't care if their biological father is blond and blue-eyed. We live in a global world. I grew up understanding that many people drew lines to shut me out. I want to make a family with you, of children who never have to know those limits. We'll build our lives around love, Simone. You and I were both made to feel less at times, but that's over. Tell me you believe that. Tell me you love me. Tell me I didn't destroy our second chance."

His life hung in the balance.

Tears rolled down cheeks that were too pale. She came to him at last, sliding her arms around his waist and resting her cheek over his heart. "I do love you, Hutch. I never stopped. And, yes…I want to marry you and make a family together."

"Thank God." He held her tightly, his own eyes damp. "I adore you. I swear you won't regret this."

After long, aching moments, Simone pulled back and looked up at him. "I'm sorry these babies aren't yours," she said, regret shadowing her gaze. "I'm so very sorry."

He shook his head, feeling everything in his world settle into his place. "That's where you're wrong, my love. Those babies *are* mine, in every way that counts. I love them, and I love you. Now hush, and let me kiss you."

Simone smiled at him tremulously. "Only a kiss?"

"Oh, no," he said, scooping her into his arms. "We have a lot of makeup sex coming our way."

His bride-to-be gave him a wicked grin, looking more like herself at last. "Then let's get started, Dr. Hutchinson. I've been waiting a long time for this."

He strode down the hall and up the stairs with his precious burden. "So have I, sweet Simone. So have I…"

\* \* \* \* \*

# A TEXAS-SIZED SECRET

MAUREEN CHILD

To the readers,
because you are the reason we have stories to tell.

# One

"What did I ever do to this Maverick?" Naomi Price kicked at the dirt, then gave a heavy sigh. "Why's he after me?"

Toby McKittrick glanced from the horse he was saddling to the woman standing on the other side of the corral fence. Even furious and a little scared, Naomi made quite the picture.

She was nine inches shorter than his own six feet two inches, but she had a lot of interest packed into her five-foot-five frame. Her long, copper-brown hair draped over her shoulders like fire, and her chocolate-colored eyes snapped with intelligence and, at the moment, worry. She wore white summer slacks and a loose, pale green shirt with some white lacy thing over it. The boots she wore were ankle-high, pale cream and fit only for walking down clean city sidewalks. Here on the ranch, they'd be ruined in a day or two. But Naomi was a city girl, so no worries.

"This Maverick," he said, "he—or *she*, for all we know," Toby pointed out, "is after everybody, it seems. Guess it was just your turn."

"Maverick" had been creating turmoil in Royal, Texas, for the last few months. Exposing private bombshells, taunting people with their innermost worries and fears, whoever it was not only knew the people of Royal, but didn't give a good damn about them.

Somehow this person—whoever—uncovered people's darkest secrets and then published them. Toby had no idea what the mysterious Maverick was getting out of all this— okay, some people had paid Maverick to keep his mouth shut—but Toby had the feeling the whole point was simply to try to destroy people's reputations. If that was it, he was batting a thousand.

"Great," Naomi muttered. "Just great."

"What exactly did he say to get you running out here first thing in the morning?" Toby gave her a long look. Usually, Naomi wasn't up and moving until the crack of noon. She didn't go anywhere unless she was completely turned out from the top of her head to the toes of her stylish shoes.

She sighed, then reached into her shoulder bag for her cell phone. "Look at it for yourself," she said, handing it over.

Toby gave the horse a pat, took the phone and keyed it up.

"It's ready to go," she said, "just push Play."

Frowning, Toby tipped the brim of his hat back and tapped the phone screen. Instantly, he saw what had Naomi as jumpy as a spider on a hot plate.

For the last year or so, Naomi had been the star, writer and producer of a small-town cable fashion show. She was making a name for herself, doing what she did best—advising women on how to look good. Naomi was proud of what she'd accomplished, and she had a right to be. She'd built herself an audience and she worked hard every day to put out the best show possible.

He scowled at the screen as the video played. Maverick had turned what she did into a parody. He'd found an actress who resembled Naomi to star in it, and the woman was cooing and sighing over a rack of dresses like she was having an orgasm on camera. Then she stepped out from behind that rack and Toby knew instantly what had *really* set Naomi off.

The actress looked about two years pregnant. She waddled across the stage, both hands supporting a belly so huge there might have been a baby elephant tucked inside.

"Oh, man…"

"Wait for it," Naomi ground out. "There's more."

A deep frown etched on his face, Toby watched and listened as the actress began talking with a slow, overblown Texas accent.

"And for summer," she said, simpering at the camera, "maternity wear just got more exciting! Our big ol' bellies won't keep us from looking stylish, ladies." She flipped long reddish-brown hair behind her shoulder, then rubbed both hands over that comically distended belly before slipping behind that rack of dresses again, still talking. "Remember, accessorizing is key. Drape a pretty belt around that baby belly. Draw attention to it. Be proud. Show the world what a fashionable pregnant woman should look like."

Toby's own temper was starting to spike for Naomi's sake.

She stepped out from behind the dress rack again to model an oversize tent dress with a gigantic black belt enveloping that belly. "Tell the world, Naomi," the woman said, smiling into the camera. "Do it fast, or Maverick will do it for you."

Gritting his teeth, Toby turned the phone off and handed it back to her. "Okay, I see what's got you all churned up."

She tucked her phone back into her purse and then reached out to grab the top rail of the corral fence. Her hands tightened on the weather-beaten wood until her knuckles went white.

"It's not just that he's threatening to tell everyone I'm pregnant, Toby," she said, her voice tight but low enough that he had to lean in to hear her. "It's that he's making fun of me. He's turning my show into a joke. He's *laughing* at me."

Toby laid his hand over one of hers and squeezed. "Doesn't matter what he thinks of you, Naomi. You know that."

"Of course I know," she said, giving him a grim smile that was brave, if not honest. "But I watched that video and wondered if I really sound like that. All know-it-all and prissy. Am I prissy?"

One corner of Toby's mouth quirked up. "I wouldn't say so, but you've had your moments…"

She looked at him for a long minute, then let her head fall back and a groan escape her throat. "You're talking about the mean girls thing, aren't you?"

He shrugged and went back to tightening the cinch on his horse's saddle. Naomi had been his best friend for years. But that didn't make him blind to her faults, either. Of course, *nobody* was perfect. Toby knew Naomi better than anyone else, and he knew that she had spent a lifetime hiding a tender heart beneath a self-protective layer of cool disdain.

"You, Simone and Cecelia have a reputation you more than earned. You've gotta admit that."

"Wish I didn't have to," she muttered and dropped her chin on top of her hands.

Shaking his head, Toby let her be, knowing her thoughts were racing. So were his own. Naomi and he had been best friends for years now. They'd grown up knowing each other in a vague, from-the-same-small-town kind of way. But in college, they'd connected when he was a senior and she a freshman. He knew her in a way not many people did, so Toby also knew that Naomi was shaken right down to her expensive, useless boots.

"Things are different now," Naomi insisted a moment later. She straightened up, and Toby was glad to see a fierce gleam in her eyes. "People change, you know."

"All the time," he said, nodding.

"Cecelia and Deacon are together now—she's pregnant, too," Naomi pointed out unnecessarily. "And Simone and Hutch have worked things out and she's pregnant with triplets, for heaven's sake." She threw up both hands and let them fall to her sides. "It's a population explosion with the three of us. We're not the mean girls anymore. We're..." She sighed. "I don't know what we are anymore."

"I do," Toby said, watching her with a smile. "You're Naomi Price—the woman who wears useless boots that cost more than my saddle..."

She laughed, as he'd meant her to.

Staring directly into her eyes, he continued. "You're also the woman who started her own television show and worked her behind off to make it a success."

"Thank you, Toby." She smiled at him, and he felt a sharp tug inside in response.

"Okay," she said, nodding to herself as she pushed away from the fence, giving that top rail one last slap. "You're right. I'm strong. I'm ready. I can do this."

"Yes, you can." Finished saddling his horse, Toby stroked the flat of his hand along the animal's sleek neck.

"I don't know how to tell them," she said, all the air leaving her body in a rush. "The whole strong, independent feminist thing just goes right out the window when I know I have to face down my parents and tell them I'm pregnant."

Toby turned, braced his forearms on the top rail of the fence and tugged the brim of his dark brown hat down low over his eyes. "You should have already told them."

"This is so not the time for cool logic," she snapped. Pacing back and forth along the fence line, she crossed her arms over her middle like she was hugging herself. "What happened to Mr. Supportive?"

"I'm being supportive," he argued. "I'm just not patting your head, because you don't need it."

She muttered something he didn't quite catch and kept pacing. If she'd stop walking so damn fast, he'd give her a hug himself. But the minute he considered it, Toby pushed the thought aside. Hell, he'd been burying his attraction for Naomi for years. He was a damn expert. She'd come to his ranch looking for a friend, so that was what he'd be for her. Which meant telling her what she didn't want to hear.

"Naomi," he said, "you knew you couldn't keep this a secret forever."

She stopped directly opposite him, with the fence separating them. A soft summer wind lifted the ends of her hair, and she squinted a bit into the sunlight, those beautiful brown eyes of hers narrowing. "I know, but…"

"But nothing," he said, yanking his hat off to stab his fingers through his hair. "Somebody else took the reins from you. You don't have a choice now in when to tell your folks. Time's up."

"How did Maverick even find out?" She took a breath and exhaled on a heavy sigh. "You're the only one—or so I thought—besides me who knows about the baby."

That sounded like an accusation. His gaze snapped to hers. "I didn't tell anyone."

"I know that." She waved that away with such casualness he relaxed again. Toby was a man of his word. Always. The one thing he always remembered his father saying was, "Without his honor, a man's got nothing." That had always stuck with him, to the point that Toby never made a promise unless he was sure he could keep it.

"You know, you're the only man in my life who's never let me down, Toby," she said softly. "The one person I can always count on."

He nodded but didn't say anything, because knowing Naomi, she had more to say.

"I tried to contact Gio again."

And there it was. Irritation spiked inside him, and Toby didn't bother to hide it. Gio Fabiani, a one-night stand who had left Naomi pregnant and wasn't worth the dust on her fancy boots. But Naomi being Naomi, for the last couple of months she'd been trying to track the man down to tell him about the baby. Even if she did finally find him, though, Toby was sure that Gio wouldn't give a flying damn.

"You've got to let that go," he ground out. "Just because the man fathered your child doesn't mean he's good enough to *be* its father."

"I know, but—"

"No buts," he said, interrupting her. "Damn it, Naomi, you told me yourself that sleeping with that sleaze was a mistake. You really want to make another one by bringing him back into your life?"

"Shouldn't he *know* that he has a child?"

"If he hadn't blown in and out of your life so fast, he *would* know," Toby said, though in truth he was damned grateful that Gio hadn't been more than a blip on Naomi's radar. She deserved better. "I did some checking of my own when you first told me about this."

"You checked? Into Gio?"

"Who else?" He calmed himself by stroking his palm up and down the length of his horse's neck. "The man's a worthless user. He goes through women like we go through feed for the horses."

She flushed, and he knew she didn't like hearing it, but true was true.

His voice low and soft, Toby added, "He's never going to stand with you, Naomi."

She took a breath and huffed it out again. "I know that, too. And I don't want him to, anyway." Shaking her head, she started pacing again. "One night of bad judgment doesn't make for a relationship. But I should tell him about the baby before this Maverick person sends that video out into the world and it goes viral." She stopped opposite him again and laid one hand against her belly. "Viral. People *everywhere* will see that awful video.

People will be laughing at me. Feeling *sorry* for me. Or, worse, cheering, because like you said, I haven't always been the nicest human being on the planet. Oh, God, my stomach's churning and it has nothing to do with the baby."

"You'll survive this," he said.

"Why should I have to *survive*? Who *is* this Maverick? Why has nobody found him yet?"

"I don't know—to all those questions."

Shooting another speculative look at his friend, Toby wondered exactly what she was thinking. With Naomi it was never easy to guess. She'd long since learned to school her features into a blank mask that could convince her disinterested parents that all was well. But usually with him, she was more forthcoming. Still, things were different now. She was more shaken than he'd ever seen her. It wasn't just the pregnancy—it was how her life seemed to be spinning out of her control.

And Naomi liked control.

"The video he sent me was just…" Her sentence trailed off as she shook her head. "If he puts that out on the internet like he threatened, everyone in town's going to know my secret in a few hours."

Toby sighed, braced both forearms on the top rung of the corral fence and waited until her gaze met his to say, "Honey, they were all going to know within another month or two anyway. It's not like you could hide it much longer."

He was repeating himself and he knew it, but sometimes it took a hammer to pound the truth into Naomi's mind when she didn't want to admit to something. That hard head of hers was one of the things he liked most about her. Which made him a damn fool, probably. But there was something about the look she got in her eye when she was set on something that twisted his guts into knots. Knots he couldn't do a damn thing about, since she was his best friend. But he did wonder from time to time if Naomi's insides ever twisted over him.

Naomi stopped pacing, spun around to look at him and blurted, "You're right."

That surprised Toby enough that his eyebrows lifted high on his forehead. She saw it and laughed, and blast if the sound didn't light fires inside him. Fires he deliberately ignored. Hell, of course his body responded as it did. She was a beautiful woman with a laugh that sounded like warm nights and silk sheets. A man would have to be dead six months to not be affected by Naomi.

"I'm not so stubborn—or delusional—I can't see the truth when it takes a bite out of me," she said. Leaning her arms on the fence rail alongside his, she said, "That's really why I came out to see you this morning. I know what I have to do, and I wanted to ask you to come with me to tell my parents."

He frowned a little, because he didn't much care for Naomi's folks. They were always so prissy, so sure of their own righteousness they put him off. Their house was like a damn museum, quiet, still, where a dust speck wouldn't have the nerve to show up. Always made him feel like a clumsy cowboy.

But he knew how they made Naomi feel, too. She'd never quite measured up to parents who probably shouldn't have had a child to begin with. From everything Naomi had told him and from what he'd seen firsthand, they'd been showing her for years in word and deed just how disappointing she was to them. The announcement she had to make today wasn't going to help the situation any.

She was watching him, waiting for an answer, and Toby saw a flicker of unease in her eyes. He didn't like it. "Sure," he said, "I'll come along."

"Thanks, Toby," she said, reaching over to lay one hand on his forearm. "I knew you'd do this for me. You really are my best friend."

A best friend probably shouldn't experience a jolt of lust with just a touch of her hand on his arm. So he'd just keep that to himself.

Naomi was nervous. But then, she'd *been* nervous since opening the email with the subject line Your Secret Is Out. She'd known the moment she saw the blasted thing in her inbox that Maverick had finally turned his talons toward her. For the last few months, she'd watched as people she knew and cared about had had their lives turned upside down by this malicious phantom. And somehow she'd managed to keep hoping he wouldn't turn on her. Now that he had, though, she was forced to tell her parents the truth and live through what she always thought of as the "disappointment stare." Again.

Her entire life, Naomi had known that she was continually letting her parents down. Oh, no one had actually *said* anything—that would have been distasteful. But parents had other ways of letting their children know they didn't measure up, and the Prices were masters at silent disapproval.

No matter what Naomi had done in her life, her mother and father stood back and looked at her as if they didn't have a clue where she'd come from. Today was going to be no different.

Thank God Toby was coming with her to face them. She glanced at his stoic profile as he drove his Ford 150 down the road toward her family's mini mansion. He was the only one who knew her secret. The only one she'd trusted enough to go to when she realized two months ago that she was pregnant. And didn't that say something? She hadn't even told Cecelia Morgan and Simone Parker, and the three of them had been close for years.

But when she was in trouble, she always had turned to Toby. Even though telling him she was pregnant because of her own stupid decision to spend one night with the fast-talking, too-handsome-for-his-own-good Gio made her feel like an even bigger idiot.

Naomi still couldn't believe that one night of bad judgment and too much champagne had brought her to this. Toby was right, though. Even without Maverick shoving his nose into her business, she wouldn't have been able to hide her pregnancy for much longer. Loose tops and a strategically held handbag weren't going to disguise reality forever.

She shuddered a little in her seat. Naomi *hated* being pushed around by some nameless bully.

"You okay?" Toby asked, shooting her a quick look before turning his gaze back on the road in front of him.

"Not really," she admitted. "What the hell am I going to say to them?"

"The truth, Naomi," he said, reaching out to cover her hand with his. "Just tell them you're pregnant."

She held on to his hand and felt the warm, solid strength of him. "And when they ask who the father is?"

His mouth worked as if he wanted to say plenty but wasn't letting the words out. She appreciated the effort.

He couldn't say anything about Gio that she hadn't been feeling anyway.

When she told Toby about the baby, he'd instantly proven to be a much better man than the one she'd slept with. Toby offered to help any way he could, which was just one of the things she loved most about him. He didn't judge. He was just *there*. Like the mountains. Or the ancient oaks surrounding his ranch house. He was sturdy. And dependable. And everything she'd never known in her life until him. Now she needed him more than ever.

The Prices lived in Pine Valley, an exclusive, gated golf course community where the mansions sat on huge lots behind tidy lawns where weeds didn't dare appear and "doing lunch" was considered a career. At least, that was how Naomi had always seen it. Growing up there hadn't been easy, again because her parents never seemed to know what to do with her. Maybe if she'd had a sibling to help her through, it might have been different. But alone, Naomi had always felt…unworthy, somehow.

Her thoughts came to an abrupt halt when Toby stopped at the gate. When he lowered the window to speak to the guard, a wave of early-summer heat invaded the truck cab.

"Who're you here to see?" the older man holding a clipboard asked.

Naomi knew that voice, so she leaned forward and smiled. "Hello, Stan. We're just coming in to see my parents."

"Naomi, it's good to see you." The man smiled, hit a button on the inside of his guard hut, and the high, wide gate instantly began to roll clear. "Your folks are at home. Bet they'll be happy to see you."

He waved them through, and she sat back. "Happy to see me? I don't think so."

Toby, still holding her hand, gave it a hard squeeze. She held on tightly, even when he would have released her. Because right now she needed his support—his friendship—more than ever.

The streets were beautiful, with big homes, most of them tucked behind shrubbery-lined fences. Even in a gated community, some of the very wealthy seemed to want their own personal security as well. Of course, not everyone's home was hidden away behind a wall of trees, hedges or stone. The palatial homes were all different, all custom designed and built. And the closer Toby's truck drew to the Price mansion, the more Naomi felt the swarms of butterflies soaring and diving in the pit of her stomach.

God, she couldn't remember a time when she'd felt at ease with her parents. It had always seemed as though she was putting on a production, playing the part of the perfect daughter. Only she never quite measured up. She wished things were different, but if wishes came true, she wouldn't be here in the first place, would she?

The driveway to her parents' house was long and curved, the better to display the banks of flowers tended with loving care by a squad of gardeners. The sweep of lawn was green and neatly trimmed, and trees were kept trained into balls on branches that looked as though they were trying to remember how to be real trees. The house itself was showy but tasteful, as her parents would accept nothing less—it was a blend of Cape Cod and Victorian. Pale gray with white trim and black shutters, it stood as graceful as a dancer in the center of the massive lot. The front door was white without a speck of dust to mar its surface. The windows gleamed in the sunlight and displayed curtains within, all drawn to exactly the same point.

It was like looking at a picture in an architectural magazine. Something staged, where no one really lived. And of course, she told herself silently, *no one did*. Instead of living, her parents existed on a stage where everyone knew their lines and no one ever strayed from the script. Well, except for Naomi.

Naomi herself had been the one time anything unexpected had happened in her parents' lives. She was, she knew, an "accident." A late-in-life baby who had caused them nothing but embarrassment at first, followed by years of disappointment. Her mother had been horrified to find herself pregnant at the age of forty-five and had endured the unwelcome pregnancy because to do otherwise would have been unthinkable for her. They raised her with care if not actual love and expected her not to make any further ripples in their life.

But Naomi had always caused ripples. Sometimes *waves*.

And today was going to be a tsunami.

"You're getting quiet," Toby said with a flicker of a smile. "Never a good sign."

She had to smile back. "Too much to think about."

She stared at the closed front door and dreaded having to knock on it. Of course she would knock. And be announced by Matilda, the housekeeper who'd worked for her parents for twenty years. People didn't simply walk into her parents' house.

And her mind was going off on tangents because she didn't want to think about her real reason for being here.

"You've already made the hard decision," Toby pointed out. "You decided to keep the baby."

She had. Not that she cared at all about the baby's father, Naomi thought. But the baby was real to her. A person. *Her* child. How could she end the pregnancy? "I couldn't do anything else."

He reached out and took her hand for a quick squeeze. "I know. And I'll help however I can."

"I know you will," she said, holding on to his hand as she would a lifeline.

"You know," he said slowly, his deep voice rumbling through the truck cab, "there's no reason for you to be so worked up. You might want to consider that you're nearly thirty—"

"Hey!" She frowned at him. "I'm twenty-nine."

"My mistake," he said, mouth quirking, eyes shining. "But the point is, you've been on your own since college, Naomi. You don't have to explain your life to your parents."

"Easy for you to say," she countered. "Your mom and sister are your own personal cheering squad."

"True," he said, nodding. "But, Naomi, sooner or later, you've got to take a stand and, instead of apologizing to your folks, just tell them what's what."

It sounded perfectly reasonable. And she knew he was right. But it didn't make the thought of actually doing it any easier to take. She dropped one hand to the slight mound of her belly and gave the child within a comforting pat. If there was ever a time to stand up to her parents, it was now. She was going to be a mother herself, for God's sake.

"You're right." She gave his hand another squeeze, then let go to release her seat belt. "I'm going to tell them about the baby and that the father isn't in the picture and I'll be a single mother and—" She stopped. "Oh, God."

He chuckled. "For a second there, you were raring to go."

"I still am," she insisted, in spite of, or maybe because of, the flurries of butterflies in her stomach. "Let's just go get it over with, okay?"

"And after, we'll hit the diner for lunch."

"Sounds like a plan," she said.

# Two

Naomi took a deep breath in what she knew was a futile attempt to relax a little. There would be no relaxation until this meeting with her parents was over.

Toby came around the front of the truck, opened her door and waited for her to step down before asking, "You ready?"

"No. Yes. I don't know." Naomi shook her head, tugged at the hem of her cool green shirt as if she could somehow further disguise the still-tiny bump of her baby, then smoothed nervous hands along her hips. "Do I look all right?"

He tipped his head to one side, studied her, then smiled. "You look like you always do. Beautiful."

She laughed a little. Toby was really good for her self-esteem. Or, she thought, he would be, if she had any. God, what a pitiful thought. Of course she had self-esteem. It was just a bit like a roller-coaster ride. Sometimes up, sometimes down. Naomi'd be very happy if she could somehow reach a middle ground and stay there. But it was a constant battle between the two distinctly different voices in her head.

One telling her she was smart and talented and capable while the other whispered doubts. Amazing how much easier that dark voice was to believe.

And she was stalling.

"You're stalling," Toby said as if reading her mind. Her gaze snapped to his.

"Think you know me that well, do you?"

"Yeah," he said, a slow smile curving his mouth. "I do."

Okay, yes, he really did. Probably the only person she knew who could make that claim and mean it. Even her closest girlfriends, Cecelia and Simone, only knew about her what she wanted them to know. Naomi was really skilled at hiding her thoughts, at being who people expected or wanted her to be. But she never had to do that around Toby.

Taking her hand in his, he started for the front door. "Come on, Naomi. We'll talk to your folks, get this out in the open, then go have lunch so I can get a burger and you can nibble on a lettuce leaf."

She rolled her eyes behind his back, because damn it, he really *did* know her. All women watched their diets, didn't they? Especially *pregnant* women? At that thought, memories of that vile video Maverick had sent her rushed into her mind again. She saw the actress waddling, staggering across a mock-up of Naomi's own television set, and she shivered. She *refused* to waddle.

Naomi swallowed a groan and took the steps to the

wide front porch beside Toby. He was still holding her hand, and she was grateful. A part of her brain shrieked at her that it was ridiculous for a grown woman to be so nervous about facing her parents. But that single voice was being systematically drowned out by a *choir* of other voices, reminding her that nothing good had ever come from having a chat with Franklin and Vanessa Price.

"You ready?"

She looked up into his eyes, shaded by his ever-present Stetson, and gathered the tattered threads of her courage. She had to be ready, because there was no other choice. "Yes."

"That'd be more believable if you weren't chewing on your bottom lip."

"Blast," she muttered and instinctively rubbed her lips together to smooth out her lipstick. "Fine. Now I'm ready."

"Damn right you are." He grinned, and her nerves settled. Really, Naomi wasn't sure what she'd ever done to deserve a best friend like Toby, but she was so thankful to have him.

Before she could talk herself out of it or worry on it any longer, she reached out and rapped her knuckles on the wide front door. Several seconds ticked past before it swung open to reveal Matilda, the Price family housekeeper and cook.

Tall, thin and dressed completely in black, Matilda wore her gunmetal-gray hair short and close to her head. Her complexion was pale and carved with wrinkles earned over a lifetime. She looked severe, humorless, although nothing could have been further from the truth. Matilda smiled in welcome.

"Miss Naomi," she said, stepping back to open the

door wider. "You and Mr. Toby come in. I'll just tell your parents you're here. They're in the front parlor."

Of course they were, Naomi thought. She knew the Price family schedule and was aware that it never deviated. Late-morning tea began at eleven and ended precisely at eleven forty-five. After which her mother would drive into town to one of her charities and her father would go to the golf course or, on Tuesdays, the Texas Cattleman's Club to visit with his friends.

Waiting in the blessedly cool entry hall, Toby took his hat off, then bent to whisper, "Always makes me twitch when she calls me Mr. Toby."

"I know," Naomi said. "But propriety must be maintained at all times." Appearances, she knew, were very important to her parents. It had always mattered more how things looked than how things actually *were*.

She glanced around the home she'd grown up in. The interior hadn't changed much over the years. Vanessa Price didn't care for change, and once she had things the way she wanted them, they stayed.

Cool, gray-veined white marble tile stretched from the entry all through the house. Paintings, in soothing pastel colors, hung in white frames on ecru walls, their muted hues the only splash of brightness in the decorating scheme. A Waterford crystal vase on the entry table held a huge bouquet of exotic flowers, all in varying shades of white, and the silence in the house was museum quality.

Idly, Naomi remembered being a child in this house and how she'd struggled to find her place. She never really did, which was why, she supposed, she still felt uncomfortable just being here.

Toby squeezed her hand as Matilda stepped into the hall and motioned for them to come ahead. Apparently,

Naomi told herself, the king and queen were receiving today. The minute that thought entered her mind, she felt a quick stab of guilt. Her parents weren't evil people. They didn't deserve the mental barbs from their only child and wouldn't understand them if they knew how she really felt.

But at the same time, Naomi couldn't help wishing things were different. She wished, not for the first time, that she was able to just open the front door and sail in without being announced. She wished that her parents would be happy to see her. That she and her mom could curl up on the couch and talk about anything and everything. That her dad would sweep her up into a bear hug and call her "princess." That she wouldn't feel so tightly strung at the very thought of entering the formal parlor to face them.

But if wishes were real, she'd be sitting on a beach sipping a margarita right now.

Her parents were seated in matching Victorian chairs, with a tea table directly in front of them. The rest of the room was just as fussily decorated, looking like a curator's display of Louis XIV furniture. Nothing in the house invited people to settle in or, God forbid, put their feet on a table.

The windows allowed a wide swath of sunlight to spear into the room, illuminating the beige-and eggshell-colored furniture, the gold leaf edging the desk on the far wall, the white shades on crystal lamps and the complete lack of welcome in her parents' eyes. It was eleven thirty. They still had fifteen minutes of teatime left, and Naomi had just ruined it.

She was about to ruin a lot more.

"Hello, Mom, Dad." She smiled, steeled herself and

released Toby's hand to cross the room. She bent down to kiss the cheek her mother offered, and then when her father stood up to greet Toby, she kissed her dad's cheek, too.

"Hello, dear," Vanessa Price said. "This is a surprise. Toby, it's nice to see you. Would you like to join us for tea? I can have Matilda brew fresh."

"No, ma'am, thank you," Toby said after shaking Franklin's hand and stepping back to range himself at Naomi's side.

Franklin Price was a handsome man in his seventies. He wore a perfectly tailored suit and his silver hair was swept back from a high, wide forehead. His blue eyes were sharp but curious as they landed on his daughter. Vanessa was petite, and though in her seventies, she presented, as always, a perfect picture. Her startlingly white hair was trimmed into a modern but flattering cut, and her figure was trim, since she had spent most of her life dieting to ensure it. Her jewel-bright blue summer dress looked casually elegant and at the same time served to make Naomi feel like a hag.

"Is there something wrong, dear?" Vanessa set her Limoges china teacup down onto the table and then folded her hands neatly in her lap.

There was her opening, Naomi thought, and braced herself to jump right in.

"Actually, yes, there is," she admitted, and glanced at her father to see his concerned frown. "You've both heard about this Maverick who's been contacting people in Royal for the last several months?"

"Distasteful," Vanessa said primly with a mild shake of her head.

"I'll agree with your mother. Whoever it is needs to

be apprehended and charged," her father said. "Prying into people's private lives is despicable."

"He's caused a lot of trouble," Toby said and took Naomi's hand to give it a squeeze.

Her mother caught the gesture, and her eyes narrowed in suspicion.

"Maverick contacted *me* this morning," Naomi blurted out before she could lose her dwindling nerve entirely.

"You?" Vanessa lifted one hand to the base of her throat, her fingers sliding through a string of pearls. "Whatever could he do to you?"

Still frowning, Franklin Price looked from Naomi to Toby and back again. "What is it, girl?"

Oh, here it comes, she told herself. And once the words were said, everything would change forever. There was no choice. Toby was right—she couldn't keep hiding her baby bump with loose clothing. There would come a time when the truth just wouldn't remain hidden.

"I'm pregnant," she said flatly, "and Maverick is about to send a video out onto the internet telling everyone."

"Pregnant?" Vanessa slumped back against her chair, and now her hand tightened at the base of her throat as if she were trying to massage air into her lungs.

"Who's the father?" Franklin's demand was quiet but no less fierce.

"Oh, Naomi," her mother said on a defeated sigh. "How could you let this happen?"

"Who did this to you?" her father asked again.

As if she'd been held down against her will, Naomi thought on an internal groan. Oh, she couldn't tell them about Gio. About how stupid she'd been. How careless. How could she say that the baby's father was an Italian gigolo with whom she'd spent a single night? But what else *could* she say?

They were waiting expectantly, her mother just a little horrified, her father leaning more toward cold anger. She'd proven a disappointment. Again. And it was only going to get worse.

"I'm the father," Toby said when she opened her mouth to speak.

"What?" she whispered, horrified.

Toby gave her a quick smile, then fixed his gaze on her father. "That's why I came here with Naomi today. We wanted to tell you together that we're having a baby and we're going to be married."

Naomi could only stare at him in stunned silence. She hadn't expected him to do this. And she didn't know what to do about it now. A ribbon of relief shot whiplike through her, and even as it did, Naomi knew she couldn't let him do this. As much as she appreciated the chivalry, this was her mess and she'd find a way to—

"We wanted to tell you before anyone else," Toby went on smoothly. "Naomi's going to be living with me at my ranch."

"Toby—"

He didn't even glance at her. "No point in her staying at her condo in town, so she's moving to Paradise Ranch in a few days."

"But—" She tried to speak again. To correct him. To argue. To say *something*, but her mother spoke up, effectively keeping Naomi quiet.

"Living together isn't something I would usually approve," she said primly, "but as you're engaged, I think propriety has been taken care of."

*Propriety.* Naomi had often thought her mother would

have been happier living in the Regency period. Where manners were all and society followed strict rules.

"Engaged." Her mother said the word again, as if savoring it. "Oh, Naomi, you're marrying Toby McKittrick. It's just wonderful."

Vanessa rose quickly, moved to stand beside her husband and then actually beamed her pleasure.

Naomi had never been on the receiving end of that smile before, so it threw her a little. Then she realized exactly what her mother had said. She wasn't thrilled about the baby, but about her daughter marrying Toby. Handsome. Stable. *Wealthy* Toby McKittrick. That was the kind of announcement Vanessa Price could get behind.

And that realization only made Naomi furious. At Toby. She hadn't expected her parents to be supportive, but having Toby ride to the rescue felt, after that first burst of relief, more than a little annoying. She'd only wanted him here for moral support. Not to sweep in and lie to save her. The whole purpose of coming here to tell her parents the truth was to get it over with.

Now not only had the moment of truth been postponed, but Toby had added to the mess with a lie she'd eventually have to answer for.

"Toby—"

He looked down at her, gave her a smile, then surprised her into being quiet with a quick, hard kiss that left her lips buzzing. Shock rattled her. He'd never kissed her before, and though it hadn't been a lover's kiss, it wasn't exactly a brotherly kiss, either.

When he was sure she was shocked speechless, he turned to face her parents. "Naomi's a little upset. She wanted to be the one to tell you about us getting married, but I just couldn't help myself. And we're heading over to her place today to start packing for the move, so we wanted to see you first."

"Understandable," Franklin said with an approving nod at Toby, followed by a worried glance at Naomi. "I'll say, you worried me there for a moment with news of a pregnancy. But since you're marrying, I'm sure it's fine."

*Great.* All it had taken to win her parents' approval was the right marriage. God. Maybe they *were* in the Regency period.

"I don't see your ring," Vanessa pointed out with a deliberate look at Naomi's left hand.

Naomi sighed, then lifted her gaze to Toby as if to demand, *this was your idea—fix it.*

Then he did. His way.

"We're going right into town to see about that. And if I can't find what I want there," Toby announced, "we'll drive into Houston." He dropped one arm around Naomi's shoulders and pulled her up close to him. "But we wanted you to know our news before you heard about Maverick's video."

"No one pays attention to people of that sort," Vanessa said with assuredness.

Naomi wondered how she could say it, since the whole town of Royal had been talking about nothing else *but* Maverick for months. But Vanessa didn't care to see what she considered ugliness, and it was amazingly easy for her to close her eyes to anything that might disrupt her orderly world.

"Now, Naomi, don't you worry over this Maverick person," her mother said firmly. "You and Toby have done nothing wrong. Perhaps you haven't done things in the proper *order*—"

Meaning, Naomi thought, courtship, engagement,

marriage and *then* a baby. Still, her mother was willing to overlook all that for the happy news that her daughter would finally be *settled*, with a more than socially acceptable husband. Which meant that when she had to tell them that she absolutely was *not* going to marry Toby, the fallout would be epic.

"We should be going now. We need to get Naomi all moved in and settled at the ranch. Sorry for interrupting your tea," Toby was saying, and Naomi told herself to snap out of her thoughts.

He was going to hurry her out of the house before she could tell her parents the truth. And she was going to let him. Sure, she'd have to confess eventually, but right this minute? Naomi just wanted to be far, far away.

"Nonsense," Franklin said. "You're always welcome here, Toby. Especially now."

Naomi muffled a sigh. All it had taken was the promise of a "good" marriage to fling the Price family doors wide-open. She could only imagine how fast they would slam shut once they knew the truth.

"I appreciate that, Mr. Price."

"Franklin, boy. You call me Franklin."

"Yes, sir, I will," Toby promised, but didn't. "Now if you'll excuse us, I think we'll just go get Naomi's things and find that ring we talked about before Naomi changes her mind and leaves me heartbroken."

Vanessa's eyes widened. "Oh, she wouldn't!"

Toby winked at Naomi, completely ignoring how tense she'd gone beside him. To her parents, this suddenly imagined marriage was very real. She knew Toby thought he'd made things better, but in reality, he'd only made the whole situation more…complicated.

"You two enjoy yourselves, and, Naomi, we'll talk

about a lovely wedding real soon," her mother called after her. "We'll want to have the ceremony before you start...*showing*."

"Oh, God," Naomi whispered.

Toby squeezed her hand and hurried her out of the house. Once outside, he bundled her into his truck before she could say anything, so it wasn't until he was in the truck himself, firing the engine, that Naomi was able to demand, "What were you thinking?"

He blew out a breath, squinted into the sun and steered the truck away from the front door and back down the flower-lined drive. "I was thinking that I didn't like the way your folks were looking at you."

His profile was stern, his mouth tight and a muscle in his jaw flexing, telling her he was grinding his teeth together. Naomi sighed a little. She hadn't thought he'd take her parents' reaction so personally on her behalf, though in retrospect, she should have. He'd always been the kind of man to stand up for someone being bullied. He took the side of the underdog because that was just who Toby was. But she didn't want to be one of his mercy rescues.

"I appreciate the misguided chivalry," she said, striving for patience. "But it just makes everything harder, Toby. Now I'm going to have to tell them that I'm not moving in with you, our engagement is off and make up some reason for it—which my mother will never accept—and then I'll still be a single mother and they'll be even more disappointed in me than ever."

"They don't have to be." He shot her one fast look. "We move you out to Paradise today. We get married. Just like I said."

Naomi just stared at him. Since he was driving, he didn't take his eyes off the road again, so she couldn't see if he was joking or not. But he *had* to be joking. "You're not serious."

"Dead serious."

"Toby," she argued, "that's nuts. I mean, it was a sweet thing to do—"

"Screw *sweet*," he snapped with a shake of his head. "I wasn't doing it to be sweet and, okay, fine, I didn't really think about it before saying it, but once the words were out, they made sense."

"In a crazy, upside-down world, maybe. Here? Not so much."

"Think about it, Naomi."

She lifted one hand to rub her forehead, hoping to ease the throbbing headache centered there. "Haven't been able to do much else since you blurted out all that."

"Then think about *this*. There's no point in you raising a baby on your own when I'm standing right here."

"It's not your baby," she pointed out.

"It could be," he countered just as quickly. "I'd be a good father. A good husband."

"That's not the point."

"Then what *is*?"

She lifted both hands and tugged hard on her own hair. Nope, she wasn't dreaming any of this, which meant she had to get through to him. What he'd just said had touched her. Deeply. To know that he was willing to throw himself on a metaphorical grenade for her meant more than she could say. But that didn't mean she would actually allow him to claim another man's child as his own. It wouldn't be fair to him.

"There are many, many points to be made, but the main one is, I'm not your responsibility," she said, keeping her voice calm and firm.

"Never said you were," he said. "You are my friend, though."

"Best friend," she corrected, still looking at his profile. "Absolutely."

"Then accept that as your friend I want to help you."

"Toby, I can't let you do that."

"You're not *letting* me, I'm just doing it." He stopped at a four-way intersection and, when it was clear, drove on toward Royal. "It makes sense, Naomi. For all of us, the baby included. You really want to be all alone in that snazzy condo in Royal? Or would you rather be with me out at the ranch? If we're living together, that baby has two parents to look out for it. And, big plus, you can stop tying yourself into knots over your folks."

"So you're trying to save me." Just as she'd suspected. "This is all some grand gesture for my sake."

"And my own," he said, then muttered something under his breath and pulled the truck over to the side of the road. He parked, turned off the engine, then shifted in his seat to face her.

His eyes, the clear, cool aqua of a tropical sea, fixed on her, and Naomi read steely determination in that stare. She'd seen him this way before. Whenever he had an idea for one of his inventions, he got that *I will not be stopped* look on his face, in his eyes. If someone told him no about something, he took it as a personal challenge. Once Toby decided on a course of action, it was nearly impossible to get him to change his mind. This time, she told herself, it had to be different.

"I'm not a saint, and I'm not trying to rescue you."

"Could have fooled me," she murmured.

He sighed heavily, turned his gaze out on the road stretched out in front of them for a long second or two, then looked back at her. "Hell, Naomi, we're best friends. We're both single, and we can raise the baby together. Helping each other. This could work, if you'll let it."

A part of her, she was ashamed to admit, wanted to say yes and accept the offer he shouldn't be making. But he was her friend, so she couldn't take advantage of him like that. "I don't need a husband, Toby. I can raise my child on my own."

Now he sent her a cool, hard stare. "You forget, my mother was a single mom after my dad died. I watched how hard it was for her to be mother and father to me and my sister. To work and take care of the house. To run around after me and Scarlett with no one to help out. You really think I want to sit by and watch you go through the same damn thing?"

She bit her lip. She had forgotten about Toby's family. His mother, Joyce, was a smart, capable, lovely woman who had worked hard to raise her kids on her own. Now Toby was not just a successful rancher, but a wealthy inventor, and his younger sister, Scarlett, was a veterinarian. "Your mother did a great job with both of you."

His features evened out, and he gave her a smile. "And we thank you. But my point is, you don't have to do it the hard way like my mom did. Mom didn't have anyone to help her. You have me."

"I know," she said, taking a breath to calm the anger bubbling inside. "I really do know. But you don't have to marry me, Toby."

"Who said anything about *have* to?" he asked. "I want to. We're good together, Naomi. There's plenty of room at the ranch. You can take over one of the bedrooms for an office. It's not far from the studio where you film your show…"

True. All true. There was a small studio at the edge

of Royal where her cable TV show, *Fashion Sense*, was recorded once a week. And to be honest, being at the ranch would get her away from most of the gossiping tongues in town, and once Maverick's video hit, she'd be grateful for that.

"It's a great idea, Naomi. Hell, even your parents liked it."

She choked out a laugh. "Of course they did. Toby McKittrick—inventor, rancher, wealthy. I'm surprised my mother didn't squeal."

He gave her a half smile and a slow shake of his head. "You're being too hard on her. On both of them."

"I know that, too," she said with a sigh. She smoothed her fingertips over her knees. "They're not evil people. They're not even really mean. They just live in a very narrow world and it's never had room for me."

He reached out and took her hand, stilling nervous fingers. "There's room for you with me."

"Toby..." Naomi didn't know what to think. Or feel. He was right in that they were good together. They were already friends, and maybe a marriage of convenience would be good for both of them. But was it fair to him? "If we're married, you can't find someone for real."

"Not interested," he said firmly with a shake of his head. "Been there already, and it didn't end well."

Naomi sighed again. She couldn't blame him for feeling burned in the love department. She could, however, blame the woman who'd hurt him enough that Toby had built a wall around his heart that was so tall and thick it had taken Naomi months to reach past it.

"Fine. You're not looking for love. Neither am I," she added in a mutter. "But that doesn't mean..."

"Think about it."

"But no one will believe it."

"Your parents did."

She waved that aside. "That's because they don't know me. My friends—"

"Are so wrapped up in their own happily-ever-afters they won't question it."

"Your family—"

He scowled thoughtfully, but a moment later, his expression cleared. Those amazing eyes fixed on her, he said, "Okay, I'll tell my family the truth. Don't want to lie to them anyway. Does that work for you?"

"They won't like it," she said, and silently added, *they'll blame me.*

"Mom and Scarlett both like you already, so what's the problem?"

"I don't know if I want to be married," she said simply. "You're my best friend, Toby. It'll be...*weird*."

He laughed and shook his head. "Doesn't have to be. Think of it as a marriage of convenience. We're together because of the baby. No sex. Just friends who live together."

*No sex.* Well, it wasn't as if she was a wildly sexual person anyway. In fact, until that single night with Gio, she hadn't been with anyone in more than a year. And since Gio, she'd avoided *all* men except for Toby. So going without sex wouldn't be that terrible, would it? Oh, God.

"I'm not saying we become monks," Toby pointed out as though he could read her thoughts. "If one of us meets someone, we'll work that out then. In the meantime, we're together."

Toby watched her and wondered what the hell she was arguing about. Anyone could see this was a good idea. Though he could admit that he hadn't come up with it until that moment when Vanessa Price gave her daughter the cool look of disappointment at news of the baby. Damned if he could just stand there while Naomi tried to explain about the baby's father and how he was a worthless player. So, before he'd really considered it, he'd blurted out the lie. And it had felt…right.

Why not get married to his best friend? Whether she knew it or not, she was going to need help with the baby. And as long as they kept things between them platonic, everything would work out fine. Yeah, he was attracted to her. What man wouldn't be? But he wasn't going to act on that attraction, so a marriage of convenience was the best solution here.

"Well?" he asked, gaze fixed on hers. "What do you think?"

"I think you're crazy," she said on a half laugh.

"That's been said before," he reminded her. "People have been talking about crazy Toby and his weird inventions for years."

Nervously, she pushed her hair back from her face, and the early-afternoon sunlight caught a few threads of copper, making them gleam. "If we do this, we'll both be crazy."

"Worse things to be, Naomi."

She smiled. "Are you sure about this?"

He tipped his head to one side and gave her a look. "When have you ever known me to say something without meaning every damn word?"

"Never," she said, nodding. "It's one of the things I like best about you. I always know what you're thinking, because you don't play games."

"Games are for kids, Naomi. Neither one of us is a kid."

"No, we're not." She met his gaze squarely and took a deep breath. "I'm a city girl. What'll I do on a ranch?"

"Whatever needs doing," he said.

She laughed shortly. "We really must be crazy. Okay. I'll marry you and not have sex with you."

He grinned and winked. "Now, how many people can say that?" Turning in his seat, he fired up the truck, put it in gear and steered out onto the road again, headed for town. "We'll go get lunch, and then we'll go ring shopping."

"No."

"No?" He glanced at her, surprised.

"No ring," she said, shaking her head. "We don't need an engagement ring, Toby, and I don't want you buying one for me when it wouldn't really mean what it should. You know?"

He understood and couldn't say he disagreed. Their marriage would be a joining of friends, not some celebration of love, after all. "What's your mama going to say?"

Smiling sadly, Naomi said, "Even if we'd gotten one, she'd have found something wrong with it anyway."

They slipped into silence. Toby took her hand for the rest of the drive but left her to her thoughts.

# Three

Toby opened the door to the Royal Diner, steered Naomi inside and stopped. Every person in the place turned to look at them, and he knew. Maverick had done as promised. That stupid video was on the internet, and it seemed clear that it was the hot topic in Royal.

The welcoming scents of coffee, French fries and burgers greeted them. Classic rock played on the old-fashioned jukebox in the corner, and noise from the kitchen drifted out of the pass-through, but other than that, the silence was telling.

"Let's go," Naomi said, and tugged at his hand.

"Not a chance," Toby countered. Then, bending his head down to hers, he whispered, "Do you really want them to think you're scared?"

He knew it was just the right note to take when she squared her shoulders, lifted her chin and stood there like a queen before peasants. Toby hid a smile, because in just a second or two the woman he knew so well had reemerged, squashing the part of her that wanted to run and hide.

A couple of seconds ticked past and then the diner customers returned to their meals, though most of them looked to be having hushed conversations. It didn't take a genius to guess what they were talking about.

He gave Naomi's hand a squeeze, then took off his hat and smiled at Amanda Battle as she hurried over. Married to Sheriff Nathan Battle, who was doing everything he could to find out who this Maverick person was, Amanda owned the diner, along with her sister, Pam.

"Well, hi, you two," she said with a deliberately bright smile. "Booth or table?"

"Booth if you've got it," Toby said quickly, knowing Naomi wouldn't want to be seated in the middle of the room. Hell, he still half expected her to make a break for the door.

"Right. Down there along the window's good." Amanda gave Naomi a pat on the shoulder and said, "I'll get you some water and menus."

They walked past groups of friends and neighbors, nodding as they went, and Toby felt Naomi stiffening alongside him. She was maintaining, but it was costing her. She wasn't happy, and he couldn't blame her. Hell, he hated this whole mess for her.

The familiarity of the diner did nothing to ease the tension in Naomi's shoulders. The Royal Diner hadn't changed much over the years. Oh, it had all been updated, but Amanda and Pam had kept the basics the same, just freshening it all up. The floor was still black-and-white squares, the booths and counter stools were still bright red vinyl, and chrome was the accent of choice. The white walls held pictures of Royal through the years, and it was still the place to go if you wanted the best burger anywhere.

Once they were seated, Amanda came back quickly, set water glasses in front of them and handed out menus. Smiling down at them, she said, "I guess congratulations are in order."

"Oh, God," Naomi murmured, and her shoulders slumped, as if all the air had been let out of her body. "You've seen the video."

Amanda gave her a friendly pat and said, "I'm not talking about the video, honey. Don't worry about that. That nosy bastard has been poking into too many lives, so everyone here knows they could be next. Looks like this Maverick is moving around pretty quick, so he'll be onto someone new before you know it and you'll be old news."

Toby could have kissed her. "She's right."

Naomi looked at him, and he read resignation and worry in her eyes. "Doesn't help much, though. The whole town knows I'm pregnant now."

"Naomi, most of us guessed anyway," Amanda said. At Naomi's stunned expression, Amanda added, "You've never worn loose shirts and long cover-ups in your life."

Toby grinned. "She's got a point."

Naomi blew out a breath and gave him a rueful smile. "So much for my brilliant disguises."

"Oh—" Amanda waved one hand "—it probably fooled the men." She gave Toby an amused glance. "You guys don't really notice much. But women know a baby bump when they see one being hidden."

Naomi nodded. "Right."

"But I wasn't congratulating you on the baby anyway,"

Amanda continued. "Though sure, best wishes. I was talking about your engagement to Toby here."

Now it was his turn to be stunned. "How did you find out about that already?"

"Remember where we live, honey," Amanda said with a shake of her head that sent her dark blond ponytail swinging behind her. "Naomi's mother called one of her friends, who called somebody else, who called Pam's sister-in-law, who called Pam, who told me."

Naomi just blinked at her. Toby felt the same way. He had always known that gossip flew in Royal as fast as the tornadoes that occasionally swept across Texas. But this had to be a record.

"We just left my parents' house twenty minutes ago," Naomi complained.

"What's your point?" Amanda asked, grinning.

Helplessly shaking her head, Naomi said, "I guess I don't have one."

"There you go," Amanda said. "And so you know, most everybody's talking more about the engagement than that video. I mean, really." She laughed a little. "Maverick thought he was being funny, I guess, but him mocking you like that? Didn't make sense. People in Royal know Naomi Price has got style. So making that woman look so big and sloppy just didn't have the smack he probably thought it would."

Toby saw how those words hit Naomi, and once again, he could have kissed Amanda for saying just the right thing. She was right, of course. Naomi, even with her pregnancy showing, would be just as stylish as ever. That video was meant to hurt her, humiliate her, but he knew Naomi well enough to know that after the initial embarrassment passed, she'd rise above it and come out the winner.

"But you two engaged," Amanda said with a wink. "Now, that's news worth chewing on."

"I hate being gossiped about," Naomi muttered.

"In a small town," Amanda pointed out, "we all take our turn at the top of the rumor mill eventually."

"Doesn't make it any easier," she said.

"Suppose not, but at least people are pleased for you," Amanda said.

"Well, it's good the news is out." Toby spoke up, getting both women's attention. "And to celebrate our engagement, I'll have the cowboy burger with fries and some sweet tea."

"Got it. Naomi?"

"Small salad, please," she said. "Dressing on the side. And unsweetened tea."

"That's no way to feed a baby," Amanda muttered, but nodded. "And not even close to a celebration, but okay. Be out in a few minutes."

When she was gone, Toby took a drink of water, set the glass down and said, "She's right. That baby needs more than dry lettuce."

"Don't start," she warned, and turned her gaze on the street beyond the window. "I'm not going to end up waddling through the last of this pregnancy, Toby."

Irritation spiked, but he swallowed it back. Naomi had been on a damn diet the whole time he'd known her. In fact, he could count on the fingers of one hand how many times he'd seen her actually *enjoy* eating. She was so determined to stave off any reminders of the chubby little girl she'd once been, she counted every calorie as if it meant her life.

But it wasn't just her now. That baby was going to need protein. And once she was living with him on the ranch, he'd make sure she ate more than a damn rabbit did. But that battle was for later. Not today.

"Fine."

"I can't believe people already know about the engagement," Naomi said, looking back at him. Reaching out, she grabbed her paper napkin and began tearing at the edges with nervous fingers.

"At least they're talking about us, not the video," Toby pointed out and took another sip of water. His gaze was fixed on hers, and he didn't like that haunted look that still colored her eyes.

Scowling, she muttered, "I don't want them talking about me at all."

Toby laughed, and laughed even harder when she glared at him.

"What's so funny?" she demanded.

Scrubbing one hand across his face, he did his best to wipe away the amusement still tickling him. Keeping his voice low, he said, "You, honey. You *love* being talked about. Always have."

When she would have argued, he shook his head and leaned across the table toward her. "You were homecoming queen and a cheerleader—at college you were the president of your sorority. Now? You still love it. Why else would you have your own TV show? You like being the center of attention, Naomi, and why shouldn't you?"

"I didn't do all that just to be talked about," she argued.

"I know that," he said and slid one hand across the table to cover hers. "You did all of it because you liked it. Because you wanted to." *And because it was the at-*

*tention you never got at home and that fed something in you that's still hungry today.*

"I did. And I like doing my show, knowing people watch and talk about it." She leaned toward him, too, even as she pulled her hand from beneath his. "But there's a difference, Toby, between people talking about my work and talking about my life."

"Not by much, there isn't," he said and leaned back, laying one arm along the top of the booth bench. "Naomi, we live in a tiny town in Texas. People talk. Always have. Always will. What matters is how you deal with it."

"I'm dealing," she grumbled, and he wanted to smile again but was half-worried she might kick him under the table if he did.

"No, you're not." He tipped his head to one side and gave her a look that said *be honest*. "You're nearly five months along with that baby, and you just now told your folks."

"That's different." Her fingers tore at the napkin again until she had quite the pile of confetti going.

"And when we walked in here and people turned to look, you would have walked right back out if I hadn't gotten in your way."

She frowned at him, and the flash in her eyes told him he was lucky she hadn't kicked him. "I don't like it when you're a know-it-all."

"Sure you do." She lifted one eyebrow again, and he had to admire it. Never had been able to do it himself. "Look, either you can let this Maverick win, by curling up and hiding out…or you can hold your head up like the tough woman I know you are and not let some mystery creep dictate how your life goes."

"Using logic isn't fair."

"Yeah, I know."

She sat back in the booth and continued to fiddle with the paper napkin in front of her. It was nearly gone now, and he told himself to remember to ask Amanda for more.

"Toby, I don't want to let Maverick win. To run my decisions. But isn't that what I'm doing by agreeing to marry you?"

"No." He straightened up now, leaned toward her and met her gaze dead-on. "If you were doing what he wanted, you'd be locked in a closet crying somewhere. Do you think that bastard wants you to be with me and happy? Do you think he wants you turning the whole town on its ear so they don't even think about his stupid video?"

"No, I suppose not," she murmured.

"Damn straight." He laid his hand over hers again and quieted those nervous fingers. "You're taking charge, Naomi."

"That's not how it feels."

"I can see that. But trust me on this—you're the one calling the shots here. You've left Maverick in your dust already, and he's only going to get dustier from here on out." He squeezed her fingers until he felt her squeeze back. "Us getting married? That's a good thing. For all of us, baby included."

She sighed. "I just don't know how this day got away from me. One minute I'm dreading talking to my parents, and the next I'm engaged to *you*."

"I don't know why you think marriage to me is such a damn hardship."

Her gaze narrowed on his. "I didn't say that—fine," she said when he smiled. "Make jokes. We'll see how funny you think it is when I'm living at the ranch with you."

He shrugged to show her he wasn't bothered. "You're a good cook and you're already pregnant, so all I need to do is keep you barefoot and in the kitchen."

She laughed then slapped one hand to her mouth to hold the rest of it inside. Toby grinned at her. God, he loved hearing that wild, deep laughter come out of such a wisp of a woman.

"You're making me laugh so I won't obsess about what a mess my life is."

"Is it working?"

Thinking about it for a second or two, she finally said, "Yes. So, thanks."

"You're welcome."

He watched her as, still smiling to herself, she looked out the window at the little town still buzzing over their news. Royal had seen a lot of upheaval over the last few months. Thanks to the mysterious Maverick, things had been changing right and left. It wasn't just him and Naomi making a major shift in their lives. Some of Toby's friends had made sudden changes that at the time had completely surprised Toby.

Hell, there was Wes Jackson for one. Toby never would have thought that man would settle down and get married, and now the man had a wife, a daughter and another baby on the way. Tom and Emily Knox had worked out their problems and seemed stronger than ever, and even Naomi's best friends, Cecelia and Simone, were happy and settled into real relationships.

Toby knew that Maverick had been at the heart of all those changes. Sure, the man had been trying to ruin people, but in a roundabout way he'd helped them instead.

Toby had stood on the sidelines, watching his friends take steps forward in their lives, and wondered when he would be Maverick's target. But the nameless bastard hadn't come for him at all, but Naomi. Seeing her worried, upset, had torn at him enough that he was willing to put aside his anti-marriage stance. And actually, the more he thought about it, the more marrying Naomi made sense. He'd get a family out of it without having to worry about getting in too deep emotionally.

All he had to do was make sure she didn't back out.

"Hey, Toby," Clay Everett called out, "you got a minute?"

"Sure." Toby glanced at Naomi. "I'll be right back."

She nodded when he slid out of the booth and walked to the table where Clay and Shane Delgado were having lunch. Toby's strides were long and easy, as if he had all the time in the world. He was tall and confident and seemed so damn sure that they were doing the right thing, and Naomi really wished she shared that certainty.

Clay, Shane and Toby were all ranchers, so no doubt they were talking about horses or grazing pastures or summer water levels. Her gaze swept them all quickly. Shane had long brown hair, a perpetual five o'clock shadow and a killer smile. He was both a rancher and a real estate developer. Clay was the strong, silent type with short brown hair, a lot of muscles and a limp he'd earned riding the rodeo circuit. After the accident that had ended his rodeo career, Clay had started a cloud computing company and had found even more success. Then there was Toby. Toby was both an inventor and a rancher and, from Naomi's point of view, the most gorgeous of them all.

She blinked at that thought and realized that for the first time she was looking at Toby without the filter of the best friend thing. And it was an eye-opener. When he looked up at her and gave her a slow smile, something inside her lit up—so Naomi instantly shut it down.

Surprise at her own reaction to him had her tearing her gaze from his and reminding herself that this marriage was a platonic one and now was *not* the time to start noting things she never had before. Toby was standing for her like no one else ever had. He was being the friend he always had been, and she should be grateful. Maybe, eventually, she would be.

But at the moment, her own pride was nicked, and Naomi hated knowing that she needed the help. He was right, of course. Raising a baby on her own was a daunting idea, but she would have done it. Now she didn't have to face the future alone. She had her best friend standing beside her. The only real question was, was it fair to *him*?

"Here's your tea," Amanda said, sliding two tall glasses of icy amber liquid onto the table.

"Oh, thanks." Naomi reached for her glass and took a sip.

"It's decaf tea for you, sweetie." Amanda tossed a glance at Toby, Clay and Shane, deep into a conversation, then looked back at Naomi. "I'd expect to see a smile on your face, just getting engaged and all."

Naomi sighed a little. Amanda Battle was a few years older than her, but growing up in the same small town meant they'd known each other forever. Amanda's blond hair was pulled back into a ponytail, and her eyes were sharp and thoughtful as she studied Naomi. "What's going on, Naomi? A woman engaged to a man like Toby McKittrick should be all smiles—and you're not."

"It just happened so fast," Naomi said, already leaning into the lie she and Toby had created out of thin air.

"Not too fast, since you're carrying his baby," Amanda reminded her.

"True." Toby had claimed the baby as his already, so that didn't even feel like a lie. Especially since the baby's actual father didn't even know about the pregnancy. "But he sort of sprung the proposal on me just this morning and I haven't gotten used to it yet, I guess." The best lies had a touch of truth in them, right?

"I know it must feel like a lot," Amanda said, laying one hand on Naomi's shoulder in sympathy. "But I was in your shoes once, remember?"

She did remember, and because she did, Naomi couldn't understand why Amanda was being so nice to her. Several years ago, Amanda had been pregnant and agreed to marry Nathan Battle for the sake of the baby. But then she miscarried and called the wedding off. Amanda had left town after that but had come back a few years later when her father died, and almost instantly, she and Nathan had reconnected and set the gossip train humming. Today, though, Nathan and Amanda had two kids and were so happily married there were practically hearts and flowers circling Amanda's head.

But back then, Naomi and her friends Cecelia and Simone were at the height of their mean girl reputations, and though it shamed her to admit it, Naomi had spread every ounce of gossip about Amanda that had come her way. Shaking her head at the crowd of memories that made her want to cringe, she managed to ask, "Why are you being so nice to me?"

Amanda threw another glance at Toby to make sure he wasn't on his way back, then she slid onto the bench seat opposite Naomi. Tipping her head to one side, Amanda studied her for a second, then said, "Because I've been the center of gossip and I know how ugly it can make you feel. And, Naomi, you're not who you were back then."

"How can you be sure?"

"Because the old Naomi wouldn't be feeling bad about any of it."

Yes, she would have, Naomi thought. Even back then, when she'd been the queen bee, guilt had haunted her whenever she allowed herself to think about what she'd said or done. Now Naomi released a pent-up breath she hadn't even realized she'd been holding. All the years she'd been coming to the Royal Diner, she'd never really had an actual conversation with Amanda. Years ago, it was because they were too far apart in age, and Naomi was too busy mocking people to make herself feel better. And then later, she'd been too ashamed of her past actions to talk to her. A small smile curved Naomi's mouth. "Thanks for that."

Amanda smiled again, shot a quick glance at the kitchen pass-through, then looked at Naomi. "Most of us did things when we were young and stupid that we come to regret." Her smile turned rueful, but her green eyes never left Naomi's. "So if you're lucky enough to grow out of the stupid, then you have a second chance to be who you want to be."

"You make it sound easy."

"It's not," the other woman said. "But you already know that. You started that fashion show—which, by the way, I never miss—and you're building a future with Toby."

"True." But if you were planning that future on a lie, did it count? Could it work? Not questions she could ask out loud. "Thanks. For the pep talk and, well, everything."

"No problem." Amanda scooted out of the booth, stood up and patted Naomi's shoulder again. "Toby's a good guy. You should celebrate."

Nodding, Naomi watched Toby laughing with his friends. Texas cowboys, all three of them. And handsome enough to have women lining up just to take a look at them. Her heart twisted as her gaze landed on Toby just as he lifted his head, caught her eye and winked. That flicker of something bright and hot sparkled inside her again, and though she fought to ignore it, the heat lingered.

In reflex, Naomi returned that smile and quietly hoped that this marriage didn't cost her her best friend.

Toby knew he'd catch his mom and sister off guard with his announcement. After lunch, where he'd finally convinced Naomi to take a small bite of his burger, Toby dropped her off at her condo to start packing. Then he'd driven straight to Oak Ridge Farms, his family ranch.

It was smaller than his own spread, but the ties binding him to the land ran strong and deep. His mother rented out most of the acreage to other ranchers and farmers, and his sister had her veterinary clinic in the remodeled barn. But no matter what changes took place, it would always be the McKittrick Ranch, and steering his truck up the drive would always make him feel the tug of memories.

He knew that he would beat the news of his engagement home, because it didn't matter how fast word was spreading throughout Royal. His mother, Joyce McKittrick, didn't approve of gossip, so she'd been cut out of the rumor loop years ago. As for his sister, Scarlett was too busy caring for the local animals to waste time or interest on gossip.

Toby had told Naomi that he wouldn't lie to his family. So after he explained the whole situation to his mom and sister, he waited for the reaction. He'd expected they'd be surprised. He hadn't expected them to be so happy about it. Especially since he'd made it clear that love didn't have a thing to do with his reasons for this marriage.

"You're marrying Naomi?" Scarlett McKittrick squealed a little, then leaped up from her chair at the kitchen table and ran around to hug her brother. "It's about time."

"What?" Toby looked at his younger sister when she pulled back to grin at him.

"Well, come on," Scarlett said. "You two have been tight for years, and even a blind person would have seen the sparks between you."

Sparks? There were sparks? Toby frowned a little as he realized that maybe all the lustful thoughts he'd been entertaining for so long had been obvious. Well, that was lowering, if his sister noticed something that he'd never seen himself—or allowed himself to see.

"Scarlett," he said, automatically returning his sister's hug, "there are no sparks. I told you it's a marriage of convenience."

"Yeah, I heard you," she countered and gave his cheek a pat as she straightened up. "Doesn't mean I believe you. I've seen the way you look at Naomi, Toby. And it's not like you're thinking *hey, good buddy*."

"That's exactly what it is. She's my friend. That's all."

Shaking her head, Scarlett glanced at the wall clock and said, "If that's how you want to play it, fine. Look, I've got to run. There's a cow giving birth, and if she manages to pull it off before I get there, people will think they don't need to call me for this stuff." She grabbed her huge black leather bag and headed for the back door.

Once there, she stopped, ran her fingers through her short honey-brown hair and narrowed wide hazel eyes on him. "But I'll want more details later, you hear? 'Bye, Mom. Don't know when I'll be back."

And she was gone. Scarlett McKittrick was a force of nature, Toby thought, not for the first time. She'd always moved through life like a whirlwind, and now that she was a vet, it was even worse. Answering calls for help at all hours, she was dedicated to the animals she loved and as caring as their mother.

Scarlett did everything at a dead run, moving from patient to patient and keeping a grin on her face while she was doing it. Most people looked at her and thought she was too slight to do the kind of work she did. But Toby had seen his sister in action. When one of his mares got into trouble during labor, Scarlett had been there to save the foal and the mother. He knew she had the strength, determination and pure stubbornness to do a job most often thought to be a man's purview.

When the door slammed behind her, silence settled on the homey kitchen. He glanced around quickly while he grabbed a chocolate chip cookie from the plate in the middle of the table. The walls were sky blue and the cabinets were painted bright white. Toby himself had painted the kitchen for his mother the summer before, and he figured she'd be ready for another change by next year. The floor was wide oak planks, and the fridge and the stove had been replaced with top-of-the-line new ones. But there were old pictures attached with magnets to the new fridge, and when he looked at the images of him and Scarlett as kids, he had to smile. His mom's old mutt, Lola, was napping on a cushion under the bay window, and her snores rattled in the room.

Toby had grown up in this house and spent too many hours to count sitting at this very table. He'd done his homework here, had family dinners, come in late from a date to find his mother awake and waiting up for him. So it made sense to him that it was here that he and his mother had the conversation he could see building in her eyes.

Joyce McKittrick was short, with golden-blond hair that fell in waves to her shoulders. Her blue eyes were as sharp as ever, and she never missed a thing. She was, he thought, beautiful, strong and smart. Hadn't she stepped up when Toby's father died, to raise Scarlett and him on her own? Thanks to her husband's life insurance, they hadn't had to worry about money, but Joyce had never been one to sit back and do nothing. She'd boarded horses and given riding lessons to local kids. And she'd encouraged both Scarlett's love of animals and Toby's inventive nature. In fact, she was the one who'd made sure he got a patent on his very first invention—a robotic ketchup dispenser he'd come up with at the age of ten.

Joyce was his touchstone, the heart of their family, and she had given his sister and him the kind of home life that Naomi had missed out on.

"When you first said you were marrying Naomi, I was pleased. She's a good person, and I'm glad she's finally letting that side of her out to shine instead of hiding behind a mean streak that wasn't natural to her."

He smiled to himself. Trust Joyce to see past the surface to the truth beneath. Not many had, really. Naomi,

Cecelia and Simone had been like a trio of mean for a long time. They had always seemed to enjoy setting people back a step. To strike quick with a sharp word or a hard look.

But times, like everything else, changed, and now the three of them seemed to be coming into their own. Naomi, especially, he thought, had done well by letting go of her past enough to carve out the future she wanted for herself.

"Should have known you'd see through all that drama she used to be a part of," Toby said ruefully.

"Of course I did." Joyce waved that aside. "Her parents are…difficult and they made Naomi's life a misery for her, I know. It says something about her character that she's come so far all on her own." She reached out and smoothed his hair back from his face. "Though she had a good friend, these last few years, to be there for her."

"I have been," Toby said, wanting her to understand. "And I'm going to continue."

"I know that, too," his mother said, sitting back in her chair to give him a long look. "But, Toby, starting a marriage with a lie isn't the best way to go."

"We're not lying to each other," he countered. "Or to you and Scarlett." He'd known she'd feel this way, and he couldn't blame her. But he could convince her he knew what he was doing. "Naomi needs me, Mom. That baby does, too. I watched you struggle as a single mother, and I don't want to watch Naomi do the same. We get along great. We're good friends."

*Apparently with sparks*, he warned himself silently, and then dismissed the warning. "We're good together, and this is what I want."

"Then I want it for you," she said, though her eyes

said different. "All I ask is that you be careful. That you really think about what you're letting yourself in for."

He grinned and winked. "I'm always careful."

"Not nearly enough," she said, laughing a little.

"Honestly," Toby said, stealing another cookie and taking a bite. No one made cookies like Joyce McKittrick. "I figured you'd have the most trouble with me claiming the baby as mine."

"Not a bit," she said, shaking her head firmly. "That baby is an innocent, and you and Naomi are doing the right thing for it. I just want to be sure it's the right thing for *you*."

"It is, Mom," he said, his tone deep and serious. "I never figured to get married..."

She snorted a laugh. "Men always seem to say that, yet the world is filled with husbands."

His eyebrows arched. "*Anyway,*" he said pointedly, "Naomi and I are good together. I think we'll make this work for all of us."

"I always liked Naomi," Joyce said, nodding. "She's got a lot of spirit and a little sass, and that's a good thing. But she's also got a heart that's not been treated very gently over the years."

"I'm not going to hurt her."

"Not purposely, of course," she said. "And she wouldn't intentionally hurt you, either. Still, I'm your mother, so I'll worry a little, and there's nothing either of us can do to stop that. But if it's my blessing you were after, you have it."

"You're amazing," he said softly.

"I just know my son." She stood up, walked to a cupboard and came back with a plastic zip bag. She dumped every last cookie into the bag and sealed it before handing it over to Toby. "You take these home with you. And when you get home, you have a good long talk with yourself. Make sure this is what you want."

"I have. I will." He reached out and patted her hand. "I know what I'm doing."

Joyce shook her head and smiled wryly. "Scarlett was right, you know. There's always been sparks between you and Naomi."

"Mom…"

"I'm just saying, don't be surprised if those sparks kindle a fire neither of you is expecting."

# Four

The next morning, Naomi was at the local cable studio outside Royal. No matter what else was going on in her life, she had a job to do—the fact that she loved her job was a bonus.

The station was small but had everything you could need. Local businesses used it to film commercials, the high school football games were broadcast from the studio, and Naomi's own show had been born there. The studio was so well set up they had community college students as interns, helping the professional staff.

She tried to focus on the upcoming taping of her show, but it wasn't easy to concentrate when she knew that Toby would be coming by her condo that afternoon to help move her things to the ranch. Naomi stopped on the walk across the parking lot, just to allow her brain to wheel through everything that was happening. She'd worked hard to buy her little condo in Royal and then to fix it up just as she wanted it. Sure, it was small, but it was *hers*. Her own place. And now she was giving it up to move to the country.

Granted, growing up in a small town in Texas, she was used to being in the country. But she'd never *lived* there. And not only was she giving up her home, but she was marrying her best friend, and that still was enough to make her bite her bottom lip and question herself.

In fact, Naomi had spent most of the night before pacing through her home, mind spinning. Was she doing the right thing? She didn't know. There were plenty of doubts, plenty of questions and not many answers. All she could be sure of was the decision had been made and there was no backing out now—since the whole town was talking about her engagement to Toby.

Of course, she told herself, since everyone was busy with Toby's lie, no one was talking much about the hideous video Maverick had put out. And today she was taping her first maternity-wear show—fighting fire with fire. Maverick had wanted to make her look foolish, but she would take his announcement and make it her own. Toby had been right about that. If Maverick wanted her crying in a corner somewhere, he was going to be really disappointed.

Truthfully, it was a relief to no longer have to hide the fact that she was pregnant. Disguising a growing baby bump wasn't easy. Loose shirts, pinned slacks and an oversize bag to hold in front of the rounding part of her body could only work for so long. Knowing her secret was out was…liberating in a way she hadn't expected.

Taking a deep breath, she headed for the building, stepped into the air-conditioned cool and came face-to-face with Eddie, the lead cameraman. He was an older man, with grizzled salt-and-pepper hair that stuck out around his head like he'd been electrocuted.

"We're ready for the run-through, Naomi." He gave her a smile and a thumbs-up. "You good to go?"

"I really am, as soon as I stop by makeup," she said. Twenty minutes later, she walked to the set, hair perfect, makeup just as she wanted it and her wardrobe displaying that bump she'd been hiding for too long.

Local cable channel or not, Naomi's show, *Fashion Sense*, was catching on. In the last year, she'd managed to get picked up by affiliates in Houston and Dallas, and just this week a station in Galveston had contacted her about carrying her show. And, thanks to social media, word about her show was spreading far beyond the Texas borders. Her Facebook page boasted followers from as far away as New York and California and even a few in Europe.

Naomi had plans. She wanted to take her show national. She wanted to be featured in magazines, to be taken seriously enough that even her parents would have to sit up and take notice. And she was going to make those dreams come true. Lifting her chin, Naomi walked in long, determined strides to the center of her set and turned to face the camera and her growing audience. The lights were bright, hot and felt absolutely right.

"In five, four," Tammy, the assistant sound engineer, said, counting down with her fingers as well until she reached one and pointed at Naomi.

"Hi, and welcome to *Fashion Sense*. I'm Naomi Price." She was comfortable in front of the camera. Always had been, a small part of her mind admitted quietly. Toby had been right about that, too. She enjoyed being the center of attention when it was *her* idea.

And she had a lot of ideas. Just last night, while she wandered her condo hoping for sleep, her mind had raced with all kinds of possibilities. To grow her audience, she had to grow the show itself. Make it appeal to as many people as possible. There were plenty of women out there, she knew, who didn't give a damn about fashion—though she found that hard to believe. But those women did care about their homes, decorating. Just look at all the DIY programs that were so popular.

Well, she couldn't build a staircase or install fresh lighting, but she knew how to find those who could. So today, she was going to announce a few of the changes she had in mind. Starting, she told herself, with the biggest announcement of all. With Maverick's video out and viral by now, she had to assume that her viewers had seen it, or would have by the time this show aired. So she was taking control of the situation.

"As you can see," she said, turning sideways to show off the baby bump proudly displayed beneath a tight lavender tank, "my own personal fashion style will be undergoing some drastic transformations over the next few months. My fiancé, Toby McKittrick, and I are both very happy about our coming baby and we're excited to greet all the new things in our future."

Smiling into the camera, she faced the audience head-on again and continued. "And to keep up with the changes in my life, I'm going to be doing a lot of shows focusing on contemporary, fashionable maternity wear, obviously."

Again, that brilliant smile shot into the camera and into homes across Texas. "But don't worry. It's not going to be all babies all the time. As our lives grow and evolve, we have to keep up. So here on *Fashion Sense*, we're going to be branching out—dipping into home furnishings and gardens and even designing your own outdoor living space." She tossed her hair back from her face and winked. "Since I'm expanding, I thought it was only right the show did a little growing, too."

Off camera, she heard a chuckle from one of the grips and knew she'd hit just the right note.

"So I hope you'll come with me on this journey of discovery. Over the next few months, we'll all be in new territory—should be fun!"

"And cut."

When Eddie gave her the go-ahead, Naomi looked at him and asked, "Well, how'd I do?"

"Great, Naomi, seriously great." Eddie winked at her. "I think you're on to something with this house stuff. My wife's always watching those home shows, coming up with things for me to do. So I already know she'll be hounding me to do whatever it is you show her."

"Good to know," Naomi said, laughing.

"We're gonna set up for the next shot. Be about fifteen minutes," Eddie said as the crew scurried around, making TV magic happen.

As long as most women felt as Eddie's wife did, this new direction Naomi was determined to take would work out. All she had to do was bring in experts to interview and to demonstrate their specialties. She could already see it. Gardeners, painters, tiling specialists. She would push *Fashion Sense* to the next level—and at the bottom of it, didn't she have Maverick to thank for the push?

Unsettling thought. Naomi wandered off to a chair in a quiet corner of the studio, sat down and turned her phone on. She checked her email, sighed a little at the number of them and wondered halfheartedly how many of them were because of Maverick's video. With that thought in mind, she closed her email program. She didn't need to deal with them right this minute, and she really didn't want to ruin the good mood she was in.

Because she felt great. She'd taken Maverick's slap at her and turned it around. She was taking ownership of her pregnancy, pushing her show to new heights—and marrying her best friend.

Okay, she could admit that she was still worried about that. Toby had been such an important part of her life for so long that if she lost him because of a fake marriage, it would break her heart. So maybe they needed to talk again. To really think this through, together. To somehow make a pact that their friendship would always come first.

The rumble and scrape of furniture being moved echoed in the building, letting her know the guys were still hard at work. So when her phone rang, Naomi checked the screen and felt her heart sink into a suddenly open pit in her stomach.

Wouldn't you know it? Just when things were starting to look up.

Answering her phone, she said, "Hello, Gio."

"Ciao, *bella*." The voice was smooth, dark and warm, just as she remembered it from that night nearly five months ago now.

Naomi closed her eyes as the memory swept over her, and she shook her head to lose it again just as fast. It wasn't easy admitting that you'd been stupid enough to have a one-night stand with a man you *knew* would be nothing more than that. And even though they'd used protection, apparently it wasn't foolproof.

Gio Fabiani, gorgeous, lying player who'd sneaked past her defenses long enough to get her into bed. Even now Naomi felt a quick stab of regret for her own poor choices. But moaning over the past wouldn't get her anywhere. She opened her eyes, looked across the room at the crew busily working and kept her voice low as she spoke to Gio. As much as she'd prefer to just hang up on the man, she had to do the right thing and tell him about the baby.

"I have your many messages on my phone, *bella*," Gio was saying. "What is so important? Is it that you miss me?"

She rolled her eyes and ground her teeth together, silently praying for patience. Behind his voice, she heard the telltale clatter and noise of a busy restaurant. With the time difference between Texas and Italy, it was late afternoon for Gio and he was probably at his favorite trattoria, sitting at a table on the sidewalk where he could see and be seen. She frowned at the mental image and then instantly shut down everything but the urge to get the truth said and done.

"I've been trying to get hold of you for months, Gio," she said softly.

"*Sì, sì,* I have been very busy."

Getting other foolish women into his bed, no doubt, and oh, how it burned to know she'd been just one of a crowd.

"Yes, me too. Gio," she said, taking a breath to say it all at once. "I'm pregnant."

Silence on the other end of the line and then, "This is happy news for you, *sì?*"

She skipped right over that. None of his business how she was feeling. "You're the father."

A longer silence from him this time, and she heard the street sounds of Italy in the background. She could see him, lounging in a chair, legs kicked out in front of him, a glass of wine in one hand and the phone in the other. What she couldn't see was his reaction. She didn't have long to wait for it, though.

"I am no one's father, *bella*," he said softly enough that she had to strain to hear him. "If you carry the baby, the baby is yours, not mine."

She hadn't expected anything else, but still, hearing it felt like a slap. How many women, she wondered, had made this call to Gio? How many times had he heard about a child he'd made just before he walked away from all responsibility? He was a dog, but it was her own fault that she'd fallen for his practiced charm. Toby had been right about him, of course. He'd called him a user, and that described Gio to a tee.

Naomi didn't actually *want* Gio in her life or her baby's. It seemed she would get what she wanted. But she had to be sure they both understood right where things were. "You're not interested?"

"*Bella*, you must see that I am not a man who wishes the encumbrance of a child."

The tone of his voice was that of a man trying to explain something to a very stupid person. And maybe she had been stupid. Once. But she wasn't anymore.

"That's fine, Gio. I'm not the one who made this phone call, Gio. I don't want anything from you," she said, flicking a glance toward the set, making sure no one was within earshot. "You had a right to know about the baby. That's it."

"Ah," he said on a long sigh of what she assumed was satisfaction. "Then we are finished together, yes?"

*Big* yes, she thought. In an instant, her mind drew up an image of Toby and what had happened yesterday. How he'd stood with her to face her parents. The difference between the two men was incalculable. Toby would always do the right thing. Always. Gio did the expedient thing. And Naomi herself? She would do what was best for her baby. And that was ridding them of the man who was, as he'd pointed out, *no one's* father.

"Yes, Gio," she said, her grip on the phone tightening until her fingers ached. "We're finished."

And she was relieved. She'd never have to see him or deal with him again. There was no worry about him coming back at some later date, wanting to be a part of her baby's life. The minute he hung up the phone, Gio would forget all about this conversation. He would forget *her*. And that was best for everybody.

*"Arrivederci, bella,"* Gio said and, without waiting for a response from her, disconnected.

She expelled a breath, looked at her phone for a long minute, then shook her head. Naomi had been trying to reach Gio for weeks, and when she finally did manage a conversation with him, it had lasted about three minutes. It felt as if a huge weight had been lifted off her shoulders. "It's over."

Of course it had *been* over for months. Heck, it had never even started with Gio, really. You couldn't count one night as anything other than a blip on the radar that appeared and disappeared in the blink of an eye. If she hadn't gotten pregnant, would she even have given Gio a single thought? "No, I wouldn't have," she said out loud.

Really, she'd have done everything possible to never think about one night of bad judgment. She looked down at the phone in her hand as a wave of relief swept over her. Gio was well and truly out of her life. Naomi knew Toby would be pleased to hear it.

*Toby.*

The familiar noises of the crew working registered in one part of her mind as her thoughts swirled as if caught in a tornado. What did it say, she asked herself, that the first person she wanted to tell about the call from Gio was Toby? That he was her best friend. That he was the one person in her life she always turned to first.

Maybe marrying him would be all right, she told herself now. Maybe it would be good for all of them. She trusted him, she loved him—as a friend—and she knew she'd always be able to count on him. So what was she so worried about? No sex? Not that big a deal, she assured herself silently. Heck, it wasn't as if pregnant women had red-hot sex lives anyway.

Was it fair to Toby? Wasn't that up to him? she reasoned. If he wanted to marry her, why shouldn't she? Yes, she could be a single mother. She was perfectly capable of raising a child on her own. But as Toby had pointed out, why deliberately take the hard route when there was another answer? And knowing that Toby would be with her, sharing it all, seemed to make the niggling fears of impending motherhood easier to conquer. But what to do with the fears she had of losing her best friend because of a convenient lie?

"We're ready, Naomi," Tammy shouted from across the room.

Pushing herself out of the chair, still wrestling with her thoughts, Naomi walked to the set. Distracted, she took her place in the center of the stage.

"Hey, hey," Eddie said. "Find your smile again, Naomi. We've got to finish this segment."

"Right." She shook off the dark thoughts, focused again on the moment and resolved to put all her energies into making this the best show she could.

Toby led the way into the stable, glancing over his shoulder at Clay Everett. As a former rodeo champ, Clay was the best judge of horseflesh in the county—not counting Toby himself, of course. Clay had left the rodeo behind after a bull-riding accident that had been bad enough to leave him with a slight limp. And a part of the man still missed it, Toby knew. The competition, the intensity of a seven-second ride that could win a trophy or break your heart. But he was settled now in Royal on his own ranch, and horses were still a big part of his life.

Of course there was more to Clay than being a successful rancher. His company, Everest, installed cloud infrastructure for corporations and was in demand by everyone with half a brain. Though Clay was a hell of a businessman, his heart was still at his ranch. The man was much like Toby in that way. Didn't matter how many inventions Toby came up with or how his business interests ate up his time, the ranch fed his soul.

There were twenty stalls in Toby's stables, but only eleven of them were occupied at the moment. Clay was here to see one of Toby's treasures—a beautiful chestnut mare called Rain.

"I brought her in from the south pasture this morning. Thought you'd want to take a close look at her before sealing the deal."

"You thought right," Clay said and stopped alongside Toby at the stall's half door. Inside the enclosure, the beautiful horse stood idly nosing at the fresh straw on the floor. When Toby clucked his tongue, the mare looked up, then moved to greet him.

"She's a beauty," Clay said, reaching out to stroke the flat of his hand along the horse's neck.

The mare actually seemed to preen under the attention. Clay laughed. "Yeah, you know you're something special, don't you?"

"She does." Toby watched Clay feed the mare an apple he'd brought along just for that reason. "She's two years old, good health—Scarlett did a full physical on her last week."

"Scarlett's word's good enough for me," Clay said, stroking the horse's nose. "Yeah, you still want to sell her, I want her."

"Deal," Toby said and gave the mare one longing look. Raising horses also meant you had to sell them, too. You couldn't keep them all. But every time he sold a horse, he felt the loss like a physical pang. Still, he knew Clay would be good to her, and Toby would get a chance to see her once in a while.

"We'll go up to the house, have a beer and take care of business."

"Sounds good," Clay said. Then he slanted Toby a look. "I hear you and Naomi are getting married."

*Getting married.* The words didn't send a clawing sense of dread and panic ripping through him. After Sasha walked out on him, Toby had pulled back from anything even remotely resembling a relationship. Now here he was, engaged, going to be a father, and it felt… good.

Toby blew out a breath, tipped the brim of his Stetson back a bit and nodded. Here it was. He was going to look into his friend's eyes and lie to him. But, hell. A lie to protect Naomi didn't bother him a bit. "When you've got a baby coming, it's time to get married."

Clay's eyebrows lifted. "Hadn't heard the baby part of the rumor. My source is slipping."

Toby grinned. "Times are sad when you can't count on the gossip chain to be thorough."

"Can't believe how the men in this town are getting caught in the marriage trap." Clay shook his head as if very sad for all his friends. The man's smile, though, told Toby he was enjoying all this. "Wes Jackson is a man I thought would never go down that road, and look at him now."

Toby had been thinking the same thing just a few months ago. Watching Wes reconnect with the woman he loved and discover he had a daughter had hit Toby hard at the time. Back then he'd felt the same way Clay did now, that somehow Wes had set himself up for pain. Funny how your ideas could change so dramatically in just a few months. Of course, he reminded himself, he wasn't in love with Naomi. This was a bargain between friends. Which was why it would work.

"He's happy." Toby braced both feet wide apart, folding his arms across his chest. Just because he wasn't looking for love didn't mean he couldn't recognize it when he saw it. "Hell, he practically *glows* when he's around Belle. And as for his daughter, Caro, he's become such a whiz at sign language he's talking about teaching it to a few of us so we can talk secretly to each other in the TCC board meetings."

Sunlight speared through the open stable doors, pouring spears of gold into the shadowy interior. The building smelled of horses and hay—one of Toby's favorite scents.

Nodding thoughtfully, Clay said, "Not a bad plan

there. But not the point of what I was saying. It's this whole wedding plague that's sweeping through Royal. It's picking the men off one by one."

"A *plague*?" Toby laughed.

"It sure as hell seems contagious," Clay said. Ticking them off on his fingers, he continued. "There's Deacon and Hutch and Tom Knox."

"Tom doesn't count," Toby interrupted. "He and Emily were already married."

"Yeah, but they were separated, now they're not," Clay pointed out. "Then there's Shane and now *you*."

Toby laughed shortly and shook his head. "I'm not sick—so not contagious, no worries there. I'm not caught in a trap, either, man. I'm marrying my best friend." And as he said it, Toby again felt the rightness of it. There was no risk in this marriage. No worry about falling for a woman and having her walk out, taking half his heart with her.

He'd already done that. Already lived through betrayal and having his heart smashed under the boot of a woman who decided some loser wannabe country singer was a better bet than a Texas inventor/cowboy. When Sasha walked out, she'd burned him badly enough that Toby hadn't wanted anything to do with women. But Naomi had been there with him, through all of it.

He didn't give a damn about Sasha anymore and figured he'd made a lucky escape in spite of the pain and fury he'd survived. And Naomi had helped him get clear of all that. So marrying her was not just a perfect solution to the current problem—it was also a way to stand by Naomi. To thank her for being there for him when he needed it most. This marriage meant he got his best friend living with him. He got a child to raise and love, and he didn't have to worry about whether or not he could trust his wife.

"Yeah, well," Clay said wryly, "she's your best friend *now*. That'll stop when she's your *wife*."

A flicker of doubt sputtered into life inside him, but Toby squashed it flat. "Not Naomi. I trust her."

"Your funeral," Clay said with a shrug.

"You talk a hard game," Toby retorted with a half laugh. "But then there's Sophie."

Sophie Prescott. Clay's secretary.

The other man shrugged, stuffed his hands into his pockets and said, "What about her?"

"Oh, man, don't try to look innocent. You can't pull it off." Toby laughed. "I've seen the way you look at her."

"Looking's one thing. Marrying's another," Clay allowed with a grin. "The rest of you may get picked off one by one, but you can bank on me being the last single man standing."

"Yeah," Toby said, heading for the house, waiting for Clay to follow, "that's what we all say. But you know what? You're going back to a cold, empty ranch, while I'll be here with Naomi."

He smiled to himself as he realized he was looking forward to having her here. To her being a part of his everyday life. Of watching that baby inside her grow. With Naomi, he could have the life he wanted with none of the dangers or risks. What man wouldn't want that?

# Five

"So," Simone asked as she set an empty box down on Naomi's bed, "how excited is Toby to be a father?"

Simone had her nearly blue-black hair pulled back into a thick tail that hung down between her shoulder blades. The woman's amazing ice-blue eyes shone with a kind of happiness Naomi was glad to see there. Simone had the kind of face that made most people think she was gorgeous but empty-headed. It didn't take her long to prove just how brilliant she really was.

"He says he's really happy about it." Which was true, but not the whole truth. A flicker of unease rippled through her as Naomi realized that to keep her bargain with Toby, keep her baby safe, she'd have to lie to her closest friends.

It wasn't that she didn't trust Simone and Cecelia both. They'd been friends forever, and heaven knew the three of them had shared so many secrets, there really wasn't much they didn't know about each other. But she had to think about her baby, too. The baby who would grow up knowing Toby as its father. Was it fair to her child to let other people in on the fact that Gio Fabiani had been her sperm donor? And that was really all he had been, she assured herself. He wasn't a father in any sense of the word, so did he really deserve to even be mentioned? Now that she'd actually spoken to him and knew without a doubt that he'd never have anything to do with the baby, wasn't it better for everyone to just forget about his involvement completely?

"I can't believe you managed to keep your pregnancy a secret. From *us*," Simone added. "I mean, you're nearly five months, right?"

"It's because she never eats," Cecelia put in, playfully sticking her tongue out at Naomi. She was any man's dream woman, Naomi thought. Gray-green eyes, long wavy platinum hair, a curvy figure and long legs. She was also driven, ambitious and funny. "She's pregnant and still skinnier than I am."

Skinny. That had been Naomi's goal for most of her life. Now her body would be doing as much changing as her life, and she found she wasn't too concerned about it. Maybe it was having Toby standing with her. Maybe it was finally accepting and being proud of the fact that she was going to be a mother. Whatever the reason, though, Naomi thought it was about time she stopped worrying so much about the scale. She had more to think of than herself now, right? Hadn't Toby said just the other day that the baby needed more than a lettuce leaf to grow on?

"Naomi?" Cecelia asked. "You okay?"

"What? Yeah. Sorry. I'm fine. I'm just—" She paused, looked around at the chaos strewn around the bedroom of her condo and realized it was the perfect metaphor for her life. "Overwhelmed."

"Easy to understand," Simone said, folding another sweater and laying it in a box. "It's not every day you get slammed in a viral video, get engaged and announce a pregnancy."

"God," Naomi whispered. "It sounds even crazier when you say it out loud."

"Yes, but you're handling it," Cecelia said, pushing her hair back and kicking back onto the bed to get comfy. She crossed her feet at the ankle, grabbed a pillow and held it against her belly. "Simone and I have had our share of crazy lately, too, remember?"

"Absolutely," Simone muttered and pushed Cecelia's feet out of the way to reach for a stack of folded T-shirts. "Honestly, I didn't know what was going to happen with Deacon, but now look at us."

Cecelia tossed Simone more shirts while Naomi zipped her cosmetics case closed.

"Heck, look at *all* of us," Cecelia said with a wide smile. "The mean girls are done, and we're all in love."

Naomi sighed a little.

"Plus," Cecelia added, "we're all pregnant at the same time. Our kids can grow up friends."

"I'm more pregnant," Simone pointed out. "There's three in here." She patted her slightly rounded tummy. "Remember?"

Cecelia laughed. "You always were a show-off."

Naomi smiled, too, because it was so easy to be with these women. They'd been a trio for so long she couldn't even imagine her life without them in it. She had great friends. Cecelia, Simone—and Toby.

Bottom line, worries and all, it came down to the fact that she was marrying her best friend. How bad could it be?

"Is it time for a break?" Cecelia asked from the bed. "Come on, let's let the new fiancé finish this up when he gets here."

"Cec," Simone said, "if you'd pack as much as you talk, we'd be finished by now."

"Talking's more fun," Cecelia said, but she dutifully pushed herself off the bed, walked to the closet and dragged Naomi's garment bag down off the high shelf. "Fine. I'll get as much of her stuff into this thing as I can. But there's no way we'll get all your clothes in one trip, Naomi."

"I know." Her condo was small, but the closets were huge. It was really what had sold her on the place. "You know what?" she said, making up her mind on the spot. "Cec, do what you can with that bag. Simone, when we fill up this box, we're stopping. That's it. I've got enough to live on, and it's not like I'm moving to the moon. Toby and I can come back to get the rest another time."

"Deal. I feel ice cream coming on," Cecelia said from the depths of the closet.

Simone sighed. "Ice cream. I love ice cream. And I'm going to be *much* bigger than you guys will be, so I shouldn't have any. But I'm weak."

"You're safe, then," Naomi told her with a shrug. "I don't have ice cream in the house." In fact, she didn't have anything fattening in the condo. She'd never seen the point in testing her own willpower.

"Oh, that's just wrong." Cecelia came out of the closet,

laid the garment bag on the bed, then picked up her purse. "I'm going up to the store for ice cream and maybe cookies. I'll be back in fifteen minutes."

When she was gone, Simone said, "Thank goodness for Cec. I really do want ice cream now."

Naomi laughed. "I guess we do have to have some priorities, huh?"

"Ice cream is top of the list," Simone said. Then she hooked one arm around Naomi's shoulders. "I know what you're thinking. Everything's changing."

"Yeah," Naomi agreed, wrapping one arm around her friend's waist, "that's it exactly."

"I was feeling the same way just a few weeks ago, but then I remembered the most important thing."

"What's that?" Naomi asked.

"Change can be *good*, too."

"You're right," Naomi said and looked around the room again.

This condo had been perfect for her once. When she was single, with nothing more to think about than the career she was trying to forge. But the condo wasn't who she was anymore.

It was time to figure out who she was becoming.

"We can't sleep in the same bed."

Later that night, Naomi was at Paradise Ranch, staring up at Toby in stunned surprise. Sure, they had a no-sex agreement, but *look* at him.

He took a breath and blew it out again in obvious exasperation. "Naomi, you know I've got a housekeeper. If Rebecca sees we're not staying in the same room, how long do you figure it'll be before the rest of Royal knows it?"

"But—" She looked at the gigantic bed against the far wall of Toby's bedroom and shook her head. Sure, it was big enough for four or five people, but was it big enough for the two of them?

The room was cavernous, just right for the master of the house. There was a black granite fireplace tall enough for Naomi to stand up in, with two chairs and a table sitting in front of the now cold hearth. Along one wall were bookcases stuffed with hard-and soft-backed books, family pictures, and framed patents Toby had received for his many inventions. Across from the bed, a gigantic flat-screen TV hung on the wall, and French doors on the far wall led out to a wide wooden balcony that overlooked the fields behind the house and the really spectacular pool.

But her gaze kept sliding back to that bed. A massive four-poster, with heavy head-and footboards, the mattress was covered in a dark red quilt that looked as if it had been hand stitched. Toby's mother, Joyce, was a quilting fiend, so she was probably behind that. And there was a small mountain of pillows propped against that headboard, practically begging a person to climb up and sink in.

The whole room was inviting, and Naomi had to at least partially blame herself for that, since she'd helped him decorate the house. But she'd never imagined herself sleeping in the master bedroom.

"I thought I'd be staying in one of the guest rooms," she argued. "You've got seven bedrooms in this place."

"Yeah." He scrubbed one hand across the beard stubble on his jaw. "But married people sleep together. That's what folks expect."

He had a point, and why hadn't she considered it before? She hadn't counted on this at all. How was she supposed to share a bed with her best friend?

"Okay, look," he said, clearly reading what she was thinking. "We'll try this. You can sleep in the room next to mine, but all your stuff stays here, in my room. That should throw Rebecca off the scent. Especially if we keep that guest room looking like nobody's been in it."

"Okay. I can do that." This was crazy and getting worse by the minute. Enforced closeness was going to push their friendship places it had never been before, and it really worried her that the relationship might just snap from all the tension.

Reaching out for him, she laid one hand on his forearm and waited until his gaze shifted to hers. "You have to promise me, Toby. You have to swear that no matter what else happens between us, we stay friends."

"That's not even a question, Naomi." He pulled her in close for a hard hug, and Naomi surprised herself by leaning into him, relishing the feel of his strength wrapping itself around her. So much was changing so quickly that he was her stable point in the universe, and if she lost him, Naomi didn't think she could take it.

"We're gonna do fine, Naomi. Don't worry." His hands moved up and down her back, and tiny whips of heat sneaked beneath her defenses. Startled by that simmering burn, she stepped away from him, told herself that she was just tired. Distracted. Vulnerable. But that heat was still there, and Naomi knew she needed some distance.

And she didn't think the guest room was going to be far enough away.

Naomi hadn't been awake at 6:00 a.m. in...*ever*. And couldn't understand why she was now.

An avowed town girl, Naomi had always believed the only reason to be up with the sun was that your house was on fire. Yet now she was going to be a rancher's wife. She was in the country, where the quiet was so profound it was almost alive. There were no cars roaring down the street, no neighbors with a too-loud stereo. Here the night was really dark and there were more stars in the sky than she'd ever known existed.

She hadn't slept well, either. Lying there in the dark, listening to the quiet, knowing Toby was just on the other side of the wall, had kept her too on edge to do more than doze on and off. So this morning, it was too early, she was too sleepy and felt too off balance. Clutching the single measly cup of coffee she allowed herself each day she stepped out onto the back porch, where the soft, morning breeze slid past her.

The only reason she was up early enough to watch the sun claim the sky and begin to beat down on Texas with a vengeance was that Toby had woken her in the guest room so she could move into his bedroom while he went to work.

Once in Toby's bed, she'd tried to get back to sleep, but the pillows carried his scent and the sheets were still warm from his skin, and none of that was conducive to sleeping. She could have stayed upstairs and unpacked, but instead she'd grabbed one of Toby's T-shirts and pulled it on over her maternity jeans—that thankfully didn't *look* like maternity jeans unless you saw the elastic panel over the belly. She wore slip-on red sneakers and left her hair to hang in a tumble over her shoulders.

Now she looked around in the early morning heat and thought how beautiful Paradise Ranch was. There were live oaks studding the yard, providing patches of shade under the already blazing Texas sun. A kitchen garden behind the house was laid out in tidy rows and surrounded by a low white picket fence in the hopes of discouraging rabbits. The corral was enclosed by a high fence, also painted white, and the barn as well as the bunkhouse used by the cowboys who worked for Toby were freshly painted in a deep brick red. Toby's workshop was on the other side of the property from the barn and was the same farmyard red as the rest of the outbuildings.

The yard in front of the house boasted a neatly tended green lawn. Summer flowers in bright jewel tones hugged the base of the big house. But the house itself was the masterpiece. Two stories, it was the kind of house you expected to see in a mountain setting, with cedar walls, river rocks along the foundation and tall windows that opened the house up to wide views of the ranchland. To one side of the house was a pool, surrounded by rocks and waterfalls so cleverly designed that it looked like a naturally formed lagoon, and the whole thing was shaded by more oaks and a vine-covered pergola. A wraparound porch held tables and comfortable chairs that signaled a welcome and silently invited people to sit and relax.

This wasn't her first visit to Toby's ranch. She'd helped him design it. Helped to decorate it. Yet it all felt…different to her now. Not surprising, she told herself, since now she was *living* here. And awake way too early.

She took another sip of her coffee and let her gaze slide across the trees, the field beyond the barn and then back to the corral where Toby was grooming one of his prized horses.

Toby stood near the fence, brushing down a golden-brown horse whose coat seemed to shine in the sunlight.

But as beautiful as the horse was, Naomi couldn't take her eyes off Toby. He wasn't wearing a shirt. She took another gulp of coffee and struggled to swallow past the knot in her throat.

His chest was broad and chiseled, skin tanned, and every move he made had his muscles rippling in a way that made her think of those cool sheets and the wide bed.

"Oh, God..." Hormones, she told herself. Had to be hormones running amok inside her. Pregnancy was making her crazy. It was the only explanation for why looking at her best friend could suddenly turn her insides to mush.

She laid one hand on her rounded belly, and touching her baby seemed to ground her. Remind her of why she was here. What she'd agreed to. And for heaven's sake, Toby was her *friend*. She had no business getting all ruffled over a muscular chest and a tight butt encased in worn blue denim. She shouldn't even be noticing how the shadows thrown across his features by his cowboy hat made his face look sharply dangerous. And if she had any sense at all, she'd turn right around and go back in the house.

"Naomi?"

*Oh, thank God.* She turned to the open back door where Rebecca stood, holding out a sturdy wicker basket. "Yes?"

Rebecca had graying red hair, bottle-green eyes and freckles sprinkled liberally across her nose and cheeks. She was a widow in her midfifties with two grown kids who lived in Houston. She'd been working for Toby for five years and lived in a set of rooms off the kitchen. And she couldn't be more excited at the prospect of having a baby in the house to take care of.

"I've got to get breakfast going, and you could do me a huge favor if you'd go collect some eggs for me."

"Eggs?"

Rebecca wiggled the basket. "The chicken coop is on the other side of the barn. Just gather what's there. Should be enough with what's still in the fridge."

Naomi walked over, took the basket and handed her now-empty coffee cup to the other woman. "You know, I've never actually gathered eggs before," she admitted, wondering why it sounded like an apology.

"Nothing to it." Rebecca was already darting back into the coolness of the house. "Just reach under the chickens and grab them up." She let the screen door slam behind her, then closed the wood door as well.

"Reach under the chickens." Naomi looked at the empty basket, then lifted her gaze to the side of the barn where she could just make out another structure. A chicken coop. With chickens in it. Did chickens bite?

"I guess I'll find out," she muttered and started walking. If nothing else, this should take her mind off Toby. For now, anyway. She was headed across the yard, in no hurry to find out what *reaching under a chicken* was like, when Toby's voice stopped her.

"Hey, Naomi, come on over here a minute."

She changed course and walked to the corral, swinging the wicker basket with each step. Toby watched her approach, and even in the shadow of his hat, she saw those aqua eyes of his shining. Then Toby flashed a grin that made her heartbeat jolt a little, and Naomi told herself to get a grip.

Honestly, she'd always known he was a good-looking man. You'd have to be blind not to notice. But did he have to be *gorgeous*? Up close, his chest looked broader, his skin tanner, and every muscle seemed to have been carved out of bronze. She swallowed hard, forced a smile and said, "I'm supposed to be gathering eggs. Do the chickens mind?"

He laughed.

"Seriously," she said. "How do you gather eggs?"

Shaking his head, he said, "You're a smart woman. You'll figure it out." Toby opened the corral gate so she could step into the paddock with him. "I wanted you to meet Legend."

The horse he held by the bridle was tall and golden brown, with a dark streak down the center of his nose. His big dark eyes locked on Naomi, and she said, "He's beautiful."

"He is," Toby agreed. "I've had Legend with me since I was a kid. He's been living out at Mom's ranch, but I brought him here to Paradise a couple months ago. He's old, and I wanted him to live out the rest of his life here. With me."

"He doesn't look old." She reached out one hand to stroke the horse, but Toby grabbed her hand and pulled her back. "What's wrong?"

"Probably nothing. You just have to be careful around him. Like I said, he's an old man now and pretty damn crotchety." Toby held the horse's bridle tightly so she could slide her hand across the big animal's neck. "He gets so he doesn't like anybody—even me," he said, with a chuckle. "So I just want you to be cautious with him."

"Oh, you're not dangerous, are you?" Naomi was no stranger to horses. It would be impossible to grow up in Royal, Texas, and not be at least comfortable around them. She'd never had her own horse and hadn't really ridden much since high school, but she'd always liked them. And Legend, she could see, meant a lot to Toby.

"You just like getting your own way, don't you?" she cooed as she stroked and petted the horse. "Well, I do, too, so we'll get along fine, won't we?"

"You the horse whisperer now?" Toby asked.

She shot him a look from the corner of her eye. "He's male, isn't he? A woman always knows her way around a crabby man."

"Is that right?" One corner of his mouth tipped up.

God, he smelled good. He shouldn't smell good after standing out in the early-morning sun, sweat already pearling on his chest and back.

"I've talked you out of every bad mood you've ever had."

He laughed again and stroked Legend's nose. "Not much of a test, since I'm not a moody guy."

"Oh, really?" She tucked her arm through the handle of the basket and looked up at him. "When you couldn't get the hydraulic lift to work on the patio table you built to go below ground?" It had been a terrific invention and one of her favorites that he'd come up with.

A picnic table that seemed to dissolve into a patio, with the push of a button, it lifted, pieces sliding into place until it was a concrete-topped table big enough to seat six. When you wanted it, there it was. When you didn't need it, it disappeared, leaving only a patio behind.

"That was different," he said, a slight frown on his face.

"How?"

"That wasn't moody. That was frustration."

"Frustration *is* a mood," she pointed out, pushing her hair back from her face. "But did I talk you out of it or not?"

That frown slid into a smile of remembrance. "You did. Took me to the roadhouse for a beer and karaoke."

"You're a terrible singer."

"But I make up for it with enthusiasm."

Naomi laughed and felt everything in her settle. This was good. Hormones aside, this was what she needed, wanted. This easy affection. They were friends, and they always would be. She'd see to that.

"Okay," she said, giving Legend one last pat, "now that I've won an argument—"

"Not an argument. No one shouted."

"A debate, then," she amended. "I have chickens to assault and eggs to kidnap. If you don't hear from me in half an hour, come and find me."

"You're taking this whole rancher's wife thing to heart, aren't you?" he asked, and his mouth was still curved in a smile.

"If I'm living here, I'm doing my share of chores," she said. "As long as the chickens don't kill me." She looked past him to the horse. "Legend, it was nice meeting you. Toby, I'll see you at breakfast."

She headed for the corral gate and stopped when Toby laughed. Turning around, she saw that Legend had pulled free of Toby's grip to follow her. "I've never seen him do that before," he admitted.

"I'm new here, that's all," she said and kept walking. But now she heard the horse's hooves plopping onto the powder-soft dirt right behind her. Naomi stopped again and this time waited for the horse to come close. Staring up into those chocolate-brown eyes, she smiled and said, "You're on my side, aren't you?"

The horse lifted his huge head then laid it gently on her shoulder as if giving her a hug. Touched, Naomi whispered to the big animal and stroked his neck as she would have a puppy.

She looked over at Toby and saw amazement on his face as he watched her. And Naomi thought that maybe this was all going to work out, after all.

# Six

The next couple of weeks were harder than Toby had thought they would be. Living with Naomi was both torture and pleasure.

She was his friend, but more and more, he was noticing her breasts, her butt, her smile, her low, full-throated laugh that tugged at something deep inside him. Lust, pure and simple, he told himself. Now that she'd relaxed about her pregnancy and he'd gotten her to loosen up and actually eat real food, she was curvier than ever, and that was giving him some bad moments.

He didn't want to feel for her. Didn't want to start feeling a need for more. But he didn't seem to have a choice in that. Cursing under his breath, Toby grabbed a screwdriver, stepped behind his latest project in the workshop and tightened the screws there. He smoothed his thumb over them to make sure they were deep set, then took a long walk around the piece, inspecting every inch before moving to test the design. Better to keep busy, he told himself. To keep his brain so full of work it didn't have time to pick apart thoughts of Naomi.

The workshop was his sanctuary. When Toby had the ranch built, he'd had this shop done to his specifications. The floor was hardwood, as it was easier to stand on for hours than concrete. The windows were wide enough to let in plenty of natural light, plus there were skylights in the roof. The walls were peppered with sketches he'd stuck there with pieces of tape. There were walls full of shelves holding every kind of supply he might need. And the wall behind his bench was covered in Peg-Board so he could hang his favorite tools within easy reach.

On the far side of the building, he had lumber, plastic, metal and vinyl and a table saw to let him cut anything down to whatever size he needed. This building was the one spot in the universe that was all his. No one came in here, so he was always guaranteed peace and quiet and the solitude he needed to spark ideas. He'd come up with some of his best stuff in this shop, and whenever he was here, his brain kicked into gear.

Until lately.

"Just keep focused." He studied the raw version of his design, looking for areas he could improve. If it worked as it was supposed to, of course, he'd redo the whole thing in finer materials and, with patent in hand, get it onto the market. It was what he did, what he'd been doing most of his life. Taking ideas and making them real. A few of those inventions had helped him amass a fortune that had allowed him to buy this ranch and live exactly the way he wanted to.

"And nothing's going to change just because Naomi's

here," he muttered. But hell, even he didn't believe that. Things had already changed.

Having Naomi around constantly was like having an itch he couldn't scratch. He hadn't counted on that. Her scent was everywhere. It was like she was stalking him. In his sleep, in the kitchen, hell, even here in his workshop he couldn't get her out of his mind. She'd invaded every part of his life, and what was worse, he'd *invited* her in. He'd done this to himself by coming up with that marriage-of-convenience idea. Now his skin felt too tight, his mind was constantly filled with images of her and she was looking at him as she always had. As good ol' Toby.

"And that's how you've got to stay," he said tightly. Once he got used to her constant presence, he'd get over the whole want-to-strip-her-naked thing and their relationship would smooth out again. That would be best. He didn't want any more from her than friendship, because anything beyond that was too damn risky. He could deal with the sexual frustration. But if she got any deeper under his skin, Toby could be in trouble. And he'd had enough female trouble to last him a lifetime already.

So he deliberately pushed everything but the moment at hand out of his head. All he needed was to keep his distance from her once in a while. Clear his head. Get some space. Like today. Some time spent in the workshop, focused on what he loved doing.

"Toby," Naomi called, walking into the workshop. "You in here?"

"So much for that idea," he muttered. "Yeah." He raised his voice. "In the back."

Sanctuary was gone now, so he braced himself for being near her. It was just as well she was sleeping in the stupid guest room, he thought. He didn't know if he could take it, having her in his bed every night and *not* touching her.

He heard her footsteps and could have sworn he smelled her perfume rushing toward him. Toby didn't dare take a deep breath to steady himself—he'd only draw more of her into him. And he was already on the slippery edge of control.

"Wow, you've been busy," she was saying as she got closer.

He turned to watch her as she approached and asked himself how any man could keep his mind on work when Naomi Price was around. Hell, she was his friend, and right now it felt like a damned shame to admit it.

Shaking his head at his own disturbing thought, he turned back to the shelf unit.

"I've got a few more projects hitting the market in the next couple months," he said.

"Like what?"

One thing he gave Naomi, she'd always been interested in his inventions. Wanting to know what they did, how they worked and how he'd come up with them.

"There's a self-leveling measuring cup—" He glanced at her as she came closer. "My mom loves to bake and complains that there are different kinds of cups. For dry or liquid. This cup does both and levels itself so you know you're always right."

She gave him a smile, and it lit up her eyes. Toby looked away fast, but not fast enough. The pit of his stomach jittered, and a little lower, his body went rock hard. Damn it.

"Your mom'll be happy. What else?"

She picked up a wood dowel and twirled it in her fingers. Those long, slender fingers with the deep red polish on the nails. He looked away again.

"Something Scarlett wanted," he said and made a minor tweak to the hydraulic system. Anything to keep his brain focused. "She keeps her vet tools in the trunk of her car and had one of those flimsy trunk organizers. The one I designed is heavy acrylic, with a hinged lid and compartments that slide out with a button push." He checked the mechanism on the back of the piece again. "I figure it'll be a hit with carpenters, plumbers, artists, even fishermen. They'll be able to keep their stuff handy and safe."

"Wow." She dropped the dowel onto the workbench. "Okay. Made your mom and Scarlett—not to mention millions of others—happy. What've you got for me?"

He looked at her in time to see a wide smile flash across her face. *What did he have for her?* Well, now, that was a loaded question, wasn't it? Rather than face it, he asked, "What do you need?"

She propped one hip against the workbench, threw her amazing long copper-streaked brown hair back behind her shoulders and said, "Surprise me."

Damn. Everything she said now tempted him, and he knew she hadn't meant it that way. "I'll do that."

"So, what're you working on now?"

"This? It's a prototype for a new piece of furniture," he said, relieved to shift his thoughts back to safe territory. He stood back, folded his arms over his chest and said, "Look at it. Tell me what you see."

Frowning a little, she moved to get a better look. Sadly, she moved closer to him, and her scent wrapped itself around him.

After a second or two, she shrugged. "It looks like

a bookcase. At least the top half does. The bottom half looks like it's a cabinet door, but you don't have any pulls on it yet."

He grinned. "Don't need them. See that switch on the side there? Give it a turn."

She did, and the machinery inside hummed into life. Naomi moved out of the way and watched, a smile on her face, as the cabinet door swung out and up until it was horizontal, jutting out from the bookcase itself. "Cool. It converts to a table."

"There's more," Toby said and, stepping forward, reached under the table and pushed another switch to one side. Instantly, hidden benches lowered from beneath the table and took their places, one on each side.

She laughed. "I love it. Table and chairs in a bookcase."

He liked that approving smile and took a seat on one of the benches as he waved her toward the other one. "In a small place? Buy this bookcase, and you have a table when you want one and it's gone when you don't."

She propped her elbows on the table and rested her chin on her joined hands. "For a man with a gigantic house, you're really into space-saving mode, aren't you?"

He ran his hand over the table surface. "I like coming up with things that can be multifunctional."

"It's brilliant. I love it." She looked at the top half. "And the bookcase stays in place so you don't have to unload it before using the table. Very cool."

"Thanks." He looked at the piece again. "There are some products like this on the market, but none that include benches along with the table and none that use hydraulics like I'm using them."

"Another patent for the boy inventor."

"Haven't been a boy inventor for a long time," he said, shifting his gaze back to hers.

For one long, humming second, the air between them nearly bristled. Toby stared into her eyes and wondered if she could read the hunger no doubt shining in his. She licked her lips, huffed out a breath and opened her mouth to speak. But whatever she might have said was lost, and the mood between them shattered, when another voice called from the doorway.

"Hey, you two! I'm on the clock here. No canoodling."

"Canoodling?" His eyebrows lifted. "Scarlett's here?"

Ruefully, Naomi smiled. "That's what I came to tell you. She's here to give Legend a checkup. I took him from the corral into his stall to make it easier on her. You know, out of the sun. It's really hot out there."

Toby shook his head again. "You mean you walked to the stall and he followed you."

"Pretty much. What can I say? He finds me irresistible."

*A lot of that going around*, Toby thought grimly. His horse loved her, and Toby couldn't stop thinking about her. Naomi Price was making life on the ranch a hell of a lot more interesting than he would have believed.

"Hello? You coming out or do I have to come in?" Scarlett's shout was tinged with laughter.

"We're coming!" Naomi called back and got up. She headed for the front door, then stopped and looked back at Toby.

Through the skylight, sunlight poured down over her like a river of gold. It highlighted the copper streaks in her brown hair and made her brown eyes glow like aged whiskey. Her body was curvier than he'd ever seen it, and the rounded mound of the baby made her seem softer, more alluring than he wanted to admit. She stood there, watching him, the hint of a smile on her face, and everything in Toby tightened into a hot fist.

"You coming?" she asked.

"Nearly," he muttered, and stood up slowly, trying to mask the signs of his body's reaction to her. "Yeah. Be right there."

As soon as he could walk again.

A few days later, Naomi had her files—folders with clippings and printouts of websites she was interested in—scattered across the dining room table. The room, just like every other one in the house, was perfect. At least to Naomi. The table was a live edge oak, long enough to seat twelve and following the natural contours of the tree it had been made from. The grain was golden and gleaming from countless layers of varnish and polish. A fireplace along the wall was unlit, and in the cold hearth were ivory candles on intricate wrought-iron stands. The windows across from Naomi gave her a view of the paddock and the fields stretching out beyond.

Naomi had the whole house to herself, since Toby was at Clay Everett's and Rebecca was in Royal doing some grocery shopping. Funny, Naomi used to be alone so much of the time she had convinced herself she loved it. Now that she lived with Toby and had the ranch hands popping in and out and Rebecca to sit and talk to, the house today seemed way too...*quiet* with everyone gone. On the other hand, she told herself, she could get some of her own work done with no interruptions.

With her new plans for the show, Naomi wanted to line up guests who could come in and demonstrate different ideas. And she knew just where she wanted to start. There was a place in Houston that specialized in faux stone finishes. It was owned and operated by a woman who'd started her business out of her garage. The show would be good for Naomi and good for the woman's company.

She shuffled through a pile of papers looking for the number, and when her cell phone rang she answered without even looking at caller ID. "Hello?"

"Ms. Price?"

"Yes." Frowning slightly at the unfamiliar voice, she said, "If this is about a survey or something, I'm really not interested—"

"I'm calling from Chasen Productions in Hollywood."

Naomi swallowed hard and leaned back in her chair. Panic, curiosity and downright fear nibbled at her. Hollywood? She took a breath, steadied her voice and said calmly, "I see. What can I help you with?"

"My name is Tamara Stiles, and I think we can help each other."

"How so?" *Wow.* She silently congratulated herself on sounding so calm, so controlled, when her insides were jumping and her mind was shrieking. Hollywood. Calling *her*.

"I've seen your show, and I'd like to talk to you about perhaps taking it national."

Naomi lurched up from her chair and started walking, pacing crazily around the long table. This couldn't be happening. Could it? Really? Her show. On national TV?

"National?" Did her voice just squeak? She didn't want to squeak. Oh, God, she couldn't seem to catch her breath and she really wanted to sound professional.

"That's the idea," Tamara answered. "Do you think you could come to Hollywood next week? I'd like to meet in person to see what the two of us can come up with."

Clapping one hand to the base of her throat, Naomi said, "Um, sure. I mean, yes. Of course. That would be great. I'd love to meet with you." *Understatement of the century.*

"Fine, then. Give me your email and I'll send you my contact information. I can arrange for your flight and hotel—"

"Not necessary," Naomi said, instantly wanting to stand on her own two feet. Sure, it would be nice if a Hollywood producer paid for her travel, but if Naomi did it herself, *she* remained in charge. They exchanged information, and then Naomi said, "I'll email you when I have particulars."

"Excellent. If you could be in town Monday, that would work well for us here."

"Monday is doable." Even if it wasn't, she'd find a way to make it work. Hollywood? Taking her show national?

People had enjoyed her local cable show, and it was getting more popular, but Naomi knew that her parents considered it more a hobby than anything else. This would convince them that she was so much more than they thought.

There were too many emotions crowding around inside her. Too many wheeling thoughts and dreams of possibilities. She was starting to shake, so she got off the phone as quickly as possible. There was no one there to tell. She needed to tell Toby, but she couldn't do it over the phone.

So Naomi just sat there in the silence. Alone. Smiling.

Later that night, Toby listened and watched as Naomi paced back and forth in the great room. She hadn't stopped talking since he got home, and honestly, he couldn't blame her. Pretty big deal getting a call out of the blue from Hollywood. Good thing the great room was as big as it was, though. Gave her plenty of space to walk off her nerves.

"Can you imagine?" she asked. "Hollywood? Calling me?"

"Well, why wouldn't they?" Toby said from his position on the couch. He was slouched low, feet crossed at the ankles, hands folded on top of his belly. "Even California's got to hear about it when a show takes off like yours has."

She stopped, threw him a grin that was damn near blinding. "You have to say that. You're my best friend."

There it was. Best friend. No lust. No need. Just pals. As it should be. If only his brain would get the memo. "You're great at what you do, Naomi. Half of Texas is talking about you, and the other half will be soon. Why not Hollywood?"

"You're right. Why not?" She started pacing again, her steps getting quicker and quicker as her words tumbled over each other. "Tamara," Naomi said, "isn't that an elegant name? Very showbizzy."

"Showbizzy?"

She shot him another wide smile. "I'm rambling and I know it. Heck, I can hear myself babbling and I can't seem to stop. Until you got home, I was talking Rebecca's ears off. She was too nice to tell me to be quiet and go away."

"Maybe she's pleased for you," he pointed out.

"She is. I know. But you're the one I wanted to tell, Toby." Naomi stopped dead, looked at him from across the room and said, "It about killed me waiting for you to get back from Clay's, because I just couldn't tell you this over the phone."

"Next time you need me," he said, sitting up, leaning his forearms across his knees, "call. I'll come home."

"Okay. Thanks. I will." She took a deep breath, laid one hand on her rounded belly and sighed. "Toby, this is just so crazy. Am I crazy?"

"Not that I've ever noticed."

"I've got to get tickets. And a hotel reservation."

"For both of us," he said, and she looked at him in surprise. Didn't she know that he would stand with her? Didn't she realize that Toby knew what this meant to her? That everything she'd been working toward for the last few years was finally coming true?

"Really? You'd come with me?"

"I'm not going to let you go alone." He shifted on the couch and dropped one arm along the back. "Naomi, I get it. This show, it's who you are. And someone noticing, wanting to talk to you about making it even bigger? I know what it means to you, so no, you're not going alone."

"You really are the best, Toby," she said, her voice soft, almost lost.

He shook his head, smiling wryly. "Who'll you talk to while you pace a hole through your hotel room floor?"

At that, she stopped pacing, darted across the room and dropped onto the chocolate-brown leather couch beside him, curling her feet up beneath her. She was so close he could see the excitement glittering in her eyes. Feel the warmth radiating from her and the scent of her, drawing him in again.

Laying one hand on his forearm, she admitted, "It was so surreal. Hollywood wants *my* show, Toby. It's a dream. And okay, maybe nothing will come of it, after all, and I'm completely prepared for that, but it's a *chance*. It tells me people are noticing."

"I know." He covered her hand with his.

"You know," she went on, "when Maverick first started all his trouble, I thought for sure the world was ending, and now look at me. I'm marrying my best friend and going to Hollywood to talk about my show."

*Best friend.* He took a breath and let it slide from his lungs. No matter what else happened, he would remain her friend, and that would be easier, he told himself, if he let go of her hand and slid just a bit farther away from her.

"Oh!" Her eyes went wide, and her mouth dropped open.

Instant panic clutched at his throat. "What? What is it? Is it the baby? Are you okay?"

She didn't answer him, just kept looking at him through wide eyes shining with something far more magical than the promise of Hollywood. Then she took their joined hands and laid them on her belly. "It moved. The baby moved, Toby."

His insides settled now that he knew she was okay. But then the baby moved again, the slightest ripple of movement beneath his hand, and he felt the magic still glittering in her eyes. "That was…"

"I know," she said breathlessly. "Wait for it."

She pressed his hand to her belly, and Toby held his breath, hoping to feel that rustle again, and when it came, they smiled at each other. Secrets shared and a moment of real wonder connected them more deeply than ever before.

"Isn't it amazing?" Naomi launched herself at him, planting a hard, fast kiss on his mouth that changed instantly from celebration to something else entirely.

Heat erupted between them, surprising them both. Toby's heart jolted into a fast gallop, and Naomi did a slow melt against him, parting her lips under his. His tongue swept in, tangling with hers, tightening the knots inside him until he was pretty sure they'd never come undone. His hands fisted at her back. Her hands stroked his shoulders and slid up into his hair, her fingers holding him tightly to her. Seconds passed, and the building heat between them became an inferno.

Toby had never felt anything like it, and he wondered how he'd been so close to her for so many years and never tried this. She moved against him, sliding onto his lap, and he knew she felt the hard proof of what he was feeling for her, because she squirmed on his lap, making it both better and worse all at the same time.

When that thought hit, Toby knew he had to end this. Before they completely crossed the line they'd agreed on to protect them both. He broke the kiss, lifted her off his lap and set her down on the couch. Then he got up, needing some space between them.

"Toby—"

He looked over his shoulder at her and nearly groaned. Her mouth was full and tempting, her eyes wide with surprise and her breath coming in short, hard gasps. He knew the feel of her, the soft curves, the warmth and eager response to his touch. And damned if he knew how he'd ignore that knowledge now.

"Just give me a minute here, Naomi," he ground out and pushed both hands through his hair. He dragged in a deep breath and shook his head.

"Why did you stop?" she asked.

Toby spun around and glared at her. "You're kidding, right?"

"No." She pushed herself off the couch and walked toward him.

Toby held up one hand to keep her at bay. Her hair was loose on her shoulders. The T-shirt she wore clung to her rounded belly, and her white shorts displayed way too much tanned leg. Her bare feet didn't make a sound on the floor, but it was as if every step thundered in his head, his chest, as a warning. Well, he was going to listen.

He'd been burned once by a woman he cared too much for, and he wasn't going to set himself up for that again. They were going to be friends. Nothing more.

"Toby, that was—"

"A mistake," he finished for her and walked to the bar in the far corner of the room. Yanking the mini fridge open, he pulled out a beer, opened it, then slammed the fridge closed again. He took a long pull of the cold, frothy brew and hoped to hell it served to put out the fire burning inside him. Somehow he doubted a beer was up to that task, though.

"Why does it have to be a mistake?" she asked. "We're engaged, aren't we?"

"Yeah," he said, taking another drink. "And it's a marriage of convenience, remember? We agreed to no sex. It'll just complicate everything, and you know it."

She scowled at him. "Nobody said anything about sex tonight, Toby. I'm talking about a kiss."

"A kiss like that?" He waved one hand at the couch where they'd been just moments ago. "Leads one place, Naomi."

"Wow. You're really sure either of yourself or of me." She tipped her head to one side to watch him like he was a bug on a glass slide. "You think kissing my brains out means I'm just going to leap into your bed shrieking, 'Take me, baby'?"

"I didn't say that."

"You didn't have to." She pushed that silky mass of copper-brown hair back from her face. The better to scowl at him, he guessed. "For God's sake, Toby, I'm not that easy."

He snorted, shook his head and took another gulp of his beer. "You are many things, Naomi, but I never thought *easy* was one of 'em."

"Right." She folded her arms across her middle, unconsciously lifting her breasts so that the tops peeked out of her T-shirt's neckline. "But you figured one hot kiss from you and I was going to toss my panties over my head?"

"You're twisting this up somehow," he said and tried to figure out exactly where he'd taken the wrong tack.

"Oh, I don't think so." She walked toward him, and as short as she was, she looked pretty damn intimidating when she had a mad on.

She stopped about five feet from him and said, "I liked kissing you—which, okay, surprised me a little—"

He snorted again and nodded. It had surprised the hell out of him, too. Hell, his mouth was still burning.

"—that doesn't mean I'm ready for more, though. But we are engaged, Toby." She wagged a finger at him. "You're the one who's waking me up at six in the morning so Rebecca won't find out we're not sleeping together."

"Yeah, so?" He frowned a little, not following her train of thought.

"Well, don't you think she'd expect to see an engaged couple kissing now and then?" she asked, sarcasm dripping from her tone. "Hugging? Looking like we're intimate even if we're not?"

He hadn't considered that, but she had a point. If he kept treating her like a pal or a little sister or something, Rebecca would notice and start wondering. "Damn it."

"Ah," she said, satisfied. "Good. Now maybe you won't freak out over a simple kiss. And you'd better get used to the idea, because we should do more of it."

Insulted, he countered, "A, I didn't freak out. B, there was nothing simple about that kiss."

"You don't think so?" she asked, turning around and heading toward the door. "For me, it was nice, but nothing special."

He stared after her, stunned. She was playing him. Had to be. Because that kiss had nearly lifted the top of his head off, and he'd damn well *felt* her heart beating a wild rhythm. No way was she as unmoved and blasé about it as she was pretending.

When she was at the door, she paused and looked back at him. "Seriously, Toby, if we're going to make Rebecca and everyone else believe this marriage is real, then we'd better practice kissing until we're good at it."

She gave him a half smile and left. Toby stared at the empty doorway for a long count of ten, then tipped his beer back for another drink.

"Practice? If we get any better at it, I'm a dead man."

# Seven

Dinner at the TCC on Saturday night was a treat. Naomi had always liked the club, and once women were allowed in as members, she'd taken full advantage of her new rights. She, Cecelia and Simone had headed the redecorating committee, and they'd done what they could to spruce up the old place.

Not that they'd been given free rein. But painting the entryway and the restaurant and the ladies' room had helped to brighten things up. They were too steeped in tradition here to willingly let go of the Texas artifacts, documents and pictures decorating the walls, and a part of Naomi understood it. She was a Texan, too, after all. But at least those walls were painted a soft gray now, with fresh white trim, and it looked brighter in here even with the dim lighting.

Sitting across the table from Toby, she took a second to admire it. The dining room in the Texas Cattleman's

Club really hadn't changed much in decades, and even with a fresh coat of paint, it remained very much what it always had been—an upscale restaurant with roots in the past. Tables were draped in white cloth, and on every table was a bud vase with a single yellow rose in it. Soft jazz spilled out of overhead speakers, and the brass sconces on the wall threw out shafts of pale light. The atmosphere was old-world, but the clientele was a mixture of the older generation and younger. Conversations rose and fell like the tides, with a sprinkling of laughter now and then to keep things bright.

Naomi looked at Toby and just managed to squelch a sigh. He wore a white dress shirt, black jacket and black slacks. His black boots were shined to perfection, and he'd capped everything off with a black Stetson that made him look like a well-dressed outlaw. Her insides shivered, and her stomach did a long, slow roll. That sensation still caught her by surprise, despite how often she'd been experiencing it lately.

Desire pumped through her and she fought it down, because really, he hadn't said a word about that kiss since it happened two nights ago, so maybe he hadn't felt what she had. Wanted what she had—did.

And maybe she'd been trying to tempt him, to remind him of that kiss when she chose what to wear tonight. Her short, bright red dress hugged her breasts and her growing curves proudly. The neckline was square and deep and supported by inch-wide straps across her shoulders. Her red heels gave her an extra three inches of height, which she was always in favor of—plus, they made her legs look great.

He'd noticed, because she'd seen the flare of approval in his eyes when he first saw her tonight. But he'd been cool, controlled, even a little distant since they sat down at the restaurant.

Two days since she'd kissed him on impulse and found so much more than she'd expected. When his mouth fused to hers and his arms came around her, every cell in Naomi's body had come alive. Sitting on his lap, she'd felt his body tighten, and just remembering it now had her shifting slightly in her seat.

But long, luscious kisses couldn't make up for the sheer panic in his eyes when he pulled away from her. When he'd announced that for her own good, he was stepping back.

Infuriating to think about it even now. Naomi made up her own mind, and she didn't appreciate him making decisions for her. After all, she wasn't the type to just leap into bed without thinking about it. Although, she thought as she glanced down at her baby bump, she'd done it at least once. And maybe that was what Toby had been thinking. That she'd slept with Gio so easily, why wouldn't she jump *him*, too?

God, that was humiliating.

Especially when it was true. If he'd made the slightest move, Naomi would have willingly gone to bed with him, and forget the bargain they'd made. She'd never felt anything like that kiss before, and oh, how she wanted to know what else he could make her feel.

"What in the hell are you thinking about?" he asked, his voice a low rumble.

"What?" She jolted a little, immensely grateful he couldn't read minds.

"Just a tip, Naomi, but poker's not your game." He shook his head. "I'm sitting here watching your expression shift and change with every thought running through your brain. Want to tell me what's going on?"

"Nothing," she said. Though she wanted to talk about that kiss *and* the way he'd pulled back and shut her down, this wasn't the place for that conversation. Not when they were surrounded by half the town. "I'm just mentally packing, preparing for the trip tomorrow."

"Right." Clearly, he didn't believe her. But he was going to accept it. "Okay. Wes said he'd have his jet ready to leave whenever we get to the airport."

Toby had arranged to borrow Wes Jackson's private jet for the trip to LA, and Naomi was looking forward to it. She was so nervous about this upcoming meeting that being able to pace restlessly on the flight was going to be nice.

Actually, Toby had taken not only their flight but their hotel reservations out of her hands and didn't mention it until it was done. She should have been irritated, since she was completely capable of making reservations, but instead, she thought it was sweet. Which only went to prove that their kiss had seriously short-circuited her brain.

"You didn't have to ask Wes for the use of his plane."

Toby shrugged. "He wasn't using it. Said it was no big deal, and it's better than flying commercial."

"It would have to be," she said and tried a smile. His eyes gleamed in the candlelight as he watched her. "I'm glad you're still going with me."

"Why wouldn't I?"

"After the other night..." There, she'd brought it up anyway, despite vowing that she wouldn't. But then again, it was hard *not* to talk about something that was constantly on her mind.

"You were right," he said, tapping his fingers against the tabletop.

"That's unexpected," she said, keeping her voice even, soft, not sure where he was going with this. "But I'm always happy to hear it. What was I right about?"

He leaned closer. "About showing affection for each other. If we want to make this marriage look real to everyone, then you were right." As if to prove it, he reached across the table and took her hand in his.

Heat skittered up her arm to settle in her chest. His thumb stroked the back of her hand, and his gaze locked on hers. "I'm with you, Naomi. For the long haul. We made a deal, and I keep my word. You know that."

"I never doubted it," she said honestly. No matter what else, Toby McKittrick kept his promises. Which meant, she thought sadly, that he would not be the one to cross that no-sex line. If the line was to break, it was up to her to do it. Now all she had to do was figure out if it was what she really wanted or not.

"Good. So we'll show affection. Make this marriage as real as we can..." He paused, then added, "While keeping to the bargain we already made." As if everything were settled, he gave her hand a pat and let her go to sit back and pick up his after-dinner coffee.

Naomi stewed quietly. How was it possible to both win and lose at the same time?

"Naomi!" Cecelia, a wide smile lighting up her face, hurried up to their table with Deacon just a few steps behind her. "Oh, I'm so glad we ran into you tonight." She glanced across the table. "Hi, Toby. Don't mean to interrupt, but I just have to tell someone."

"What's going on?" Naomi asked, standing to hug her friend.

Cecelia gave her a squeeze, then reached back for Deacon's hand before looking at Naomi again. "We just found out today. We're having a girl." Her eyes filled with tears that she blinked furiously to keep at bay. "God, I've been tearing up all afternoon. Can't seem to stop myself. Don't really want to. I'm going to have a daughter, Naomi."

Happy for her friend, Naomi pulled her in for another hug and then kissed Deacon's cheek. "Congratulations, you two."

"Yeah," Toby said, "add mine to that." He shook Deacon's hand. "That's great news. Really."

"Yeah, it is," Deacon said, pulling Cecelia to his side and holding on to her as if worried she might try to make a break for it. "And if she's half as gorgeous as her mother, she's going to be a beauty."

"Deacon..." Cecelia sighed a little and went up on her toes to give him a kiss. "When will you find out, Naomi? Can't wait to see what you're going to have."

"I was thinking about being surprised," Naomi admitted, only because she couldn't say that up until a couple of weeks ago, she hadn't really allowed herself to think about the baby.

"Oh, how will you get things ready?" Cecelia asked. "No, you've got to know. The suspense would kill me."

Laughing, Naomi said, "I'll think about it."

"Okay, good. Now, we're going to have dinner and plan our baby girl's future, right up through college," Cecelia said, laughing. "Oh, Naomi, you can help me with the design and furnishings for the nursery..."

"I'd love to." It would be great practice for setting up a nursery at the ranch. She hadn't even begun to think of that, but that was not surprising, since there'd been so much more to concentrate on lately.

"Okay, we'll talk soon."

When Cecelia and Deacon walked off to their own

table, Naomi sat down again and watched Toby as he reached for the check folder.

Cecelia was in love and lucky enough to have Deacon love her back. Naomi shot a sidelong glance at Toby as he tucked several bills into the folder for their waiter. He loved her, she knew. But he wasn't *in* love with her, and that was the difference between her relationship and her friend's. Still, Naomi was lucky, too. Toby was here. With her. He'd changed his life around to be there for her.

And they'd had that kiss that had stirred up feelings she'd never suspected she had for him. Was there something more than friendship between them? Was it worth the risk of losing him to find out?

Los Angeles was big and noisy and crowded, and Naomi loved it. From the packed freeways to the mobs of tourists wandering down Hollywood Boulevard, everything was so different from what she knew that Naomi felt energized. Of course, being with Toby had that effect on her, too.

From flying on Wes Jackson's private jet to their penthouse suite at the Chateau Marmont in West Hollywood, it was as if she and Toby were wrapped up in some fantasy together. The two-bedroom suite was decorated in pale grays, with hardwood floors, beamed ceilings and glass tables. There was a tiled terrace off the living room and a waist-high concrete balcony railing. The gas fireplace in the main room flickered with dancing flames, because though it was June, it was also Southern California. The damp air coming in off the ocean meant the fire was welcome as well as beautiful.

Naomi spent that first night alone in her bedroom,

unable to sleep—not just because she was nervous about her meeting with the producer the following morning. But because Toby was right there with her and still so far away.

He'd been as good as his word, making small, affectionate gestures in front of Rebecca and the hands who worked for him. But when they were alone, he was careful to be..._careful_. He didn't seem to be having any difficulties keeping his distance from her. So maybe she was wrong about all this, she told herself. Maybe she was the only one who couldn't stop thinking about that kiss. Who couldn't help wondering what more might be like.

"How'd the meeting go?" Toby sat across from her, a sea breeze ruffling his hair as he watched her, waiting. He'd loosened the dark red tie at his neck and left off his steel-gray suit jacket. The long sleeves of his white dress shirt were rolled back to the elbows, and his long legs were stretched out, crossed at the ankle. Toby was probably the only man she knew who could pull off black cowboy boots in Los Angeles.

They were on the terrace of the penthouse suite, and evening was settling in. On the glass-topped table between them was a pitcher of iced tea and two tall glasses provided by room service. It had been a long day. Naomi'd had her meeting with the producer, and Toby had taken care of some business with his patent attorneys. This was really the first chance they'd had to talk since breakfast in the restaurant that morning.

Naomi took a breath and sighed it out. How did she explain what it had been like to hear Tamara Stiles praising _Fashion Sense_? All her life, she'd been striving to matter. Maybe it had started out as an effort to finally earn her parents' pride, but at some point her motivation had shifted. It wasn't only about them anymore, but about Naomi herself. She'd wanted to prove to everyone—including herself—that she was more than a rich man's daughter. That she had more to offer.

Okay, a cable television show about fashion wasn't curing cancer or ending nuclear war, but she *was* helping people, she told herself silently. Giving them ideas on how to improve not only their looks, but their lives. Looking your best meant that you *felt* your best. Sure, she enjoyed what she did, but knowing that other people did, too, was what made it all so good.

Now, here in Hollywood, she'd reached the very thing she'd been aiming for. There were people here who wanted to produce her, make the show bigger, get a larger audience, really help Naomi be *heard*. And she wasn't thrilled. She should be. This was the pot of gold at the end of her own personal rainbow. This was the X marks the spot on her private treasure map.

Looking at Toby, she tried to tell him what she was feeling, but she couldn't explain it, since she wasn't sure herself yet. Maybe she just needed time to think. Distance to put it all in perspective.

"Naomi?" His features reflected concern. "It didn't go well?"

"No," she answered quickly with a shake of her head. "It went fine. She loves the show—said it has great potential."

He frowned a little at that. "Potential? What's that supposed to mean? It's already a hit in Texas. Hell, it's why she wanted you to come talk to her."

"Thanks. That's what I thought, too." Naomi tried to settle and couldn't, so she stood up and walked the length of the private terrace. He was right when he'd once said she needed room to pace when she was thinking. But this time, she felt as though she could walk all the way back to Texas and things still wouldn't be clear.

When she came back up to the table, she didn't look at Toby, but instead turned to face the valley view, her hands flat atop the wide concrete rail. "Tamara says for the show to go national we'd naturally have to make changes. To the sets, the kind of shows we do, pretty much everything."

"If she loves it, why does she want to change it?"

She looked over her shoulder at him. "Funny, I asked myself that same question."

"You should." He stood up, too, and joined her at the railing.

A sea breeze drifted through Hollywood and brushed past them like a damp caress. Naomi pushed her hair back and lifted her face into that soft wind before looking up at Toby.

He was so steady. So strong. And she was so grateful he'd come with her. She was out of her element here. In Royal, even in Houston, she was fairly well-known. But here she was just one of a crowd of supplicants trying to take that next step up on a Hollywood ladder.

Resting one hip against the balcony rail, she said, "Tamara says the show had something on its own—and that the Maverick video and all the hype that happened after on social media really gave it the kind of push they need to bring up a local show."

"Okay…"

"But," she said, shifting her gaze again, out to the valley and the smudge of ocean she could see in the distance, "to go national, the show has to be polished, have less of a small-town feel, so that it will appeal to everyone."

"Small town?" he asked. "Houston, Dallas—they've signed on already. They're not exactly small town, and it works for them just as it is."

"It does," she said, and again, Toby was saying pretty much what she'd said to herself after leaving the meeting. "She says that with a bigger studio and professional crew—not to mention scriptwriters—we *might* make it big."

"Might."

"Well, she can't guarantee it, of course," Naomi admitted. "And I wouldn't have believed her if she'd tried. But I never saw a problem with our studio in Royal."

"Seems to work fine," he agreed.

"And the crew are very professional. Even the interns from the college know what they're doing." She'd already made these arguments to Tamara. Gone over them time and time again by herself after the meeting, too. But it didn't change anything.

"They do."

"She said," Naomi added after a long minute, "that at first, they'd want to do the taping here. In Hollywood."

He went still. "So you'd have to live here."

"That was part of it, yes." She looked at him again and tried to read what he was thinking. But except for the flash in his eyes, his features were cool, blank. "They would, in theory, tape a short season all at once, so I'd have to be here in California for at least a few weeks."

"Weeks." He nodded thoughtfully but didn't say anything else.

Seconds ticked past into minutes, and still the quiet between them grew. Naomi's own mind was racing, going over the meeting again, what living in California for weeks at a time might mean to her. To Toby.

The baby. There were too many questions and too few answers.

"This is Hollywood, Toby," she said a little wistfully. "They're the experts. And this chance, it's what I've been aiming for."

"Sounds like you got it." No inflection to his voice, giving no clue to what he was thinking.

"I don't know," she said softly. What was more, she didn't know if she wanted it anymore.

Yes, LA was exciting. Hollywood had such cachet, deserved or not. Even their hotel, the Chateau Marmont, was a legend in a town filled with them. Movie stars as far back as the '20s had stayed in this hotel, and it was as if their spirits remained, because the hotel felt...out of time somehow. The stars still flocked here—movie stars, TV actors, singers all flocked to this place, this city.

Dreams were born, lived...or died, all in this one city.

And Naomi didn't know anymore if she wanted what was offered here. "This all comes back to Maverick's video," she mused, shaking her head at the irony of having something she hated be at the base of what could be the realization of her dreams.

"Well," she amended, "I guess it was more about how we handled the video than the video itself. That's what caught her attention, really. Tamara said she liked how we turned it around, used that video to spark more changes on the show..."

"Not we, Naomi," Toby said softly. "*You.* You did it. You faced Maverick down, took that ugly video of his and made it work for you."

She smiled to herself and pulled a lock of windblown hair from across her eyes. "You know, I really did. But, Toby, without you I don't think I could have. You're the one who helped me see that hiding wasn't the answer. You were right there. Standing with me. Helping me. You gave my baby a father."

His eyes darkened, swirled with emotions that flashed past too quickly for her to read. And suddenly, she didn't care what he was thinking, feeling. Right now all she knew was what *she* felt.

"Ever since we kissed," she said softly, sliding her hand along the railing until she found his and covered it with her own. "I've been thinking about more."

"Me too." He looked down at their joined hands, then into her eyes.

"That no-sex line you talked about?" she said, despite the tightness in her throat, the galloping of her heart. "The one you said we shouldn't cross?"

"Yeah?" His eyes darkened again. A muscle in his jaw twitched.

"I want to cross it."

"Me too." Toby reached for her, and she went to him eagerly. He pulled her in close, locked his arms around her and kissed her with a raging hunger that shattered every last thread of control she might have clung to.

Naomi lifted her arms to hook around his neck and held him to her as his mouth took hers. Their tongues tangled together in a silent dance of passion that sent tingles of expectation skittering through her veins. Better even than the kiss that had filled her dreams for days, this one promised more than just a few minutes of heat. This kiss promised an inferno to come, and Naomi readily jumped into the flames.

She lost herself in the wonder of the moment, of having him touch her, hold her, kiss her. For days she'd been hoping to feel this again. For days she'd watched him try to keep a safe distance between them. And now at last, the wall separating them was coming down in a rush.

His hands swept up and down her back, and Naomi wanted to peel out of her sleeveless sunshine-yellow dress. She wanted his hands on her skin—those strong, rough hands that showed such gentleness. She wanted all of him against her, inside her.

He tore his mouth from hers, and for one horrible second, Naomi thought he was going to pull away from her again. To back off from what was happening. Breath catching in her lungs, heart pounding in her chest, she looked up at him and knew she needn't have worried.

"That's it," he muttered thickly and bent to scoop her up into his arms.

"Toby!"

"Quiet," he ground out through clenched teeth. "We're too far gone to stop now, Naomi. I swear I will stop, though, if you say no," he added. "So don't say no."

She shook her head, cupped his cheek in the palm of her hand. "I'm not. I'm saying hurry up."

"That's my girl."

# Eight

He marched through the living area and straight into the big bedroom. There were two in the penthouse suite, and last night they'd been in those separate rooms. Not tonight, though, Naomi thought. Tonight, things would change. He walked to the wide bed, reached down and tugged the silky gray duvet off and let it slide to the floor. Then he set Naomi on her feet but kept a firm grip on her as if half-afraid she'd disappear if he stopped touching her. But she wasn't going anywhere.

Naomi turned in his grasp, pulled her hair to one side and said softly, "Help me with the zipper?"

He did, his fingertips trailing along her spine as the material fell open. She shivered when he bent to kiss the base of her neck, and an instant later, her dress was sliding off her body to lie on the floor like a puddle of sunlight. Wearing just her cream-colored bra and panties and a pair of three-inch taupe heels, she stood in front of him, letting him look his fill.

She was a little nervous, because her body was so different now. Naomi had been so careful for so long, counting every calorie, watching every bite, but since Toby's proposal, he'd been coaxing her to eat more. Now Naomi was rounder, fuller, and the mound of the baby was distinct enough that she actually thought to cover it with her hands.

He stopped her, though, holding her hands in his and tugging them aside. "No, don't hide from me." Shaking his head, he let his gaze sweep over her, top to toe and back again. A slow smile curved his mouth. "You make a hell of a picture, Naomi."

What she saw in his eyes made her feel beautiful. Desirable. She released a breath she hadn't known she was holding and reached for the buttons of his shirt. Then she pulled the tie from around his neck and tossed it onto a nearby chair. "You're wearing too many clothes," she whispered.

"Yeah, we can take care of that." He did. In what felt like a blink, he was undressed, laying her back on the bed and covering her with his body.

She sighed at the first contact of skin to skin. God, it felt good. Right. The cool sheets at her back, Toby's hot skin against the front of her. Sensations swarmed inside her, and she fought to breathe past the rush of them.

She smoothed her palms across the broad expanse of his chest, and he hissed in a breath in reaction. Naomi smiled, loving how much he was affected by her. Knowing that he was as swept away as she was. She rubbed her thumbs across his flat nipples until he groaned deeply, then dipped his head to take one of her hard nipples into his mouth.

Her smile slipped away, lost in the rising tide of heat enveloping her. His tongue swirled across her sensitive skin, and he ran the edge of his teeth across her nipple as well. Naomi moaned softly and arched her back, moving into him. When he suckled at her, she whispered his name, threaded her fingers through his hair and held him to her.

She didn't ever want him to stop. Naomi's eyes closed on a wave of heat swamping her senses. She'd never known anything like this before. The feel of his mouth on her was incredible, and when he ran one hand down the length of her body, she shivered. His hands, so scarred and callused from years of hard work, touched her skin with a rough tenderness that left her breathless.

He lifted his head, and she nearly whimpered at the loss of his mouth against her breast. But she stared up into his eyes and felt herself falling into that churning aqua sea of sensations. How had she gone so long, never knowing what they could create together? Never knowing what it felt like to have his hands on her skin?

"I've wanted this for a while now, Naomi," he whispered, stroking one hand across her breasts, down her rib cage. "But you've gotta be sure."

She actually laughed a little, to think that he was giving *her* a way out this time. But no, they were through turning from each other. For tonight, for now, all that was important was the two of them. She didn't even want to think about tomorrow, but there was one thing she had to reassure herself on.

"I'm absolutely sure. But, Toby—" She paused and took his face between her palms. "Remember what we promised each other. No matter what else happens, we stay friends."

"Honey, right now I'm feeling *real* friendly." He grinned, took her mouth in a long kiss that had her insides melting into a puddle, then said, "Yeah. Friends. Always."

She nodded, because she was too full of emotions to speak. Naomi couldn't even identify everything she was feeling. All she knew was that in this moment in time, she was right where she wanted to be. But neither of them needed words right now. All they needed was to *feel*. To explore. Experience.

As if he heard her thoughts, he slid one hand down her body to stop over the curve of the baby she carried. Naomi went perfectly still, wondering what he would do, what he was thinking. Pregnant women couldn't be very alluring, right?

"Stop thinking," he ordered in a hush.

"What?"

"You're worrying. About how you look, of all things." Toby shook his head as his gaze met hers. "Can't you tell that I think you're the most beautiful thing I've ever seen?"

"Toby—"

He smoothed his hand across her baby bump, then bent to kiss both her and the child within. There was so much tenderness in the action, in his eyes, that in that instant, Naomi was lost. Her heart filled to bursting, she felt the sting of tears in her eyes and impatiently brushed them away. She wanted nothing to blur this image of him. Instead, she etched it into her heart and mind so she'd never forget.

He looked up at her, his eyes shining, and all she could

think was that she loved him. Beyond friendship, beyond sense, beyond anything. Naomi was in love with Toby. With her best friend.

When had it happened? Had it always been inside her, just waiting to be recognized? And what was she supposed to do about this realization now? If Toby knew what she was feeling, he'd pull away again, and Naomi knew she wouldn't be able to stand that. So she'd hide what she felt. Keep it locked up inside her so she wouldn't have the pain of seeing him turn from her.

Reaching for him, she stroked her fingers over Toby's cheek, then across his lips, defining them with the lightest of touches. There was so much she wanted to say to him and couldn't.

Finally, though, when she was sure her voice wouldn't break, she said only, "You're going to make me cry."

"Oh, no," he assured her, giving her a slow smile and a wicked wink. "I'm going to make you scream."

"Promises, promises," she said, keeping it light, not wanting him to guess at what she'd just discovered.

"I always keep my word," he reminded her, then shifted his hand down to cup her center.

Naomi gasped and instinctively lifted her hips, rocking into his touch, wanting more, *needing* more. And he gave it to her. His thumb caressed that one sensitive spot while he speared two fingers into her heat. Within and without, Naomi felt on fire. She wouldn't have been surprised to see actual flames licking at the mattress beneath her.

She grabbed at his shoulders, her fingers flexing to hold on as gentle exploration gave way to desperation.

He kissed her, touched her, lavished attention on Naomi's breasts, her neck, her inner thighs, driving her wild with a kind of need she'd never known before. She'd never thought of herself as particularly sexual, but right now her body was pleading for release and the only man who could give it to her was bent on drawing out the torture of expectation.

"You smell so damn good," Toby whispered against her throat. "Your scent stays with me everywhere I go." He kissed her neck, licking, tasting. "You're there in my sleep, Naomi. I can't shake you."

"Then stop trying to," she told him, and he lifted his head to look at her.

"Yeah," he said, "I'm done with that. You're here to stay."

One breathless second passed, then two before he kissed her, taking her mouth in a celebration of need and passion. God, she wanted to drink him in, drown in him and what he was making her feel. She couldn't touch him enough. Hair, face, shoulders, back. She loved the feel of his muscles shifting beneath her palms.

Then he moved to kneel in front of her, and Naomi held her breath as he entered her. One long, slow thrust and he claimed everything she was, and she sighed as a shiver slid through her body. Lifting her legs, she wrapped them around him and pulled him deeper, higher.

His body moved in hers, in a rhythm that moved faster and faster. She groaned, sighed, at the luscious feel of his hard length taking her so completely. Silently, he offered her more, demanded the same. He looked down into her eyes, and she couldn't have looked away from that heated stare if it meant her life.

Anticipation coiled in the pit of her stomach as tension settled even deeper within. Naomi moved with him, racing to match his rhythm, rushing toward whatever was waiting for her. Always before, sex had been a quick bout of stress release. A subtle pop of pleasure that had left her mildly satisfied and silently wondering what all the big fuss was about.

Then she found out. His fingertips stroked her core while his body moved in hers, and she shattered, clawing at his back, whimpering his name through a throat so tight air could barely pass. Mind spinning, she held on to him and rode the pulsing flashes of brightness that seemed to blind her.

"Toby!" Her hips were still rocking with the force of that climax, and before she had time to adjust, to understand, he was pushing her past that pleasure to a place she'd never been before.

Her body felt raw, too sensitive, too *everything*, but Toby was relentless. "I can't," she whispered, shaking her head, looking up at him. "I mean, I already—"

"Again," he said tightly and drove himself deep inside her. He lifted her hips, tossed her legs over his shoulder and went even deeper than he had been.

Naomi wouldn't have thought it possible, but while her body was still quivering from the most amazing climax she'd ever experienced, she felt it preparing for another. She could barely breathe and didn't care. Her head tipped back into the mattress as her hands reached for his thighs. She was lifted so high she had no way to match his movements. She was at his mercy, and he was showing none.

Naomi had never been so at the mercy of her own body. She'd never known the kind of overwhelming sensations that were taking her over. Had never been so out of control with a man. Never let any man take her over as Toby was doing. And she hadn't even guessed that her body could feel so much.

He was unstoppable. Indefatigable. His hips were like

pistons, pumping into her, pushing her past all boundaries, all restrictions. Naomi stared up at him, licked her lips and knew that nothing would ever be the same again. Not after this. Not after Toby.

"Come on, Naomi," he whispered, voice low. "Let me watch you fly. Let go, Naomi. Just let go."

"I am, Toby," she said breathlessly, as her heels dug into his back. He was battering away the last of her defenses. Tension clawed at her. That first orgasm was as good as forgotten in her body's rush to claim another.

"Now, Naomi," he whispered, his big hands holding her bottom, squeezing soft flesh, giving her one more sensation to add to the mix. "Come now."

She laughed a little, but the sound came out as a sob for air. Her hands slapped at the sheets, clutching the fabric as if looking for a way to hold herself in place. "You're not giving me a choice. I feel—"

"Look at me," he said, and she heard the fight for control in his voice.

She opened her eyes, met his, and while their gazes were locked, he pushed her over the edge of desire into a completion that was so foreign to her that she was lost in the sweeping tide of it. Naomi stared into those aqua eyes as her world rocked and her body splintered. She screamed, unable to stop the wild rush of release as it grabbed her and shook her down to the bone.

Naomi watched him, lost in those eyes, as her body, still trembling, held on to his and cradled him as he let himself go.

When he collapsed on top of her, Naomi held him tightly. Their hearts raced in tandem, their bodies quaking as if they were shipwrecked survivors clinging to each other for safety. But it was so much more than that.

He rolled to one side, taking her with him, and Naomi laid her head on his chest, listening to the steadying beat of his heart. Loving him was going to be hard, she knew, but there was nothing she could do about it. He was in her heart forever. And she would never, for as long as she lived, forget what they'd shared here tonight. On the night she knew she loved him.

Toby lay there like a dead man. If the hotel had been on fire, he'd burn to a crisp because there was no way he could move. He doubted his legs still worked.

Hell, he'd been with plenty of women in his time, but not once had he experienced anything like what had just happened between him and Naomi. He scraped one hand across his face and stared at the ceiling. He'd crossed a line. Hell, he'd *erased* the line. And he didn't give a good damn. All he could think about was that he wanted her. Again. Now.

She curled on her side and slid one leg across his, and the silky glide of her skin against his stirred him into need in a flat second. Who knew that there would be such heat between them? He rubbed one hand down her back, and she cuddled into him, sliding her palm across his chest. She was…amazing. More than that, but he didn't have the words. What he had was need that only she could meet.

That was dangerous territory, though, and he had to lay out some signposts before they headed farther down this road. Now that the line was gone, new ones had to be drawn. To protect both of them.

"Toby…"

She whispered his name on a breathy sigh, and instantly his body tightened. Didn't seem to matter that he barely had his breath back from the most incredible sex of his life—his body was apparently raring to go again.

But right now he had to give his brain the upper hand. If he could manage it while she was looking at him through soft eyes, her tongue running across her bottom lip. *Oh, man.*

"Okay, we need to talk," he said and winced because he'd just sounded like a damn cliché.

"No, we don't," she said and smoothed her fingertips across his nipple.

"That's not helping." Muffling a groan, Toby caught her hand in his and held her still. If she kept touching him like that, talking would be the last thing on his mind. "Naomi, this changes things."

She chuckled, tipped her head back and looked up at him. "It sure does."

"Not funny," he warned, going up on one elbow and rolling her over onto her back. Still, seeing the softness and the humor in her eyes, he nearly smiled back. Then he remembered the line. Smoothing her hair back from her face, he ran his fingers through the long, silky threads and had to fight to concentrate. "We have to talk about what this is going to mean between us."

She sighed, stiffened a little, then said, "That it'll be even easier for us to show affection toward each other?"

Oh, he wanted to show her some affection right now. But before anything else got started, he had to make sure she knew there was a limit on how much he was willing to give. How much he was willing to risk.

He looked into her eyes—eyes that shone like warm whiskey—and shook his head. Taking a deep breath to center himself, he said, "Sure. Yeah. That's a good point.

But what I want to say is..." Hell. What *was* he trying to say?

Naomi pushed herself up slightly, bracing one hand against his chest. "Want me to say it for you? That I shouldn't let my little heart fall in love with you because you're not interested in love?"

"Naomi..."

"Or is it that you don't want me to make the mistake of thinking that our marriage is going to be real all of a sudden?"

"That's not what I was going to say," he argued, though he had to admit it was pretty damn close.

"Right." She tipped her head to one side. "You can stop panicking, Toby. We were friends and now we're friends plus. That's all. I get it. That about sum everything up?"

Sounded like it did. Although why it bothered him that she was being so reasonable about it all, he didn't know. He hadn't expected calm, and he should be grateful for it. Toby wasn't even sure why he felt oddly...disappointed. "Yeah, I guess it does. Look, the point is, we had the no-sex agreement, and that's shot to hell—"

"Not going to say I'm sorry about that," she put in.

"No, me either," he admitted. They could at least be honest with each other. "But I have to make sure you know that sex doesn't mean—"

She pushed herself off his chest into a sitting position, shoved her tangled hair back and looked him dead in the eye. "For heaven's sake, Toby. I'm not going to throw my heart at your feet. I know you, remember? I know that Sasha messed your head up so bad you don't even want to hear the word *love*."

His frown deepened. Was it a blessing or a curse that

Naomi knew him so well? "This isn't about Sasha," he ground out.

"Oh, please. It's always about Sasha. That miserable excuse for a woman was never right for you, and," she said, lifting one eyebrow meaningfully, "if you'll remember, I told you that at the time."

"Yeah. I remember." His expression soured. "Thanks for the *I told you so*."

"No problem." She scooted off the bed, stalked to the window and stared out at the deepening twilight.

The growing darkness seeped into the room as well, shadows filling every corner. Toby's gaze followed the line of Naomi's back and down to the curve of her behind. The woman had a great behind. Then, when she turned to look back at him, she was profiled and her breasts were high and full, the rounded outline of the baby on full display. She was beautiful. Even the fire in her eye couldn't dim his reaction to the woman.

Then she started talking. "Sasha leaving was the best thing to happen to you."

He gritted his teeth. "This isn't about Sasha."

"It's all about her," Naomi continued. "Has been since the day she walked out with her pretty-boy country singer. She's gone, Toby, but you're still caught up in that drama."

He sat up and leaned against the headboard, the sheet pooling at his hips. "What the hell are you talking about?"

"You." Naomi walked back to the side of the bed and glared down at him. "She's moved on, Toby, but you're still running your life by what happened to you with her."

"No, I'm not."

"Really? You haven't been involved in a single relationship since she left." She crossed her arms beneath her breasts. "Why?"

"Not interested."

"Liar." Now she frowned at him. "At least be honest and admit that you won't let yourself trust anyone anymore."

"I trust you," he pointed out. And why did he suddenly feel as though he had to defend himself?

She sighed as if disappointed, but damned if he knew what the problem was.

"Toby, you're cheating yourself out of maybe finding something amazing, all because Sasha convinced you that feelings weren't to be trusted." She bent down and tapped her index finger against his chest. "Well, you're wrong to give her so much power."

"How did this get to be about Sasha?" he asked, shoving himself off the bed to stare down at her. "She doesn't run my life. Never has. Never will. I stopped thinking about her the day she left Royal. I live my life the way I want to, Naomi."

"You're probably the most stubborn man I've ever met."

"Thanks."

"Not really a compliment." She sighed a little and chewed at her bottom lip.

He dropped both hands to her hips and pulled her in closer. She had to tip her head back to meet his eyes, but she did. "I trust *you*. That's good enough for me."

"Okay," she said, nodding, watching his eyes. "I just don't want you to be sorry one day for marrying me and cheating yourself out of love somewhere down the line."

"We're getting married, Naomi." He smiled softly. "And hell, if we get sex, too, all the better."

Her returning smile wasn't wide, but it was there. "Yeah, that works for me, too."

"I do love you, Naomi. Always will. I just don't want you to think of what we have as more than what we have."

"Got it. You're not in love with me."

"Right." He didn't know what the hell he was feeling at the moment, but it wasn't the kind of love that people built dreams around. He knew that much.

"Fine. Don't worry about it." She shook her hair back and said, "Oh, stop looking like you're kicking a puppy. I'm a big girl, Toby. I walked into this with eyes wide open, and I didn't ask for undying declarations of romantic love."

No, she hadn't, he realized. In fact, she was acting like what had happened between them was no big deal. And he didn't know how he felt about that. Damn it, Naomi had a way of turning everything around on him so that Toby didn't know whether he was coming or going, and she'd just managed it again. Was he worried about nothing?

"So, are we finished talking?" she asked, running one hand down his chest, across his abdomen and lower still, to curl her fingers around the thick, hard length of him.

He hissed in a breath through his teeth. "Yeah, I think that about covers everything."

"Good to hear," she said and kissed him while her fingers moved on him, sliding, caressing. "So don't just stand there, cowboy. Show me what you've got."

"Challenge accepted," he muttered. He felt like he was going to explode. How could he want her so desperately? Lifting her, he half turned and braced her back against the closest wall. "Not slow this time, Naomi. This time it's gonna be hot and fast."

She leaned into him, wrapped her legs around his waist and nibbled at his neck. "Show me."

Hard and aching, he slid inside her and instantly felt her body tighten around his. Silky heat surrounded him, and he groaned as Naomi scraped her nails across his skin and hooked her ankles behind his back. She met him eagerly, hungrily, and his brain short-circuited as he stared into the eyes of a woman he'd thought he knew.

Her body, his, moving together, in a mad, wild tangle of desire and need that gripped them both. One corner of his mind yelled at him to lay her down, take his time with her. But that calm, reasonable voice was shouted down by the other half of him demanding that he have her. Now.

"Toby, Toby..." She twisted her hips on him, increasing the friction, increasing the need until he thought he'd go blind with it.

"Come on, baby." He kissed her, hard and long and deep, and took her breath as his own, devouring her as she was devouring his body. "Come with me. Come with me now."

He felt her body tighten, felt the first flickering pulse of her climax and watched her eyes glaze. And while she rocked with the orgasm shaking through her, he forgot about control and emptied himself inside her.

Caught in the web spinning between them, Toby knew that in spite of what he'd said before, nothing would ever be the same.

# Nine

After a few days in LA, Naomi was ready to be home in Texas. Now that she was back home, she might miss Hollywood a little, but it was good to be back. As summer heated up and June inched toward July, the days got longer and the people moved slower. It was an easier pace than the big city, and that was part of its appeal. She'd heard people say that anyone could live up north, but it took real character to make it through a southern summer.

Naomi wasn't so sure about that. But one thing she did know—she was grateful the Royal Diner had AC. The minute she and Toby's sister, Scarlett, stepped inside, Naomi almost whimpered.

"Oh, it's going to be one ugly summer," Scarlett said as she signaled to Amanda and then tugged Naomi to a booth.

Naomi flopped onto the red vinyl bench seat and

stacked her shopping bags beside her. "I let you talk me into buying too much."

"It's never too much," Scarlett said. "Besides, you're getting married. You need…stuff."

*Stuff* didn't begin to describe all the things Naomi had picked up that morning. She and Scarlett had spent the last several hours at the Courtyard Shops, a great collection of eclectic shops where you could find anything from antiques and crafts to fresh local produce. But there was also a new bridal shop owned by Natalie Valentine.

And *that* shop was where Scarlett had pushed Naomi into going a little nuts. She was only carrying a few of the things she'd bought. The rest were being delivered to the ranch. Naomi wanted a small wedding, in the evening, maybe, out at the ranch. She hadn't talked to Toby about it yet, and she knew her mother wouldn't be happy with the venue, but Naomi was. A small, simple wedding, with just their families and friends there, made the most sense to Naomi. After all, it wasn't as if this was ever going to be a *real* marriage.

Her heart ached at that thought, but she had to acknowledge the truth, no matter how painful. Toby was never going to know she loved him. Never going to love her back. And she had to find a way to be all right with that. If she couldn't…then maybe marriage wasn't the answer. For either of them.

"I love the dress you picked out," Scarlett said. "That pale yellow just looks gorgeous on you, and knee length will keep you from passing out in this heat."

"Thanks," Naomi said. "I like it, too. My mother will no doubt want me in yards of lace and tulle, but that doesn't make sense for a backyard ceremony. And besides," she added wryly, "it's tacky to wear white on your wedding day when your baby bump is showing."

Scarlett laughed a little, then shook her head. "You're going to be a beautiful bride. But are you really sure you want it held outside? Even in the evening it'll be hot."

"I'm sure," Naomi said. "We can have the reception by the pool, and if it gets too hot, people can go into the house for a break. Of course, I haven't talked to Toby about any of this yet, so he may have different ideas…"

Scarlett waved one hand at her. "He'll be good with whatever you want. He loves you, right?"

Sighing a little, Naomi leaned toward the other woman and whispered, "Scarlett, you know the truth. I know Toby told you."

"Sure, I know," she said. "And I know my brother. He's a great guy, Naomi, but he's not going to marry someone just to do her a favor. He cares for you. I can see it."

Care was a long way from love. Too long. Since they got back from California, they'd shared a bed and shared each other, every night, every morning and one memorable afternoon in the workshop. But they hadn't talked about Hollywood. Hadn't talked about their wedding. Hadn't talked about anything important. It was as if they were both holding back, and Naomi didn't know what to do about it.

"Hey, Naomi, you okay?"

"What?" Sighing, she shook her head. "Sorry. I drifted."

"To somewhere nice? Maybe cooler?" Scarlett asked.

"No, stayed right here in Royal. Scarlett, can I ask you something?"

"Sure."

"Are you good with this?" Naomi asked. "I mean, me and Toby getting married. You're okay about it?"

"Absolutely." Scarlett paused when Amanda Battle walked up to their table. She slid two tall glasses of ice water onto the table, and Scarlett sighed. "Bless you, my child."

"Thanks, I'll take it," Amanda said, laughing. "You two been running around buying out Royal's shops?"

"Just put a dent in a few of them," Naomi assured her. Her stomach rumbled, reminding her of why they'd come to the diner. And a salad just didn't sound the least bit appetizing. "Can I get a turkey sandwich? Potato salad?"

"Oh, me too, please," Scarlett said.

Amanda nodded and hurried off to tend to other customers. So when they were alone again, Scarlett took a long drink of her water, then said, "Anyway, why wouldn't I want you married to Toby? You're way better for him than Sasha was."

"Low bar there, but thanks," Naomi said drily.

"What's going on?" Scarlett watched her for a long minute. "You don't seem as excited as I thought you'd be over everything. I mean, you're engaged, pregnant and have Hollywood knocking on your door."

"It's complicated," Naomi said and thought that might be the understatement of the century. She still didn't know what she was going to do about the offer from Tamara Stiles, and she had to let them know soon.

But if she took it, she would be giving up the kind of control that had made the show *hers* in the first place. And did she really want to live in Hollywood for weeks at a time? If she did, what about Toby? Would he move there with her? Stay on the ranch? And what about when she had the baby? What then? Would she be dragging the baby from state to state?

"Wow. Judging by your expression, wish I could buy you a beer."

Naomi sighed. "Me too. Or the most gigantic glass of wine in the state of Texas." She took a long drink of her ice water, letting it soothe her dry throat. "There's just so much going on right now, and I'm still getting emails from people about that stupid video—"

"No one who knows you cares about that thing, Naomi," Scarlett said.

"I know, but millions of people who don't know me have seen it." Just thinking of that made her want to cringe. Didn't matter if she'd managed to turn the tables on Maverick. That she'd taken his vicious attack and made it work *for* her.

Whoever Maverick was had tried to ruin her life, and knowing that person was still out there made her nervous. He'd wanted to make her life a misery. Wouldn't it infuriate him to realize that he'd inadvertently helped Naomi rather than hurt her? Wasn't it likely that he'd try something else in order to make trouble for her?

"Okay, yeah," Scarlett allowed, "millions of people saw the video, but now they're tuning in to your show, so hey. Win for you." She picked up her water glass, waited for Naomi to do the same and then clinked them together in a toast. "Seriously, don't let that weirdo bother you. I'm sure Sheriff Battle's going to find out who Maverick is and stop him. Soon."

"I hope so," Naomi confessed. "I can't help wondering if he's going to be frustrated at how the video worked for me and try something else."

"I understand why you'd be worried about that, but

honestly, I don't see it happening." Thoughtful, Scarlett looked at her. "Why would he? There're still plenty of people in Royal to screw with."

"Talking about Maverick?"

Both women looked up at Gabe Walsh. He was tall and gorgeous and his hazel eyes always held a gleam of humor. His dark blond hair was militarily short, and he had a lot of intricate tattoos. Formerly FBI, he now owned a private security firm based in Royal.

"Sorry," he said, mouth curving into an unrepentant smile. "Didn't mean to eavesdrop, but I heard you talking as I was walking to my table. Maverick the subject of interest?"

"Who else?" Scarlett asked.

"Everyone's talking about him," Naomi said. "Especially those of us he's already attacked."

Gabe winced. "Yeah, I get that. And I know the guy's caused a lot of misery around here. But I just left my uncle Dusty, and I swear all the intrigue and mystery surrounding this Maverick guy is really sparking my uncle's will to live. It's even making his cancer treatments easier for him to deal with."

Dale "Dusty" Walsh was in his sixties and used to be a big bear of a man. But Naomi had seen him not so long ago, and the chemo he was undergoing had whittled him down until he hardly looked like himself anymore.

"I'm glad to hear he's doing better," Naomi said, knowing nothing she said could make things easier on Dusty's family.

"I don't know about better," Gabe admitted sadly, stuffing his hands into the pockets of his slacks. "But Maverick has sure perked Dusty up. The mystery of it has him intrigued and more interested than anything else has been able to do. I think he's trying to figure out who the guy really is."

"I hope he does," Naomi said with feeling. "I won't feel really safe until he's caught."

"He will be," Gabe assured her before he left to meet his friends for lunch. "No one can stay hidden forever."

Naomi wondered, though. For months, Maverick had proven elusive enough to avoid being caught. Who was to say anything would change? And if he came after her again...

Scarlett's cell phone rang, and when she glanced at the screen, she said, "It's Toby."

Naomi listened to the one-sided conversation, and when Scarlett hung up she asked, "What is it?"

"It's Toby's horse, Legend." All business now, she looked worried. "Toby says he's gone down and won't get up again. Sorry about lunch, but we have to get to the ranch." She waved a hand at Amanda and called, "We have to cancel. Sorry."

Naomi was already gathering her things, and when she pushed herself out of the booth, Scarlett was right behind her.

Toby hated feeling helpless.

Legend's labored breathing filled the air and brought Toby to his knees beside the failing horse. Fresh straw littered the floor and rustled with every movement. Toby rubbed his hands up and down the big animal's neck. He felt each shuddering breath and the thready beat of Legend's big heart. Hell. He was old. The horse had had a long, great life. Toby had brought him to live with him at the ranch because he knew that Legend's life was coming to an end. And God, Toby wished he could do *something* to change what was happening.

He heard his sister's approach before he saw her and recognized the quick, lighter steps of Naomi coming in with her. He'd hated to interrupt their day out together, but he didn't want Legend to suffer. He owed his old friend that much. And damn it, he'd wanted Naomi with him.

Scarlett came into the stall with her doctor's bag and instantly went to work. Toby stood up, making room, and walked to where Naomi stood at the open door. She didn't say a word, just wrapped her arms around his waist and nestled her head against his chest. Toby held on to her like a lifeline in a churning sea and felt everything inside him settle.

Holding Naomi, he watched his sister examine the horse, and as he looked at Legend, he saw his own life flash in pictures through his mind. The day Legend arrived at Toby's home. The first time they rode off together, down back roads and out through the fields. He could still feel the excitement of being astride Legend and pretending to be everything from a great explorer to a Western outlaw. Life had been easy and full of possibilities, and Legend had been with him through all of it.

That horse had been the most important thing to him for a lot of years, and now it was time to let him go. Toby didn't need the sympathy shining in his sister's eyes to know Legend had run out of time. His heart ached with the truth.

"I can put him down gently, Toby," Scarlett said. "He'll just go to sleep."

"Oh, God..." Naomi's voice was a whisper, but he heard the pain in it and was grateful she was with him.

"Give us a minute with him first, okay?"

"Sure." Scarlett stood up, kissed her brother's cheek and said, "Call me when you're ready. I'll be right outside."

"Thank you." Naomi squeezed Scarlett's hand as the woman slipped out of the stall.

Toby walked to Legend's side and held out one hand to Naomi for her to join him. The horse's breathing was more labored, and his eyes wheeled as if he were trying to understand what was happening.

"Poor Legend," Naomi whispered, then bent to kiss the horse's forehead. "You're such a good boy. Such a good horse."

"He loves you," Toby said simply, watching as Legend tried and failed to rest his head in Naomi's lap.

She lifted tear-drenched eyes to Toby's. "I'm so sorry. So sorry you have to lose him."

"I know. I am, too." He stroked the horse's side, then back up to his neck and face. Bending down to look into the big brown eyes of his oldest friend, he said, "We had a great life together, Legend. And I'll never forget any of it."

The horse jerked his head as if agreeing, then tried to stand, failed and fell back into the straw again. It broke Toby's heart to watch the valiant old horse try so desperately to stand and be what he once was.

"Easy, boy," he said quietly. "It's all right. You can go on now."

Naomi never stopped stroking him, whispering to him as the horse labored on until Toby couldn't stand it any longer. Glancing at Naomi, he saw her tears and felt his own. But it did none of them any good to drag this out. Best to say goodbye and let Legend go on to the next adventure.

"Scarlett?"

"I'm here." She stepped into the stall, sympathy etched into her features.

"Do it," Toby said. "But I'm staying with him."

"*We're* staying with him," Naomi said, gaze locked with his.

"Yeah. We." Toby nodded, his throat too full to speak.

"Not a problem," Scarlett said. "It won't take long and he won't suffer. I promise."

Toby tuned his sister out. He didn't want to think about it. Didn't want to watch her end the old guy's life, even though it was a blessing for Legend. Toby looked again into his horse's eyes, and he could have sworn he read a silent thank-you there.

Legend's breaths came slower, slower, then stopped, and the silence was almost unbearable. He was gone. A huge piece of Toby's life had just ended, and he felt like he'd been kicked in the gut. Naomi took his hand and held on. Scarlett kissed him again and silently left them alone.

"I'm so sorry," Naomi whispered, turning into him, wrapping her arms around him.

"I know," he said and held on to her, burying his face in the curve of her neck.

He'd wanted her there, with him, when he realized that Legend was dying. Toby had needed Naomi, and she'd come. Just as she always had. Her hand in his, he felt her warmth pouring into him and clung to it.

After the trip to California, things had definitely changed between Naomi and him. Sure, the sex was great. Amazing, even, but out of bed, he felt the strain between them. They hadn't talked again about the offer she'd had, and he had no clue what she was thinking. Planning. So he had to wonder what she was considering. Did she want that offer badly enough to leave Texas? Move to Hollywood? And if she did, what then? His life was here. In Royal. Living in California wasn't part of his game plan, but was it in Naomi's? That producer had offered a dream. Was she going to take it?

And if she wanted to, then maybe they shouldn't get married, after all. Was it fair to her?

*That's bull*, he told himself. All of it. He wasn't thinking about what was best for Naomi. It was about *him*. What he was feeling. Every time they had sex, he felt himself sliding farther down a steep cliff. Pretty damn soon, he'd find himself loving a woman and risking everything he'd promised himself he never would again.

Straightening up, he looked into those whiskey-gold eyes and knew he was in trouble. He just didn't know how to avoid getting in deeper. "Thanks, Naomi. For being here."

"I'll always be here, Toby."

He hoped so, but there was some serious doubt. Toby caught her cheek in the palm of his hand and realized that Naomi was really the only woman outside his immediate family whom he trusted completely. Why, then, was he so cautious about letting his feelings for her grow? Was it himself he didn't trust? Or was he just too damned cowardly to risk loving again?

Either way, he didn't come off too well.

Standing up, he drew her to her feet and said, "Come on. I have to get out of here."

"Okay." She held his hand and followed him out of the stall, where they both stopped and looked down at Legend one more time.

Then, together, they left the stable, and the pain, behind.

# Ten

Two days later, Naomi was furious.

The text she'd received an hour before ran through her mind again.

Naomi, we must speak. Come to Oaks Hotel in Houston as soon as you can. Gio

The fact that he'd practically ordered her to come irritated her only half as much as the fact that she was going to see him at all. Why had Gio come to Texas? Why had he texted her out of the blue after making it perfectly clear he wasn't interested in her or her baby?

Temper spiked inside her. Naomi hadn't told Toby about Gio's text, because she knew he'd tell her not to go meet the man. But she had to, didn't she? Had to find out what he was up to. Why he was here. Had to tell him to go away and never come back. Once she had it all settled, she'd tell Toby about it, of course. She wasn't going to lie to him about this.

Over the past few weeks, Naomi had put Gio out of her mind completely. He had nothing to do with her or her baby. Toby was the man who would be her child's father. Toby was the man she loved. The man she was about to marry. Gio had no place in their lives. And the only reason she was going to see him was so she could tell him that to his face.

It was time to banish her past so she could go forward with her future.

She parked her car on the street, fed the meter and then hurried toward Gio's hotel. It was plush, of course, with a liveried doorman and a red carpet stretching from the sidewalk to the polished brass front door.

Naomi smoothed her palms over her cream-colored slacks, then tugged at the hem of her pale green blouse. The fabric was light but clung to the outline of her baby bump proudly. The doorman hurried to open the door for her, and she smiled at him as she stepped into the blessedly cool interior.

The spacious lobby was all wood, dark fabric and glass, giving the impression of old-world money and cool elegance. Naturally this was the kind of place Gio would stay. Looking around, she spotted the bar and headed for it. She was right on time for this meeting, and she didn't want to be here any longer than she absolutely had to.

The elegant bar held a luxurious hush. A long mahogany bar stretched along one side of the room, and a dozen or more small round tables dotted the gleaming woodplank floor. Her gaze swept the room, and since there were only a handful of people in the room, she spotted

Gio instantly. He had a table in the back, in a shadowed corner, and Naomi sighed. If he thought this was some kind of assignation, he was in for a disappointment. The only reason she'd agreed to meet him was that she wanted to look him in the eye and tell him to get lost.

Gio had been a blip in her life. A moment out of time in her past. He had no part in her future, and that was what she'd come to tell him. As she approached, her heels tapping on the floorboards, he noticed her, and Naomi stiffened in response. She still couldn't believe she'd been foolish enough to spend the night with the man, but in her defense, just look at him.

Not as tall as Toby, Gio had long jet-black hair, blue-green eyes and always just the right amount of beard scruff on his cheeks. He wore black slacks, a cream-colored silk shirt and looked, as always, very self-satisfied. The man was gorgeous, but he was as deep as a puddle.

"*Bella*," he crooned as he stood to meet her, "you are so beautiful."

"Thanks, Gio." She avoided the kiss he aimed at her cheek and pretended not to notice his clearly false look of hurt and disappointment.

"Can I get you something to drink?" he asked, already signaling to the waitress.

"No, thanks."

He waved the waitress away again as Naomi took the seat opposite him at the small round table. She glanced around the room, making sure she didn't know anyone there, then focused on Gio again. Waiting.

"I'm so happy you came to meet me," he said and managed to look both pleased and disappointed.

"Gio," she said, "I don't know what this is about, but I'm only here to tell you I don't want anything from you—except," she added as she had a brain flash, "to have you sign away your parental rights to the baby."

"*Sì, sì,*" he said, waving his hand as if erasing the very thing she'd just asked for. "We will speak of all this. *After* we speak of something else…"

Okay, so it wasn't the baby he was interested in. No big surprise there, after the way he'd reacted when told he was going to be a father. So what had brought him all the way from Italy?

The room was quiet, and so was Gio's voice. He leaned toward her across the table, and Naomi had a moment to really look at him and wonder how she could ever have been attracted to the man in the first place. He was handsome, but in a stylized way that told her he spent a lot of time perfecting his look. The just long enough hair, the right amount of scruff on his face, the elegant, yet seductive pose he assumed, half lounging in the chair. He couldn't have been more different from Toby.

Toby was a man comfortable enough with himself that he didn't need to set a scene so that a woman would admire him. All he had to do was walk into a room and his confidence, his easy strength, would draw every woman's eye.

No, there was no comparison between Gio and Toby. And now all she wanted to do was wrap this up and get back to the man she loved.

"The baby is growing, yes?"

Hard to miss that, she thought, since her top clung to the rounded curve of her belly. And as if the baby was listening, it gave her a solid kick, as if to say *Let's get out of here, Mom. Go home to Dad.* She smiled at the notion, and Gio smiled back, assuming her expression was meant for him.

Shaking her head a little, she said, "Yes. Everything's fine. And no, I don't need anything from you, Gio. I'm getting married, and *he* will be my baby's father."

Gio tapped one manicured finger against his bottom lip, then gave her a reluctant smile. "Yes, I have heard of your marriage plans." When she looked surprised at that, he shrugged. "Gossip flies across oceans, too, *bella*. You have the marriage with a very rich man. I wish you well."

Frowning now as a ribbon of suspicion twisted through her, Naomi said, "What are you getting at, Gio?"

"Ah, so you are in a hurry. *Che peccato*—what a shame," he translated for her. "All right, then. I will sign your paper for you—"

"Good. Thanks."

"—*if*," he said, "you are willing to do something for me."

A cold chill swept along her spine, twining itself with the suspicion and quickly tangling into greasy knots that made Naomi shiver in response. Gio's eyes were fixed on hers, and she saw the speculative gleam shining in their depths.

"What do you want, Gio?"

"Ah. We will be businesslike, yes?" He smiled, and she saw briefly the man she'd slept with before he disappeared into a sly stranger. "*Bene*. We will be frank with each other. Is best."

"Then say it." She folded her hands together on the table in front of her and kept her gaze fixed on him.

"I will be quiet, *bella*, about being your bambino's daddy," he said with a wink, "*if* you agree to finance my next film."

She blinked at him. The one thing she hadn't expected

to hear from him was a threat of blackmail. Gio was a filmmaker, but she knew his last two films hadn't done well. So apparently, he was having trouble getting backing. Enough trouble that he was willing to fly to America for the sole purpose of blackmailing *her*.

Naomi was so furious with him, with herself, she could hardly draw breath. But Gio was oblivious of her thoughts and feelings, and went on outlining his business plan.

"Since you told me about the bambino," he said, "I felt it my duty to check on you. And I have found that your fiancé is the man who invents so many wonderful things..." He gave her another of his *I'm so disappointed* looks and said, "He is very rich and yet you did not mention this to me. Why is that?"

"Because it's none of your business?" she ground out.

"But yes, it is." He leaned toward her again, reached out and covered her hand with his, and smiled into her eyes. "You will marry this man soon, yes?"

"Yes." One word, squeezed past the knot of fury and humiliation lodged in her throat.

"Then you are able to afford to help me, *sì*? I have a film in production, and I want you to finance it for me. We will be business partners, *bella*!" He released her hand, sat back and smiled benevolently at her. "You, me, our bambino."

Blackmail. Plain and simple. It was an ugly word, but it was the only one that fit. Naomi felt like an idiot for ever involving herself with this sad, shallow man. She could only hope that her genes would wipe out whatever of Gio was lingering in her baby. But even as she thought it, she realized that Toby would be her child's father. He would be the role model her child needed—the guiding hand, the understanding heart—and that would more than make up for Gio's faulty genes.

"Do we have an agreement, *bella*?" He pursed his lips, shook back his hair and positioned himself in the single slice of light piercing through a window. "I will keep your secret about the baby. I will not demand my fatherly rights. All you must do is help me with this. Is not such a bad bargain, *si*?"

Naomi took a deep breath, shook her head and said, "No, Gio. It's not a bad bargain."

He smiled, clearly delighted with her.

"It's a terrible one."

His smile disappeared. "*Bella*, do not be foolish."

"You know when I was foolish, Gio?" she asked. "When I looked at you and saw more than was actually there. I'm thinking clearly now." Leaning across the table toward him, she said, "I won't give you a penny. You'll get nothing from me, Gio. Ever.

"So, you do your worst. Tell the world you're the baby's father. In fact," she said, as brilliance flashed in her mind, "I approve. Go ahead. Take out an ad in every paper...splash it across cyberspace, claim my baby as yours. It'll be easier to sue you for child support."

He gaped at her, his mouth opening and closing like a fish on a line. Oh, he hadn't expected this. He'd thought that Naomi would roll over and do just what he wanted to protect her own name. But she'd learned something with Toby's help. You stood up to bullies. You didn't let them dictate your actions. So she was taking a stand here, to protect herself *and* her baby.

He looked absolutely stunned, and the knowledge that she'd caught him off guard gave Naomi a huge rush of pleasure. Pushing up and away from the table, she looked down at him. "My husband will be my baby's father, and no child could ask for a better one. So do what you have to do, Gio. But you'll never get a dime from me."

Smiling, she turned around and stalked out of the plush bar. She felt…liberated, and she couldn't wait to get home to the ranch and tell Toby all about this meeting and how she'd handled it.

Naomi never noticed the man in the corner who'd been surreptitiously taking pictures during her encounter with Gio.

When his phone signaled an incoming text, Toby checked it, expecting to hear from Naomi that she was headed home from Houston. He opened it, stared and felt his stomach drop to his feet.

A picture of Naomi and a dark-haired man seated at a table together, looking cozy, as the man held her hand and looked meaningfully into her eyes. The message accompanying the photo was short and to the point.

You're a fool. She's meeting Gio Fabiani behind your back.

Gio. Her baby's father. Toby actually *saw* red. His vision blurred and darkened at the edges as he stared at the damning photo. Naomi was meeting the man who'd gotten her pregnant and turned his back on her. The man she'd claimed she didn't want anything to do with. Yet they looked pretty damn friendly, with him staring into her eyes while he held her hand.

She'd told Toby she was going to do some wedding shopping in the city. Instead, she'd gone to meet another man. She'd lied to him. So what else had she lied to him about? His heart felt as if it were being squeezed by a cold, tight fist. He couldn't breathe, because the cold rage rising inside was choking him.

This was exactly what he'd worried about. Getting closer to Naomi only set him up for the pain he'd felt the last time he allowed a woman into his life. Naomi knew what Sasha had put him through, and now she herself, the woman he'd thought of as his best friend, was doing the same thing?

Why was she meeting Gio? Was she playing both of them against each other? Was she planning on walking out on him in favor of the guy who'd gotten her pregnant?

"What the hell, Naomi? What the hell is going on?" He couldn't stop staring at the picture.

Maverick was behind this texted photo, he knew. Who the hell else would be watching Naomi and making sure Toby knew what was happening? Bastard had a lot coming to him when he was finally caught.

Shutting his phone down, he stuffed it into his pocket as if he could wipe the image of Naomi with another man from his mind if he just didn't have to look at it. Pain stabbed at him. This was so much worse than when Sasha had walked out. It cut deeper because Naomi was a part of him. She'd been his friend. His lover. His fiancée.

And now she was...what? He didn't know. All he was sure of was that he had some thinking to do. He wouldn't hold her to their engagement if this Gio was what she really wanted. But he'd be damned if he'd wish her well with the guy. Betrayal stung hard and settled in the center of his chest.

"Damn it, Naomi," he muttered. "What the hell were you doing with him?"

After all they'd shared, all they'd planned, she went to Gio in secret? Why? Naomi was *his*. They were building a damn life here. Didn't that mean anything? He had half a thought to drive to Houston, hunt down this Gio and beat his face to a pulp. But as satisfying as that would be, it wouldn't change the fact that Naomi had sneaked off to meet him.

Toby needed time to think. Space to do it in. Slamming out of the workshop, he stalked to the stables and saddled a horse. It'd be best for all involved if he wasn't at the ranch when she came back. Because he wasn't sure how he would handle it if she looked him dead in the eye and lied to him. Again.

Good thing he wasn't in love with her—or this would be killing him.

Astride the big black stallion, Toby headed out, and the horse's hooves beat out a rhythm that seemed to chant, *it's over, it's over, it's over...*

By the time Naomi made it home to the ranch, her anger at Gio had dissipated and she felt as if she was thinking clearly for the first time in days.

It was time to stand up to all the men in her life. She'd sent Gio packing, and heck, maybe she'd scare Toby into taking off, too. But she was tired of pretending, living a half life.

She was in love with Toby McKittrick, and today she was going to tell him just how lucky he was to have her. She didn't care if he wasn't in love with her right now. Naomi could wait. Because he loved her for who she was, and that was enough for her—for now. She had no doubt that he would come to feel the same way she did. He was only protecting himself after what Sasha had done to him.

Hardly surprising that he would keep his heart safe after having it crushed by betrayal.

But she was going to show him that love didn't have to be about pain. And she would *make* him listen.

She steered her car into the long, curved drive toward the ranch house and realized that in the past few weeks, Paradise Ranch really had become home. Her heart was here. In the wide-open spaces. In the stupid chicken coop and with Legend, lying buried under a live oak at the rear of the property.

Her heart was with the man who had always been her friend and was now her lover. The man who had offered to be a father to her child. How could she *not* love him and everything they'd found together?

She didn't need Hollywood. She didn't need dreams of fame and fortune. She didn't even need her parents' approval anymore. All she needed was Toby.

When she parked the car, Naomi raced into the house, calling for him as she went from room to room. She'd been longer than she'd planned and so she expected him to be in his office, as he was most afternoons, working on plans for another amazing invention. But he wasn't there, so she headed to the kitchen and tried not to hear how the heels of her shoes sounded like a frantic heartbeat against the wood floors. "Toby?"

"He's not here," Rebecca said, poking her head into the room from the walk-in pantry. "Took off on that big black of his a few hours ago. Haven't seen him since."

Disappointed, Naomi asked, "Do you know where he went?"

"Nope." Rebecca shook her head, then went back to whatever she'd been doing before. "He took off like a bat outta hell, though. Must be something bothering him."

Worry replaced disappointment, and Naomi chewed at her bottom lip. What could have happened while she was gone? "Okay, thanks. Um, I'll try his cell."

"Phones on horses," Rebecca muttered. "It's a weird damn world..."

Naomi called him as soon as she was in the great room, and she listened to the ring go on and on until finally his voice mail activated. She didn't leave a message, just hung up. And as she looked out the window at the sprawl of the ranch she considered home, she wondered where he'd gone. And why.

An hour later, Toby opened the front door and stalked into the house.

She'd tried to reach him a dozen times, but his phone went to voice mail and her texts to him went unanswered. By the time she heard him enter the house, Naomi's nerves were strung so tightly she could have played a tune on them.

She followed the sound of his footsteps and found him in his office, pouring scotch into a heavy crystal tumbler. He glanced at her when she walked into the room, but there was no welcome on his face.

"Toby? Is everything okay?"

"Interesting question," he said without answering at all.

The only light in the room came from the dying sun drifting through the wide windows at his back. He was a shadow against the light, and even at that, she saw the tightness on his features, the hard gleam in his eyes. And she wondered.

"I was worried," she said, walking a little closer.

"Yeah?" He laughed shortly, took a long drink of

scotch and said, "Me too. So, did you find some great wedding stuff in Houston?"

"Actually, that's what I wanted to talk to you about."

"Is that right?" His hand tightened around the glass, and even at a distance, she could see his knuckles whiten.

"I didn't really go to the city to shop."

He snapped his gaze to hers. "Yeah, I know. See, you weren't the only one texting me today."

"What do you mean?" Worry curled in the pit of her stomach and sent long, snaking tendrils spiraling through her bloodstream.

He pulled his phone from his pocket and held it out to her. "Here. Tell me what you think."

Naomi suddenly didn't want to know what was on his phone. What had made his eyes so cold and his mouth so relentlessly grim. But she forced herself to walk to him, take the phone and turn it on. The photo was already keyed up.

She and Gio at their shadowy table, leaning toward each other, his hand covering hers. They looked…cozy. Intimate. If she didn't know what had happened between them, she might believe that they were lovers, intensely focused on only each other.

Oh, God. What he must have thought when he saw this. She took a breath, looked up at him. "Toby—"

"You lied to me." His features were colder, harder than she'd ever seen them. Even when Sasha left him, he hadn't looked this closed off. Untouchable.

"I didn't lie."

"Semantics. By not telling me you were meeting Gio, you lied to me," he ground out through gritted teeth. "Damn it, Naomi."

He whirled around and threw the glass tumbler into

the empty fireplace, where it shattered, sounding like the end of the world. Despite the heat of that action, Toby was coldly furious. When he whipped around to look at her, his sea-blue eyes were stormy and glinting with banked fury. "You're meeting Gio behind my back?"

"It wasn't like that."

"Really?" He pushed both hands through his hair. "Because that's just what it looks like in that picture. Maverick said I'm a fool, and I'm starting to think he's right."

Stunned, she stared at him. "Until now, Maverick was a lowlife. Now you're ready to take his ugliness over what I'm trying to tell you?" She took a step toward him. She hated that he stepped back, keeping her at bay. "Gio texted me. Said it was important that I meet him. So I went there to tell him to leave me alone."

"Yeah?" He cocked his head and gave her a sour smile. "You needed a quiet little romantic corner to do that?"

"It wasn't romantic, Toby." She couldn't believe she was having to explain this. And wanted to kick herself for keeping it from him in the first place. "I don't want Gio. I want you."

"What's the matter? Gio not interested? Or, hey, maybe you're going to keep us both dangling. Is that the plan?" He shook his head and said, "Don't bother answering that. I don't need another lie."

"I'm not lying to you," she countered. God, she'd handled this all wrong. She should have gone to him, asked him to go to Houston with her. To face down Gio together. Instead, she'd wanted to clean up her own mess, and now it looked as though she'd simply traded one bad situation for a worse one. How could she make him see? Make him understand that he was wrong about all this?

Then she realized what she had to do. What she should

have done weeks ago when she'd first admitted the truth to herself. "Toby, I love you."

He laughed, but the sound was harsh, strained, as if it had scraped along his throat like knives. "God, Naomi, don't. You really think telling me that is going to convince me?"

Stung, she swallowed the ache and demanded, "Well, what will?"

"Nothing," he said, staring at her as if she were a stranger.

Naomi's heart hurt, and her breath was strangled in her lungs. She was losing everything and didn't know how to stop it. Toby's gaze was locked with hers, and through her pain, Naomi realized that she wasn't just hurt, she was *insulted*. She was closer to him than to anyone she'd ever known. He *knew* her and he was still going to take Maverick's word over hers?

She had to reach him. Had to fight for what they had, because if she gave up now, he'd never believe in her. Never accept that she loved him.

"You know me, Toby," she said and saw his eyes flash.

"Thought I did," he acknowledged.

"Well, thanks for the benefit of the doubt." She crossed her arms over her chest and hugged herself for comfort.

"What doubt? That picture says it all," he said.

"That picture says just what Maverick wanted it to say," she countered. His eyes were shuttered, his mouth tight and grim, and every inch of his tall, muscular body looked rigid with tension. She wasn't reaching him and she knew why. This wasn't Maverick and his nasty tricks. This went back much farther than that.

"This all comes back to Sasha," she said tightly.

"It has nothing to do with her." Toby stalked across

the room, as if he needed some distance from her. As if shutting her out wasn't enough. Then he turned around to face Naomi. "She's gone. Been gone for years."

"And she took your heart with her," Naomi said, though it cost her to admit it.

"Please." He snorted.

"I'm not saying you're still in love with her," she said, voice cold as steel. "I'm saying that the part of you that was willing to trust, to take a risk, left with her. You loved her, and she walked out."

"I don't need the recap," he said. "I was there."

"Yes, me too," she reminded him. "I was there for you. I saw what you did to yourself to get past her. You closed off a part of your heart. Your soul. You didn't want to trust anyone because you were afraid to be hurt again."

"Afraid? I'm not afraid."

"Come on, Toby," she said. "At least be honest."

"Oh, like you?" he asked with a snort of derisive laughter.

She winced, because even she knew she'd had that shot coming.

"Today was the first time I've ever lied to you, Toby, and I didn't like it. You know me. So whatever it is you're feeling right now isn't about me meeting with Gio."

"Is that so? Then what is it about, Naomi?"

"It's about you using Maverick's photo as an excuse to back away from me before I get too close."

If anything, his features tightened even further. "That's bull."

"Is it?" She stomped across the room, stopped right in front of him, tipped her head back and looked into his dark, angry eyes. "I didn't do anything wrong. Well, okay," she admitted, "I should have told you that I was meeting Gio today."

"Yeah, I'd say so."

"But," she continued as if he hadn't spoken at all, "other than that, I've done nothing to earn your mistrust, Toby. You're my friend. My lover. The man I trust to be a father to my baby."

A muscle in his jaw twitched furiously, but he didn't speak. That was fine by Naomi, because she wasn't finished.

"Sasha hurt you so badly you don't trust anybody."

"I trusted you," he said quietly. "Look where that got me."

"You didn't. Not really." Funny, she was only just seeing it now. "You've been holding back all along. Waiting for something to go wrong. For me to screw up. To prove to you that I was no better than Sasha."

"Not true."

"Of course it's true," she snapped. "My mistake was playing into it. I was afraid to tell you how I really felt because I thought you'd shut me out even more if you knew."

His eyes narrowed. "Knew what?"

"I should have told you in California, when I realized it for the first time," she admitted. "I *love* you, Toby. I'm *in* love with you."

"I don't want to hear this."

"Too bad," she said. "You need to." Naomi shook her head and stared up into his eyes, willing him to see the truth. "I'm not going to pretend anymore. I love you. If you don't believe me, I can't do anything about that.

"But I knew you'd react this way, and that's why I didn't tell you. I thought I could wait, that you would eventually come to love me back." She cupped his face in her palms and held on when he would have shaken her off. "I'm not so sure of that now, and you know what? I'm not going to wait for crumbs, Toby. I deserve more. We both do. I can't be with someone who doesn't trust me. Doesn't believe in me. Doesn't love me."

Turning around, she walked to the door, hoping with every step that he would stop her. Ask her to stay. But it didn't happen, and disappointment welled up inside her until it dripped from her eyes.

She paused briefly at the threshold to look back at him. So tall, so strong, so determined to cut himself off from love. Sadly, Naomi told herself she had nothing to gain by staying except more pain—and she'd had enough of that for one day.

"Congratulations, Toby," she said sadly. "You found a way out of this marriage, and you convinced yourself it was my fault. A win-win for you, right? You're using my stupid meeting with Gio as your excuse to not have to feel. It's easier that way. If you hold yourself back, you don't risk anything."

"Why did you meet Gio, then?"

She smiled sadly. "You should have just asked me that first, Toby. You should have trusted me. Believed in me. But you didn't. This marriage was a bargain. An act. But that's not enough for me anymore. I want it all. Or I don't want any of it. I deserve more. So does my baby." She took a breath and let it out. "Toby, so do you."

She didn't wait for an answer. Instead, she walked out, grabbed her purse off the hall tree in the entryway, then left the ranch, closing the door quietly behind her.

# Eleven

"She's right, you know."

Toby looked over at his sister as she gave one of his pregnant mares a checkup. "Figures you'd say that. You're female."

Scarlett bit back a smile. "True, females are far more logical than males, but even a man should be able to see the truth here. You're just not letting yourself."

Why the hell had he talked to Scarlett about this? Answer? He hadn't slept, and he'd been on edge since the day before, when Naomi walked out, left him standing in his office, more alone than he'd ever been in his life. Temper still spiking, he'd roamed through his house like a ghost, haunting every room, seeing Naomi wherever he looked. Maybe *she* was the ghost, he corrected silently.

Either way, he felt like his head was going to explode with all the thoughts running through it. Then Scarlett had shown up, and he'd blurted it all out before he could stop himself. He and his sister had always been close. He'd expected some support. Instead, he was getting his ass kicked. Figuratively speaking.

Stubbornly, though, he reminded his sister, "She went into Houston to meet that sleaze Gio and didn't bother to tell me."

"Did you give her a chance to when you came home?" Scarlett asked. "Or did you just jump down her throat with accusations?"

He frowned and asked himself when Scarlett's loyalties had shifted to Naomi. Female solidarity? Made a man feel like he was standing outside, pounding on a door for someone to notice him.

When he didn't answer, Scarlett said, "Yeah, that's what I thought."

"I saw the picture, Scarlett," he argued, remembering that hard punch to the gut that had hit him when he first saw the photo Maverick had sent him.

"You saw exactly what that bastard Maverick wanted you to see," she corrected.

He looked at her and waited, because he knew she wasn't finished.

"Damn it, Toby, that guy's been creating chaos all over Royal for months and you know it." She smoothed her hands up and down the mare's foreleg to make sure the strain she'd suffered a few days before was healing well. When Scarlett stood up again, she said, "You reacted just the way he wanted you to. My God, could you be any more predictable?"

That was irritating, so he didn't address it. "Maverick's been hitting people with *truth*, hasn't he?"

"Uh-huh. The truth was, she met with Gio. She didn't

fling herself at him and run off to the closest hotel room. You're the one who filled in that blank."

He scowled at her, but she didn't stop.

"And you know, Maverick hit Naomi with truth and you stood by her." Tipping her head to one side, she stepped around the mare, running her hand across the animal's back as she moved. "You think maybe Maverick might have been ticked that she didn't fall apart? That her life wasn't ruined by his vicious little attack? You think it bothered the hell out of him that you went riding to the rescue?"

He scrubbed one hand across his jaw. His brain started working even through the sleep-deprived fog, and he had to admit that she might have a point. "Maybe."

"Uh-huh. And maybe he was mad enough to go after *you* this time? To get you to turn from Naomi so she could be as crushed as he'd planned in the first place?" She leaned her forearms on the stall's half door and looked up at him. "And then *you*, being male and not exactly logical when it comes to the women in your life, react just like he wanted you to."

Well, if any of that was true, it was damned annoying. Toby hated the thought that he'd done just what Maverick had wanted him to do. Hated being that predictable. He remembered the look in Naomi's eyes and wondered if Scarlett was onto something. Had his sister instantly understood something that he'd been too blind to see? Then Scarlett started talking again, and he was feeling less magnanimous toward her.

"Naomi was right about you and Sasha."

He shot her a single, hard look. "Leave it alone."

"Yeah, that's gonna happen," she said with a laugh as

she swung her hair back from her face. "You know Mom and I were worried about you when Sasha took off."

He did know that, and it didn't make him feel any better to recognize it. Sure, he'd taken it hard, but anyone would have. He remembered his family trying to make him see that Sasha leaving was the best thing that could've happened to him. But he hadn't been willing to admit that then.

"Yeah, so?"

"Naomi was the one you turned to back then."

"I know that, too." He remembered how Naomi had drawn him out of the dark fury that had held him in a grip for weeks after the woman he thought he'd loved left with another man. She'd stuck by him no matter what he'd done to make her leave. She'd stayed to be insulted when he was rude to her.

Naomi had just flat refused to leave him alone to brood. Instead, she'd dragged him out to the movies, to dinner, to picnics. He'd remembered how to laugh because of her. And eventually, he'd admitted that it hadn't been Sasha he had missed, but the idea of her. Of a wife. Family.

"But you're still holding on to what Sasha made you feel, Toby."

"The hell I am." He brushed that aside, stepped back and opened the stall door so his sister could exit. When she was out, he closed and locked the door behind her.

Sunlight speared through the open stable door to form a slash of pale gold along the center aisle. The scent of hay and horses was thick in the air, but it didn't give Toby the sense of peace it usually did. Hell, there was never peace when Scarlett was on a tear.

"You don't even realize it," his sister said, "but ever

since that woman, you've looked at everyone else like you're just waiting for them to turn on you. To prove themselves dishonest. Untrustworthy."

He shifted uneasily. He was long since over Sasha, but the lesson she'd taught him had remained fresh. "So being cautious is wrong?"

"That's not cautious, Toby," she said, laying one hand on his chest. "That's cowardly."

"Oh, thanks very much." He turned and headed for the next stall, opening it for her and holding it even when she didn't step inside.

"What would you call it if someone refused to care again because they might get hurt? Refused to trust again because they might be let down?"

He wanted to say careful, but he was afraid she had a point.

"Naomi loves you."

"How the hell do you know that?" he demanded. "She only told *me* last night."

"And you let her leave anyway?" Scarlett's eyes went wide in astonishment. "God, you really are an idiot. Of course she loves you. She always has. If you weren't such a stubborn *male*, you would have noticed it on your own."

She walked into the stall and slammed the door closed behind her.

"Love wasn't part of our deal," he argued, even knowing it was weak.

"Love isn't a bargain, Toby. It's a gift. One you just returned." She shook her head again and turned away to do another physical on the next mare. "Idiot."

Toby watched her but stopped listening to her frustrated muttering. He had a feeling it wasn't real flattering to him anyway. And maybe he didn't deserve flattery. Maybe he was the idiot his sister had called him.

And maybe, he thought in disgust, he'd tossed aside something he should have been fighting for.

When her cell phone rang, Naomi grabbed it, hoping to see Toby's name on her screen, and felt a swift stab of disappointment when it wasn't him. She answered on a sigh. "Hi, Cecelia."

Her friend started talking in a rush. "Naomi, you remember that guy Gio you told me and Simone about when you came home from that big fashion show?"

Naomi rolled her eyes and dropped into a chair. Curling her feet up underneath her, she said wryly, "Yes, I remember him." *Just saw him yesterday*, she wanted to add but didn't. "What about him?"

"I was watching that gossip channel on cable just now, and he's all over it." Cecelia paused for dramatic effect. "Can I just say wow? You didn't tell us how pretty he is."

"He's not that good-looking in person," Naomi assured her. Especially, she added silently, when you added in his personality. His character. Compared to Toby, Gio Fabiani was simply an attractive waste of space.

"Well, he looks good on camera," Cecelia said. "Except he's not looking real happy right now."

Naomi sighed again. She was tired, since she'd been up half the night reliving that argument with Toby. And the other half of the night, her dream self had done the same thing.

This morning, she'd been on the phone handling dozens of things, all the while letting the back of her mind work on what she would say to Toby when she talked to him again. Because they *were* going to talk. She wasn't going to let him end what they'd just so recently found because of a stupid lie. Should she have told him about meeting Gio? Sure. In hindsight, it was perfectly clear. But at the time, she'd been trying to handle things on her own. Clear up her past and set up her future. Why was that so hard to understand?

Resting her head against the back of the chair, she stared up at the ceiling and asked listlessly, "Why's he on the news?"

"Get this," Cecelia said, clearly settling in for a good gossip session. "There are *three* different women suing him for child support."

Surprised, but somehow comforted by the fact that she wasn't the only foolish woman to have landed in Gio's bed, Naomi chuckled a little to herself. "Really?"

"Oh, yeah, apparently it's huge news in Italy. He even left the country to get out of the spotlight for a while."

"If he's on the news, doesn't sound like that plan worked."

"I know, right? And you know what's weird?" Cecelia asked, and didn't wait for an answer. "Some photographer caught him at the airport in Houston. He was running to catch a plane headed to England. He was right here in Texas. Can you believe it?"

And now he was gone, Naomi thought with a pleased smile. Obviously, he'd taken what she said to heart and wasn't waiting around to see if she'd change her mind. "Well, I hope those women catch up to him."

"I think they will," Cecelia said. "He's got to go home sometime, right? Anyway, I just thought it was weird, seeing him on TV and knowing you'd met him—"

"It is weird." Beyond weird. But it explained why Gio

had been desperate enough for money to give extortion a try. The upside here was, with three other women and children to worry about, the man would certainly be willing to sign over his parental rights, so that was good for Naomi and her baby.

Cecelia was talking, but Naomi was only half listening. Instead, she was thinking about Toby. Maybe she should have stayed at the ranch last night and just had it out with him. But he'd hurt her, damn it. Hurt her by dismissing her when she told him she loved him. It had been a big moment for her, opening herself up like that, and he hadn't believed her.

Hadn't trusted her, and that, she thought, hurt most of all. He'd been waiting, or so it seemed to her, for Naomi to let him down. To prove that what they had couldn't be counted on. Scowling, she thought about the night before, and then something dawned on her.

A part of his mind and heart had been convinced that she would leave him. Walk away. To protect himself, he'd held back, committing to a marriage he didn't believe would work so that when it failed, he wasn't blindsided by it.

With a jolt, Naomi sat up straight. And what had she done? Walked away in the middle of an argument. She'd walked away. Just as he'd expected her to do. "Oh, God."

"Naomi, are you even listening to me?"

She winced. "Sorry, Cec, I'm just really distracted."

"Everything okay with you and Toby?"

She hesitated and almost lied but didn't want to get into the habit, so she said only, "It will be. We're just working out a few things."

*Like our lives.*

"Oh, I totally get it. Between weddings and babies

and the rush of hormones...we're all half-crazed these days. I'll let you go, sweetie. I just wanted to tell you about that Gio guy."

"And I appreciate the update," Naomi said. "We'll talk soon."

When the call ended, she stood up and walked through the condo, realizing that this wasn't her place anymore. Her place was with Toby. Whether he knew it or not.

Grimly, she turned her phone on and made a call. When a woman answered, she said, "Scarlett, this is Naomi. Where's your brother?"

"An hour ago, he was at the ranch, and he was pretty damn crabby, too."

Naomi smiled. "He's about to get a lot crabbier."

"Yay!"

Naomi drove straight to the ranch, telling herself if he wasn't there, she'd wait. She wasn't going to leave again without making him see the truth of what they had. What they *could* have. And if she'd just stayed right there last night, they'd be through this already. *Mental note: no more walking out.*

Her hair twisted wildly in the wind blasting through her open window. The Texas summer sky was a brassy blue with only a few stray clouds drifting aimlessly, looking lost and alone in that vast expanse. There was no traffic on the road, so she pushed the car as fast as she dared. The baby was moving around excitedly, almost as if he or she knew they were headed home. Naomi smiled fiercely and caught her own eye in the rearview mirror.

She was going to make Toby listen. Make him believe. Make him love her as much as she loved him. Naomi had waited for love her whole life, and she wasn't going to settle for less.

Gravel flew up from behind her tires as she took the long drive to the ranch. Her gaze swept the familiar, looking for Toby, and then she spotted him, getting into his truck.

"Oh, no," she murmured, "you're not leaving yet." She pulled to a stop directly in front of the truck, blocking him from leaving. Then she threw the gear into Park, jumped out and walked toward him with long, determined strides.

Toby's breath caught in his throat. When he saw her car flying down the drive, he thought he'd never seen anything that beautiful. She was coming home on her own. But now, watching the woman who held his heart, he had to admit that she looked both gorgeous...and dangerous. There was fire in her eye, and what did it say about him that he found that damned sexy?

It was so good to see her. To catch her scent on the wind. He wanted to tangle his hands in that thick hair of hers, slant his mouth over hers and feel that rush of *rightness* that always went through him when they were together.

Since she walked out the door yesterday, he'd felt only half-alive. Through his anger and pain, there was a constant ache for her. In spite of distrusting her, he wanted her. In spite of everything, he'd missed her.

And after talking to Scarlett today, he'd realized that he'd handled that talk with Naomi all wrong. He hadn't even listened to her, because he'd been so wrapped up in the surety that he'd been right to keep his heart locked away.

But he was wrong. About all of it. And it was long past time she heard everything he'd been keeping inside.

"You're not leaving, Toby," she said when she was close enough.

"No need to now," he said affably, one corner of his mouth lifting as her eyes spit fire at him.

"Not until we get a few things straight," she said, then asked, "What did you say?"

"I was coming to you, Naomi, so, no," he said, "I'm not going anywhere now."

Some of that temper that had been driving her melted away. He could see it in the way her shoulders relaxed some. "You were really coming to me?"

"Couldn't take the silence here, Naomi. The emptiness. I needed you to come home. And you have."

He grabbed hold of her, yanked her in close and kissed her, letting his body tell her everything that was so hard to say in words. She leaned into him, and he felt whole for the first time in hours. This was where he belonged. Right here, with her. The world righted itself, and every last, lingering doubt hiding in the shadows of his mind dissolved in the realization of what he had—what he had almost lost.

When he finally lifted his head, he looked down into her eyes and said, "I'm sorry."

"Excuse me? You're sorry?"

He grinned a little. "Is it so surprising?"

"Well," she admitted, "yes. I didn't expect you to say that. I thought we'd finish our argument and that I'd have to hold you down to make you listen to me. An apology wasn't in the game plan."

"I was wrong, Naomi. Expected or not, I am sorry. I never should have let Maverick get to me." He released her, jammed his hands in the back pockets of his jeans and admitted, "I reacted just the way he wanted me to. I shut you down. Wouldn't listen. Hell, I didn't even listen to myself, because of course I trust you, Naomi."

She blew out a breath, then pressed her lips together in an attempt to steady herself. Toby knew her even better than he knew himself, and that was just one more reason why he'd been the idiot his sister had called him.

Naomi didn't cheat. Naomi would never hurt him.

"Thanks for that," she said and gave him a tremulous smile.

"I saw that picture and I lost it," he admitted, jerking his hands free and tossing them in the air helplessly. "I didn't think. Didn't remember that the bastard's whole point is to create chaos and tear people apart."

"It wouldn't have done anything to us if I had just told you about Gio wanting to meet with me in the first place, Toby." Her eyes were shining as she looked up at him. "I should have asked you to go with me."

Watching her, he asked what he should have the day before. "Why didn't you?"

"Because I wanted to handle it myself." She laid both hands on the curve of the baby and rubbed, as if soothing the child within. "I wanted to kick him out of my life, *our* lives. Once I was there, I was wishing for you, though, if that helps."

"A little," he admitted. "I get you wanting to do it yourself, Naomi. But you could have told me."

"And should have, I know." She pushed her hand through her wind-tangled hair and sighed. "He wanted money. Threatened to tell the world that he's my baby's father if I didn't pay him off."

Toby felt a hard punch of anger and gritted his teeth against the helpless flood of it. He really wished he had five minutes alone with the man. "What did you say to that?"

"I told him to go ahead. It would make it easier to sue him for child support."

A laugh shot from Toby's throat. "You did?"

"Yes, and he wasn't happy," she said, smiling now. "But according to Cecelia, he's got bigger problems at the moment."

"What?"

"Not important," she said, shaking her head. "I'll tell you later. Toby. Why were you coming to see me?"

"Because sometime between last night and this morning, I finally figured something out." He reached for her again, laid both hands on her shoulders and held on. "I was coming to tell you that I love you, Naomi."

She gasped and clapped one hand to her mouth. Her eyes filled instantly with a sheen of tears. "Really?"

"Yes." His gaze moved over her face, taking in every detail. In the sunlight, the bright streaks in her hair shone like polished copper. Behind her hand, her mouth was curved in a small smile, as if she wanted to believe him but couldn't quite manage it. And her eyes, her beautiful eyes glittered with love and hope.

"I love you, Naomi," he said again, willing her to trust him. To believe him. "I was a jackass yesterday. I was so worried about losing you I forgot to fight to keep you."

"Toby…"

He had no clue what she was going to say, but Toby was determined to speak first. To tell her everything he should have told her when he first suggested they get married.

"I shouldn't have shut down like that yesterday. I do trust you, Naomi. It was my own stubbornness that didn't let me tell you that I think I've always loved you." He ran his hands up and down her arms, kept his gaze locked with hers. "I'm lucky enough to be in love with my best friend."

She pressed her lips together and reached up to impatiently swipe tears from her eyes. "When I left yesterday, Toby, I wasn't really *leaving*, you know. I always planned to come back."

"You walking away is something I never want to see again, Naomi. Don't think I could take it." Just the thought of losing her was enough to bring him to his knees.

When Sasha left, anger had driven him. If he lost Naomi, he'd lose his soul.

"You don't have to worry about that," she assured him, stepping in to wrap her arms around his waist. "I'm not going anywhere. I'm exactly where I want to be."

He held on to her for several long minutes, relishing the beat of her heart against his chest, the scent of her shampoo flavoring every breath and the thump of their child, kicking to get attention.

Finally, though, he pulled back, caged her face between his palms and said, "I want to adopt your baby, Naomi. As soon as it's born, I want to be its father. So that baby will never doubt that he or she belongs. That we're family."

"Oh, Toby…" Tears trickled down her cheeks, but she smiled through them, and his heart turned over to see the love beaming in her eyes.

"And about the California thing," Toby added quickly, wanting to say it all now while he was holding her close. "If you have to be there for weeks on end to tape your show, we'll manage. We can buy a house in the hills there and we'll have a California base for whenever we need it."

"You'd do that for me?" she asked.

"For *us*," he corrected, wiping her tears away with his thumbs.

"It means so much to me that you would," Naomi said and went up on her toes to kiss him, hard and fast. "But you don't have to. I called Tamara today to tell her thanks but no, thanks."

Now it was his turn to be surprised. "What? Why would you do that?"

"Because I don't need it in the desperate way I used to," she said. "Before, I wanted my show to succeed so badly so I could prove myself. To my parents. To myself. Because the show was all I had, I poured everything into it.

"But these past few weeks, I've discovered I'm more than my show, Toby. I don't need to make a point. I need you. *Us*."

"But, Naomi, this was your dream."

She shrugged and smiled. "If Tamara Stiles can get *Fashion Sense* on stations around the country, so can I. And doing it myself means it gets done my way. I don't have to leave Texas, leave what makes my show what it is to make it succeed. I'll get there. It'll just take a little longer."

"You're amazing," he said quietly. He'd always seen her strength, and he was glad she could see it now, too. "I believe in you, Naomi. You wait and see. In a few years, your show is going to put Royal on the map."

She grinned. "As long as you're with me, then everything will be perfect."

"Oh, I'm with you, honey. And you'll never shake me loose now."

"Good to hear," she said and moved to kiss him again.

He stopped her cold with a shake of his head. "Not yet. We've got something else to settle first."

"What's left?" she asked, but she was smiling and he was grateful. He never wanted to see her cry again.

"Just this." Toby went down on one knee in front of her and pulled a simply set sapphire ring from his pocket. Holding it up, he saw more tears and told himself this one last time was okay. "You didn't want an engagement ring before because it wouldn't have been real. I hope you'll take this one, though. This ring belonged to my grandmother, Naomi. It symbolizes the fifty years of love she and my grandpa shared."

"Toby…"

His gaze locked on hers, Toby said softly, "I'm offering you this ring, Naomi. I want to give you my name, my love and the future we'll build together. Marry me for real, Naomi. Trust me with your heart, with your baby. Give me more babies. Fill this big empty house with the kind of love that lasts generations."

"Oh, Toby, my heart hurts it's so full," she whispered brokenly.

"That's a yes, then?"

"Yes, of course it's yes."

He slid the ring onto her finger, where that cool sapphire caught the sunlight and winked up at both of them. Then he lifted the hem of her shirt and pressed a gentle kiss to the mound of her belly and heard her sigh as she stroked her fingers through his hair.

Then he stood up and looked into her eyes as he pulled

her into his arms. "I love you, Naomi," he whispered. "Always have. Always will."

She sighed again, smiled and lifted one hand to smooth his hair back from his forehead. "I love you, Toby. Always have. Always will."

"Good to hear," he said, lowering his head for a kiss.

Naomi grinned. "Talk, talk, talk. Show me what you've got, cowboy."

He grinned back, and then he showed her.

* * * * *

# COMING SOON!

We really hope you enjoyed reading this book. If you're looking for more romance, be sure to head to the shops when new books are available on

## Thursday 25th July

To see which titles are coming soon, please visit
**millsandboon.co.uk/nextmonth**

MILLS & BOON

# Want even more ROMANCE?

## Join our bookclub today!

'Mills & Boon books, the perfect way to escape for an hour or so.'

Miss W. Dyer

'Excellent service, promptly delivered and very good subscription choices.'

Miss A. Pearson

'You get fantastic special offers and the chance to get books before they hit the shops'

Mrs V. Hall

**Visit millsandbook.co.uk/Bookclub
and save on brand new books.**

MILLS & BOON

# LET'S TALK
# *Romance*

For exclusive extracts, competitions
and special offers, find us online:

- facebook.com/millsandboon
- @MillsandBoon
- @MillsandBoonUK

**Get in touch on 01413 063232**

For all the latest titles coming soon, visit
**millsandboon.co.uk/nextmonth**

# JOIN THE MILLS & BOON BOOKCLUB

* **FREE** delivery direct to your door
* **EXCLUSIVE** offers every month
* **EXCITING** rewards programme

**50% OFF YOUR FIRST PARCEL**

## Join today at
Millsandboon.co.uk/Bookclub

# MILLS & BOON

MODERN

# Power and Passion

Prepare to be swept off your feet by sophisticated, sexy and seductive heroes, in some of the world's most glamourous and romantic locations, where power and passion collide.

Eight Modern stories published every month, find them al

## millsandboon.co.uk/Modern

# MILLS & BOON
## *True Love*

## Romance from the Heart

Celebrate true love with tender stories of heartfelt romance, from the rush of falling in love to the joy a new baby can bring, and a focus on the emotional heart of a relationship.

t True Love stories published every month, find them all at:
## millsandboon.co.uk/TrueLove